Pleasant Hill

Driskill Horton

For Lindsay

AUTHOR'S NOTE

Although the Red River Campaign, culminating in the Battles of Mansfield and Pleasant Hill, are historical military events of the American Civil War, this is a work of fiction. I have used artistic license to change some of the more trivial aspects of the time period and the conflict itself. This was done for entertainment purposes only, not political. My apologies to all die-hard historians.

Prime acknowledgment and eternal gratitude goes out to my mother, Betty Westmoreland, whose patience, hard work and tolerance contributed greatly to the creation of this novel. I could not have done it without her. Thanks Mom. I love you.

A special thanks goes out to Gary Joiner at LSU Shreveport, who was kind enough to point out some of the more glaring flaws in the manuscript.

I would also like to acknowledge Eileen Lass and her excellent editing process, priceless assistance for a beginner.

And finally I want to thank my brother, Mark Horton, for his support and the stellar effort he put into formatting the text.

Driskill Horton

"When I was a lil' bitty baby, my mama use'ta rock me in da cradle in dem ol' cotton fields back home."

Old Negro Folk Song

"Today, men, you will see blood till you are satisfied!"

Confederate officer before the Battle of Mansfield

PROLOGUE

Louisiana 1864

Like some cold baptism of ancient rites, the Confederate finally got his feet wet in the chilling water of the Mississippi, uttering a mild curse as the icy waves jolted his senses. All the way across the great river he had been trying very hard to keep them dry, but now that he was almost home it just didn't seem to matter. Mud oozed through the cracks in the soles of his boots and still he did not care. Reaching down he gathered up some of the red mud in his hand, smearing it on his face like a child. Coppery pungent smells filled his nostrils bringing him even closer to the home he'd left some two and a half years ago. Temporal afterthoughts concealed in the terrain. Shaded haunts of yesterday conjured at the waters' end.

Snow had blanketed northern Virginia when they first started on their journey south, just days after the beginning of the New Year, a little over a month ago. They were the only able-bodied survivors of a once proud, strong cavalry battalion that had left Louisiana in the fall of 1861. A newly-formed outfit full of daring young men ready to charge even the bête noire in hopes of capturing glory and all the trappings of victory. Chivalrous waves of pageantry coursing specter-like from the trees, hills and back roads, granted authority by the dreaded angels of war to spill the blood of their brothers, staining the common soil of their cause. Crescendos of a rebel yell now all but wasted and dashed with the last hopes of the South against their ever-growing, ever-learning adversary, the Union cavalry.

At Manassas they had been able to catch a ride on a train, having to sleep in the same car as their horses, their furlough papers not being enough for a proper coach set. Not even for an officer. A crowded, smelly jaunt in a boxcar listening to the dreary clacking drone of the rail. They had been told they would be taken all the way to Atlanta, but men from the War Department boarded in Charleston, demanding to see their papers. Loud unreasonable men of authority, pompous blowhards thinning the chaff. They would have to get off unless they wanted to wave the furlough and join the fight for South Carolina. No, they had done enough fighting and were going home. Fortunately their documents bore the signatures of both Generals Stuart and Longstreet, otherwise they could have been mandated and forced to fight. States' rights still had its precedence, but not against the weight of two corps commanders, especially ones of such status.

They had kept to the wider traces just south of the Carolina-Tennessee line cautiously zigzagging through Georgia and Alabama, now well acclimated to the cold. In Mississippi they passed through a twenty-mile-wide swath of destruction. Charred remains of still- smoldering homesteads were all along that blackened stretch of land where the winter crops had grown. Rotting animal carcasses littered the barnyards. What few people they met told them Sherman's army had recently marched across the state from Vicksburg to Meridian, burning and destroying all that could not be taken, including livestock.

They were eventually given the name of a man who could get them across the river, but there were no guarantees. Since the fall of Vicksburg last summer, the Mississippi was under the control of the Union Navy. Lincoln's wishes dissecting the homeland. They met the man at a secluded spot fifty miles upriver from Natchez, a privateer whose only loyalty was coin and cash. Their predawn voyage across the water had been uneventful save the floundering vessel itself. A large pontoon boat with a steam engine listing precariously through the mighty river's powerful currents, water lapping over its sides, men and horses swaying nervously to its unsteady pitch and yaw. Finally running aground with a dull scraping thud scaring off a flock of white egrets roosting in the wet brush.

"Yer horse, Major," a voice said from behind the Confederate, breaking him from his reverie.

Major David Hawkins turned to see his first sergeant, Steven Jenkins, handing him the reins to a large, beautiful red stallion with a thick, unruly black mane.

"Easy, Jackson," said Hawkins to the magnificent creature. Not the beloved charger he'd left Louisiana with, but certainly one he'd become quite attached to. "It's not Virginia, but you'll never know the difference."

As he led Jackson up the riverbank, Jenkins and two other men guided their horses off the pontoon boat. The vessel's pilot and mate then shoved off, vanishing into the cold February mist like a ghost. The other two men were heading south to their homes near Winnfield, brave souls who'd done their duty with little ceremony. Jenkins handed them a wad of money, Union currency, spoils from the better days of their tour.

"Why, that there's Yankee money," said one of the men.

"There's nearly a hun'erd dollars here, Sergeant," said the other. "We can't take all this."

"You take it," said Jenkins. "You'll need it."

The man nodded, then looked up to see the major off in the distance with his arms around his horse's neck. He looked to be whispering something to the animal.

"He gonna be aw'right?" asked the man with genuine concern, a mix of envy and sympathy pooling in his eyes.

Jenkins turned and smiled. "Yeah, he's aw'right. The major's just real fond'a that horse."

The man smiled weakly, nodded again and waved before heading off with his friend. As they disappeared through the trees, their horses' steps added sounds to the life and scenery all around, a chorus of crickets, scampering squirrels and chirping birds fluttering by. A cold wet breeze. The dull steady whoosh of the river.

Jenkins walked up behind his commander who was still hugging and whispering to Jackson, a bizarre moment he was reluctant to interrupt. "Ya wanna get go'n, Major, or ya wanna rest a spell?"

Keeping his arms around the horse's neck, Hawkins turned to Jenkins, his face still coated with the drying mud. "Nah, let's get go'n."

Both men were in their mid-thirties and had known each other since they were very young, but had not become close friends until after the war began. Hawkins was a career military man with red curly hair that fell to his shoulders. A big man, he stood about six-three and was a bit light at 210 pounds. He had been wounded seven times and walked with a slight limp, favoring his left leg. Over the years he had developed a habit of changing the way he talked, suiting his diction and accent to the people and places he encountered. In a relaxed setting with his men or with casual friends, an obvious drawl could be detected. When angered or excited this accent became even more pronounced. In the company of high-ranking officers or the elite well-to-do, his voice took on the disarming twang of fine Southern nobility. Serving out West before the war, he had spoken with fewer words, vehemently cutting off his phrases in sharp commands and quick exclamatory remarks. Prior to Lee's first invasion of the North, Hawkins had been chosen with a handful of other men to ride a few days ahead in civilian clothes, gathering intelligence on Union troop deployments. Dangerous work, once even dining in a fancy Baltimore restaurant. The men had been specifically selected for their ability to hide the southern drawl and duplicate the more neutral northern accent.

Jenkins had dark hair, was about six inches shorter than Hawkins, and had a stocky build that allowed him to sit in the saddle like a bag of grain. He too had been wounded numerous times, but showed none of the outward signs of disability save the scars. Jenkins had also volunteered for the quick bit of espionage, but no matter how hard Hawkins coached him, his thick backwater accent was a dead giveaway. Still, to Hawkins, Jenkins was the perfect subordinate.

"Did ya really eat snails in 'at fancy restaurant, Major?" Jenkins had asked back in Maryland shortly before Sharpsburg.

"Yep," answered Hawkins. "Mighty tasty, too. They cook'm in white wine, butter'n garlic. Kind'a like some frog legs I had once in New Orleans."

"Frog legs, huh?" Jenkins's eyebrows had risen sharply in a short moment of approval, then fell back suddenly, furrowing together with aversion. "But snails?"

As they rode away from the river, the Mississippi sun began to creep over the Louisiana sky. It broke across the treetops in tenuous gossamer rays, shifting the dark purple firmament to a soft, welcome blue. Rarefied honey-colored light streamed through the mist casting long shadows on the fallen leaves and pine straw. All seemed eerie and surreal juxtaposed with the familiar thoughts of home. Moss hung thick from the trees, swaying, waving senseless at the land, an enigmatic curtain of shrouded mysteries awakening their numbed senses. Small rolling hills etched by wetlands dotted with white cranes and blue heron. Cattails innumerable, all in review. More inland was drier, cueing a frosty southern morning. Birds still flew south in their crooked V-shaped flocks. Something large trolled across a bayou into the marsh by the bog. Cypress trees like ancient elders. Oaks like houses. Yellow pines like summer. Magnolias, willows and soft maple. White-tailed deer. Some running off. Some just looking.

There had been so much fighting it was often hard for Hawkins to remember one engagement from the next. Bits and pieces of retrospect, disjointed, out of place and time. Horrible battles in lonely places stuck in his mind, wandering next to memories he only wished he could choose from. Fenced-in meadows near fields and crests where men wait to die. Wait, pondering their existence in the martial design or just wait at the fitting, much-talked-about places where they killed each other and ask why, but never answer. Queries, unknowable and obscure. Home is the best place to die, he thinks, on a quiet afternoon perhaps, or a morning such as this one.

Sometimes he would find himself trying to recall the name of a friend who had been killed early in the war. A promise made as they died in his arms. Maybe a glimpse of their final moment ruined and broken, taken suddenly and quick. Or simply a word of their demise by the bye. The faces he still had locked away in the boxes of his mind, but the names were gone, like a part of his childhood he could not quite see anymore, a plaything he no longer had interest in. Other times a certain sound, a song or smell was all it took and he was back reliving moments most extreme, calling men to bear, seeing their brave yet terrified faces. Some of them so young as to never know the touch of a girl, not even a kiss. Dead virgins, still virgins.

At Fredericksburg he had watched from a distance as the enemy charged Marye's Heights, headlong into musket fire like children playing tag with new rules and new devices. The deadly limits of insanity thought clear. A plan for success sprung from the mouth of folly. It was like watching a man attempt to destroy a meat grinder by shoving his arm into the working end of it. Then, after the arm is chewed up to the shoulder, the man screaming all the while, he grits his teeth as if perseverance is all that is needed, straightens his cap and shoves in the other arm. Senseless undertakings come to fruition by the thoughtful disregard of fire, lead and powder fingers. The numbers meant nothing but ink for the press. Asinine calculations chalked up to a new math done with the pen and paper of scapegoats. The baneful milk of politics.

Within an hour they came to a small crossroad; at its northwestern corner was a ghastly sight. A layer of crows and buzzards swarmed around a man hung nailed to the width of a massive oak. His arms were stretched out crucified to the tree's thick off-shooting upper limbs, his legs spiked tightly to the mid-section of its vast trunk. The gory, medieval work of marauders. He looked to have been dead for several days, his features long since eaten away by the birds and other creatures of the woods. Completely oblivious of the two live men, the thoughtless scavengers continued to peck and gouge, displaying their work with little bother. A lipless mouth agape in mute protest revealing two rows of rotting teeth. The familiar odor hung like a wet sheet slapping them across the face, reminders of a lost war yet to be finished. Above the man a sign read:

Jayhawkers Beware

Suddenly Hawkins saw the dead man's face change, eerily shifting to the visage of Christ Jesus. A crown of long sharp thorns was embedded into his scalp, spilling rivulets of blood down a countenance of anguished responsibility. Hawkins slowly made the sign of the cross, drawing a sideways glance from Jenkins.

"Ya aw'right, Major?" asked the sergeant.

For a moment Hawkins said nothing, his eyes fixed on this vision of the Christ. The stricken Messiah seemed to be trying to say something, mouthing words of counsel. Or a warning perhaps. Hawkins wiped his face with a cupped hand. When he looked again the vision was gone. Only a luckless jayhawker nailed to a tree, food for carrion crows and turkey buzzards.

"Major," repeated Jenkins. "Ya aw'right?"

"Did you see that?" Hawkins asked, still keeping his eyes on the rotting corpse.

"See what?" Jenkins frowned and looked back at the dead man. "This nasty business here?"

What was this? Hawkins wondered. Another visitation of the Man in White, that noble presence that had called on him half-a-dozen times or more, often in the midst of furious battle?

The two Confederates were silent for a moment, taking in the hideous display of malevolent lust. After witnessing so much carnage on the battlefield, their senses had become somewhat dulled, but still they wondered what kind of men could do this to another. And what might this man have done to deserve so gruesome a fate? They glanced at each other, then back at the horrible spectacle before them. Finally without a word they turned west, moving on, the sun now high at their backs. Hands on their side arms. Mindful of the trees. Looking. Looking.

Warfare comes in different schemes. Shades of chivalry tossed to the wind. Cutthroats shining at your back. A blind rendering of what one wants to be right. And a stark, unflinching glare at what one hopes to be wrong.

Hawkins often wondered about his moments with the Man in White, and the other strange, surreal happenings he'd witnessed in the fighting back east. Blood raining from the sky. A sky that would sometimes light up the color of bright luminescent blue, momentarily halting epic battles as if God Himself had called a brief intermezzo. There had also been great visions in the sky; arks, columns of fiery chariots, legions of angels, and the Christ himself clothed in the sun. Other things bizarre and unknown had been displayed up above for all to see, yet spoken of by so few.

After the Battle of Malvern Hill, Hawkins had some time with a chaplain, a delightful old gentleman from Ireland whose voice reminded him of his father. The wise chaplain told Hawkins of a phenomenon called the Man in White. He explained that the strange occurrence is as old as warfare itself, a myth fabled in stories and poems, predating even the Greeks and Romans. In moments of utterly turbulent combat, just when all seems lost, an unknown person appears out of nowhere rendering aid to a desperate warrior in his weakest hour. Then, after the tide has turned for the better, this unknown presence departs, leaving the warrior to wonder if the mysterious person had been there at all.

At a small creek hidden in a grove of trees, Hawkins and Jenkins watered their horses. As they looked into the distance, riders could be heard coming from the west, many of them, twenty, thirty or more. Suddenly, across a large clearing just beyond the trees, no fewer than forty men on horseback moved quickly back toward the river. Hoof beats bounding through the air, shaking the earth. They wore plain clothes and rode with the determination of desperate men.

"Ours, ya think?" whispered Jenkins.

Hawkins just shook his head and shrugged his shoulders. After a moment they moved west again, keeping to the trees.

By early afternoon they spotted a small group of seven men clad in gray and followed them for nearly an hour before deciding it was safe to make contact. They were Confederates patrolling near the river zone for Jayhawkers, Red-legs and other Unionists, doing what they could to keep it safe for the few who'd chosen to remain there. Ever since the fall of Vicksburg, the area near the river had turned into a constant war zone with a few small towns burned and many of the people moving west. Violence and mayhem had spread like a plague, and anywhere near the river one could encounter savage marauders with allegiance to the North or the South or to no one.

As their small group continued west they met up with more and more Confederates, all eager to hear firsthand news of how the war was going back east. But Hawkins and Jenkins had little in the way of encouraging reports. Not only was talk of the war itself daunting, but for every single man they were asked about, old friends and family, all they had to offer were grim condolences. Hawkins listened as one young private, shades of peach fuzz still on his face, rattled off name after name to Jenkins as they rode along. At first all the sergeant could do was slowly shake his head to each inquiry. Then he heard the name of a man he thought might still be alive and turned to his commander.

"Billy Albright, Major, you 'member him?" asked Jenkins. "I think he was with eff troop. Tall fella with blond hair an' freckles. Played harmonica an' sang a bit."

"He's my cousin," said the young private. "I'm Charlie Albright."

Hawkins looked up and slowly nodded, now seeing a resemblance in the boy. He recalled Albright playing music and singing songs for the men in his troop, a lively character with an affable personality, quite brave, daring, and a bit reckless. Shortly before Gettysburg his left arm and leg were badly mauled in a clash with Union cavalry at Brandy Station. Both had to be amputated and he was transported to a hospital in Richmond. Weeks later as the defeated Southern Army limped back into Virginia, Hawkins received word that Albright had contracted pneumonia and died.

"I'm sorry, son," he said, grimacing. "He was very brave."

The young private nodded and slowly rode off to the side to be alone, a lost and dazed look on his face. Later he would be seen weeping silently. A healthy reaction, thought Hawkins. It was the ones who could not cry that would suffer the most, keeping it bottled up inside to fester like an unclean wound.

By sunset there were twenty-five of them. In the twilight the party made camp along the bank of a small lake. One of the men had a cast net. He kicked off his boots and rolled up his pant legs, then began twirling the net into the water, all the while quoting scripture from the Gospels. Blending with the first stars of the night, ripples of pink and purple played across the lake, giving its colors back to the sky. Charlie Albright pulled out a harmonica and began playing a slow weighty melody, a sad tune for his cousin. As brim and catfish roasted over a fire, Hawkins ran his hands across Jackson's reddish-brown coat, the horse chomping at a foot-high pile of oats and molasses. At first light the camp was struck and the small band of Confederates began skirting around the lake to the west.

A few miles before they reached Shreveport, Hawkins noticed a simple yet prominent skyline had emerged over his childhood home. A high water tower was surrounded by a series of five looming smoke stacks belching their waste over a structure that stretched just north of the city. He had been too tired to ask and was in no mood for conversation. Besides, he knew what it was - foundries for the Confederate Naval Shipyard on the southern bank of Cross Bayou's mouth to the river, completed in his absence on land that had once belonged to his father.

Shreveport was the Confederate capital of Louisiana; Baton Rouge and New Orleans had been surrendered to the North early in the war. It was also the headquarters of the Trans-Mississippi Confederacy, which encompassed Louisiana, Arkansas, Texas and any legitimate part of the Confederate States of America west of the Mississippi, now all but cut off from any significant support from its dying main body.

The sun was low in the western sky when the group of Confederates, now numbering more than thirty, crossed the rickety pontoon bridge over the Red River into Shreveport's wharf area. The hustle and bustle of city life, a large presence of soldiers, teamsters and slaves groping with the never-ending tasks of the day. After showing their papers at a checkpoint and a quick salute, Hawkins and Jenkins bid their traveling companions farewell and headed on into the town.

"In case ya forgot, David, headquarters is back 'at way," said Jenkins, jerking his thumb over his shoulder as they rode down Commerce Street. "Papers say we're 'posta check in soon as we get here."

"Well I reckon 'at can wait, Steve," said Hawkins, looking at the man. "Them boys back at the river didn't do nothin' but give our papers a once-over. Go an' see your family. Tell Jenny I said hey."

"You sure are a compassionate type, David," said Jenkins, grinning ear to ear as he rode off down Crockett Avenue, looking back over his shoulder to shout, "Good to be alive, huh!?"

"Hey, Steve!" Hawkins yelled, causing Jenkins to stop and turn his horse. "All this time you've been call'n me major, even when I ordered ya not to. So why are ya just now call'n me David again?"

"Cuz we're back home, by golly!" shouted Jenkins, swatting the horse's butt with his hat to turn again and sprint down the street.

Good to be alive indeed, thought Hawkins.

As he turned off Spring Street and crossed the old wooden bridge over the bayou, his eyes scanned the shipyard. Three-story buildings jammed into a corner of land he had ruled as a child, its construction begun only days before the war. Occasionally his lovely Emily would tell him of its progress in her letters as viewed from their small cotton farm on the opposite corner of the two waterway's nexus.

"Oh, David, it's such a dreary, awful sight. And the noise, a most infernal racket. Why on earth couldn't they build it on the other side of the river?"

A faraway din of metallic clanks, pings and banging echoed through the air, reverberating under the bridge, bouncing off the murky water below. A thick cloud of stygian smoke issued from the looming stacks, scarring the pristine sky.

On the other side of the bayou, he looked out across Grimmet Field at the old levee that ran the length of his property, and more memories came flooding back. The many priceless correspondences with Emily, a treasury of endearment. Since Vicksburg the letters had stopped and he ached for her touch. How he longed to fill their bed with fresh picked flowers, kisses and sweet words. To lie gazing into her loving eyes, listening to the soft tones of her healing voice.

They had met almost ten years ago on an Easter Sunday during the egg hunt at the First Methodist Church. A little girl dressed in pink had dropped her egg, cracking the prized gift. The child began to cry quietly, trying ever so hard not to be disappointed. But the egg was so pretty, pink like her dress. Hawkins, who was just back from West Texas in his U.S. Cavalry uniform, happened by and noticed the little girl crying.

"What's the matter, my darling?" he asked, bending over to console the small child.

"I broke my egg," said the little girl in a voice so soft Hawkins could barely hear it.

"Well here, little one," he said, spying a blue egg inside the bushes to the right. Gently, he picked it up and placed it in the girl's tiny cupped hands. "Surely this one will do. Careful now, don't drop it."

The child stopped crying but still looked sad, glancing back and forth between the baby blue egg in her hands and the cracked pink one on the ground.

"But it's not as pretty as that one," she said looking up at Hawkins.

"Well, this egg comes with a special attachment." Hawkins unclipped a small, frilly, white tassel from one of the ribbons on his uniform, a well-deserved commendation for one of his many grueling duties out West. He clipped it to the side of the little girl's basket and watched as her eyes opened wide, a sweet smile spreading over her tiny face.

"What is it?" she asked with delight.

"Peter Cottontail himself gave me this when I was a little boy," lied the tall soldier. "He told me I could give it to whomever I liked. And now I'm giving it to you."

The little girl's mouth opened wide, her lips curling inward as she gave a tiny gasp of surprise.

"Well, you certainly have a way with the ladies."

Hawkins turned and stood almost at attention.

"Aunt Emily, look," said the little girl, holding up her basket in one hand and the blue egg in the other. "I got an egg with Peter Cottontail's tail, see?"

She was wearing a yellow dress, holding a matching parasol over her head. Her long dark hair was pulled back away from a strikingly animated face, her lips pressed slightly together as if trying to stifle a laugh. Deep brown, happy eyes, inquisitive yet knowing. Her head was bowed down a bit to her niece, eyes looking up occasionally at the tall soldier standing before her.

"And where did you get this bunny tail?" she asked shifting her full attention to an obviously smitten Hawkins.

"That nice man in the blue suit gave it to me," the little girl said.

"Lieutenant David Hawkins, Madam," he snapped to, bowing slightly, never taking his eyes from hers. "At your service. Ladies in distress always have a way with me."

"Indeed, they do," she said, offering her hand. "Emily Rains. So nice to make your acquaintance, Lieutenant Hawkins."

"You'll have to excuse me if I don't release you," he said, after kissing the delicately gloved hand. "My feet are no longer touching the ground, you see, and I'm afraid I might simply float away into the far reaches of space, never to see you again."

"Oh, how distressing," she giggled. "Do hold on tight."

And hold on tight he did, courting her for less than a month before getting married in that same church. That spring they would run along the old levee for the first of many countless times, holding hands as their young legs worked the ground. Laughing as they went, talking about the little goings-on of the town, like whether or not Old Man McBride's barn would be painted in time for next weekend's social dance. He said it would, she laughed and said it would not, too much lollygagging. At a tall pine where a trail led off into another grove of trees they would follow honeysuckles, white and yellow, sweet with aroma and buzzing with bees. Ducking through the harmless swarm where blackberries grew thick and twined with their small stickers on the stems, waiting for summer to be picked and eaten or made into pies or jam or wine. Round they went till they came to their special place under a large oak tree, its canopied boughs guarded by brush and other trees. It was here that they really knew each other, laid out on a blanket over the soft clover, naked and alone, smiling innocent, running their hands along their bodies, finding it so good to be so young and so free.

When they were done, exhausted, they would just lie vulnerable looking into each other's eyes, not talking, still gently touching, and caressing one another. Then, as their heartbeats settled back down, they would tell one another how good it had been, neither really finding the right words. But that did not matter; they trusted and believed in each other entirely. Sometimes they would spend the rest of those moments just talking of very simple things, their faces and bodies so close.

14

Other times, like maybe when the moon was full or when the day had been short, they would have each other again and maybe again, finding new frontiers for their joy and passion. And this would sustain them through their times apart, and even through their times very far apart.

As a child he would run that levee, crossing the bridge, following its traces along the south bank of the bayou to its mouth at the river, past the fish market and the wharf. From there he would run along the trails into the town, taking the long way as children do because they don't yet know how short time is. Sometimes he and his baby brother, Paul, would run the trail with their friends to the mouth of the bayou, where just a short hike upriver they had a swing tied to a large cypress tree. Most of the year it was warm enough to go into the water. They would swing out on the rope, letting go at just the right time, crashing into the eddy that had formed there away from the strong currents. They would swim back to quickly scurry up the muddy grassy bank or just stay out to frolic and play in the water. They were all strong swimmers and played rough with each other in those days, many times inflicting pain, but never serious injury. They would fish almost daily and hunt the woods to the north taking coons, squirrels and gray back doves. In winter deer were plentiful and could be seen from across the water running in small herds. That levee and the bayou feeding into the river and the woods and clearings that surrounded it, he claimed as his own. Deep, way back in his strong fervent memories of home were the places of his dreams.

At the farm Hawkins was surprised to see things looked as good as they did. He had expected disarray and clutter. The two-story house his father, brother and he had built over fifteen years ago had a fresh coat of whitewash, three dormers spaced evenly between its long steep gables. An ample sweeping porch ran the whole length of the house, wrapping around the right side all the way to the back. Two massive oaks stood guard to the left, their strong sturdy limbs reaching out toward each other creating a voluptuous domestic sanctuary.

Out front a well-worn footpath circled inside the thin drooping bare branches of a willow tree. And to the right facing the porch waited a grand magnolia, its own little refuge nestled in the twilight. Hawkins stopped in front of the house, surveying the scene of his home. Beyond the house was a large barn and stable. Next to it was the slave quarter, a thirty-by-fifty-foot log cabin with its own shaded porch. Behind that were two smaller cabins used as storage sheds.

Most everything looked in order, hens strutting around just outside their coop, hogs lolling quietly way off back in their pen. A familiar old horse named Nitney grazed in the corral. The field was ready for spring plowing. Two old dogs looked up from their nap under the magnolia: Caesar, a blue heeler that was the epitome of ever-alert-cool, and Jacko, a light-brown collie-retriever mix with white patches and a perpetual canine grin flanked by a long floppy wet tongue. The former let out one solitary bark, then raced low and deliberate toward his long-gone master. The latter, always a half-step behind but made up for it with boundless howling enthusiasm.

Hawkins was just about to call out for Emily when a small black boy about seven came from around the side carrying two buckets of water, followed closely by a little black girl about four, sucking her thumb.

"Stop fall'n me Rachel!" he shouted at the little girl, "an' shut up Jacko!" When he saw Hawkins, he dropped the buckets wasting the water on the ground, staring in disbelief at the master he barely knew.

"Hey there, Noah. Didn't mean ta scare ya. How ya been?" said Hawkins as he dismounted Jackson, who was totally oblivious of the two dogs that swarmed the Confederate. Caesar glanced up at the horse between pats and rubs. Jacko demanded more than his share of attention, and Noah stood speechless.

"Who dat is?" cried Rachel, taking her thumb from her mouth as she stared up wide-eyed at Hawkins.

"Is that little Rachel there behind ya? My, ya'll sure have grown." Hawkins removed his hat, swatting a cloud of dust from his uniform. "Well, where's Emily at? I need a big hug and a long kiss from that girl."

Suddenly Noah broke off into a run toward the slave quarters with Rachel hot on his heels, Jacko sprinting after them momentarily, then turning back to Hawkins.

"Momma! Pappa!" he cried. "Massa David's back! Massa David's back!"

"Momma! Pappa!" mimicked Rachel. "Matta Dava back! Matta Dava back!"

At the slave quarter their mother, Sarah, stuck her head out the door. She was in her early forties and wore an expression of utter disbelief as she wiped her hands on her apron.

"Oh, my Lawd," she whispered to herself, then moved out to meet her son. "Go'n get ya pa and granpap, dair in da barn. Hurry now!"

In a blur the boy was off running toward the barn as Sarah gathered up Rachel, looking at the man she had helped raise.

"Hey, Sarah, how are ya?" said Hawkins coming closer, still looking over the place. "Things look pretty good 'round here. Bout'ta start plow'n I see."

She tried to speak, but could say nothing. Finally from out of the barn came Noah, his father Jacob and his grandfather Isaac. Seeing them she mustered up some strength.

"Didn't s'pect ya back so soon, Massa David."

"Got a little sidetracked up in Tennessee, I guess." Hawkins laughed, then turned to greet Jacob and Isaac. "And there they are, the real men of the family."

The relationship between Hawkins and his small family of slaves had always been good. Never had they been abused or neglected, the adults playing a significant role in young David's nature and nurture. Sarah had been like an older sister to him, and her children more like nieces and nephews. They all worked hard and lived quite well on the seventy-five-acre farm. At its peak, the Hawkins farm had been over two-hundred acres. When Hawkins's father, Ira, fell on hard times before the war, he sold bits and pieces of the land to pay off debts. Not once did he sell or beat a slave. During Hawkins's absences out West, and while he'd been off fighting the war, neighbors had tried to persuade Emily Hawkins to hire an overseer. But she'd refused, saying they got by just fine. In truth, they were more like family.

After a few awkward moments, Sarah's oldest child, a beautiful fifteen-year-old girl named Ruth, came from around the slave quarters. She had always adored Hawkins and often considered Miss Emily the luckiest woman in the world. Seeing him, her hands came up to her mouth as tears welled up in her eyes. Hawkins looked up and saw Ruth crying, standing off to the side with a painful, troubling look on her face. Hawkins was just about to call out to her when he noticed the solemn looks on all their faces. Noah stood at his father's side, a strong hand on his head, and Rachel in her mother's arms still sucking her thumb, her little head nuzzled against Sarah's neck. Caesar and Jacko sniffed the ground at Hawkins' feet.

"Where's Emily?" he asked. "She go into town? Did I miss her come'n in?"

"Oh, uh…" Jacob choked, trying to speak.

"David," Sarah said, painfully.

"What is it? Where is she?"

No one spoke. Isaac looked at the ground. Jacob fumbled with his hands trying to find words. A tear fell from Sarah's eye, running down the length of her cheek.

"She was so good," Isaac finally said in a soft voice.

"What'a ya mean?" Hawkins asked sternly. "Where is she?"

He moved close to Jacob, looking intently at the man's face, a man he'd known all his life. Jacob could not meet his eyes. Hawkins had never handled one of his slaves roughly. It surprised even him when he grabbed Jacob by his shirt, violently jerking him around in a half-circle.

"WHERE IS SHE?!" he screamed.

Finally Jacob met Hawkins' gaze, slowly pointing with his left hand backward over his right shoulder as tears streamed down his face.

"I'm so sorry, Massa David."

The Confederate shifted his eyes from Jacob's, looking over the black man's shoulder off into the distance. He gently pushed Jacob aside and slowly started to walk toward the edge of the field. Isaac held back Jacko as Caesar trotted sentry-like behind and to the left of his master. There, at the far end of the field surrounded by a clump of trees, were seven gravestones. When he had left two-and-a-half years ago there had been six. His parents and younger brother were buried out there. He'd been gone when each of them died, out West in the U.S. Army, or off on some errand. Also buried there were Sarah's parents, and Isaac's wife, Jacob's mother. Another sign of the Hawkins's intimacy with their slaves; they were buried with them.

By the time Hawkins got to the small plot his legs were shaking and could barely hold him. For a moment he lied to himself, imagining that it would not be her. Then he saw her name. His hat fell to the ground as he dropped to his knees, weeping. Caesar let out a short audible whine, glancing back and forth between Hawkins and an epitaph that read:

Emily Hawkins
1835-1864
With the Angels

He thought of the last time he had seen her, that autumn day of another world. She had worn her favorite blue dress, the one he liked so much. Her arms stretched out toward him, holding tight to his hands, not wanting to let go. A cool breeze blew through her raven colored hair hanging down past her shoulders. Her beautiful, bold features never betrayed the sadness in her eyes.

"I need for you to be careful," she had said, as he parted in his gray uniform.

"I was careful, Emily," he said caressing her gravestone. "I was so careful."

I

Shortly after his 20th birthday David Hawkins's childhood sweetheart married the son of a wealthy cotton broker. Brokenhearted and disenchanted with farm life, he ran off and joined the Army. After nine months in an infantry battalion, constantly drilling and marching about, he began to think he had made a huge mistake. But one day a high-ranking officer saw Hawkins breaking in a horse that no other man could ride. His reputation for fighting and expertise with firearms had already made him a bit notorious, and soon he was transferred to the cavalry. After nine more months of training, consisting of long journeys through Texas and Indian Territory, he was promoted to corporal and sent to far-off New Mexico Territory. From there he went on countless expeditions through the newly acquired territories and California, exploring and helping bring civilization to a wild, reluctant land. He chased outlaws and banditos. Made friends with most Indians, fought and killed others.

Though tough and rugged, he was also very bookish, reading almost constantly in his spare time. His study habits were very acute, never letting an unknown word or phrase slip past his eyes, digging and researching until he had a full grasp of its meaning. He loved studying military geniuses like Julius Caesar, Alexander the Great and Napoleon. He often wondered why all men of war and conquest seemed sinister and wicked, with only degrees of good and right, regardless of loyalties. Thoughts like this would haunt him throughout his career. His favorite authors were Victor Hugo, James Fennimore Cooper and Herman Melville. He was also intrigued by the exchange between Emerson and Thoreau when the former visited the latter in jail for refusing to pay a war tax. And though he disagreed with the philosophy of *Civil Disobedience*, Hawkins found the man's intentions quite admirable. Occasionally a taste of the bizarre suited him and he would indulge in the likes of Mary Shelley or the strange short tales of Edgar Allen Poe. He once read *The Tell-Tale Heart* aloud to a group of Comanche while struggling with the translation, coaxing horrified glares of wonder from the natives. Another time he sat up all night with a group of friends drinking scotch, discussing the merits of *Frankenstein* and whether or not life could actually be reanimated through science. Such pointless debates entertained him, helping him unwind after a week or two of hard soldiering.

The son of a benign slaveholder, Hawkins was aware of the cruelties of slavery, but he was shocked when he read *Uncle Tom's Cabin*. It seemed strange to him that slavery in the modern world had become distinguishable by color, especially in a nation contending with the very definitions of freedom. Talk of a possible war between the North and South was not uncommon in those days. There were many issues that could lead to war: states' rights, free navigation of the Mississippi River, trade with Europe and expansion westward. But all of these, Hawkins realized, could be negotiated. Some sort of compromise could be reached. There would be no sitting down at a table and discussing the issue of slavery. It would only be solved by violence because violence was what kept it in place as an institution. Hawkins was in favor of freeing the slaves, but realized until the system itself was radically changed this would not happen. In some parts of the South there was simply no such thing as a free black.

After four years in the military, Hawkins's superiors saw him fit to be an officer and he was commissioned to the rank of second lieutenant. He did not disappoint his commanders, stepping into the role of a confident leader of men as if born to it. His troop showed much promise, accomplishing one successful mission after another. He imagined his future as a victorious high-ranking officer of honor and renowned, gaining peers of status and prestige. But a year after he received the commission, his mother passed away and he returned home to Louisiana.

He was temporarily posted in Shreveport at Fort Turnbull to be near his family. It was then that he met Emily Rains and took her to be his wife. Not long afterwards tragedy struck again. A barn was being raised at the Hawkins farm and David had gone into town to get more supplies. While he was gone, his brother Paul slipped and fell from the top rafters, breaking his neck killing him instantly. Ira Hawkins was devastated. Though he loved his eldest son, Paul had always been his favorite. For it was Paul who had stayed on the farm, never complaining, always working feverishly to bring in the crops or do whatever it took to keep the place up and running.

Two more times Hawkins was sent out West. Once to help negotiate treaties with the Apache and Navajo Indian tribes. The natives knew him now and trusted him. He was affectionately called Barbarossa or Red Beard by both tribes and was openly welcomed to many of their seasonal celebrations. By this time many of the tribes living on land recently gained by the war with Mexico were already somewhat leery of white men, another terrible stain of European conquest. Although most initial contacts were peaceful, U.S. relations with the Indians always became strained at best. Hawkins hated the obvious way the natives were constantly being lied to and cheated out of their land, but short of treason there was little he could do about it. He also despised the general way in which the Indians were judged by most whites.

Some were bad, but most were good, just like all people. In most cases those that feared them were driving them to their hostile nature.

While he was gone he corresponded with Emily almost constantly, at times both receiving and sending out small bags of mail. He wrote to her in great detail about the vast painted land out West, referring to it in very intimate terms.

It is a red-brown, dry cracked land, my love. Open, forever changing by the second, by the tick of the sun, by the dance of the moon. It greets me with howling wolves and coy dogs. There are grizzlies, wild cats and herds of bison with no end. Great birds of prey, song and scavenge. A kingdom of insects, snakes, scorpions and spiders. Huge unreal mountains like infinite cathedrals. Canyons, breathtaking and otherworldly. Heat to shrink the soul and slow the spirit, and cold like I've never felt, speechless and biting. Waterless for weeks and months on end, then deluges and floods from nowhere.

Emily responded in kind, keeping him abreast of all the local activities and the silly community gossip, and soon they both had trunk-loads of letters and cards.

In 1856 Hawkins's unit was dispatched to a northern section of Indian Territory to deal with a minor uprising by a small group of Cheyenne when his outfit briefly crossed into Kansas. They watched from a distance as a bunch of crazies fired at each other from across a cornfield. It was then that he first heard the name John Brown. The Army had orders not to interfere with the insanity, pro-and anti-slavery men bleeding the state, gearing up for the war to come. Three years later, on his last tour out West, Hawkins was helping oversee the protection of a gold mine in a very remote part of Colorado Territory. Suddenly, news was told of a violent insurrection at a place called Harper's Ferry, Virginia, by the abolitionist John Brown. It was the beginning of the Confederacy.

For over a year, Hawkins remained loyal to the Union. But when Louisiana seceded he resigned his commission. Just six months earlier he had taken a position as a surveyor at a Cherokee reservation in the southeast corner of Indian

Territory, only a day's ride from his farm. It was there that he received word that his father had died, suddenly collapsing on the porch while reading the newspaper. By April of 1861, David and Emily Hawkins had somewhat settled into their modest estate and he was even considering retiring from the military altogether. Then one morning a rider came, delivering news that Beauregard had fired on Fort Sumter. The war had begun.

For six months he had stayed in the area training men who already knew how to ride and shoot. He thoroughly taught them the basics of practical military necessity, strategies and tactics, morale and structure of command, turning them into disciplined soldiers, at least on the training ground. But how, he often wondered, would they react when brushed against a regiment of the enemy to play for keeps, strangling one another in a house divided. Most every night he was able to ride home to Emily and discuss this as they lay holding one another in bed.

"They're so eager to go and fight," he said, as she nuzzled her face in the nape of his neck, running her hand gently across his chest. "Some are even worried the war will end without them firing a shot."

"Somehow," she purred in her hypnotic tone. "I don't see the worry in that."

"They only want to be part of history, my darling," he said, running his hand through her long dark hair, lifting it away to let it fall in soft strands across her shoulder. "And they're afraid it will pass them by."

"I can do without the history," she said nibbling on his ear. "What I can't do without is you."

Eventually word came that his regiment was being transferred to Mississippi to await deployment elsewhere. The days leading up to his departure were especially hard for Emily. She would stand close, pressed up against him, rarely leaving his side. Sometimes she would just embrace him, not saying a word, holding him tight, feeling the warmth of his hard body. Other times she would simply hold his hand, gazing at his face, occasionally looking off as if searching for some danger lurking there in the distance.

Before sunset their last evening together they walked along the levee, holding hands like so many times before, the dogs trotting along as they took the trail to their special spot under the old oak. The weather was always so nice in northern Louisiana that time of year, the oppressive heat of the summer gone, and the wet cold winter not yet arrived. A cool, crisp breeze blew through the grove as they reclined in the clover, propped on their elbows facing one another. Jacko snuggled tight at Emily's feet, while Caesar walked a perimeter check.

"What's going to happen, David?" she asked running her fingers down his forearm.

"I don't know, my dear." He brushed a lock of long dark hair away from her face.

"When do you think you'll be back?" It was a question she had never asked before. He had always told her beforehand, letting her know of his approximate return.

"I'm sorry, my love, but it could be some time yet."

She didn't say anything, just looked up at him, holding his gaze for a moment, then laying her head across his arm.

"I'm so sorry, Emily," he said, reaching to pull her close to him as the last glimmers of dusk played through the trees. "You've deserved so much better than this. I've been gone far too often."

"Well, I guess I could forgive you," she pouted playfully, "if you'll only come back to me."

The next morning they gathered to see him off. Emily stood to one side as he mounted his horse, stroking the animal's dark chocolate mane. Sarah, Jacob, Isaac and their children stood to the other side, looks of worried fascination on their faces. Jacko, showing rare solemn reserve. Caesar, as stoic as ever.

"Bring him back to me, Tempest," Emily said to the horse. "In one piece, if you please."

And so, David Hawkins left his wife and home again, this time traveling east to fight a war he truly felt was for the sovereignty of the South. Even then, deep in his personal thoughts, there was something unsettling about his choice of loyalties. But what was he to do? Draw his gun against his friends and neighbors? The terrible thought had entered his mind in those early, infant days of the war. But those thoughts soon faded as he passed through south lands he had never seen before, meeting the proud Southern folk rich and deep with their heritage and traditions. And though he already had his baptism of fire way off in The Territories, he would soon be totally immersed in something far more incendiary; warfare unlike any he had never imagined.

She had taken ill with a fever. For days she had been complaining of headaches and dizzy spells, unable to sleep or eat. About the time David Hawkins was leaving Virginia to return home, Emily had collapsed in the kitchen and was found there by Sarah. Twice the doctor came, but could do little. For over a week she laid in bed delirious with fever, calling out his name. Some felt surely he was killed, his presence visiting her, beckoning her on to his new world, lonely and wandering. Then one morning she simply did not awake, passing on in her sleep. The previous night she had cried out quietly, Sarah sitting off to the side by the window.

"I can see him through the trees," was all she said.

For days and weeks Sarah pondered her family's fate. There was talk of them being auctioned off to one of the large plantations in the area, brutal places where their small family unit would be shattered by the constant leering eye of the overseer and his arbitrary lash. Taken without voice from the sweet, simple home they had known all their lives. David Hawkins had not been heard from since last spring and rumor was spreading that Louisiana troops were suffering heavy losses in the fighting. Then suddenly he arrived, haggard, exhausted and so glad to be home. And even though they were happy to see him, it broke their hearts to see his heart break so.

It was dark. Sarah and Isaac sat on the porch of the slave quarter looking out toward Miss Emily's grave, out toward the graves of the Hawkins family. Their family. They could not see him, but they knew he was still there, talking to her, crying, wondering what happened. Even they did not know.

"He been out dair an awful long time," said Sarah

"He's griev'n, baby," replied Isaac. "Dat takes time."

Sarah stood and moved to the post by the steps. "He looks so much like Massa Ira. I 'member when 'es little. I'd wash'm an' feed'm an' play wit'm."

Jacob stepped out on the porch. "Noah wants ya to kiss'm good night."

"What 'bout da baby?" asked Sarah, still looking out into the darkness.

"She'sleep."

Sarah turned and walked over to her husband. "Honey, please go'an check on Massa David. Please."

For a moment he said nothing, just looked out toward the field. Then Sarah caressed and kissed his shoulder. "Please, baby,"

"Aw'right, shugga." He looked at her. "I will."

She went inside as Jacob moved to the post. For a while the two black men just stared off into the darkness.

"Think he'find out?" asked Jacob finally.

"Oh, he'find out," said Isaac. "Jus'a matter of time."

He was utterly delirious with grief and exhaustion, still on his knees, his cheek pressed against the gravestone. His hand caressed her name, eyes moist with tears, staring off seeing only her. All the while Caesar and Jacko were huddled at his side.

"It was real pretty in Virginia," he said softly. "Leaves all change color up there. You'd like it. But it gets real cold. Colder than here. Pennsylvania was pretty too, but I didn't like it there. Bad things happened." He paused. "I missed you so much."

From off in the distance a light was coming. Sensing their master's urgency, Jacko stayed by Hawkins as Caesar quietly ran off to inspect. The light moved along the edge of the field coming closer and closer to Hawkins. He looked up and saw Jacob standing over him with a lantern in his hand, Caesar close behind.

"Iss cold out, Massa David," said Jacob through a thick plume of steam. "Lem'me help ya inside. Don't need ya get'n sick."

When he finally got the tired soldier up and headed toward the house, Hawkins began speaking incoherently, disjointed ramblings with a faraway look. "Sergeant," he said, Jacob looking at him strangely. "Sergeant, we must fall back and regroup. Colonel Prescott is dead and Major Bennings is badly wounded. We must fall back. The enemy is moving on our right flank. Sergeant, where are you, Sergeant?"

"I'm here, sir," said Jacob. "I'm here."

Someone else had been there, too. Someone holding Hawkins on his right side. Someone strong and constant, a Presence of another world. Later, Hawkins would ask about this Person. Who had it been? But Jacob would tell him there had been no one else, except Sarah and Isaac. The three of them had been able to put him to bed. But days later, Hawkins would swear there had been a fourth Person.

He'd slept all that night, but by morning a fever had taken hold of him, deep and festering. For three days he lay in bed. The doctor came and gave him a dose of laudanum, but still the fever held. Sometimes he would wake screaming for Emily, having to be restrained by Sarah and Jacob. Other times he would call out deliriously as on the battlefield: orders and replies, warnings and pleas for support. There he hovered in a vortex of sweat and nightmares.

During that time Sarah stayed at Hawkins's bedside, sometimes just holding his hand while she kept a damp rag on his forehead, quietly speaking to him in pleasant tones. Other times, after one of his horrible fits, she would kneel and pray with all her might, even lying prostrate on the floor, begging God to intervene, crying painful tears of petition.

"O Lawd Jee'zuss," she would cry with solemn earnestness. "Please, Lawd, send ya angels to help Massa David.

He needs ya Lawd. I know he wants to be wit' Miss Emily. But please, Lawd, please don't take'm, Lawd. We needs'm."

On the fourth morning the fever finally broke and Hawkins's condition took an encouraging turn for the better. He was resting peacefully when the rooster crowed announcing the dawn twilight, waking him out of a sound sleep. Sarah and Jacob were in the kitchen when he slowly shuffled in wearing his long night shirt. He sat at the table, looking utterly despondent. After putting her hands to his face and forehead, Sarah poured him a cup of coffee. Jacob stood before him, hands clasped together in a gesture of service.

"What can I do fer ya, Massa David?"

He said nothing, just stared at the kitchen floor.

"Day fo' yesta'day," Sarah said. "Isaac kilt a lil' shoat. Dair's pleny'a bacon an' eggs. Grits, too. Lem'me fix ya sump'n ta eat, Massa David."

"Just coffee," he whispered, slowly shaking his head.

"Papa, Papa!" Noah's voice came from outside, as the dogs began to bark. "Somone's come'n, Papa!"

"I'll go'n see who it is, Massa David," said Jacob, leaving the kitchen.

As he sat staring at the floor, tears began to well up in Hawkins's eyes. He looked up at Sarah and tried to speak, but his mouth only moved; the words would not come.

"Oh, David," said Sarah, moving to hold him like an older sibling or an aunt. "I'm so sorry, baby. We loved'r so much."

She held him close, stroking his hair as he cried, his arms wrapped around her, sobbing desperately. He knew only the grief that seemed to rip at his heart, like something jagged and sharp suddenly torn through it. The pain coursed through his body like bits of glass in his blood, no longer isolated to one part, spreading, seeking all the empty places deep in the corners of his soul.

Anytime he could, little Noah would stand right next to his father. Looking, watching, and taking in what he could of the world around him. Hoping to learn without asking too many questions or getting hurt or in trouble. Most of the time, when he was busy, Jacob would tell him to run along or find something productive for him to do. But sometimes he would let him stand right there, his little shoulder touching, pressed up against his father's hip. When he did this, Jacob would always rest his hand palm down on his son's head. A covering of love reassuring the little boy it was all right for him to be there. He was doing it now as they watched a rider slowly approaching up the road that led to the Hawkins farm.

"Who dat is, Papa?" asked Noah.

"Dunno, son," said Jacob. "Could be a friend'a Massa David's."

The rider wore a Confederate uniform and looked familiar to Jacob. He stopped in front of the man and his boy and nodded, the two dogs sniffing at the horses' hooves.

"Howdy, Jacob," he said. "David here?"

"Why, yessir." Jacob squinted his eyes. "You be Mista Jenkins. Ain't dat right?"

"Yeah. Been a while, huh?"

"Yes, it has, sir," said Jacob. "Massa David's here, sir. But he's feel'n awful poorly."

"I heard. Maybe you could just tell'm I'm here. I think he'll wanna see me."

After a short hesitation, Jacob asked, "You da sergeant, sir?"

"Yeah, dat's right."

"Why don't you come on inside? Give the boy here ya horse."

In the kitchen Hawkins was beginning to pull himself together. Sarah sat facing him, holding his left hand in both of her hands. When she saw Jenkins she stood and gave a slight bow.

"Iss Sergeant Jenkins, Massa David," said Jacob.

"Morning, David." Jenkins said, taking off his hat.

Hawkins barely nodded.

"Would ya like some coffee, sir?" asked Sarah. "Iss good'n hot."

"That'd be fine, thanks."

Jenkins sat opposite of Hawkins, studying his commander with genuine concern, while Sarah poured him the coffee.

"We'll be outside, Massa David," said Jacob.

"Just holler if'n ya need me, David," Sarah said as they left.

After a long moment of silence between the two men, Jenkins said, "I'm so sorry, David. Jenny didn't even know. I found out the day after we got back. I would'a come earlier but Jenny's brother got killed a few weeks ago, so things are kind'a bad at home."

"Sorry 'bout Jenny's brother." Hawkins paused and looked around the kitchen, still half in a daze. "Are ya hungry?"

"No, thanks. I'm not stay'n."

"Well, I should get dressed," said Hawkins, beginning to stand. "We still gotta report in at headquarters."

"No, David." said Jenkins. "Sit back down. I've taken care of all that. They want you to rest."

Hawkins settled back in the chair and looked up. "Thanks, Steve. I … uh …"

"David, please. Don't worry 'bout nut'n. Just get ya some rest."

After another long moment of silence, Hawkins said, "I'll be need'n an extra plow horse soon."

Jenkins frowned and stared at the man. Then he began to laugh, slowly shaking his head, leaning forward to prop his elbows on the table.

"Well," said Hawkins with a stern, serious look. "Nitney's get'n too old to do all the plow'n by'm self."

"Don't ya worry none, David. We'll get ya 'nother plow horse." He stood, looking down at his commander. "I gotta run along. They got me help'n out at Fort Turnbull. Train'n dem green ree'crewts."

"Ya didn't drink your coffee," said Hawkins, motioning at the cup.

"Oh, yeah." Jenkins picked up the cup and gulped down the hot liquid. "Aaaahh!" he went, gasping, shaking his head. "Boy, she's right. Dat's good'n hot."

Hawkins managed a slight laugh. Jenkins stopped at the door and turned back.

"There is something I guess I ought'a tell ya," he said with his hand on the door jam. "Met'a lieutenant colonel named Hackwith at headquarters. Said you and him served out West together."

"Grady," Hawkins whispered.

"Yeah," said Jenkins. "That was it. Lieutenant Colonel Grady Hackwith. He was miss'n an arm. Didn't say what happened. Was it like that when you knew'm?"

"No," said Hawkins, slowly shaking his head, looking down.

"Well, he told me dem Yankees down south might be head'n up dis way."

"What?" said Hawkins. "Here?"

"Didn't say much about it. Said it could be a campaign to take Shreveport. Was all he told me. Gotta feel'n he knew more than he was let'n on." Jenkins waved his hand. "I'll be see'n ya, David. Gotta run."

After Jenkins left, Hawkins sat there staring at his coffee. Sarah came in and stood before him.

"Everything all right, Massa David?"

He nodded as Jacob came in carrying his saddle bags.

"I almost forgot deez, David," said Jacob. "I'll jus' set'm here on da table."

"Lem'me fix ya somp'n ta eat, David." said Sarah. "Ya needs ta eat, baby."

"Maybe later," he said. "I'll be all right. Y'all run along, now. Don't mind me."

Sarah and Jacob looked at one another, then slowly headed toward the door. Just before she stepped out Sarah looked back over her shoulder, a worried look on her face. Hawkins was sitting dazed, staring off into nowhere.

For a while his hand fumbled with the coffee cup, slowly turning it in circles on the table. Then he glanced at the saddlebags to his right. Without much thought his hands found the old leather bags. He could not remember where he got them or what was inside. The first thing he found was a small pistol, an old short-barrel .32 from before the war. Then he found a small bundle of papers, orders, dispatches, cash and some of Emily's letters. Maps. A Bible. A pair of field glasses. A flask half full of brandy. A comb. A tin of tobacco. A thick leather-bond journal. Deck of cards. More papers. Then he saw something that he did not recognize at first. Pulling it out and shaking it loose, he saw that it was a blood-stained Rebel cap. Instantly his thoughts were taken back to a horrible battle and a promise he had made almost two years ago.

II

Adam McRay was a brawler. Besides working in lumber mills and chopping down trees in the woods south of Shreveport, he earned his money by fighting. Bars, back alleyways, wharfs and loading docks. Any place where a man could walk in penniless and say, "I can wup any man here," and other men would pay to see it happen. Just shy of six feet, he possessed a robust frame of intimidating proportions, muscular and compact, with the fluid swagger of a jungle cat. Very little was known about him, but he was rumored to have been orphaned at a young age and raised by the wife of a river pirate down in New Orleans. In and out of trouble with the law, his life was going nowhere until he fell in love with a pretty young girl named Carla. She tamed him somewhat, and Adam McRay settled down somewhat, to the remnants of the domestic life of a husband and a father. His drinking and brawling ways changed little, but he always provided for his family and, with the exception of a night or two spent in jail, he always came home to his wife and child. Carla became pregnant again, but tragically she and the infant died in childbirth. Though still a good father to his son, Johnny, Adam McRay's drunken debauchery increased after his loss. And just before the war began he got into a little trouble in Shreveport.

"She was the best!!" he screamed, after riding his horse into a saloon on Texas Street. "The best, I tell ya!!"

When the proprietor refused to serve him, taking exception to his unorthodox method of entry, McRay commenced to thrashing the barroom to pieces. A mallet was harmlessly broken across his granite cranium before the barkeep was pitched through the window, bouncing into the street like an empty bucket. He mowed through the crowd of local tough-guys as if taking an afternoon stroll, their punches having no effect while he obliterated everything in his path. Heaps of splintered tables and chairs littered the establishment. The piano, a wooden Indian and half-dozen spittoons were all overturned, sprawled about like clutter. Pictures and mounted animal heads were knocked from the walls. Shrieking table girls fled for cover as shattered glass flew everywhere, bottles, mugs, more windows and a fifteen-foot custom-made mirror shipped all the way from Boston.

Seven men were sent to the doctor's office that night and it finally took the sheriff and all his deputies to restrain the raging lumberjack. He was going to get four years hard labor for the stunt, but an old friend who always made money betting on his fights was able to pull a few strings. He got McRay conscripted into the Confederate Cavalry instead. He would end up in the 13th Louisiana's Company "E", commanded by a Captain Gregory Rivers. Second in command, First Lieutenant David Hawkins.

When Hawkins first resigned from his commission as a U. S. Cavalry officer, he had hopes of joining the Confederacy as a captain or possibly even a major. But he was given his same rank of first lieutenant. He had never been **that** type of officer, an inner circle man, a company man. He had come up through the enlisted ranks. When he was finally made an officer, he led by pure example and demonstration. He could outride, outrun, outfight and outshoot any soldier in his charge. And during the first few years of his commission, was required to do so quite often, dealing with insubordinate and unruly types with his own hand. Isaac, who was more like an uncle to Hawkins, had been a champion pugilist in his youth. He had taught young David many tricks of the fight game. Over the years Hawkins had also become quite proficient in the art of swordplay. He once won a duel against a much-feared opponent from France, skewering the man through the shoulder, a stunt that cost him a night in the stockade.

Though his formal education was more than adequate, Hawkins was by no means scholastic. He was, however, extremely well-read and would often shine in situations where a war of wits was required. He had very few close friends, and for the most part kept his own counsel, avoiding the covertly hostile pseudo-intellects that seemed to proliferate the junior grade ranks. He was considered by many both soft and outspoken, the latter causing him trouble on more than one occasion.

Just days after Lincoln was elected President, Hawkins was at a small officers' party in Fort Worth. Talk of secession was thick in the air. He strongly disapproved of the direction in which the North was taking the South, seeing no need to snarl her ties to the international community with trade tariffs and petty meddling. But when the topic of slavery was discussed, he saw things differently than his fellow Southern officers. Freeing the slaves and giving them small plots of land and small percentages of the profits would yield more growth in the long run than the whip and the chain. This, Hawkins thought, would also produce a kind of morale within the black community that had never really existed because of the lack of choice.

"And this," he expounded, after a few too many cognacs, "would create a huge conscription base that could be used to defeat the North, winning Southern independence."

"You've gone mad!" blurted a tall, strapping lieutenant from South Carolina. "Nigger soldiers! How utterly vulgar!"

"I've known some to ride and shoot quite well," said Hawkins. "Follow orders, too."

"Ride and shoot!" the man bellowed.

"Oh, I've seen how you mount a horse," retorted Hawkins. "Don't worry, my friend; we'll only let them become officers over their own."

"Officers!" screamed the man before throwing his drink in Hawkins's face. "I'll be waiting in the courtyard."

Hawkins made short work of the South Carolinian, who flailed madly at him with both arms. A noble effort against amateurs and street brawlers. But Hawkins was no amateur. He threw only three punches. A long hard jab, bloodying the man's nose. A quick, searing right follow-up to the jaw. And the finishing touch, a short wicked hook to the side cracking two of the man's ribs, dropping him like a sack of laundry. Though he easily won the duel with his fists, it was his words that alienated him from his peers. After he joined the Confederacy, even after the war began, this incident would come back to haunt him, slowing his climb up the chain of command.

Twice Hawkins briefly had the opportunity to join the Confederacy as a captain. The first came shortly before Sumter as a staff advisory liaison officer to Governor Moore. The posting would allow him to stay in Louisiana, assisting in the state's military development, reporting only to the Governor and his top generals. But rumors were spread of his true position on slavery and he was denied the appointment. The second came just days after the war began. He was being considered as a candidate to command a company in the 3rd Louisiana Cavalry. As he met with the unit's colonel, discussing his qualifications, he noticed an unwelcome, familiar face among the staff, the sneering South Carolinian. Hawkins would eventually be assigned to the 13th as executive officer to "E" Company.

The 13th Louisiana Cavalry was a rough, tough gang of over 1500 mounted men that was formed shortly after the state seceded from the Union. It was made up of seven companies, each with over 200 country boys who were all eager to go and pick a fight with the first bunch of Yankees they could find. Hawkins, who had seen quite a bit of combat out West fighting

Indians and outlaws, knew deep down inside that his past experiences would pale in comparison to what was about to happen. His men were more than willing and ready to fight, but they lacked the practical knowledge that came only from combat itself. At first Hawkins saw potential in Adam McRay. He could ride and shoot better than most, but it was his strength and toughness that really caught Hawkins's eye. He would soon learn, however, that McRay was big trouble. He stayed drunk and always seemed to be getting into fights. He was insubordinate and gave a damn about no one but himself. Once he was caught passed out under some bushes when he was supposed to be helping dig latrines. As punishment Hawkins ordered McRay to dig the latrines by himself. A few hours later McRay was found sleeping in the bushes again. Hawkins was just about to have him put in shackles, when it was brought to his attention that the latrines had been dug to his exact specifications. McRay had done the work of three men in less than half the time. Another time Hawkins caught McRay intentionally picketing a troop of horses in a spot known for flooding. A storm was coming, so he had the man move the whole line of over forty horses to higher ground. By the time the rains came, Hawkins was stunned to learn that McRay had moved the whole company's herd of horses, some 215 animals, to higher ground, all staked down and tied in. As McRay sat laughing atop his own horse, whiskey bottle in hand, Hawkins could not decide whether to have the man arrested or promoted. He chose the latter. McRay was made a corporal with four men under him.

By 1862 the battles of the war began taking on a more epic scope. In its first few months many a political speaker would scoff at the notion of a long, bloody war. Even Frederick Engels, on a European speaking tour, said that the war in North America would amount to very little. Fort Sumter was almost bloodless, a mule being the only casualty. The first real battles were quite small, pitting a few hundred men against a few hundred men. First Manassas changed all that. Now armies of thousands were slamming into each other with frightful results, using antiquated, small-battlefield tactics against powerful weapons that killed from great distances, enlarging the field as well as the violence.

A large Union force was moving through western Tennessee attempting to drive out the Confederate Army. The 13th Louisiana Cavalry was sent to northern Mississippi to help stop the Union advance. At Corinth, Hawkins and McRay would have another confrontation. This time he found the man fighting for money. McRay had easily taken all four of his men's hard-earned weekly pay, almost forcing them to fight. When Hawkins demanded he give the money back, McRay refused. A dark look came over Hawkins as he calmly took off his coat, preparing to square off with the grinning McRay. Though four inches shorter than his commander, McRay matched Hawkins in overall size and weight, and was deceptively quick and agile. He also had no qualms about harming an officer and Hawkins knew this. From the start the fight was a violent crowd pleaser, most of the men rooting for Hawkins, a few rooting for McRay. "E" Company's executive officer fought with surgical precision, landing beautifully timed blows to the corporal's rock-hard jaw. McRay landed fewer punches, but their jarring effects were evident and soon both men's faces were bloody and swollen. Suddenly, Captain Rivers happened upon the crazed mayhem.

"What in God's name is this!?" he screamed. "Lieutenant Hawkins, please explain yourself!"

The two men stood weary before their superior, swaying and unbalanced.

"A demonstration, sir," lied Hawkins. "Corporal McRay and I were simply showing the men some of the finer techniques of close quarter fighting, sir."

"Nonsense!" growled Rivers. "If either of you is unable to perform your duties, I'll hold you responsible, Lieutenant!"

Later the ever-insolent McRay approached Hawkins feigning fatigue and injury.

"I'm not feel'n so good, Lieutenant," he said. "Might need to go see the doctor, huh?"

It was all Hawkins could do to restrain himself from pulling his sidearm and shooting the man on the spot.

Less than a week later, Confederate Commander-in-Chief Albert Sidney Johnston moved his three consolidated corps back into Tennessee with plans of crushing Ulysses S. Grant's Army at Pittsburg Landing. Two months earlier Grant had invaded Tennessee, capturing Forts Henry and Donelson, rocking the whole framework of Confederate defense in the western theater of the war. Southern forces abandoned Kentucky, and Nashville was lost. Now the Rebels would do what they could to drive out the Yankees. Over 100,000 men would clash in the beautiful, scenic hillsides surrounding Shiloh Church, bringing something very new to the American way of war: monumental wholesale slaughter.

Many had said the 13th was doomed from the onset, having been given the very number of ill fortune. At dawn they raced across the west end of the peach orchard. Pink blossom petals began to fall, knocked loose by the concussive explosions of gunfire, drifting down in moving sheets of pastel to blanket the field and blind the view. The ill-fated battalion would be all but wiped out by a series of terrible mishaps. First, they ran headlong into a Union artillery barrage. Then, still reeling, they were charged by over a thousand fresh Ohio infantrymen. Then they were picked apart like cornstalks by Indiana and Iowa sharpshooters, only to be charged again and again.

Hawkins's left leg was badly broken during the cannon attack and he was pinned under his dead horse. Just as he was about to be bayoneted, helplessly run through by a screaming Yankee, Adam McRay sprang from the encircling chaos. Now a murdering do-gooder, he played the martyr card, rectifying his sins in a last-minute reprieve. With casual truculence he shot the Yankee through the head, then stood his ground fighting to protect his commander. McRay was well within his element, a juggernaut of inexorable might repelling every entreaty. A screaming, howling wreck of havoc, run amuck on the enemy like a secret weapon.

During a slight lull in the fighting, McRay pulled Hawkins out from under his horse and began carrying him through the madness toward the tree line. Repeatedly he had to lay the man down, better to fight, dispensing his wrath in turns. Then they moved on, crawling and stepping over men in heaps. Dodging the fray where they could, tangled piles of human wreckage, they glanced in horror at the vast pandemonium strewn to the cardinal points. A seething labyrinth of corporeal fury, apocalyptic and rabid, stretched to the horizon. A deafening roar permeated the atmosphere, a thousand-thousand shouts at the devil, multiplied by all the lamentations of Jeremiah in sackcloth and ashes.

Suddenly there was a loud clap of thunder and the entire sky lit up. From horizon to horizon it blazed the color of bright blue flame. At that moment something very strange happened; the fighting ceased. The Battle of Shiloh came to an abrupt intermission. Every man stopped his killing work and looked up, scanning the heavens in awe. The silence was deafening. Men began to point. There was something in the sky. It was the image of a Man with His arms stretched out wide. He was enveloped, but not consumed, by the brilliant blue flame that had become the sky. Then it began to rain. Only it wasn't water. It was blood, thick drops of crimson pelting the combatants below. Then the sky began to fade back to its original cloudscape, dimming, obscuring the image of the Man until He vanished. The blood-rain then turned to water, washing the airborne blood into the soil, mixing with the blood of the fallen. The rain then stopped, rays of sunlight cueing the inevitable. An unbearable tension seemed to rise out of the earth, the vast plethora of soldiers all looking at one another. Then, as if the vision had never happened, the killing resumed with a vociferous mingled roar.

McRay continued to carry Hawkins, traversing the ravaged field till they reached the tree line. They rested a moment in the shade, the battle churning before them just yards away. McRay was shot and both had been lacerated, bleeding badly, in need of medical attention. Hawkins looked to his left and right noticing hundreds of emerald green caterpillars inching their way across the crimson-stained grass, crawling here and there over the corpses of men, who just moments ago had crawled off to die alone in peace. The tiny larva meandered in and out of rifle barrels, up and down the edges of sword and bayonet blades, leaving tiny red trails streaked across the faces of the dead.

"I don't know what dat was," said McRay, not taking his eyes off the fighting, "but I know I ain't the only one dat seen it."

He looked at Hawkins, who was slumped against the base of an oak tree, still watching the green caterpillars as they crawled through the bloody flora. He too wondered what he'd seen out there, but was in such pain it was hard to get his thoughts together. Watching the caterpillars felt tranquil, and he suddenly thought of staying there till he died.

"Come on, Lieutenant," McRay said. "Let's get go'n."

"Leave me," he told McRay. "I can't go any further."

"Ya want me ta go'n get yer nanny, Lieutenant?" taunted the corporal.

"Save yourself," said Hawkins, closing his eyes.

"Get ya ass up," said McRay as he lifted his screaming commander by the armpits.

They traveled only a short distance before coming to a small creek, one of the many tributaries in the area that flowed into the Tennessee River. Its banks were sparsely lined with the dead and dying, blood swirling in its ripples. From behind them the sounds of battle reverberated through the trees, at times rising to a dire cacophonous peal, echoing in great coughs like some gigantic beast stirring off in the distance. Just as McRay was helping Hawkins get a drink from the water, four Union soldiers appeared at the creek, emerging out of the brush not twenty feet away. For a moment the two groups stared at each other, fear and surprise showing on their faces, even McRay's. Then, as one of the Yankees raised his rifle, McRay drew his pistol. Shots rang out as he quickly rolled to his right and charged the four men. Hawkins lay helpless, watching from the creek's edge as the corporal engaged the enemy with all that was left of his ebbing strength. At one point he seemed done for, teetering at the brink of defeat and death. But then, with almost inhuman reserve, he sprang back, scrapping bellicose from deep within. Crushing blows. Violent knife strikes. And finally, grappling a fallen pistol from the last man, shooting him in the face. Utterly exhausted he crawled back to Hawkins, strained to lift him, then moving on following the flow of the creek.

McRay was totally spent, and it wasn't long before he could go no further. He fell to the ground, causing Hawkins to cry out in pain. The two of them lay there, helpless, breathing heavily, not speaking. Through the brush voices could be heard. Suddenly another team of Union soldiers was on them, half-a-dozen or more. They raised their rifles touching McRay and Hawkins with the tips of their bayonets, poised to run them through. But suddenly a Man appeared out of nowhere, stepping to gently push aside the sharp bayonets. He wore a white tunic and ash-colored pants. His hair was long and His face was like that of an angel. The Union soldiers stepped back in fear, turned and disappeared into the brush.

They next thing Hawkins knew, he was being carried along the creek again by McRay, the unknown Man nowhere to be seen. They soon heard a shout and looked up. A small band of walking-wounded Confederates was moving through the trees to their right headed for the creek. A row of men with their heads, arms and legs wrapped in bloody bandages, limping and crutching their way from the dreadful battlefield. After drinking their fill of water the men helped Hawkins and McRay as best they could, and eventually they found a makeshift Confederate hospital.

Hawkins and McRay lay bleeding on the ground, staring at one another. All around them horribly wounded men screamed and pleaded for help. Blood pooled in the grass mixing with the sudden April rain scattered throughout the hills. To the side, arms and legs were hacked off at the surgeon's callous disregard to the men's hideous shrieks of pain. Held down, sometimes by teams of three or more, as they flailed and begged. Limbs tossed into piles like so much cordwood.

Somehow through all the chaos, McRay had been able to keep his cap. Reaching out, he handed the blood-soaked garment to Hawkins.

"Please, sir," he said, very weak. "If ya live, take my cap to my boy in Pleasant Hill. His name's Johnny. Johnny McRay. He's only eleven. Please, sir….please."

No sooner had Hawkins taken the cap than he was lifted up, screaming, and laid on a stretcher.

"I will," he gasped, looking down into McRay's pleading eyes. "I promise." The last thing he noticed, before he was carried off, was McRay sighing with something like relief and closing his eyes.

On a table Hawkins's trousers were cut off, revealing a small nub of bone jutting from his left calf. A piece of wood was shoved in his mouth as one man held him under his armpits, while another pulled on the broken leg. Just before he passed out Hawkins screamed silently, his voice now gone, biting hard on the stick as the nub of bone receded back into his leg with a sickening crack. Because he was an officer, Hawkins received faster care and his leg was set clean and saved. The man who saved his life repeatedly that day bled to death waiting.

Later, after he came to, Hawkins looked out and saw a long row of dead being prepared for burial. He then noticed a Man carrying Adam McRay's lifeless body. The Man turned and looked directly at Hawkins from across the distance. It was the Man who had saved them from the Union soldiers. The Man then turned and gently laid McRay in the row of dead, momentarily placing His hand on the dead Confederate's forehead. At that time a column of soldiers marched by obscuring Hawkins's view. When they had past the Man was gone, McRay lying at the end of the row of corpses.

That night a terrible storm raged as if God Himself was rebuking the conflict. From the back of a packed ambulance wagon, Hawkins watched in horror as brilliant lightning strikes illuminated the battlefield. Silhouetted images of hogs were seen feeding off the ungathered dead, fighting over the corpses. After Shiloh the 13th Louisiana Cavalry was so decimated it was disbanded, its remnants absorbed into another Louisiana regiment, which was soon sent to Virginia, just in time for the Seven Days.

Sitting at the table, staring at the cap in his hands, Hawkins realized he had not thought of that day since it happened. So many terrible things had occurred since then. Had that been the first time he encountered the Man in White? He wasn't sure. Perhaps he was simply going mad. He did feel something, however, something he thought just moments ago was gone from his life forever. Purpose. Direction. A reason to carry on. Honor and a sense of duty. He had a promise to keep.

"Sarah!" he shouted. "Jacob!"

When they entered he was on his feet stuffing everything back into the bags.

"Sarah, where's my uniform? I need it now." He looked up at them as if everything were normal, showing renewed vigor and life in his movements.

"Why, it be hang'n in ya room, David," she said. "It was sump'n filthy, but'iss good'n clean now."

"Jacob, go'n get Jackson ready for me, please."

"Ya mean Jacko?" Jacob frowned. "Dat crazy ol' dawg?"

"No," said Hawkins. "Jackson. My horse, man, my horse."

"Oh, yessir," said Jacob, looking a little confused. "You go'n somewheres, David?"

"Yes, I have business at attend to." He turned to Sarah. "I'll take you up on that breakfast now. Remember how I like my eggs?"

"Ah' course, David," said Sarah, moving to crack some eggs. "Over runny. But ya can't go nowheres now. Ya needs ta rest."

"Please, Darling, just do as I ask," he said, looking at them both. He then turned and walked from the kitchen leaving the two confused slaves to wonder what on earth the matter was.

They had no idea why or where he was going, but since he had made up his mind to go, they would do their best to help him look his best. Water was heated so he could take a hot bath after he ate. He shaved off his beard leaving the mustache and goatee. Noah polished his old, weathered boots and Sarah trimmed his hair. After he was dressed he stood in front of a full-length mirror admiring himself on attention.

Outside Jacob had Jackson by the reins, holding the beautiful animal at a distance. The sun shined off his dark reddish-orange, well-muscled body, its long unruly mane so black as to almost appear blue. The horse seemed giddy with anticipation, snorting, neighing and tossing its head side to side when Hawkins stepped outside. Just as he was about to mount the beautiful charger, Ruth ran up with a long brownish-red feather in her hand.

"I founds it down by da bayou, Massa David," she said, smiling sweetly at him. "Fer ya hat."

"Red-tailed hawk," he said in a pensive tone, as if the item had suddenly conjured up some distant memory. He removed his hat, setting the feather in its band before placing back on his head.

"Thank ya, Ruth. How's it look?"

"Mighty fine, Massa David," said Ruth, half-spinning back and forth, grinning up at Hawkins. "Ya looks real impo'tant."

"Ya be gone long, David?" asked Jacob.

"No, I should be back later this evening."

"Where ya's go'n, David?" asked Sarah.

"Now, shugga," said Jacob, looking at his wife. "Where Massa David's a go'n ain't none'a our lookout."

"I'm go'n down to Pleasant Hill," said Hawkins. "Won't be gone long."

He tipped his hat to his small family of slaves and headed off, Jackson moving in an effortless, graceful trot.

"Wonder why David's go'n to Pleasant Hill?" asked Jacob out loud to himself. "Ain't nut'n down nair."

"Well, I don't know," said Sarah. "Ain't none'a my lookout."

"Watch it, girl," Jacob said swatting his wife on the butt as their children giggled, "'fo I takes ya back behinds da shed an' gives ya what fo."

"Oh, I'm always watch'n you," she said walking away, looking over her shoulder. "Take me behind dat shed. I ain't scare't none."

III

Pleasant Hill was a small town of about 300 that sat at the base of a gentle rise sixty miles due south of Shreveport. It was an affluent community within the sphere and influence of a few prosperous cotton plantations, a center of refinement and education with a bank, a post office and a nice hotel. It was a well-kept hamlet with two small colleges, one for girls and one for boys. There was a little museum and art gallery, a theater and several thriving businesses. To the north, alongside the road that ran into the little village, was a small schoolhouse that was situated a bit off, somewhat isolated from the rest of the town. About a hundred feet to the side of the schoolhouse was a large pecan tree that was a favorite gathering spot for a few of the lesser-privileged children who lived in the area. In Pleasant Hill even the lesser-privileged lived quite well. After school or on weekends or whenever their parents would let them, they would meet at the large tree, playing games, gathering up fallen pecans and just talk about the things children talk about.

Today 13-year-old Bobby Bernard had an audience. And when he had an audience, there were two things he loved to do, run his mouth and fight. The former he had been doing for the better part of a half-hour, telling another embellished tale of how his father had been single-handedly reducing the Yankee population of Louisiana. The latter was just moments away.

"Dare was 'bout four'a dem damn Yankees left, see," Bernard drawled with grave exaggeration to the small crowd, whose ages ranged from four to fourteen. "An' dey had my pa cornered, see. An'ees da last man stand'n, with only four bullets left." Bernard hesitated for effect, then continued. "He lifts his hands like 'ees gonna surrender. Den, fast as light'nin, he whipped out his pistol an' shot'm all right twixt da eyes. Dead'r dan dawg roots."

A collective "Ooooh" rose from the crowd of youngsters. Only one seemed unimpressed with Bobby Bernard's tall tale, 13-year-old Johnny McRay.

"You're such a liar, Bernard. I swear."

"Whad'ju say?" said Bobby, jerking his head around at Johnny.

"Your pa was part'a dat patrol dat went after dee'serters," said Johnny. "He ain't done no fight'n."

"Watch yer mouth, McRay," said Bobby, moving close to Johnny, "or I'll wup ya, just like last time."

Bobby was a few months older than Johnny and they were about the same height, but Bobby was a bit stouter. They disliked each other so much, they only called one another by their last names. Several times they'd gotten in fights over the past couple of years, with Bobby always edging out a win. Not because Johnny couldn't fight; Bobby was just a little too strong for him. Still, Johnny refused to observe the pecking order, and Bobby always did what he could to provoke an incident.

"Yer pa never fought no Yankees," said Johnny, looking Bobby right in the eye. "All 'ee did was arrest men who came home without'a fur'low. I did hear'ee shot a man once, but it weren't no Yankee. Just some fella 'round Doyline way, want'n to see's wife'n kids. An' your pa shot'm, Bernard."

"Oh, yeah," said Bobby. "Well at least my pa's good 'nuff to stay alive."

Johnny's eyes narrowed, growing dark with anger and rage. "Take it back Bernard, or I'll …"

"Or what, McRay?" Bobby moved closer, his face only inches from Johnny's. "Or what?"

Johnny's father had taught him how to fight, how to twist his back foot, turning his arm, all the while throwing the punch in a tight straight line. And that's just what he did, crashing a textbook right cross to Bobby Bernard's jaw, knocking his head around 180 degrees like a loose shutter. But the bigger boy absorbed the blow, wrestling Johnny's arms into a clinch. As the two youngsters tussled to the ground in a cloud of dust, the rest of the kids went berserk. Eventually, Bobby got Johnny in a headlock and began pummeling his face with punches.

Just then, Jake Watson, the owner of the local general store came looking for his son, Mark, needed back at the family business to help stock some leather goods from Texas. Watson was a huge, fat tank of a man with no neck, and arms like a picnic roast. When he saw Johnny and Bobby fighting on the ground, surrounded by the small pack of screaming children, he rolled his eyes and waddled as quickly as possible over to the kid-world commotion.

"You two, again!" he shouted, after jerking the two juvenile brawlers off the ground and holding them at arm's length from each other. "I don't believe it!"

"He started it!" cried Bobby, pointing at Johnny, who was still red with rage, a trickle of blood from his nose, silent and glaring at the other boy.

"Yeah," Watson said cynically. "And I'll bet ya did nothing to provoke'm, huh?"

"Me!?" Bobby blurted, playing the innocent victim. "He trew da first punch! Axt anyone!"

Suddenly, Bobby was distracted by something. He looked off behind Watson, away from the small crowd of children. "Hey! Look at dat!"

The group turned to see a Confederate soldier riding up the road that led into Pleasant Hill. He was superbly mounted on a magnificent horse the color of sunburnt ocher with a long flowing sable mane. When he spotted the small group gathered under the spreading boughs of the pecan tree he detoured their way. After stopping in front of them, the regal horse turned sideways as if to display its master. A long feather, almost the color of the horse, jutted from the soldier's hat, presenting quite a sight for small-town folks, especially children.

"Howdy, sir," said Watson, not sure what else to say. "Is there any trouble? Something I can help ya with?"

At first the Confederate said nothing, just looked at the little crowd of awed on-lookers. Then he straightened his hat and sat up in the saddle.

"I'm look'n for a young fella named Johnny McRay."

In unison, Watson and the other children all turned to look at Johnny, who stood staring wide-eyed at the majestic sight before him.

After a moment, while the Confederate's eyes scanned the small group, Watson's hand gently released Johnny and the boy slowly stepped forward.

"I'm Johnny," he softly said.

The soldier slowly dismounted and reached into his saddlebags pulling out a Rebel cap, most of its butternut-gray discolored a dark shade of rust. With his elbows propped up against the horse, he held the cap in both hands just above the edge of the leather bag, staring at it as if it possessed some kind of special gift or dark secret. He then turned and walked over to Johnny, holding out the cap for the boy to see.

"I'm Major David Hawkins, and this here cap belonged to your pa. He gave it to me almost two years ago at Shiloh. He asked me, if I lived, to please bring it to you." He handed the cap to the boy, but did not let go. "Your pa died saving my life."

Johnny took the cap, looking at it for a long while before looking back up at Hawkins.

"Thank ya, Mister."

The small group was silent for a moment. Then Watson began tending to the children.

"Aw' right, now," he said. "y'all run along. Mark, go on up to the store and help ya ma. Get them goods all sorted out."

As the children dispersed, Bobby Bernard, who was almost green with envy, looked over his shoulder at Johnny. But Johnny was looking at his father's cap, studying the splotches of long-since-dried blood stained into its threads. Watson introduced himself to Hawkins and the two made small talk, while Johnny glanced back and forth from the cap to the tall soldier who had brought it to him. Finally, Watson headed back into the town, leaving the boy and the Confederate alone to talk.

They walked side by side in a large clearing near the pecan tree. Hawkins cracked two of the nutty fruits in the palm of his hand while Johnny still examined the cap, turning it over and over as if expecting to find some other remnant effect of his father's. Behind them, Jackson trailed freely, nibbling at patches of grass here and there as his reins traced the ground.

"Is dis my pa's blood or yours?" asked Johnny, looking up at Hawkins.

"Might be a bit of both, son," answered Hawkins, "but I'm sure most of it's your pa's."

For a long while the two were silent. Then, without being prompted, the boy began to talk about his life when he had both a mother and a father. Hawkins learned that in his early years, before his mother passed away, Johnny's life had been quite good. Carla McRay had kept a simple yet loving home with fresh-baked biscuits every morning with butter and honey. In the afternoon a peach or apple or blackberry cobbler would be cooling by the window. She baked sugar cookies and muffins he liked to eat with molasses or jam. Sometimes she would make gumbo or jambalaya, chicken stew or meat pies. They would play games together like checkers or hide-and-go-seek, or take long walks through the woods holding hands, playing word games or 'I Spy.' At night she would sing him to sleep with sweet lullabies, stroking his hair until he dreamed off to be awakened by her cheerful encouraging voice.

Although Johnny knew of his father's carousing ways, he never saw it firsthand at home. Hawkins heard the boy talk of a man very different from the one he knew in the 13th. A man who never once raised a hand to Johnny or his mother. A man who brought home gifts and jovial stories of the day. An upbeat jocular man of boundless energy, always willing to help others, wanting little or nothing in return. Occasionally, Adam would take the three of them into town, or on a daylong outing at one of the many lakes in the area.

Only once did Johnny and Carla come close to witnessing Adam's potential rage. He had taken them to Shreveport one weekend, with a nice room at the Remington Hotel, dinner at Straughn's and a carriage ride along the river. It was early evening and they were walking back to the hotel on Spring Street when three drunken cowhands staggered by using foul language, a forgivable offence if a simple apology was offered. But the cowboys only leered momentarily at Carla before moving on.

"Fellas hav'n a good time, are ya?" Adam coolly remarked after they had passed. The three men stopped and turned, looking more carefully at the McRay family. Carla had on a nice autumn dress. Seven-year-old Johnny and his father were each wearing a new coat and tie.

"Why, sure," said the biggest, four teeth showing through his crooked grin, eyes back on Carla. "An' how y'all do'n?"

"Well, we were do'n just fine, up till now," said Adam, taking a step toward the man. "Sir, I realize yer not dressed at the height of fashion. But if ya don't take yer eyes off my wife an' apologize for yer mouth, I'm gonna hit ya so hard, when ya come to, your clothes are gonna be outta style." By the time Adam said the last words his face was only inches from the taller man.

"Now, Adam, don't you hurt those men," said Carla, placing her hand on her husband's rock-like shoulder. "You yourself said this dress was gonna make everyone look at me."

After a tense moment the three men tipped their hats, humbly apologized and went on their way.

"Dat ol' feller never knew how close he come to be'n chewed up an' spit out like a bad piece'a pie crust," Johnny said to Hawkins, who raised his eyebrows and nodded, pensively rubbing his chin.

"Sometimes pa'd come home with 'is face all busted up, like he'd been fight'n." Johnny looked at the cap. "He'd smell like whiskey. But he'd never act mean or nut'n'. Ma'd act kind'a funny, quiet an' all. But really, she didn't seem to care. Cept'a couple'a times, pa didn't come home 'cause he's in jail. Then ma chewed'm out good, but pa didn't say nothin' bad to'r. Just kissed'r an' said it won't happen no mores. He loved me and ma."

Two years before the war started, when Johnny was only eight, Carla died and Adam started back drinking almost every night. She had been far along in her second pregnancy when terrible, shooting pains caused her to collapse in the yard. Adam was sent for at the mill twenty miles away in Mansfield. But when he arrived the baby had already been stillborn. Carla had hemorrhaged badly, the doctor unable to control the bleeding. Later that night she died while Adam held her, weeping like a child. Financially Adam still took good care of Johnny. But he soon began staying away longer and longer, leaving the boy with Carla's cousin, the local schoolteacher just returned from college.

"Pa use'ta take me fish'n over dat way," Johnny told Hawkins, pointing at a small trail that led off into the woods, obviously wanting to change the subject of his mother's death. "An' on da utha side's some good hunt'n. We'd always shoot us a coon or two. Whole heap'a squirrels and rabbits. Seen me some deer run'n jus' dis morn'n."

Hawkins forced a smile. His thoughts were on Emily and he suddenly missed her very much. They both often wondered why they had not been able to have children. He imagined her there walking with them now. And even though Johnny was a bit too old, he suddenly imagined him as the child they never had.

"What's ya horse's name?" asked Johnny, turning to pet the calm animal.

"I call'm Jackson."

"Jackson?" Johnny said, screwing up his face at the soldier. "Funny name fer a horse. Why'd ya call'm dat?"

"I got'm at Chancellorsville," said Hawkins, running his hand over the magnificent horse's black mane. "Same day Stonewall Jackson fell. So I named'm Jackson."

"You knew Stonewall Jackson?" asked Johnny, looking up at Hawkins in wonder.

"Well, sort'a. I once delivered him a very important message."

"Wow, really!? Did he say thanks?"

"Not sure." Hawkins laughed. "Things was pretty loud at the time."

At that moment a large red-tailed hawk plunged from the sky like an apparition. With chilling accuracy it snatched up an unsuspecting old hare scampering across the clearing. Without missing a beat of its wings, the raptor swooped the helpless creature up into the tall pecan tree. The Confederate and the boy watched silently as the majestic bird began tearing the rabbit to pieces. Talons deep in the poor coney's flesh. Entrails hanging from the hawk's blood-splattered beak.

"How'd my pa save yer life?" Johnny suddenly asked as they both continued to watch the gory spectacle in the tree.

Hawkins took a deep breath, then began telling Johnny what happened that wet spring day in Tennessee. He told how his company was wiped out almost to the man. How his leg had been badly broken when his horse was shot out from under him during the initial cavalry charge. How Adam had saved him from almost certain death. And how he stood and fought with uncommon bravery and skill, single handedly defeating one enemy soldier after another. He told Johnny how his father carried him to the safety of the trees, even after being shot himself. Then on to the creek, where he tenaciously fought again, outnumbered four to one yet emerging victorious, only to have to carry his commander even further before finding help. And finally, he told Johnny of their intimate moment in the terrible hospital when his father handed Hawkins his bloody cap. How he pleaded with him to take it to his son. It was then, looking back on that day, Hawkins realized he had met the Adam McRay that Johnny knew. A man who had loved and lost his wife with the same passion and pain as he felt for Emily. A man, who if dealt by fate a slightly different hand, could have fittingly been Hawkins's superior.

When Hawkins had finished with the painful account, he looked at Johnny standing to his left. The boy had finally put on his father's cap, but kept his eyes on the savage display in the tree. Locks of golden-blond hair fell out from under the cover, touching the light brown freckles that dotted his nose and cheekbones. He seemed to age, taking on the likeness of his father. The deep-set, penetrating hazel eyes. The wide, generous mouth, buttressed by a strong, square jaw. Hawkins guessed that his mother had been somewhat tall, for Johnny stood only a few inches shorter than his father. He would surely grow much more over the years, filling out to become a large, powerful man. But it was the look in his eyes that touched Hawkins most. Unlike his other features, which still held fast to the wondrous years of youth, his eyes seemed to be seeking something. Wanting the type of knowledge that taxed the soul, leaving vacuums the older man would try to fill with ill-formed vanities of the mind.

They continued their walk following the perimeter of the clearing, coming back around to the opposite side of the schoolhouse. As they approached, a woman in her late twenties stepped out on the porch. She wore a dark blue dress and had long brown hair that fell around an honest face with just a hint of mischief and curiosity.

"Aunt Amy," Johnny called out. "This here's Major David Hawkins. He brought me Pa's cap from the war."

"Oh, hello, Major," she said with a charming smile, unabashedly admiring the man in his uniform. "Good to meet you. Amy Bolton. Actually, I'm Johnny's second cousin, but he insists on calling me aunt. His mother and I were first cousins."

The three chatted for a while making casual pleasantries. Randy Randall then appeared and asked Johnny if some of the boys could see the cap. Johnny excused himself and ran off with Randy to show his gift to the boys who were waiting under the pecan tree.

"It's very nice of you to bring him his father's cap, Major," said Amy as they watched the boys from the porch.

"Please," he said turning to her. "Call me David."

"All right," she smiled. "David. You knew Adam well?"

"He was in my company," said Hawkins. "As far as knowing him well, I doubt that anyone in the whole battalion knew him very well. He was a bit difficult at times. But I can say that he was a very brave, strong man. I'd be dead if it wasn't for him."

"Where did this happen?" she asked, tilting her head slightly to the side. Hawkins looked at her lovely face, for a moment unable to speak. Her dark brown eyes matched the color of her hair. They gleamed with a thoughtful, radiating warmth that stirred the Confederate. A compassionate glow emanated from her countenance causing him to realize the subtle seduction. He could not look away.

"Shiloh," he finally said.

"Oh, my goodness," she replied, bringing one hand to her mouth, the other gently touching the sleeve of his coat. Most of the civilized world knew about Shiloh. At its time it had been the largest battle in the Western Hemisphere, one of the greatest in history. Since then it had been reduced to part of a list, a declaration for the many battles that were worse.

"A tough day for the regiment," was all he could say.

Their eyes could not pull apart, a fascination of something new and uncomplicated yet still fleeting. Tangible, within reach yet chased by doubt and fear. His alone.

"Yes," she said, yielding to his sad, constant gaze. "Would you like some tea?" She motioned to the door of the schoolhouse, showing something that might have passed for awkwardness.

"Sure. A cup of tea would be nice."

They sat at a small table by a window watching Johnny and his friends as they passed the cap around, each trying it on for size. For a while the soldier and the teacher conversed of simple things, people and places familiar to both. Then Amy asked Hawkins if he had any family. He hesitated, looking out the window at the boys still standing and jostling with each other around the pecan tree.

"My wife passed away about a month ago," he said, looking back at her.

"Oh, I'm so sorry," she said, again touching his arm sending a warm sensation through his body. "But didn't you say that you only got back four days ago?"

"Yes," he said quietly. "That's when I found out."

"Oh, how sad." Their hands touched, gently wrapping around one another. For just a second they both hesitated and she pulled back slightly, embarrassed at the advance. "I'm so sorry. I ..."

"No, please." He took her hand back, gently pulling it to the center of the table as tears showed in his eyes, his voice wavering yet calm. "I don't know what to say. To go through all that hell and come home and ...," he hesitated, the grief still showing in his eyes. "I miss her so much."

She reached out and touched his face, suddenly feeling lost herself, a witness to his pain as she quietly spoke. "You don't have to say anything, David."

Her words compelled him to lift his hand and touch her cheek with his fingertips. She smiled softly, and for a long while they gazed into each other's eyes, caressing and feeling the sweetness of the affection. He held her face in his hand, his thumb touching the soft part of her ear. His fingers ran gently back and forth across her cheek, tracing the line of her jaw. She closed her eyes just slightly, her smile growing brighter, but not forced. The room seemed to light up as she tilted her head back, his fingers moving in slow little circles down her neck. He leaned in close, unable to look away from her mouth, her lovely, beautiful mouth. She smelled of lilac, cinnamon and lavender. How long they kissed he did not know, their lips seeking the other's softness. Eyes closed, they became lost in the warmth of one another, arousing sensations neither had felt in years.

"Aunt Amy, can I go'n show da cap to some'a da udder kids?" Johnny had called out just before entering, but they pulled apart too late and he caught a glimpse of their intimacy.

"Oh, uh … yes, Johnny, go ahead," said Amy, standing trying to recover from the awkward moment. "But tell me again, in proper English, what you are going to do."

For a second Johnny stood there not knowing if he was supposed to see what he had just seen. Then, he straightened himself and squared his shoulders.

"I'm going to show the cap to some of the other kids." Johnny said this as if he were practicing lines to a play.

"Very good, Johnny. And …," said Amy, glancing at Hawkins.

"Oh, yeah!" Johnny stepped forward extending his hand to Hawkins. "Thank you very much Major Hawkins for bringing me my pa's cap. It was good to meet ya and I hope your leg gets better. Would it be all right if I came and visited ya sometime?"

"Sure, Johnny," said Hawkins. "Drop by any time. I'd like that."

After Johnny left with his friends, Hawkins and Amy stood for a while not saying anything. Then he looked away and moved toward the door.

"Miss Bolton, I'm sorry. I should be going. Thank you very much for the tea."

"Please," she said. "You don't have to go."

He did not meet her eyes as he left the schoolhouse, crossed the porch, descended the steps and mounted Jackson. Without Hawkins's lead, the animal took two steps to where Amy stood at the edge of the porch and began nuzzling her hands. Since he had first acquired Jackson in Virginia nine months earlier, he constantly spoke to the horse of Emily, whispering stories of his love in the sorrel's ear.

"What a beautiful horse," said Amy, stroking the animal's face.

"Another who saved my life," said Hawkins, staring at the ground.

"Please, come again," she said as he touched his hat, still not looking at her, gently spurring Jackson into a trot.

At a slight bend in the road just outside the town limit he stopped, keeping his eyes straight ahead. He actually feared what he might see if he turned back. Surely she would have stepped back inside, undaunted by his curt departure. Finally, he looked over his shoulder and she was still there, standing on the porch a hundred yards away through the trees. Still gazing after him, just as he had left her. Even from a distance he could make out her thoughtful smile, the ends of her mouth turned upward, responding to his decision to stop and look back. Her hands were held together, hanging loosely against her blue dress. A graceful posture of hope. Again without command or gesture, Jackson, who had also looked back, turned and began to walk toward the schoolhouse. Hawkins let out a sigh as his horse veered off the road through the trees, straight toward the innocently esoteric Amy Bolton, as if drawn to a new friend or some merciful source.

"Did you forget something?" she said, again tilting her head for effect, acknowledging the return of his presence and his eyes, reaching out to greet the ever-coquettish Jackson.

"I think my horse likes you," he said, still looking and feeling so awkward. Although he dismounted slowly, letting Jackson's reins slip to the ground; before he knew it he was back up on the porch, again unable to take his eyes away from her and her soft supple smile.

For over two years he had been faithful to Emily, never once bowing to the temptations of the women who followed the soldiers. Was this just something he needed? The physical touch of a woman. Or was it something more than that? It really didn't matter now. Still he felt so awkward. He suddenly thought of the Man in White and looked around, his eyes scanning the trees.

"What's wrong?" she asked, thoughtfully.

"Miss Bolton, I uh…" He looked back at her.

"Please," she said, stepping close to him, her hands inside his elbows, his hands touching her hips. "Call me Amy."

"Amy," he said softly, caressing her face like silence after a long dreadful noise, a soothing quiet so welcome and hoped for.

Their lips came together again. She let out a soft purring moan as he ran his fingers through her chestnut hair. She led him to a small back room where she kept a bed for times when a child might become ill. That bed was seldom used except for her to take an occasional nap. But today she used it to bring a near-dead soldier back to life. They spent most of the afternoon in that room, touching and exploring each other, not caring what anyone outside might think. It was a special time for both of them, talking little, holding and looking into each other's eyes. Looking for something, something lost long ago. Something in their dreams. Something beautiful, innocent and still free.

When the time came, she did not want him to go and he did not want to leave. They parted without episode or empty promises. Still looking and smiling, almost like children. From the porch of the schoolhouse, her hair roughed up, falling on her blouse. From over his shoulder, till he could see her no more for the trees.

All the way back into town his conscience whispered to him. Did this mean he'd sinned in God's eyes? Who was he to question that? He knew that he would repent. Just as he'd repented for all the killing he'd done. One thing was for sure; a dear lover had come to sooth a pain that ran so deep and lighten a load much too heavy to bear alone.

IV

At the Headquarters of the Trans-Mississippi Confederacy, Lieutenant General Edmund Kirby Smith stood looking at a large map of Louisiana on the wall behind his desk. Seated in front of the desk, sipping brandy and nibbling peanuts, were two well-dressed men in civilian clothes, and a man wearing the uniform of a Confederate full colonel. All three were spies, agents for various orders of Northern wealth and power. Their primary motive, however, was greed; military intelligence was merely a secondary means to that end. One of the men in civilian clothes was Samuel Casey, a former U.S. congressman from Kentucky. He had just paid $200,000 in Yankee greenbacks for 20,000 bales of cotton. The other man was Frank Butler, a cotton speculator for Skinner Textile Mills of Massachusetts. He'd also just made a very large purchase with U.S. dollars. The man dressed as a Confederate colonel was actually a Union major named Andrew McMillan. He was currently head of purchasing in the Trans-Mississippi's Cotton Bureau, secretly slipped into the position early in the war. His older brother was a personal friend of both Abraham Lincoln and U.S. Treasury Secretary Salmon P. Chase. McMillan had just brokered the two transactions and was guaranteed twenty percent of the cotton once it arrived safely in Union-controlled territory. The man was so brash he hadn't even bothered to change his name.

Standing off to the side was a one-armed lieutenant colonel, his left coat sleeve folded neatly at the elbow, pinned to his lapel. He had listened to the entire proceeding, a bit surprised at its brazenness.

Confederate spies in New Orleans had recently sent word that a large Union expedition would soon be underway to capture Shreveport. General Smith and his staff had been expecting such a campaign for nearly a year. Shreveport offered an excellent staging ground for the invasion of Texas, which Lincoln desperately wanted before the November elections. It was now known that the Red River Expedition, as it was being called, would be launched within a week. The main objective was still to occupy Shreveport and prepare for the invasion of Texas. Of equal importance as noted in a primary executive order was the confiscation of the huge stores of cotton on the many plantations of Northwest Louisiana. Textile mills throughout New England had sat dormant for nearly two years due to the lack of cotton, causing a staggering rise in unemployment. The value of the cotton just purchased by Casey and Butler would easily quadruple once it reached New England.

The two men would receive no bill of sale of course, or a receipt. They would, however, have in their possession an official U.S. document signed by President Lincoln ordering all military commanders to provide safe passage for them with any cargos they may bring. They would also have an affidavit signed by McMillan swearing to the authenticity of their specific claim. Casey and Butler would be traveling with the Union expedition, along with dozens of cotton speculators. As the other speculators haggled over the cotton, Casey and Butler would simply produce their papers to a certain brigadier general, another confidant of the McMillans', who would then see to the procurement of their product. If all went as planned and the expedition made it to Shreveport, Andrew McMillan would change into his Yankee uniform for the return trip back down the Red River. As stated in Lincoln's document they would be taken unmolested with their cargo up the Mississippi all the way to Illinois. And they would be allowed as many return trips as they pleased until the end of hostilities with the Confederacy.

"Even if Banks fails to get this far," said McMillan, reassuring his two cohorts, "there's plenty of cotton between here and Alexandria. Isn't that right, General?"

"Yes," said General Smith, after a slight hesitation as if in deep thought, turning from the map to face the men. "There is plenty of cotton."

"We thank you for your hospitality, General," said Casey, standing with his brandy. "I'm sure you're right. There'll be more than enough cotton. However, we are pressed for time."

"How right you are, Samuel," replied Butler, also standing. "We must be off, General. So nice doing business with you. Perhaps in the future we will have more opportunities like this."

"I hope so," said the General Smith in a monotone voice that seemed to be hiding something; but only the one-armed lieutenant colonel would have detected this. "I truly do."

After a short round of small talk the three men left the general's office. Butler and Casey had travel passes to get them down to Baton Rouge. McMillan would see them off, after another drink of course, showing them his office at the Cotton Bureau, telling them to hurry back.

"What will you do with all the cotton here, General," asked the young lieutenant colonel with one arm, "if the Yankees do get this far?"

"I'll burn it, Grady," said Smith, looking out the window. "I'll burn it. Now, please, go and put that money in a safe place."

At least a dozen nervous-looking men waited to see the general as Lieutenant Colonel Grady Hackwith walked through the crowded corridor that led from Smith's office. In his only hand he carried a large carpetbag, obviously with some weight

64

to it. He turned left and just outside his office he saw a major, an old familiar friend, arguing with one of his lieutenants.

"No, I don't have an appointment," said the major. "He's a personal friend."

"David?" said Hackwith, dropping the carpetbag to the floor.

Hawkins turned in surprise.

"Grady, ol'boy!"

The two embraced, then Hawkins noticed Hackwith's missing arm.

"Aw, don't worry," said Hackwith. "I've got it on ice. They're making huge strides in medicine these days. By the time the war's over, I'll be able to get it reattached. If I can afford it, that is."

Hawkins forced a smile, glad to see his friend had kept his sense of humor. Hackwith reached down for the carpetbag.

"Here, let me get that, Grady," said Hawkins, also reaching for the bag.

"Indeed, no," replied Hackwith, lifting the bag. "I lost my arm, not my dignity."

He showed Hawkins to a small office with a single window view of the street. After securing the carpetbag in a large safe behind his desk, Hackwith produced a bottle and two glasses.

"Sorry, all I've got is this Arkansas sour mash," he said. "But it's better than the moonshine we got last month. Killed one man and blinded four others."

"Too many twigs in the pot?" asked Hawkins.

"More like a railroad tie," replied Hackwith, lifting his glass. "Well, here's to the cavalry. The first and the most."

"The first and the most, indeed," said Hawkins. After swallowing his drink, his eyes momentarily glanced at his friend's missing arm.

"Port Hudson," Hackwith said, noticing Hawkins's eyes. "Yankee bullet caught me right in the elbow. I knew it was gone the moment it happened."

Hawkins pressed his lips together, slowly nodding.

"Funny thing about it, though," said the young lieutenant colonel as he looked out the window.

"What's that?" asked Hawkins.

"Didn't hurt nearly as bad as when they cut it off."

Hawkins said nothing, just looked at his empty glass, fumbling with it in his hands.

"I'm so sorry about your wife, David," said Hackwith, after a few moments' hesitation.

Again Hawkins said nothing. He looked out the window at a column of troops marching down Market Street, the setting sun turning their gray uniforms to a brownish-orange. The afternoon love-making with Amy Bolton had definitely improved his mood. But in the back of his mind he wondered if he'd committed adultery, fornication or both. How would he justify this to the Lord? He couldn't and he knew it. He also thought of Emily. He knew she would want him to be happy. But in the context of all that had happened to him, he was at a loss to put a moral justification on his recent moment of sexual intimacy. The experience had been wonderful, but his heart still ached for Emily. And his conscience? What about his conscience? What about God? This caused him to think even more of Emily. He wanted so badly to hold her while she nuzzled her face in his neck like she always did. Or chase her playfully across one of the clearings, gently tackling her to the ground to lie for hours gazing up at the fluffy clouds. Even to hear her complain about fixing the leak in the roof over the upstairs guestroom. Or how Jacko, who she always referred to as "that dog," had gotten into her perennials again. Anything, just to have her at his side.

"David," Hackwith finally said, "is there anything I can do for you?"

"No, thank you," Hawkins said coming out of his reverie, "I'm alright, Grady."

"Well, then. Have you heard anything about this Red River Expedition?"

"Is that what they're calling it?"

"Very fit'n, I think."

"Sure," said Hawkins. "Steve Jenkins, my first sergeant mentioned something about it."

"Aw, yes. I met him. Seemed like a decent fella."

"He is," Hawkins said. "Told me the Yankees might be trying to take Shreveport."

"That's right."

"Who's in command?"

"Banks. Porter's giving him a ride."

"How many?"

"About forty thousand men."

Hawkins raised his eyebrows and looked back out the window.

"Porter's got at least twelve ironclads," said Hackwith. "Maybe more."

"Ironclads?" Hawkins looked back at Hackwith. "When are they due to set out?"

"Any day now." Hackwith looked at the calendar on the wall. "If the rains come early, those boats could be here by the end of March."

"What can I do to help?"

"Nothing for now. I want you to rest. We may need you later. How's the leg, by the way?"

"It's making progress. Lucky to still have it. Five months after I broke it, I took a bullet in the thigh at Sharpsburg. A doctor in Richmond told me all the riding may be cutting off the flow of blood, slowing the healing process. So I do a lot of walking every chance I get. Seems to help."

"How are things on the farm?"

"Great. Things look good. Gonna be look'n to buy me a plow horse soon."

"You own a few slaves, right?"

"Three adults and three young'uns."

"If you need any help with'm, I could send a man out to watch over'm."

"No, Grady," Hawkins said, standing to leave. "They work just fine, thank you."

"You're sure? Won't cost you a penny. Just give the man something to eat and he'll make sure your slaves are good'n busy."

"Yes, I'm sure, Grady. Thank you."

"Well, you don't have to leave, David. At least have another drink with me."

"No, thanks, Grady. I really gotta be go'n. Heard ya were here and just wanted to say howdy, old friend. Drop by the farm some time."

The two men shook hands, chatting a bit more as Hackwith walked Hawkins out to the street.

"Where on earth did you get this fine piece of horse flesh?" asked Hackwith, immediately taking notice of Jackson.

"He's a beauty, ain't he?" said Hawkins, stroking Jackson's thick jaw muscle. "Got'm in Virginia, at Chancellorsville. Best horse I've ever had."

"What about that dark brindle you had out West?" Hackwith asked, still admiring Jackson, petting the animal's black mane. "The one that saved us from those Apaches. Wasn't as pretty as this, but that was one helluva horse. Tempest, I think ya called'm."

"Tempest was a great horse," said Hawkins. "And here is the only one that could've ever bested'm."

"What happened to Tempest?" asked Hackwith, turning to Hawkins.

"Lost'm at Shiloh. Died a good warhorse's death. Quick and bloody."

"Shiloh? Good God, David. You're not just lucky to still have your leg. You're lucky to be alive."

Hawkins didn't respond, just kept looking at Jackson, caressing his exquisite neck. He wanted to tell Hackwith about the other horrible engagements, or at least he thought he did. But the words wouldn't come.

"I tell ya what," Hackwith said, looking back at Jackson. "I'll give ya a thousand Yankee dollars for'm right now."

"I wouldn't sell this horse for all'a God's green earth." Hawkins mounted Jackson. "Where ya get'n Yankee dollars from, Grady?"

"Oh, they're everywhere, my friend," Hackwith said with a grin. "They're everywhere."

Hawkins nodded goodbye, then turned Jackson down the street, falling in behind a line of wagons packed with supplies.

There was much work to be done on the farm and he was on recuperative leave. Because of Emily's passing, his wounds, and all the campaigning he'd seen, he could easily put in for an early discharge. But that was unthinkable now knowing the enemy could soon be upon his very own hometown. He had seen what war did to hometowns, a thought that did not sit well with him. He'd had enough of war. But if the Yankees came he would fight them once again.

As he approached his farm Hawkins thought of Johnny, an eerie dusk bidding its welcome. Giving the boy his father's cap seemed more than just a good deed. Keeping this important promise gave him a unique sense of accomplishment. It seemed to have set him on a course that otherwise would have eluded him. Whiskey and spirits had been a problem time and again for Hawkins. While gone he had abstained from sex, but not from alcohol. He rarely drank socially anymore. During lulls in the fighting, he would go on long benders lasting days, even weeks. Had he not rummaged through his saddlebags and found Adam McRay's cap, surely he would have taken to the bottle and daily, round-the-clock drinking. His thinking would have dwindled away, his identity thwarted, staggering headlong into oblivion. But now he could work, regain his health and plan for his new future. If the Yankees would let him.

Sidney Brooks had been waiting over two hours outside of General Nathan Bank's temporary headquarters in Opelousas, one of the larger towns on the Bayou Teche where very little English was spoken. Brooks was a reporter from New York City, commissioned to cover the campaign by Harper's Weekly. He was having trouble securing the proper papers to travel with the Army. Instead he'd lagged behind tagging along any way he could. He had brought with him three different two-piece suits, changing them out every day. But the constant traveling, sleeping wherever and whenever he could, and the Louisiana humidity had them each looking rumpled and stained with sweat. Normally clean-shaven, he now sported a month-old beard offset by a pair of round spectacles fronting weary eyes. Although his spirits were still high and his wits intact, he now looked much older than his twenty-five years.

Three weeks ago he'd been in New Orleans, arriving from New York after a nine-day ocean voyage. He found buying information there quite easy and soon learned Banks's army was at Morgan City, a busy port in the Atchafalaya Basin. After a long series of ferry and coach rides through the swamps crossing water, then land, then water again, over and over until he lost count, Brooks finally arrived in Morgan City. But the army had moved inland by then, plodding along the Bayou Teche. He caught up with them at Grand Coteau, but was constantly hassled by soldiers for not having a travel pass. Almost out of money, he gave five of his last twenty dollars to a master sergeant who allowed him to enter the town hall-turned-Yankee Headquarters at Opelousas.

Just as he was about to step outside for some fresh air, the huge set of double doors that had been closed since he first arrived opened wide. At least a dozen Union officers filed passed him from out of the room. None of them even looked at him. A young major finally stepped out and glanced around the foyer. Brooks felt his heart beat faster, knowing it was now time for him to put on a show and lay it on thick.

"Hello!" he said in a loud, clear voice, stepping into the doorway. "I'm Sidney Brooks reporting for Harper's Weekly. I'd like to speak to General Banks, please."

"Let'm in," said a voice from the room.

Banks was standing at a long table with two other generals, looking over some maps when Brooks entered the large conference room. At another table off to the side were five other men, colonels and majors, also studying maps while they smoked cigars, drank tea, cursed and spat on the floor.

Brooks got straight to the point, explaining his problem to the three-time Massachusetts governor. He also told the general that he could help with his future political aspirations. It was no secret that Banks wanted to be president. If successful in his summer campaign to capture Shreveport he would be a prime candidate against Lincoln in the fall.

"You see, General," said Brooks. "I'm having trouble traveling with your army. I cannot get the access I need to do my work. One of your officers even accused me of espionage."

"My apologies, Mr. Brooks," said General Banks with attempted aplomb. At first glance he appeared quite dapper, cavalier even. But on closer examination he possessed the aspect of a worried man, a man out of place. His hair was a bit ruffled and he had dark circles and bags under his eyes, adding to a slight hangdog expression. "Reporters are often considered spies. Tell me who it was and I'll see that he's reprimanded."

"Oh, that's not important, General," replied Brooks, waving off the thought. "And there's no sense telling tales if it's just hearsay. Besides, the man was obviously drunk at the time. What's really important is documenting the Red River Expedition." Brooks paused and removed his spectacles, breathed on them, then began to polish the glass with a handkerchief as he continued to sell himself. "I can also be most beneficial in letting the public know the true heart and character of the great General Nathaniel Banks."

Brooks said the last words as if he were running for office, a tone of challenge in his voice. For a moment Banks almost seemed to forget himself. The effect Brook's words had on him were not unlike a child being handed a large multi-colored lollipop. His eyes grew open wide, his lips pressed tightly together in a grotesque pucker. His hands seemed to be strangling one another with glee.

"I will take care of your problem, Mr. Brooks," said Banks, his subordinates looking at him strangely. "Don't worry. You will have all the access you need."

A hundred and twenty miles south of Shreveport, Major General Richard Taylor sat on a tree stump at the peak of a small hill, whittling a stick he'd found on the ground. He would occasionally stop and look up, his thoughtful eyes scanning the 8,000 Confederate soldiers camped at Hinestown, thirty miles west of Alexandria. General Smith, Taylor's only superior west of the Mississippi, had recently sent written orders for him to concentrate his scattered troops and prepare for the Union invasion of Northwest Louisiana. Taylor had been expecting this invasion for over a year. After reading the order he'd quickly written back a formal compliance, attached with an informal request, "I'll need more men, Edmund."

Although he had no formal military training prior to the war, Richard Taylor was no stranger to the drama of strategic military administration. He was the son of former U.S. President Zachary Taylor, 'Old Rough-and-Ready.' He was also brother-in-law to Confederate President Jefferson Davis. Both a Harvard and a Yale man, Dick Taylor was made a colonel at the outbreak of war, commanding the 9th Louisiana Infantry. Six months later he was promoted to brigadier general. He campaigned under Stonewall Jackson in the Shenandoah Valley, where he'd faced Nathan Banks at the Battle of Cedar Mountain. Union forces had surged early that day, overwhelming the Confederates along the base of the mountain, shooting and bayoneting many of the men who tried to surrender. As the Yankees pillaged the overrun Rebel works, Jackson and Taylor unleashed their reserves routing the Federals, handing Banks a humiliating defeat. Taylor was again promoted and sent back to Louisiana, where he was needed. Banks, the politician-turned-soldier, was sent to the Louisiana to get him out of the way.

Just as Taylor was putting a nice point on his stick, a young strapping lieutenant approached him with a piece of paper in his hand.

"Sir, we've received a dispatch from our man in Baton Rouge," said the lieutenant, glancing at the paper. "Banks's men are currently moving up the Bayou Teche. They're to rendezvous with Admiral Porter and A.J. Smith's division at the mouth of the Red."

"A.J. Smith?" Taylor queried, raising his eyebrows.

"Yes, sir. Porter's ferrying him down from Vicksburg. Sherman has apparently loaned Smith to Banks until late April. But he wants the division back for his summer campaigns, wherever they may be."

"Any word of how many men?" asked Taylor.

"Yes, sir. It's believed that Smith has about ten-thousand men. Banks has well over twenty-thousand that we know of, maybe more. Add that to Porter's sailors and marines, and it will probably be over forty-thousand." The lieutenant paused briefly, allowing his commander a moment to digest the information. "We're also being told that Porter has over a dozen ironclads, and over a hundred large transports with enough horses, supplies and munitions to sustain a very long campaign."

"Any good news?" Taylor asked as he continued to whittle.

"Oh, yes sir." The lieutenant perked up a bit. "General Polignac will be arriving soon. Should be here by nightfall. And General Magruder's cavalry has left Austin. In less than a week they'll be here, sir. That should give you at least five-thousand more men."

Taylor nodded, his blade sending a large chip of wood flying from the stick, arcing down to bounce off the lieutenant's boot. "Find Mouton. Tell him to come see me once he gets his men settled. And also send a party to meet Polignac. See to it that his men get across the river post haste, Lieutenant."

"Yes, sir," said the lieutenant, holding up a finger. "There is one other thing, sir."

Taylor stopped whittling and looked up.

"General Walker would like to know if he should continue with the work on Fort DeRussy?"

Taylor stood and turned looking south, arms at his side, knife in one hand, stick in the other. He was a short man who came up just past the lieutenant's shoulders. He wiped the back of his knife hand across his thick mustache, then casually waved the blade in front of him. "Send word to General Walker to continue with the work on Fort DeRussy. And to increase patrols at the mouth of the river. I want three daily reports; morning, noon and evening." He turned to the lieutenant, still keeping the knife pointed the other direction. "I wanna know beforehand when the enemy enters the Red. See to it, Lieutenant."

"Yes, sir." The lieutenant saluted, turned on his heel and marched down the hill into the encampment.

"Ironclad gunboats on the Red River," Taylor said to himself, tossing the stick he'd been whittling back to the ground.

V

Shortly after David Hawkins left for the war in October of 1861, a runaway slave named Clem and his pregnant wife Noel happened upon the farm at sunset one evening. They were hiding in the bushes by the bayou and saw Ruth walking down a trail that led up to the back of the farm. "Hey, lil'sista," Clem called out to her. "How's about a lil'somp'n to eat?"

"Who you is?" she asked, peering at them quizzically as they lay huddled together wrapped in a single dirty blanket.

"We's hungry," said Noel. "Dat's who we is."

"You go'n have a baby," said Ruth, noticing Noel's swollen belly.

"Ya think?" mocked Noel.

"Please, lil'sista," said Clem. "We been walk'n all day, an'we ain't et nut'n."

Ruth turned and looked toward the farm, then jerked her head back to Clem and Noel. "I be back," she said before quickly sprinting up the trail.

Ruth soon brought back a small basket full of apples, peaches, bread and cheese. She then watched in amazement as Clem and Noel gorged themselves, mumbling indiscernibly, moaning and groaning the pleasures of the famished suddenly satisfied. Both were only seventeen and told Ruth they were from Palestine, Texas, about 140 miles southwest of Shreveport. They had gotten married just seven months earlier when they first found out Noel was pregnant. But just last week, the owner of a large plantation where they lived and worked sold Noel to pay off a debt from a card game. Fortunately Clem and Noel learned of their master's shrewd dealings from another slave just moments before they were to be separated. With no provisions whatsoever, they quickly slipped into the woods. Bloodhounds were soon set upon them, but the runaways zigzagged across a creek, confusing the dogs and their scent was lost. They wandered northeast for several days, living off wild blackberries, with no idea where they were going until Providence brought them to the Hawkins Farm.

Later that day, Ruth snuck more food and blankets out to Clem and Noel. But Sarah followed her daughter, wondering what she was up to and discovered the runaway couple. After some discussion between Sarah, Jacob and Isaac, they decided it was safe to bring the matter to Miss Emily.

"Where are they?" she asked in surprise.

"A lil'ways behind da barn, Miss Emily," said Sarah as she stood with Jacob and Isaac.

"Well, bring'm in the barn for heaven's sake," said Emily moving to get her coat. "Poor things. Can't let'm get found out. That'd be terrible."

In the barn, Emily was even more surprised when she saw Noel's condition.

"Oh, Lord," she said, putting her arm around the pregnant girl. "You're about to bust, aren't ya? Sarah, go'n get more blankets."

"If'n ya can, kind ma'am," said Clem, "please jus' let us rest a day or two, den we be on our way."

"Nonsense," Emily said. "She can't travel. Besides you'll just get caught and I know ya don't want that."

Two days later Noel went into labor. Emily wanted to move her into the house, but the baby wouldn't wait. After a bunch of screaming and fussing, Noel gave birth to a healthy baby boy they named Aaron. Emily was actually planning on forging papers of ownership for Clem, Noel and baby Aaron, with a clever story of how she obtained them from a relative in Little Rock. But less than a week after the baby was born, Jacob came in from town one day with frightening news. A group of runaway-slave-hunters was in Shreveport looking for a male and a pregnant female that may have recently given birth. Clem, Noel and little Aaron would have to go if they wanted to stay together.

"What we go'n do, Miss Emily?" asked Sarah.

"Don't worry. I'll think'a something."

Emily knew of a kind elderly couple that lived in the mountains of central Arkansas. After some careful planning, she headed out before sunrise in a wagon with Sarah, Jacob, the two runaways and their baby. Isaac stayed behind with the children. A note from Emily was left for anyone who might drop by, saying she had gone to Texarkana to buy a horse and should be back in a day or two. They traveled all that day and through the night until they came to Rich Mountain where a Mr. and Mrs. Charles Etheridge had a small farm. The Etheridges were old friends of Emily's parents, and she had visited the farm several times as a little girl. They had a handful of slaves and were known to treat them quite well.

"They were gonna sell'r, Charles," said Emily to the burly old man, whose face wore a constant thoughtful smile. "She just had the baby and slave hunters were in Shreveport look'n for'em. I just couldn't leave'm to fend for themselves."

"Of course not!" bellowed Etheridge, smiling. His chubby, ruddy-red cheeks were accented by a pair of round spectacles and a large straw hat. A large man of boundless energy, Charles Etheridge always spoke with great enthusiasm, his arms stretched out like he was ready for a hug. "And praise God, ya brought'm here! How's about something to eat and we'll get ya settled in!"

The Etheridge's had actually freed their slaves before the war, an illegal act in most parts of the South. However, all five of them chose to stay with the kind couple. When Clem and Noel met these happy, content workers, they knew they had found a safe home to start their family. There was plenty of work to do and the place was so isolated it was doubtful that any slave hunters would ever find them. This was the beginning of the Hawkins Farm's connection to the Underground Railroad.

Little girls do not know how to keep secrets and young Ruth, who had just turned thirteen after helping out the runaways, was no exception. That same year, Emily Hawkins and her slaves had been invited to the Christmas celebration across the river at the Belcher Plantation in Bossier Parish. It was a huge annual occasion with a reenactment of the Nativity Scene and a fireworks display that could be seen all the way to the Texas line. After watching the three wise men bring gifts to the baby Jesus, Ruth was playing with her friend, Pearl, the granddaughter of the Belcher's head housemaid, a feisty old slave named Clair. Though almost two years younger than Ruth, Pearl was a bit precocious and fancied herself an actual blue-blood because aristocrats owned her. She always seemed to be provoking Ruth into an I-know-something-you-don't-know game. But on this night Ruth knew something Pearl did not.

"We had a lil'baby born in our barn," Ruth told Pearl.

"Na'ugh, when?"

"Rat fo' Punk'n Day."

"Where dat baby is?" asked Pearl, looking around. "I wants to see it."

"Iss gone. Ma'n Pa'n Miss Emily tooks it away someplace safe so's da hunters won't gets it."

"Where?"

"I dunno," said Ruth, shrugging her shoulders. "But 'deys left early'n da moan'n, an'didn't get back till late-late night afta da nex.'"

And that was pretty much all it took. Sometime between Christmas Day and New Year's, Pearl spilled the beans to her grandmother as inadvertently as Ruth had to her. Clair and Sarah had known each other for nearly three decades. They seemed to have a grown up version of Ruth and Pearl's relationship, a big mansion house slave looking down her nose at the small farm slave. For over two months Clair kept what she knew to herself, then one day she got word that a young slave named Tim was going to run. Slaves running from big plantations like the Belcher's was not an uncommon occurrence, especially if they had somewhere and someone special to run to. But more often than not, they were brought back battered and beaten, sometimes even maimed by the brutal slave hunters.

"Where ya think ya go'n, boy?" Clair asked the young man. "Ya jus' gonna run off an' get drug back like an ol' dawg."

"I got's me a brotha' up in Springfield, Illinois," said Tim.

"How ya know dat?"

"He tol' me dats where'es go'n when he run off be'fo da war."

"Who yo brotha' is?"

"My brotha' be Sooky Joe, run off from da Marshall farm in Ruston, 'bout near a year ago."

"I 'member Sooky Joe," said Clair. "He really yo brotha'?"

"Yes'm, sho'is."

"You even know how ta gets ta Springfield, Illinois, boy?"

"I knows it's up dat way." Tim pointed north.

"Boy, ya don't go nowhere's till I tell ya. Ya hear?" Clair said, pointing her finger in the young man's face.

"Yes'm."

Not long after the last freeze of 1862 came through Northwest Louisiana, Clair sent word to the Hawkins farm that she needed to see Sarah. Jacob, who would go into town almost daily, was given the message by one of the Belchers' slave boys who made last-minute supply runs across the bridge.

"Wond'a what dat ol' bat wanna see me fo'?" said Sarah with a puzzled look on her face.

"Dunno, baby," said Jacob. "Lil' Boosy didn't say. Jus' tol me ol' Clair said it was im'potant. So I tells'm you gonna be in town Fry'dee when Miss Emily's a get'n fitted fo' dat dress at da shop on Lake Street."

They met at midmorning on the corner of Lake and Market, just down from the store where Emily Hawkins was buying her dress. Clair had asked permission to go for a short stroll around the block. Sarah never had to ask to take a walk; she would simply step outside for some fresh air. Clair wore a nervous, pretentious smile as she approached Sarah, who stood calmly nibbling on a handful of peanuts.

"Mo'nin Sarah."

"Mo'nin to you, Miss Clair," said Sarah, only glancing at Clair. "Wha'chew wanna see me 'bout?"

"Now Sarah, dairs no need to be rude."

"Wha'chew want, ol'girl?" Sarah said, impatiently turning to look Clair in the eye. "Ya hadn't said five words to me in as many years. Da only thing I can fig'r ya might be want'n, is ta fix my baby, Ruth, up wit one'a dem cotton pickas' ya gots cross da river. Well, she's too young fo' dat, an' ya's ought'a know dat."

"Dat what ya be think'n, Sarah?" said Clair with a wide grin. "Dat'm play'n matchmaker fo' ya young'un."

"Well, whad'is it, den?"

"I heard tell dat da ol' stork paid a visit to da Hawkins barn late las' year," Clair said, as Sarah's eyes grew wide with fear. "I also knows dat dem hunters be 'round here 'bout dat same time, look'n fo' a couple'a runaways. An' one'um had'm a bun in da oven."

"Who tol' you dat?" Sarah said, glaring at the old housemaid.

"It don't matter none who ..."

"Yes it do!" snapped Sarah. "You wanna gets my family strung up an' good Miss Emily trown in jail?"

"Miss Emily?" balked Clair. "Why, I never said nut'n..."

"I'm gonna ax ya one mo' time what ya want, Clair. An' if'n ya don't gimme a right good answer, I'm walk'n away. An' den, if'n ya say anything else 'bouts it, I'm gonna knock ya right down in da gutta here, fo' da whole street to see."

Clair stood erect and stared sober faced at Sarah. A female slave hadn't spoken to her in that tone of voice since she was a young girl, and she was very rarely talked down at by even the meanest of male slaves. Even most whites spoke to her only in pleasant tones. She finally turned away from Sarah, looking off reflectively down Lake Street toward the river.

"Long time ago," she said softly, "you was jus' a little girl. I weren't much older dan Ruth is now. I had me a beau named Jesse. Strong'n handsome as all day long." Clair turned back to Sarah with tears in her eyes. "I loved'm so much, it hurt whenever I couldn't reach right out an' touch'm. One day he says he gonna run off to a place called Canada. Said'eed send fo' me later. I tries to stop'm, but I didn't tries hard 'nuff. Truth is, I wanted to go wit'm, but I's jus' too scare't." She paused for a moment and looked away again. "Dey caught'm da nex' day. Didn't even make it to Arkansas. Cut off part'a 'is foot so he couldn't run no mo'. Part'a me died when dey brung'm back, all beat up, bleed'n, laid over a horse like a dead goat. Couldn't gimme no love'n fo' nearly a year. One day he was move'n too slow an' da boss man hit'm upside da head wit'a big ol'rock. Few days later da good Lord took'm in 'is sleep."

Sarah reached out and gently touched Clair's arm. "What is it ya want Clair?" she asked quietly. "Jus' ax me."

"Dair's a boy gonna run," she said, looking at Sarah. "He jus' kinda reminds me'a Jesse, I guess. Says he wants ta go ta Springfield, Illinois. Wherever dat is. I jus' wants to see dat'ee gets a good start." She took Sarah's hand. "Please Sarah, can ya maybe points'm in da right way to go?"

At first Sarah didn't know what to say. She thought about it a minute, then told Clara that pointing the boy in the right direction was about all she could do. A day and time was arranged for the boy to be at a spot just north of the Hawkins farm. After that there be no turning back, except in chains.

As the two black ladies parted, Clair turned back to Sarah. "I know'd it seems I always looked down on ya, Sarah. But truth is, I always wanted to be you. When it all comes out'n da wash, yo' massa be rich'a din mines."

On the way back to the farm Sarah sat quietly while Emily drove the buggy. As she wondered how to approach her master about another imposition, she noticed two dresses had been purchased. The one she had seen Miss Emily try on was canary yellow. The other was baby blue. She was just about to inquire about the dresses when Emily broke the silence.

"Sure are quiet, Sarah," she said in her usual sweet voice. "What's a matter?"

"Sump'n I need ta ax ya, Miss Emily."

"Well, you don't have to ask me if you can ask me something," Emily said, turning to smile at Sarah. "Just ask me."

For a minute Sarah couldn't speak. The dear lady had literally exhausted herself helping Clem and Noel. Now Sarah was so hesitant to ask her to help another runaway. It was dangerous to everyone involved. She looked again at the dresses hung neatly behind her.

"What ya buy two dresses fo', Miss Emily?"

"Oh," said Emily, looking back at the garments. "Did I buy two? Well, I guess you can have that blue one. Jacob might like it, huh?"

"But Miss Emily, you gives me a dress fo' Christmas. An' ya gimme one fo' summer time, too. An' I still gots dem ones we made from dat material you gimme few years back. Don't need no mo' dresses. I got's fo' now, dis make five."

"There's no law says you can't have five dresses, Sarah. Besides, the dresses we made were pretty'n all, but don't you think Miss McBride does'm a little better?"

Sarah turned her head to look at Emily, then brought her hand up to her mouth and began to giggle. Soon they were both laughing very hard.

"Jacob did say da skirt was a bit too long, an'ee couldn't see 'nuff my legs."

"And remember," said Emily, still laughing, "the sleeves on the green one didn't match."

"Yeah," Sarah said. "Da left sleeve wa' kind'a droopy."

They laughed together a little while longer, then Emily turned back to Sarah.

"Now, you gonna tell me what's really bothering you, Sarah."

Again she was quiet, looking off across Grimmet Field at the new flowers springing up along the levee.

"Miss Emily," she finally asked. "do ya thinks ya could draw me a map'a hows to gets to dat place we tooks da runaways to las' year?"

Emily pulled over and stopped the buggy, looking intently at Sarah.

"Sarah," she said. "You need to talk to me and tell me what's going on."

She told Emily everything that Clair told her. How she found out about the runaways through Ruth and Pearl's innocent indiscretion. The plan to somehow help the boy flee his life on the cruel plantation. And the hope of a new life with his brother somewhere free up North. Emily Hawkins did not complain or show any fear. She even asked Sarah if she told Clair to pack the boy enough food for two of three days, also asking if he was strong enough to make the trip on foot. By the time they got back to the barn, Emily had taken on the project like a crusade of sorts.

"You need to have a long talk with that daughter of yours," she said, handing Sarah the blue dress. "Make sure she understands not to let the cat out of the bag again."

"Oh, I can't take da dress Miss Emily," said Sarah, "on account'a cause'n ya so much trouble."

"Sarah, please don't talk to me like that," she said, thoughtfully. "It hurts me inside. Besides, you're no trouble. You and your family are a blessing to me."

"I'm sorry, Miss Emily. I ain't never wanna hurt ya. I just..."

"It's gonna be alright, Sarah," said Emily, placing her hand on Sarah's shoulder. "You just gotta have faith in the Lord. He's do'n all the planing anyway. And now I need to go draw that map. Why don't you go and bake a sweet potato pie for that boy to take with'm."

"Dat's a good idea Miss Emily. I'll makes da crust extree tick so's it'll keep longer."

Sending word through Jacob, Emily postponed the date for a week, allowing them more time to prepare. Ten nights later Emily, Jacob and Sarah walked to a clearing at the northernmost edge of the Hawkins property. Sarah and Jacob had tried to talk Emily out of coming along, but she insisted. She wanted to make sure Tim understood some of the details of the trip he would be taking.

"This is a compass," said Emily, holding the device up for the young man to see. "Follow the blue line I drew on the map all the way to Eldorado, Arkansas, right here. From there go straight north for about a day. Keep this arrow here on the 'N' and you'll be going north. When you get to the mountains you'll see a sign on the side of the road that says, Rich Mountain."

"But, Miss Emily," said Tim. "I don't knows how ta read."

"It's alright, son. Look, I wrote it down for you." She showed him a piece of paper with the name written on it. "Study this real good, and when you see these words follow the road the sign points to. It goes to the right." She grabbed his right hand. "When your look'n at the sign, this way is right. Got it?"

"Yes'm, I got's it."

"The road winds round and round up that mountain about five miles. Then, at the end of the road, you'll come to a small farm. Folks there are real friendly and they'll help. The man's name is Charles Etheridge. He's a real good man. He and his wife will give you food and a place to sleep. You'll have to work for it, but you can leave whenever you want. From there you'll be on your own again. And when you do leave, you've got to promise not to tell anyone about the place. Unless it's people that need help, like you. Do you understand everything I've said?"

"Yes, Miss Emily. I understands."

"How old are you, Tim?" she asked.

"I tink I'm 'bout twin'ee," said Tim. "But I ain't sure."

"Well, make sure and stay away from any people you see on the road, especially white folks. And don't go through any towns. Go around'm. I don't know what else to tell you, except that I'll be pray'n for you, Tim."

The four of them then held hands in a circle and said a long powerful prayer. Emily opened, then each one of them petitioned the Lord for Tim's safe passage. David Hawkins's name was lifted up more than once. "Send angels," Emily said. When they were done praying, Emily hugged Tim, squeezing the boy tight for a long moment. Tim just stood there, awkward, his arms down at his side, afraid to put them around a pretty white woman.

"Sarah here's got some food and a coupl'a blankets," said Emily, holding the boy at arm's length.

"Dair's some sweet potato pie, cornbread, chicken, biscuits, blackberry jam, a piece'a ham, fo' apples an' tree peaches," said Sarah, handing Tim a small duffle bag. "Blankets an' a coat, too."

After Tim gave Sarah a hug, Jacob pulled out a long knife in a leather scabbard and handed it to the boy.

"Got dis here knife some years back," he said. "It's sharp as a whisker, but it best be used as a tool. Don't use it ta hurt no one, less'n ya gots to. An' don't be bopp'n down da middle'a da road like it's Sunday after church. Stay to da side. Keep ya head low and ya eyes peeled fo' trouble. Go'on now boy. An' God be wit'ya."

The three of them watched as the young black man disappeared into the darkness of the trees. He wouldn't be discovered missing until sunup. By that time, he would be very close to the Arkansas line. In his heart he was already a free man, unafraid of the fear before him. As he stretched his legs and churned his arms, looking up at the starry night sky, he knew he was no longer a slave, but a man to capture and keep his own destiny. A man to find with his own hands and see with his own eyes the faith, hope and love inherent to the rites of passage.

VI

Eight days before Tim went on the run, Emily mailed out two letters. One was to Mr. and Mrs. Etheridge up on Rich Mountain, letting them know that they would soon have another visitor. The other was to a man named Daniel Tucker, who was the pastor of a small church just south of St. Louis, Missouri. Tucker and his wife had once been slave owners, but in the decade before the war they joined the abolitionist movement and freed their slaves. Some they kept as hired workers in their small upholstery business, the rest they gave money to travel north. In her letter to the Etheridges, whom the Tuckers knew quite well, Emily Hawkins asked that they give young Tim the Tuckers' address when he was ready to leave their farm. She did not tell Tim this because she wanted him to stay focused on the first part of his dangerous journey. In her letter to the Tuckers, she gave them details of the situation, asking that they correspond with the Etheridges and assist Tim in the last leg of his search to find his brother. And of course in both letters she asked them to please pray unceasingly. "Always be praying," she wrote.

Late in the afternoon after Tim's flight to freedom, three white men showed up at the Hawkins farm. One was the local sheriff, Austin Wilhyte, a childhood friend of David's. The other two were top overseers from the Belcher plantation, mean, nasty-looking men with grim, sour looks on their faces. They both carried scatterguns and pistols. One had shackles attached to a length of chain slung over his shoulder.

"Howdy Austin," said Emily, from the porch. "What can I do for you?"

"Emily," said Wilhyte, dismounting his horse and removing his hat. "We got us a problem. A slave boy done run off from the Belcher plantation."

"We found one'a da Belchers' rowboats down at da mouth'a da bayou," said one of the overseers, also dismounting, but leaving on his hat. "We go'n have'a look around, Emily."

Emily reached inside the front door and pulled out her own scattergun.

"I don't usually make promises to men I don't know," she said, raising the weapon to her eye, aiming at the overseer's crotch. "But I promise, if ya take one single step on my property or address me common again, I'll put a load a squirrel shot right between your legs. Now get back on your horse and let the sheriff here do his work."

"Do like she says, Ben," said Wilhyte when the man hesitated, his gun hand twitching. "I'll have'a look around, if ya don't mind, Emily."

"Course not, Austin," said Emily, lowering the gun as the overseer got back on his horse, his face flushed with fear and humiliation. "Go right ahead."

After a quick look through the barn and stable, Wilhyte stopped at the slave quarter and spoke briefly with Sarah, Jacob and Isaac; he'd known them since he was a boy. He glanced around the trees that bordered the field, then walked back to his horse.

"He's not here," he said calmly. "Sorry for the trouble, Emily."

"He could be in that house," said Ben, glaring and pointing toward Emily.

"He's not in the house," Wilhyte said angrily, before turning back to Emily, tipping his hat. "Sorry to bother ya, Emily. Heard from David lately?"

"Got a letter from him just the other day. They're in Corinth, Mississippi. About to head up into Tennessee."

"Well, I hope he's aw'right."

"Me too, Austin. Me too."

Through the spring and summer Emily received more letters from David. She learned of the terrible defeat at Shiloh and her husband's broken leg. Though greatly relieved he had survived such horrific carnage, she could not understand why he had not been sent home after such an injury. News of the 13th's demise hit the area like a sinister, ominous wind. At street corners she would often come face-to-face with new widows, bereaved and tearful. For days she spent hours alone praying and weeping, her arms wrapped around herself, imagining him there holding her. Wanting only to reach out and touch him, comforting his wounded body. To lie with him, whispering sweetly, calling him darling.

By summer she got word that her husband's leg had healed to a large degree, but he was in Virginia holding the rank of captain commanding of his own company. He told her of daring raids made deep into Union-controlled areas, riding circles around his former boss, the U.S. Cavalry. She also heard of horrible battles in places like Mechanicsville, Fraysers Farm and Malvern Hill. Great and terrible days of saga. In one letter he explained in great detail his first time seeing the new general in command of the Confederate troops.

Imagine, if you can my dear wife, Santa Claus in a gray suit with a brimmed hat. Off his food for a bit and lacking the jolly demeanor. Perched atop a pale, ash-spotted horse, instead of being pulled in a sleigh by flying reindeer. That is Robert E. Lee. Though by no means warm or affectionate, his eyes possess a thoughtful glimmer of wisdom and cunning, appropriate to our cause. Surely he will emerge as one of the great generals of history. His heart, however, remains a mystery. In the end, I fear, it will be found stony at best.

As the papers told of more epic battles in the east, she agonized alone, never showing this to her slaves. Then a letter would come, grasped like a precious stone, held tight to her breast as she looked up crying quietly to the sky, "He's alive. He's alive."

By late September, word of the Emancipation Proclamation reached Louisiana. Emily read what she could about Lincoln's decree, but the Southern slant on the Proclamation was confusing to her. Then she got a letter from Daniel Tucker stating that Tim had recently crossed the Mississippi River into Illinois wearing a new store-bought suit with a pocket full of hard-earned-cash. In the envelope was also a copy of a St. Louis newspaper that had the words of the Proclamation printed in it. After she read it, she went outside and told Jacob, Sarah and Isaac to take the day off. They were all invited to the house that night for dinner.

"I want to see that blue dress on you, Sarah," she said. "Come on up to the house about five o'clock. Door'll be open, just come on in."

They showed up right on time looking a bit awkward in their Sunday-go-to-meeting clothes. But Emily put them at ease with her warm smile and delightful charm. She had a baby chair set up for little two-year-old Rachel, something she bought herself years ago when she thought she was pregnant. Noah, who was then only five, had a couple of thick books and a pillow in his chair so he could sit up at the table. After Emily said the blessing, they enjoyed a juicy pot roast dinner with stewed carrots, mashed potatoes and gravy, turnip greens with ham hocks and cornbread. And for dessert, apple and peach cobbler. When everyone was finished eating, Emily cleared the plates, then came back with a bottle of blackberry wine for the adults, and a bottle of sarsaparilla for the children. She also had in her hand the St. Louis newspaper.

"Today is a very special occasion," she said.

"Well, we knows dat, Miss Emily," said Isaac with a big grin. "We jus' don't knows what fer."

"Yeah," said Sarah. "Dis is aw'mos like Christmas."

"Or da Foth'a Jew'ly," Ruth said.

"Actually it's bigger than both of those." She held up the paper. "I'm gonna read y'all something. It's called the Emancipation Proclamation and it's the official words of President Abraham Lincoln. Emancipation means to set free from bondage or slavery. A proclamation is an official statement made into law."

She read them the whole decree, realizing they would understand little of its words. But when she got to the part that said, "Thence forward and forever free," she added emphasis, paused and looked at them from across the table.

"Do y'all understand what this means?" she asked.

"Dat mean we free, Miss Emily?" asked Jacob.

"That's right," she said. "Now, it won't actually be official here in Louisiana till the first of the year. And maybe not until the war's over. But what I've decided is to take y'all up to that farm up in Arkansas. I also know a man in St. Louis who'll give y'all jobs making furniture. You can make money and learn a trade. And if you want, you can cross the river into Illinois, where there hasn't been any slavery for a long, long time."

They were silent for a while, looking at one another, then back at Emily. Finally Sarah stood with a sad, hurt look on her face. She fumbled with her hands, looking at Isaac, then her husband, then her three children.

"Miss Emily, 'member when I didn't wanna take dis here blue dress, an' ya axt me not ta talks to ya like dat. An' ya saids it hurt ya inside?"

"Yes, Sarah. I remember that."

"An' ya said we weren't no trouble, an' we's a bless'n." Sarah paused, looking at Emily. "Well, I wish ya wouldn't talk to us like dat. Hurt me inside, an' I tink it maybe hurt dem inside, too. You'sa bless'n ta us. I don't wanna go nowheres else. I wanna stay here wit' chew, Miss Emily."

Emily Hawkins stood silent, tears showing in her eyes. Slowly she sank into her chair, put her face in her hands and began to cry very hard.

"I'm so sorry, Sarah," she sobbed. "I wouldn't know what to do if y'all left. But I can't just keep ya here, if ya wanna go. I miss'm so much. I miss David so much."

They had never seen her like this. Falling apart right in front of their eyes. They gathered around her as she slumped in the chair crying like a child. Sarah slowly laid herself across Emily's back, wrapping her arms around the poor distraught woman. Jacob, Isaac and Ruth placed their hands on her, as if trying to heal her of some dreadful disease. Little Noah and Rachel also stood close by, touching their sibling, transferring what small energy they might have, doing their part to cast out the grief that had befallen their sweet master.

"We ain't go'n nowheres, Miss Emily." Sarah whispered into her ear. "Don't ya fret none. We wants ta stay here. Dis be our home."

"Das right, Miss Emily," said Isaac. "An' don't fret none 'bout Massa David need'r. He go'n wup all dem Yankee-mens all bys'm self."

"Yeah, Miss Emily," said Ruth. "Dem Yankees don't stan'a chance 'gainst Massa David."

"Please don't takes us nowheres, Miss Emily."

When she heard little Noah's voice she looked up, for the child very rarely spoke. She wiped the tears from her eyes and reached out, taking the boy's tiny black face in her hands.

"I'm not gonna take ya anywhere ya don't wanna go, Noah," she said. "You're gonna grow up a freeman and do great things."

"Ma'n Pa named me aft'a dat man dat built dat big boat so's he could save all da animals from da flood rains."

"That's right, they sure did," she laughed, still holding back tears. Finally, she sat up in the chair pulling herself together. "Well now, it's time for some wine and sarsaparilla for the children."

Over the next year four more slaves were helped to freedom through the Hawkins farm. Two were another young couple from a large farm near Minden. They were afraid of being separated, so they were taking their chances on the run. Two more were brothers who had no immediate family. They were owned by the town blacksmith, a cruel man that beat and burned them for even the pettiest infractions. Both of these flights went off without a hitch, as they were planned even more carefully than before, bringing no suspicion to the farm. Emily would later learn that all four runaways made it safely to the Etheridge farm to wait out the winter. In the spring the young couple chose to stay at the farm, while the brothers headed for St. Louis to work in Daniel Tucker's upholstery shop.

With amazing regularity, David Hawkins still wrote to Emily, sometimes in bundles of a dozen or more. Even though the South had won impressive victories at Fredericksburg and Chancellorsville, the wins had come at a great cost to the beleaguered Confederate ranks. The men and material they were losing could not be replaced fast enough, while the North seemed to have unfathomable reserves of both.

At this rate, he told her despairingly in one letter, *we could win every battle and still lose the war.*

David's letters began taking on a more grim light, and she feared for him daily. By 1863 the relentless General Grant was moving down the Louisiana side of the Mississippi River, maneuvering his army into a position to take Vicksburg. The letters then slowed to a trickle. In late-June she received his last letter that got through, which had been mailed a month earlier. He was riding under Jeb Stuart in Pennsylvania along the Maryland line, the Mason-Dixon line. In that letter, David seemed surprisingly upbeat and hopeful. But less than a week later, Lee was defeated at Gettysburg, and Grant finally took Vicksburg.

The cotton harvests of '62 and '63 were quite plentiful along the Red River. But since the capture of New Orleans, the crop was no longer floated down to be held in the great warehouses of the South's most prosperous city, to be sold and shipped all over the world. Instead, all of the cotton in

Northwest Louisiana was stored anywhere it could be kept safe and dry. Occasionally, moderate loads of the commodity found their way southwest through Texas on what was called "The Cotton Trail," which wound its way from Dallas to Galveston at the coast. From there it was transported by land or sea to French-controlled Mexico. For a short while, Louisiana and Texas cotton had been floated down the Sabine River to the Gulf of Mexico. But the Yankees soon got wise to that and a more inland route was taken. The Cotton Trail, however, was very dangerous; cargos were often bushwhacked by murdering gangs of outlaws, who in turn sold them to the indifferent French. Little by little, warehouses and barns in the Shreveport area began to bulge with the surplus cotton.

"What on earth are we gonna do with all this cotton, Jacob?" Emily asked, as she inspected the barn, which was completely packed with 200-pound bales of the precious fiber. Two narrow aisles crisscrossed the barn's center, with the bales stacked to the rafters. "How many bales got wet from the rain last night?"

"Bout nine, Miss Emily. I fixed da roof where da rain got in, but we's gonna need us a whole new one. Nudd'r bad storm come, iss go'n leak again." Jacob looked at the ground scratching his head.

"If ya got an idea, Jacob, I'm all ears."

"Well, I heard Ol'Man Lawler, over on Hearn Road, got space in his barn, Miss Emily. It's a good, big ol'barn. An' it's a lil' closer to town. But he be want'n a penny a bale a month."

"A penny a bale a month, huh?" said Emily after a long sigh. "Think you an' Isaac can get it all over there this weekend? We gotta make room for the next year's crop anyway."

"Ain't nut'n fo'a step'a, Miss Emily," he said with a grin. "Nut'n fo'a step'a."

She smiled. "What would I do without ya, Jacob?"

About a year after the Emancipation Proclamation, Emily received a letter from Daniel Tucker saying a former slave would soon be arriving at her farm by way of the Etheridges' place. The letter was brief, the man's name not being mentioned, and Tucker advised her to destroy it once it had been read. As Emily burned the letter she wondered why a former slave would be coming to her farm from the North. Less than two weeks later, she received an identical letter from the Etheridges, and told Jacob to be on the lookout for a stranger. Two days later, Sarah was startled by a young black man who called to her from the bushes behind the barn.

Joshua Dubear was twenty-one, handsome but seldom smiled, a bit awkward and wore thick eye glasses. He told Emily he had run away from a farm way down in Houma shortly after the war began. Houma, sixty miles southwest of New Orleans, was now under Union control and Dubear planned to reunite with the family he had left over two years earlier. He had met Daniel Tucker through the black underground, occasionally working for him at the upholstery shop. When Dubear mentioned his planned return to Louisiana, Tucker offered to help, letting him know about Charles Etheridge and Emily Hawkins.

He stayed on the farm several days resting after his long journey. Once Emily saw him in the barn scribbling vigorously in a journal. Upon first meeting Dubear she had noticed something strange about the way he spoke, as if he were intentionally trying to sound less intelligent that he really was.

"Doing a little drawing, huh?" said Emily, as Dubear tried to hide the journal.

"Uh, yes ma'am," he said. "Just a little draw'n."

"May I see?"

"Aw, it's nothing really."

"I had a cousin named Herman Melville who used to draw a lot."

Suddenly Dubear's eyes opened wide and he stood, pointing at Emily. "You're related to Herman Melville?"

"Yeah," she said, laughing. "Moby Dick, too."

Suddenly, Dubear realized he had been baited into revealing his true intellect. He looked at the ground for a second, hands on his hips, then he glanced back up at Emily.

"You fell for that one, hook, line and sinker, didn't ya?" She stopped smiling, her face taking on a much more serious aspect. "You wanna tell me who you really are, and what you're do'n down here?"

"Like I told ya, ma'am, I'm go'n to see my family down in Houma."

"About a year ago," said Emily, "they caught a spy down in Alexandria. I heard about all the terrible things they did to him before they hung him." She paused for affect, "And he was a white man."

"Maybe I should be on my way," he said, starting to gather his things. "When it gets dark, I'll be head'n out."

"You'll do no such thing," said Emily. "It's bad enough having slave hunters come around here. And unless it's my husband, I'd rather not have Confederate soldiers snooping around asking questions. I have a friend down in Ringgold. You and Sarah and I'll be going down there tomorrow. You'll be the man I borrowed from Mister Dyson to do some fix'n around here. Can you remember that, Mister Dubear?"

"Mister Dyson in Ringgold," he said, before she turned and walked out of the barn.

The trip to Ringgold and back took most of the day. Only once was Emily questioned about Dubear. Without hesitation a soldier at the bridge bought the story of the unknown black man being a hired-out slave from another master. With enough food for three days, they dropped him off at a secluded wooded area outside of Ringgold, forty miles southeast of Shreveport.

"In case you forgot, Mister Dubear," Emily said, pointing south as he hopped off the buckboard. "Houma's that way, and if I were you, I'd travel at night. At least until you get good ways past Alexandria. If you can make it to Lafayette, I think you'll find the roads safe to travel into Houma. Godspeed to ya, Mister Dubear."

"Thank ya, Ma'am," he said, humbly nodding before trudging off into the woods.

"Dat man seem kind'a spooky, Miss Emily," said Sarah on their way back.

"Kind'a spooky indeed, Sarah. Kind'a spooky indeed."

Joshua Dubear would be the last black man Emily Hawkins would help traveling secretly through her farm. She would often wonder what became of him and what his true purpose was in Louisiana.

Not long after Christmas Emily began to have headaches and dizzy spells. At first she kept this from Sarah and Jacob. Every day she hoped for a letter from David, but none came. Though she tried hard to fight against it, despair and weakness began to take a toll on her body. She could not eat and tossed and turned all night, her body aching with fever. After Sarah found her collapsed on the kitchen floor, it was thought to be a spider bite or maybe food poisoning. Only once were the slaves held in suspicion of foul play. The absurd accusation came from old Debra Kaiser, the town laudanum addict. Everyone, especially Sheriff Wilhyte, quickly dismissed it. Emily Hawkins's uncommon kindness toward her slaves was common knowledge throughout the area. Still, there was something very unsettling about her death. She was laid to rest beside David's mother, father and brother.

"Oh, Miss Emily," Sarah wept, standing by her grave that night. "What po' David go'n do wit'out ya?"

VII

The Union flotilla moved into the Red River Valley like a steely bluish-black serpent leaving its lair to expand its hunting grounds. It had taken nearly two weeks for the two groups to finally meet up and converge as one, blending into a massive corps of expedition. As seen from a distance it sparkled and clanked of metal and iron, moaning, stretching its rattling scales along the traces of men and nature. Its body kept to the water and the land, breathing in the air, amphibious and lurking, deliberate and lethal, trampling out a bittersweet vintage with esters of melancholy. Up close it seemed much greater than the sum of its parts, scenes and looks of all sorts, panoramic in their scope. Views to a campaign. Disembarked outfits shortcutting swaths of destruction through the land where the river went as if warden to its flow. Quaint homesteads falling victim to the incendiary instincts of the damn Yankee man. Vistas parading en masse, sullen and morose. A scythe of belligerence slithering behemoth-like toward a not unknown prey.

Sidney Brooks finally got the spot he liked. He had been allowed to ride on one of the lead gunboats, macabre vessels that until recently did not exist. Elemental floating hulks decked with protruding cannon barrels, fore, starboard, port and aft. Looming stacks spewed thick clouds of rolling gloom. Men lumbered on the deck, wraith-like, wet and grim. A hanging murk of dark angles hissing its toxic warning, obtuse and sinister, progressive, dirty and monstrous, rendering all other navies obsolete. All guarantees in question save mayhem. The crew itself was a morbid lot and he could spend little time below, the stink of smoke and men being much too awful. Tight dank catacombs of foul industry and metallic clamor. Nauseous vertigo. Above deck was tolerable and it felt romantic knowing all his suffering would pay off with a story that might bring men to tears. A splendid narrative possibly read throughout the whole civilized world. He looked off into the distance, his head puffed full of his own self-satisfaction. The low late-winter sun glinted off the water, causing him to squint as he posed vain and meaningless on the prow. To his left, right and behind him men struggled with their painful, never-ending tasks. The vulgar work of the ignoble and the simple.

Before Bank's army had left Opelousas Brooks paid a visit to a local brothel, taking advantage of the V.I.P. treatment bestowed upon him by the general. The young lady who spent the afternoon in his service told him that she had heard of two spies being sent north to learn what they could of the defenses at Shreveport. One was a white man posing as a former planter who'd had his farm burned by the Yankees. He was said to be dangerous, cunning and very good with a knife. The other was a black man posing as a slave who had some knowledge of the Shreveport area. Brooks did what he could to find out more about the two spies but got nowhere. Dangerous work, he had thought to himself as the Army arrived at Simmesport to rendezvous with Porter's fleet.

Besides the twelve ironclads, there were several monitors and over a hundred large boats carrying horses, supplies, weapons and men. Packed cargo vessels and transports churned their way upstream, soldiers milling about the decks in an eddying mass of humanity. Alongside the river marched thousands of men far from home, most from the Northeast, some from the Mid-west. They appeared lost, dazed in a world of strange accents, climates and landscapes. Horses pulled wagons loaded with even more supplies. Entering enemy territory, the Union campaign became a hoard of acquisition confiscating goods as they went; weapons, livestock, produce, cotton and anything of value taken as contraband. Liberated slaves running amuck. Cannons were pulled like unwilling servants glaring back at their soon-to-be-forgotten homes. Everywhere up and down the line, men shouted orders, breathing in the kicked-up dust. Mumbled curses. Whispers of home and loved ones. Lonely, homesick men burdened with duty and thankless toil. All to be written off to the ages, scribbled down as afterthoughts to an executive decision run rampant.

David Hawkins had his plow rig turned upside down, propped up against the barn door. Jacob and Isaac held it steady while he ran a large file across its blade. He had been trying to focus his energy on the farm, but so many things clouded his mind. He would still look up half-expecting to see Emily standing there with her hands on her hips, giving him a wink and a smile, always letting him know he was the light of her life.

Every morning and evening he would visit her grave, standing silently for a long while before saying a few words. He would also acknowledge his mother, father and brother, feeling deep in his heart they were truly at rest together some place special. His thoughts would drift to Amy Bolton and the afternoon he had spent with her. Every time he looked out to see Jackson trotting around the corral he was tempted to saddle up the horse and head back down to Pleasant Hill. He would then think of Johnny and the time he had spent talking with the boy. He wondered how the kid was doing and hoped that taking him his father's cap would somehow bring closure to his pain and loss, a loss to which he was deeply connected.

He wanted so much to become part of Amy and Johnny's life, but knew the war could soon come to the area. And that was his final distraction.

"Riders com'n, Massa David," said Isaac.

Hawkins looked up to see two men on horseback coming up the road. Even from a distance he could tell one man was white and the other was black, not an uncommon sight. He did not recognize them, and as they drew closer he could tell they were strangers. As he walked from the barn, Isaac and Jacob trailed behind, looking nervously at one another. The white man looked to be about Hawkins' age, maybe a bit older. He wore a floppy wide-brimmed hat with a long red rooster feather, a gaudy-red shirt with a blue-patchwork design and a dark green sash around his waist. 'A Cajun,' thought Hawkins. The black man wore spectacles, looked to be in his early 20's and was dressed plainly in dingy browns and dark faded blues with a shabby-looking grey hat.

"Howdy," the white man said. "My name's Gabriel Heartshorn. But folks call me Gaby. Dis here's my slave."

"What can I do for ya, Gaby?"

"Well, I heard tell in town dair, ya might be'a need'n a bit a help 'round here."

"Someone told you that?" asked Hawkins.

"Well, yessay'did. Said ya might need a bit'a help plow'n an' plant'n an' fix'n up'a bit. Me an' Jimmy here, we work real hard. Had me my own little farm down 'round Houma. But da Yankee man burned it."

"Sorry to hear that," said Hawkins. "But who was it that told ya I needed help?"

"Oh, I don't recall da man's name," said Gaby, sticking his hand under his hat to scratch his head. "Jus' somebody dat pointed dis'a way when we asked where dair might be some work, ya see. An' a'course ya ain't gotta pay dis'n here," he pointed at the black man, "on a count'a he's my slave, ya see."

"Well," said Hawkins. "I could sure use the help, but I can't pay ya anything till the crops come in, and that could be awhile."

"What ya be grow'n out here?" said Gaby, looking around the place.

"Cotton, mainly," said Hawkins. "But I grow a lil'a just about everything."

"I tell ya what, Mister ...uh..."

"Hawkins. David Hawkins."

"Mister Hawkins, if'n ya can promise me an' Jimmy here three meals a day an' a place ta lay our heads, we'll give ya a steady grind sunup ta sundown. An' when da crops come in, jus' gimme a fair shake an' I'll be happy. How's 'at sound?"

Hawkins looked at the man for a second, then at his slave. He noticed the young black man was looking past him with a bit of concern in his eyes. Hawkins turned to Jacob and Isaac, taking note of the odd look on their faces.

"Don't worry, son," Hawkins said turning back to the young black man. "They don't bite hard, just often." He turned back to Gaby Heartshorn. "Food won't be a problem, but you'll have to bed down in the barn's upper loft. Got some extra blankets if ya need'm."

"Why, thank ya, Mister Hawkins," said Gaby, dismounting and extending his hand to Hawkins, who then noticed the large Bowie knife tucked into the left side of his sash. He was almost as tall as Hawkins with a leaner build and a strong iron grip. His face bore the scars of many knife fights and his teeth were rotten, causing Hawkins to look away when he smiled. "We'll jus' put our things up in da barn an'..."

"While you're up there," said Hawkins walking back to his plow, "have a look at that pulley, will ya. Pair'a pliers there by the barn door."

In the stable Jacob and Isaac stood looking at the young black man they knew to be Joshua Dubear. As he took care of the horses, he could not make eye contact with the two older black men. When he was done, he looked up to see Jacob standing close, glaring at him.

"Ya got some nerve come'n back here, boy."

"What hap'n to ya family?" asked Isaac, a little less hostile.

"My pa died some years back," said Dubear. "My ma, brotha's an' sista's got taken as contraband and were shipped up North. Dat's what I was told."

"Who dat man is?" asked Jacob, stepping closer to Dubear. "An' don't lie ta me, boy. I can smell me a lie a mile away."

"Met'm north'a Lafayette. It was dangerous, me traveling alone, so I took up with'm."

"An' brung'm up here", hissed Jacob.

"He jus'a man look'n fo' work, is all."

Jacob looked at Isaac, then back at Dubear, stepping close, his face only inches from the young man. "If'n dair be any trouble, boy, I kill ya myself."

Amy Bolton had just finished grading some of the homework she had recently given to her older students. She had asked them to write a page or two on what they wanted to be when they grew up. Without exception every student, both girls and boys, made reference to Major David Hawkins, either wanting to grow up and be like him or marry him. Only Johnny McRay's paper differed from the rest. It read like a personal letter to Amy. He wanted to grow up with David Hawkins and Amy Bolton as their adopted son. With innocent, thirteen-year-old candor he told how he saw them kissing, even apologizing for the accidental sneak-peek. *Sorry 'bout see'n y'all kiss. Didn't mean to.* He hoped that they would get married and the three of them live together on Hawkins's farm. He wanted to join the Confederate cavalry and fight side by side with his *step-pa, wup'n the Yankees.* Also, he hoped some kind of plaque or statue of his father might be put up in the town *so folks would know he really wasn't such a bad guy.*

When she got to the end of Johnny's paper, she let out a quiet laugh of relief. He had ended off with a note saying that when he read the paper in front of the class, which was always required, he would leave out the part about her and Hawkins kissing, and them hopefully getting married and adopting him, *so's I don't embarrass ya or nothin'.* Instead he would focus on telling the class how his pa had saved Hawkins's life, and what a brave man he was.

Amy Bolton had been born in Natchez, Mississippi, and had briefly lived in Shreveport as a young girl. She and Carla McRay had been very close growing up, spending their adolescent years living in Pleasant Hill. Amy had actually been with Carla in Shreveport the day she first met the broad-shouldered Adam McRay. The two girls had gone into town with Carla's mother. At the corner of Milam and Marshall their buckboard hit a big hole in the road, badly cracking one of its wheels. At that moment, a sober McRay happened by. When he saw the pouty, disappointed look on Carla's face, it was love at first sight. After purchasing a new wheel with his own money, he effortlessly hoisted the wagon's axle onto his shoulder while in a squatting position, then set it in place without breaking a sweat. Two months later he proposed to the nineteen-year-old girl after paying countless calls to her home in Pleasant Hill. Amy, who was seventeen at the time, stood as maid of honor missing the bouquet by mere inches. She too was spared seeing Adam's bad side, but heard of it often enough to know that it indeed existed.

As a teenager Amy had been thin and gangly, not blossoming physically into a woman until she was almost twenty. By then she was studying literature at the college in Natchitoches, where she had earned a scholarship by winning first place in a state-wide essay contest. It was there that she met her first and only other love interest, a young man from Kentucky who courted her for over a year. Their sexual encounters were exciting and quite fulfilling, but did not compare with the experience she had just days ago with David Hawkins. Eventually her suitor graduated and returned to Kentucky to run the family business. At first Amy took this in stride, but when he failed to return her letters, the crush of rejection hit home. Carla died a year later. Amy then returned to Pleasant Hill, immediately taking on the job of helping raise eight-year-old Johnny.

After Carla's death Adam McRay began spending even more time away. When he was home he was aloof to everyone except Johnny, and always smelled of whiskey. However, he did provide for the boy, always bringing home cash and material essentials. For over two years he spent his time chopping down trees and fighting for money, sometimes staying gone for a week or more. Then he would show up out of the blue, gather up his son for a long hunting and fishing excursion, only to disappear again when the money ran out. But he always left a little extra with Amy, and during that time she and Johnny grew very close. Considering the circumstances, Johnny grew into a fairly well rounded boy with a good natured disposition. But when Adam was arrested for busting up the bar in Shreveport, Johnny became distant to everyone, even Amy.

For over a month Adam McRay had languished in jail. But just days after the war began, his situation changed significantly. An old drinking buddy who'd been his fight manager paid him a visit. Bucky Morris was a one-eyed professional gambler from Memphis who had gotten McRay his more lucrative fights, and taught him the true art of the bluff.

"Never let folks know how good ya really are, son," Morris had told McRay when they first met at the fights under the old trestle bridge off Cotton Street. "Ya wupped that last fella too easy. Hell, I just lit this cigar, only took two puffs an' ya done put'm to bed. Can't make any money that way. Nobody'll bet against ya. Gotta at least make it look like a struggle." Morris had then leaned in close to McRay, handing him a flask of whiskey. "Ya gotta learn ta play with ya toys. Put on a show. Makes folks more apt to spend their money."

After making a few nice easy purses, Morris tried talking McRay into going down to New Orleans, where the big fight money was. But McRay refused, saying he would never go back to that God-forsaken city. Besides, there was Carla and Johnny to think about.

Morris was the kind of man that seemed to know everyone everywhere. He showed up at the jail in his usual three-piece suit, top hat and eye patch, sipping from a flask. "Adam, Adam,

Adam," he said, looking through the bars at the sulking McRay. "Well, I got good news. You're probably not gonna like it, but it's better than the alternative."

The next morning he was allowed out to see Johnny. That day they went fishing at their favorite spot, catching a huge batch of catfish and brim. They cooked up the fish for a small get-together in Pleasant Hill. Adam McRay was in rare form his last night in the small town, up-beat, warm and even a bit gregarious. Two days later he reported to Fort Turnbull to enlist in the cavalry. For weeks after Adam left, Amy would see Johnny standing by the road, looking off where he had last seen his father calling back to him as he slowly rode away.

"Don't ya worry none, Johnny. This ain't go'n take long. Adam McRay go'n straight'n everything out. Be back 'fore supper time."

In the past whenever he'd left to go work and fight, Adam never told Johnny when he'd be back, it was simply understood that he would be back. The boy always took everything his father said to heart, and when he wasn't back by supper Johnny began to worry.

Adam McRay wasn't much for writing, and the few letters he did send were vague and hurried. But each letter contained a special little gift. A small, bluish-gray arrowhead. The tip of a timber rattler's tail, and a mangled Union mini-ball pulled from a pine tree. The latter was wrapped in a note that read: *Bounced right off my head.*

Amy had often wondered to herself, might Adam have been better off serving the four years in prison? Maybe he could've survived that type of hell. Word of his death did not reach Pleasant Hill until five months after Shiloh. No specific location was given as to where he had been killed, just that he had been counted among the dead somewhere in Tennessee. At first Johnny took the news as well as any eleven-year old could. A mild look of shock in his eyes, followed by tears, breaking down and weeping painfully, shamelessly in Amy's arms. Soon afterwards, Johnny seemed to retreat into a shell and seldom come out, except when provoked to anger. The arrival of

Hawkins with his father's cap had definitely cracked open that shell, and Amy Bolton was determined to pry at its loose parts, doing what she could to reach the troubled boy.

"Johnny," she said to him at dinner later that evening. "I read your paper."

He looked up at her, his lips greasy from a pork chop smeared with honey. She could tell by the look in his eyes that what he had written to her had slipped his mind until now, but not what he had written about.

"You really like Major Hawkins, don't you Johnny?"

"You like'm, too, don't ya, Aunt Amy?"

"I like him a lot, Johnny, but that doesn't mean we're going get married."

"I know, but ya's told us to write what we wanna be when we grow up, an' I wanna be you an' Major Hawkins's son."

She smiled, hesitating awkwardly, then reached over to brush some of the hair from his eyes. "That's really sweet, Johnny. But it's not that simple."

"I could go'n talk to'm. Tell'm that ya like'm a lot."

"Don't you dare do that, Johnny." She pulled her hand back and sat up straight in her chair. "Besides, I think Major Hawkins knows I like him, but he's going through a lot right now. His wife died recently, and he just got back from some terrible fighting."

"I know," said Johnny. "An' you could help'm forget all that, could'n ya?"

"He doesn't want to forget his wife, Johnny. They were together a long time and she must have been a wonderful lady."

"I didn't mean like that, Aunt Amy. I mean the bad fight'n from the war, an' all."

"I wish I could help him forget about that," she said, looking thoughtfully across the room. "But it's not that simple either. They say things like that can trouble a man all the days of his life."

"Bad things happened to'm huh?"

"I think so, Johnny," she said, turning to look at the boy. "War is a terrible thing."

Johnny looked down at his food, then back up at Amy. "I wanna go'n fight in da war."

"What?" she blurted. "And get killed like Adam?" As soon as she said the words, she wished that she could somehow reach out and take them back. "I'm sorry, Johnny. I didn't mean to say that. But you're way too young to even be think'n of going off and fighting in a war. It's just men killing each other."

"Like they killed Pa," he said, standing up from the table.

"Johnny, you don't know what really happened. That battle was huge. Even Major Hawkins probably doesn't know everything, and he was there."

"Yes, he does!" Johnny shouted. "He told me! Dem Yankees ganged up on Pa! But he wupt'm, anyhows! Pa died later 'cause he bled out while he's tote'n Major Hawkins wit'a broken leg across't da battlefield! Pa's a hero!" He snatched his father's cap off the table and headed for the door. "Dem Yankees prob'lee shot'm in da back. I'm go'n kill me a Yankee someday, you'll see."

"Johnny, please, I didn't mean to upset ya. Come on back, baby," she called after him, moving to the door. But it was too late. He had already slipped off into the darkness. She hadn't realized how much in detail Hawkins had told Johnny of Adam's death. But she knew he would go to either Robert Driggers's or Randy Randall's house, where he spent most of his time anyway.

Amy sat back down at the table, bowed her head and began to pray. She'd already asked the Lord to forgive her for her intimate moment with David Hawkins, not totally clear why because it had felt so right. She wished her faith was stronger. She loved the man and wanted dearly to spend the rest of her life with him. But now she was praying for Johnny. To somehow sooth the rage in the poor boy's soul. To bring him somewhere near the face of God.

VIII

Johnny McRay looked down at the twelve-by-fifteen-foot raft that floated near the bank of the Red River. Behind him stood Robert Driggers, Randy Randall and Bobby Bernard, now best buddies with Johnny. Behind the boys was Grey Stump, a big old easygoing gray mule that would pull just about anything for a carrot or a turnip. They had swiped the mule from Old Man Ebarb's farm, just east of Pleasant Hill. Their plan was to hitch the animal up to the raft with a long rope, getting a pull upriver to Hawkins's farm. It was a Saturday morning and the boys would be missed, but with no great urgency. They would often disappear on the weekends without telling anyone.

After running off the night before Johnny had gone straight to Robert Driggers's house, telling him of his plan to pay Hawkins a visit. Soon Randy and Bobby were in the mix, and the little venture began taking on the characteristics of an actual expedition. Bobby knew where there was a raft big enough for the four of them. And they all knew Old Man Ebarb wouldn't mind if they borrowed Grey Stump, as long as the animal was returned alive and in one piece.

"Ya sure dat raft's still dair, Bobby?" Johnny had asked when they started planning.

"Yep," he answered in an unusually agreeable tone. "Me an' Uncle Coco went'n fished off it jus' las' week."

"An' iss good? It floats?"

"Why, heck yeah. Good'r den gravy, Johnny. Why, we could take dat dair raft all da way ta da Guff'a Mezco."

"It'll be easy den," said Randy. "My pa's gotta bunch'a rope..."

"An' we can go'n get Grey Stump at Ebarb's field ta do some pull'n," Robert interrupted, his young eyes full of excitement.

After rustling Grey Stump by the moonlight, the four boys piled on the mule and starting riding east all night to the river fifteen miles away. Bobby complained the entire trip because he had to ride the mule's rear end. His legs were bowed out around the animal's wide butt, his arms wrapped tight around Randy who held on to Robert, with Johnny at the helm.

The night was clear and a bright three-quarter moon played on the water, casting a blueish-gray light on the boys' faces as they looked at the raft bobbing back and forth against the riverbank, eyes gleaming, whispering their secret plan.

"Ya think it'll hold us all?" asked Robert.

"Heck, yeah," said Bobby. "Uncle Coco weighs as much as'n ol'hog. Watch'iss." He sprang out from the bank, landing in the center of the raft, causing it to launch out into the water a short ways before catching on a rope that held it to a cypress stump. "See," he said, spinning around with his hands out, his feet doing a quick little jig. "Good'r den gravy, jus' like I said."

While Randy and Bobby tied the rope between Grey Stump's harness and the raft, Johnny and Robert gathered a few long sturdy tree branches to use as push-poles. After feeding the mule a burlap sack full of vegetables, they let him get his fill of water. Robert then began leading the animal along a trail at the top of the bank that wound upriver. The other three used the poles to keep the raft off the bank as it was pulled against the current. Once he got Grey Stump into a good steady pace Robert sprinted down the bank, timing his leap so that he landed on the raft just as the boys let it drift in close to land. By first light they had fallen into a slow easy rhythm, taking turns at the poles pushing away from the bank every moment or so to keep it from running aground. The raft would swing out twenty or thirty feet until they could not touch bottom. Then it would drift back with the old mule's strong constant pull against the river's current, to be pushed out again.

Every once in a while Grey Stump would get caught up on a tree or some brush. One of the boys would have to jump off the raft and run up the bank to untangle the animal. Eventually they came to a long stretch where the mule walked unimpeded for over an hour. During this time Randy kept the raft off the bank while the others broke out the food they had brought: a loaf of bread, a slab of cheese and a big chunk of ham. A few leftover corn fritters cooked the day before by Robert's mom. An apple apiece and a jug of sweet tea with lemon. They talked with their mouths full about the different girls they had finally started noticing with an interest other than for pulling harmless pranks.

"Cindy Duncan's got da purdiest face, but she kind'a fat."

"Donna Smith's purdy'r dan Laura Stucky, but Laura Stucky's nicer."

"I kissed Laura Stucky over behind Old Lady Sutton's lemon tree."

"Na, ya didn't. When?"

"Rat 'fore New Year's. She let me."

"Kim Johnson's always smile'n at me."

"She's always smile'n at everyone."

"I's at da store las' week, an' Stacy Watson said hey."

"She says hey to everyone."

After eating and talking about girls, the conversation changed to a more serious matter.

"Did'ee tell ya how yer pa saved 'is life?" Robert asked, taking his turn at the pole.

"Said 'is leg was broke real bad," said Johnny as he trailed a twig in the raft's wake. "An' most everyone else was dead. Pa found'm dat way, an' picked'm up an' carried'm a'ways till dey got jumped by some Yankees. Major Hawkins said he was hurt so bad'ee couldn't do nut'n but lay dair, bone stick'n out 'is leg. But pa kilt all dem Yankees anyhow. Den'ee carried Major Hawkins som'ors till dey come across some good'ol Rebels who took'm to a hospital. 'At's where Pa give'm da cap'n ax'm ta bring it to me." He took the cap off and looked at it, then looked up river. "Said pa's buried up dair at Shiloh somewheres. Said it's real purdy. Real, real purdy."

For a long time no one spoke. Robert and Randy pushed at the poles while Bobby sat cross-legged at the front of the raft watching Grey Stump. Johnny tossed the twig into the water and held the cap in both hands, staring at the dark, rust-colored patches of dried blood that covered over half of the bluish-grey denim. Finally Bobby stood and walked over to Johnny who was now looking off across the river.

"Hey, Johnny. 'Member dem things I said 'bout yer pa dat day Major Hawkins came'n brung ya da cap?"

"Yeah," said Johnny, keeping his eyes off in the distance.

"Well, I jus' wanna say I'm real sorry I said dat. An' ya was right 'bout my pa. All'ee does's go'n get men who wanna go home wit'out'a furlough. Dat's why no one likes'm. He's a no-good. Anyway, I jus' wanted ta say dat I shouldn'ta ought'a said dat 'bout yer pa. An' I'm sorry."

Johnny looked at Bobby, who had his hand out.

"Dat's okay, Bobby," said Johnny, shaking his hand. "I'm sorry I punched ya, an' dat yer pa's a no-good."

"Yeah, me too." Bobby looked down at the cap in Johnny's other hand. "Say, can I wear da cap for a bit, Johnny?"

"Aw'right, but don't ya dare drop it in da water." Johnny handed the cap to Bobby.

"Aw, thanks Johnny." Bobby smiled, putting on the cap.

By noon the pontoon bridge crossing the river into Shreveport was in sight. They decided to pull the raft up on the bank and ride Grey Stump the rest of the way. They took a well-worn trail that ran through the tall grass by the river into the town. At the edge of the train yard a group of soldiers stopped them. It looked a little strange, four boys they'd never seen before riding into town on a mule.

"Where'd ya get da mule, boy?" said one soldier.

"We barr'eed it from Old Man Ebarb down 'round Pleasant Hill," said Johnny.

"Barrowed it, huh?"

"Yessir."

"Where ya go'n wit' it?"

"Major David Hawkins's farm on Cross Bayou."

"I know Major Hawkins," said another soldier with sergeant stripes. "He just got back and I heard his wife died."

"Dat's right," said Johnny. "An'ee needs dis here mule ta get da crops in da ground 'fore da rains come."

The sergeant looked at the four boys straddled on the mule, laughed and waved his hand. "Y'all, go on."

When they got to the wharf area, the boys dismounted Grey Stump and walked the mule past the crowded docks. They soon found another trail running between the shipyard and the town, not knowing it was a trail Hawkins had blazed when he was half their age. The trail darkened as it dipped down into a cave-like passageway completely shaded by a canopy of oaks, cypress trees and towering patches of fallow sugar cane. Through the gnarled undergrowth a large bayou was visible running into the river from the west. The dense spring vegetation twined together three feet above the trail, causing the boys to push it aside as they went. At one point the trail ran directly along the water's edge creating a landing for any small boats to venture out onto the bayou. They stopped for a moment, admiring the eerie scenic view across the water to the edge of Hawkins's land. Just before passing under a wooden trestle bridge that was partially obscured by the overhanging tree limbs and dried-out cane poles, the path forked up and to the left like a tunnel out of the thick canopy below. Reemerging into the sunlight, the trail then connected to the road that crossed the bridge over the bayou. On the other side, about a hundred feet past the bridge, the road forked off to the right, leading to Hawkins's farm. Just before the fork was a sign that read: **Texarkana 70 miles**, with an arrow pointing up the North Market Road. To the side of the bridge Johnny noticed another trail that crossed over the levee, running down the length of the bayou. They took the trail, following it back down to the bayou's mouth, where it turned north upriver. Soon a small farm could be seen through the trees on the other side of the levee.

Nitney had been a good horse. Not too fast and not too pretty, but he had been a good strong worker, never shying away from pulling a load. He had been born on the Hawkins farm while David was on his first tour out West with the Army. Nitney had done most of the plowing in those years before the war. He had taken Ira and Dorothy Hawkins to church every Sunday. It was Nitney that took Clem and Noel up to the Etheridge farm in Arkansas, and Joshua Dubear down past Ringgold last fall. But now the poor old horse was dead. Gaby Heartshorn and Joshua Dubear had been plowing the back end of the field when Nitney suddenly let out a neigh and a snort. The horse then fell on his left side, kicked his legs in pain before going totally limp.

"I do believe his heart give out, Mista Hawkins," Gaby said as they stood there looking down at the dead horse.

Hawkins knew he was going to have to get a new plow horse soon, but wasn't expecting it to be this soon. He always hated rushing into buying livestock and knew if he used Gaby's horse, the man would want more money when payday came.

"Want me to get Juno, David?" asked Jacob.

"No, that's your horse," replied Hawkins. "I guess we'll hafta rotate Ursa and Hugger for a while."

"Dey won't las' long," Jacob said, raising his eyebrows. "Dem horses was over ten years old when Nitney was born." He pointed toward the corral. "Don't mind none usin' Juno, David, but what 'bout dat red horse ya got dair?"

"That's a warhorse, not a plow horse, Jacob," said Hawkins, but couldn't honestly say he hadn't thought of the idea himself.

"Seen me some soldiers look'n mighty hungry back dair at da river when I came inta town, Mista Hawkins," said Gaby, scratching his chin as he looked down at Nitney. "I could butcher'm up fer ya. Go'n sell da meat. I'd say half would be a fair shake."

Hawkins took off his hat and looked up at the sky. "I'm not selling a dead horse for food."

"Look like we might be in luck, David," said Isaac, pointing off toward the levee.

They turned to see four young boys and big gray mule walking from the levee toward the back of the farm. Hawkins smiled and looked at Jacob.

"Go'n tell Sarah we got company for dinner."

"Who dat is, Massa David?" asked Jacob.

"A friend, Jacob," said Hawkins, clapping the man on the back. "A friend."

After a few introductions, Hawkins put Grey Stump to work. Not plowing, but transporting Ol' Nitney to a spot for burial. First they had to take one of the barn doors off its hinges. Then they hitched it up to Grey Stump and dragged it out to the field next to Nitney. Then they rolled the big horse over onto the door. Grey Stump then pulled old Nitney to a nice little place near the levee behind the field. After everyone pitched in with shovels digging Nitney's grave, they grabbed his legs and rolled him into the big hole with a dusty thud. Hawkins then said a few words, a reverent prayer on the creature's behalf.

"Dear Lord, Nitney here was a good horse. He worked hard'n strong for me and my family for a long time. Never caused any trouble and he was always ready to go. I ask that you give'm a peaceful rest up there in horse heaven. Amen."

Hawkins gave everyone the rest of the day off and he spent the afternoon visiting with Johnny and his friends. After showing the boys around the farm, he took them in the house and brought out some of the strange items he had collected over the years. Dozens of hides and furs, some from animals they'd never even heard of. An assortment of bugs, flowers and rocks from all over the country. A vast array of Indian artifacts. His gun, knife and sword collection. He pointed out a photograph of Emily he'd recently had framed and hung on the wall near his favorite chair. She'd had it taken in town and sent to him in Colorado, a close shot of her looking slightly to the side, her lips formed into a gentle smile.

"She's real purdy, Major Hawkins," said Johnny.

"Yeah," he said, smiling back at the picture. "She sure is."

Soon the boys began telling Hawkins of their little journey to his farm. They all laughed together as Johnny told him how they borrowed Grey Stump from Old Man Ebarb, riding the mule quadruple all the way to the river and hitching him up to the raft to pull them along like a ferry ride. He explained with even more laughter how Grey Stump would get hung up and how they took turns jumping back on land to free the animal. And how they left the raft just south of town on the riverbank to ride the rest of the way on the mule.

"Some soldiers stopped us by da train yard an' axt us 'bout Grey Stump," said Johnny, still laughing. "Soon as dey heard yer name an' dat we's bringing'm here, dey let us go."

"Ya think y'all can make it back all right without the mule?" asked Hawkings, pulling out some money.

"Well, yeah, but …." Johnny looked at the other boys.

"Here's forty-five U.S. dollars," said Hawkins. "Give forty to Mr. Ebarb and ask'm if he wants to sell Grey Stump. If he does, that'll be a down payment and I'll give'm the rest in a few days. If he doesn't wanna sell'm, tell'm to keep the forty dollars an' I'll bring'm back by the end of next week. Ya think he'll mind that?"

"Well, no, sir," said Johnny, looking at the money. "But what'sa udder five dollars fer?"

"That's y'alls. Split it four ways. Buck'n a quarter apiece."

"Sure, Major," Johnny said, smiling. "We can do dat. An' we don't need Grey Stump ta get downriver. We go'n haf'ta walk a ways, but dat ain't no big deal."

When the issue of Grey Stump was settled, Hawkins took them for a walk over the levee by the bayou. He showed them a hidden shortcut they could've taken, and the places where he used to run and play as a boy. He pointed out the boundaries of his property, explaining that the land his father had bought when he was a small child was almost three times what he owned now. He showed them the spot where he killed his first deer. And where his brother Paul and he had treed a crafty old coon that had been stealing eggs from the chicken coop one winter. The boys listened and laughed as Hawkins told them about his many failed attempts to beat his brother in fishing contests that he himself had initiated over the years. And about the first raft they had built, which stayed afloat less than a minute before capsizing fifty feet from the bank on a cold winter day.

Just off a rust-colored dirt trail that ran along the river, about a quarter mile north of the bayou, the Confederate laid his hand on the trunk of a large cypress tree that grew out over the water at a slight tilt. When he looked up the boys followed his gaze, noticing an old frayed rope swaying from one of its upper limbs, the hemp obviously rotten and now well out of reach.

"Shimmied up this here tree an' tied 'at rope myself," he said with a thoughtful smile, his eyes still upward, "'bout twenty-five years ago."

They stayed at the spot for a while. Hawkins told the boys it was where he had spent many'a hot summer day after his chores and schoolwork. Then he took them down another trail that led away from the river.

"What's 'at?" asked Johnny after they had traveled a good distance, pointing at what looked like a mound the size of a small cabin overgrown in a thicket of grass, trees and vines.

"Oh,…uh," replied Hawkins, hesitantly. "An ol' Indian man use'ta live there. Died when I'sa lil' boy, younger than y'all are now."

"Wow, a real Injun," said Bobby. "Let's go'n look."

"No," said Hawkins, putting his hand on the boy's shoulder as he started to move, yet keeping his eyes on the loamy relic. "My pa told us to leave it just like it is and never disturb it."

For a long while, the five stood silently admiring the crude artifact, hints of its man-made qualities showing through the under growth in a vague arrangement. The Confederate's eyes scanned the area as if watchful of a ghost or bogeyman.

"Why'd yer pa let'a Injun live on yer land?" asked Johnny, breaking the silence.

"Cause he's a purdy good fella," answered Hawkins, looking at the boy. "'At's why."

"Which one?" Johnny asked further, a slight frown showing on his face. "Yer pa or dat Injun?"

Hawkins hesitated, regarding the boy with some consideration. "Well, they's both purdy good, Johnny. But I's refer'n to the Indian. He's here first, ya know."

For a short while the boys made casual observations about the site. Then Hawkins said, "Come on. Let's head on back."

They took a trail that skirted well away from the little ruin before cutting back south through the trees. Soon the smell of Sarah's cooking was in the air. As they headed back, the boys began to ask questions about the war, a subject Hawkins was reluctant to discuss.

"How many Yankees ya kilt?" asked Bobby, causing Hawkins to jerk his head around at the boy.

"That's not something I like talk'n about, son. Kill'n a man ain't like go'n out squirrel hunt'n. Besides, folks up north are a lot like us down here, but where they live's a bit colder, so their moods'r different." After Hawkins said this, everyone was quiet until they came to a field that led up to the farmhouse.

"So what's kill'n a man like?" Johnny asked, breaking an awkward silence.

Hawkins glared harshly at the boy as they walked. "Any man that brags about kill'n another man is an animal that'll soon get what's come'n to'm. How would ya feel if ya knew some fella up north was brag'n 'bout kill'n your pa, Johnny?"

"Well, I ain't gotta worry 'bout dat none," said Johnny, looking back defiantly at Hawkins. They stopped walking and continued to glare at one another. "Cause you said my pa kilt all dem men dat kilt him. An' ya couldn't help none, cause ya's hurt, lay'n on'a ground. Ain't dat what ya said?"

"Yeah, that's what I said." Hawkins spoke it words quietly, almost in a whisper to himself. It was all he could say. For a second he wanted to reach out and strike the boy. But as quickly as it came, the anger suddenly left him. With a pained expression on his face, he stared at the boy who just moments ago seemed to almost worship him. He never told Johnny of the bad dealings he'd had with his father. But now, he suspected the boy knew all along about the fight and Adam McRay's attempts to kill him with cynical valor. He now saw something familiar in Johnny's eyes. Something that suddenly spoke volumes about the man that died saving his life. Something about loss, fear and redemption. Finally he forced a smile, turned and walked away. "Come on, let's eat."

Robert, Randy and Bobby looked at one another, then at Johnny, who was still glaring after Hawkins.

"Come on, Johnny. Let's go eat," said Robert as they started walking, Johnny trailing slowly behind.

It was a nice day. Sarah and her whole family had worked diligently to get the meal ready. She often kept large pots of vegetables stewing on the stove, but they rarely had guests for supper. Two large picnic tables had been brought out of the barn, set up end-to-end in the grass under the magnolia next to the house. A large sumptuous spread had been prepared and laid out on the tables. After they buried Nitney, Isaac went to his secret spot on the bayou and caught a bunch of catfish. Sarah fried them up along with four chickens. There was skin-on buttermilk mashed potatoes, poke salad with ham hocks and green beans, candied yams, cornbread and red-eye gravy, apple cobbler and sweet tea.

Since the last time he was here, Ruth had grown a bit sweet on Dubear. Sarah and Jacob had spoken at length with her and Noah about not mentioning his first visit to the farm last fall. They explained that because of the war, and Miss Emily's passing, it was only something that would trouble Massa David further. All of them, Sarah especially, disliked keeping secrets from Hawkins. But at this point none of them saw the need to reveal what Emily had done in helping runaway slaves reach freedom. This secrecy, plus the somewhat overbearing Gaby Heartshorn, had caused a gnawing tension among them, now made even more pronounced by the sudden rift between Hawkins and Johnny. By the time they all gathered around the tables, a rancor seemed to linger over the small party.

"I ain't eat'n wit no niggers." The words came out of Johnny's mouth like bile. "Dem Yankees dat kilt my pa's fight'n ta free dem niggers, an' I ain't gonna eat wit'm none."

"Watch ya mouth, boy!" growled Hawkins, pointing at Johnny. "This here's my family and ya got no call to talk to'm like that!"

"Yer family!!?" yelled Johnny. "If my pa'da known ya's a no-good nigger lover, he'd a left ya lay'n out dair on dat field. Den maybe he'd still be alive! Dem Yankees might not'a even kilt you none! Heck! Why don't ya go'n take up wit'm, dress up like a damn Yankee an' …!"

Before he knew it, Hawkins lunged and backhanded Johnny hard across the face. The boy didn't go down but staggered back, spinning around, his father's cap falling to the ground. Johnny slowly turned, glaring hatefully at Hawkins, a trickle of blood from his nose. He snatched up the cap and slapped it back on his head. Taking two steps backward, the boy kept his eyes on the man, the strength of his hate growing. He then turned and sprinted for the levee. The other three boys just stood there, blank looks on their faces. Then, one by one, they turned to follow Johnny.

Ruth had her hands at her mouth and was beginning to cry. Rachel stood sucking her thumb, her other little hand holding tight to Sarah's dress. Noah stood by his father, Jacob's hand on his head. The others looked awkwardly at the ground as Hawkins watched the boys disappear over the levee. He wanted to go after them but he could not move, his legs frozen in place, arms down at his side.

A small flock of crows had gathered. And as the little party stood speechless, the birds began to land and peck at the still-hot, untouched food.

IX

Ira Hawkins had been born Bolivar Dunnydon in Belfast, Ireland in the early 1790's. At the age of five he was suddenly orphaned when his parents and older sister died of cholera. Learning struggle at a young age, he then spent five very formative years at a Catholic monastery orphanage. He received a moderate education before running off to find his niche in the world. Eventually he found his way to the shipyards, growing up tough and strong, working the docks, running the wharfs and dirty backstreets, carving out a meager existence. By the time he was thirteen, he was the top ringleader for a gang of boys that worked the docks pilfering goods for the local thugs and various riff-raff. A wily, pan-eyed naughty boy laughing over a shoulder draped with loot, plying his sharp-witted tricks of the trade, always one step ahead of the snare. However, his name occasionally got out to the authorities, and he already had several dangerous enemies among Belfast's many roving bands of ne'er-do-wells.

So Bolivar Dunnydon decided it was time to leave Ireland. He and two cohorts, Tom and Peter, stowed away on a ship bound for America. Mercy's Wind was a Dutch cargo vessel that had briefly ported-in to pick up a large shipment of whiskey, before catching the trade winds to the Gulf of Mexico. On the first half of the journey across the Atlantic, the three boys were able to keep themselves well hidden in a little nook between the whiskey barrels and large crates of furniture. But Peter used his knife to gouge open a crack in one of the barrels. Soon the boys were passing round a cup as the wet spirits spilled to the floorboards, making up their own song of *Flying to America on Irish Whiskey Wings.* The singing got louder and eventually the boys were discovered, sick as dogs, and made to swab the deck in the sweltering heat of a tropical sun.

Two weeks later, at the busy port of New Orleans, the voyage's financier brought charges against the boys. They were then pressed into ten years of indentured servitude at the man's large plantation just west of the city. From the very start they were forced to work long, grueling hours. They sometimes picked cotton, loading the raw crop onto large basket-like carts to be hauled to the river, where it was floated in barges to the mills in New Orleans. But mainly they worked the sugarcane fields, hacking away with hooked collar blades, toting heavy bundles of the thick, sticky poles, also to be hauled off for the short transport downriver.

Because they were white, they were given a little more freedom than the black slaves, who were bit more confined. But still, the three boys were miserable. They'd been told early on that an escape attempt would not only lose them what little privileges they had, but could also add to their years as a servant. Besides, there was nowhere to run. They would easily be found in New Orleans, and outside the city was nothing but more plantations, swamps and wilderness. If they joined up with any pirates or outlaws, they ran the risk of being betrayed. Their master would very likely put a handsome price on their heads, adding even more time to their misery.

Tom and Peter had simple, easy-to-remember names. But Bolivar's name was unusual, so he was called Ira because of his thick, syrupy accent and his nationality. At first he hated the nickname. He often got into fights with those of equal pecking order who called him by it, especially Tom and Peter. Then one day after a bad storm, he found a fledgling red-tailed hawk that had been blown from its nest. He named the baby raptor Chéri and raised it to adulthood. While the hawk was still young he fed her a sundry of small creatures; worms, cicadas and crawfish. As she grew larger Ira fed her mice, fish, even whole chickens and rabbits. Ira would occasionally let the majestic bird perch proudly on his shoulder as he went about his daily duties, flapping her wings whenever he would run or jump, or hold her out high on his arm. Chéri became a bit of a fixture on the plantation in those days. A vigilant creature with intense, shimmering eyes that darted back and forth in utter fascination of all that surrounded her.

During this time, for well over a year, many of the other slaves and servants began calling Ira "Hawk" or "Hawk Boy". Soon, he decided to simply take the name Ira Hawkins. His companionship with Chéri helped Ira adjust to his new life, allowing him time to accept the realities of his situation. And as a ceremonial gesture to his own hoped-for freedom, he released her back into the woods. Sometimes he would glimpse the great bird soaring above the trees of the plantation. Beautiful Chéri - now master of the sky, circling free as the mid-day sun shone through her thick, roughed-up, reddish-brown plumage, waving her graces to the servant that raised her.

For over four years, Ira's life was very routine, up before sunrise, working the fields till dark. Once in a while there were lulls in the work and he was able to catch a short nap, or do something on his own time, like read a book. Sometimes he would take a walk down by the river to just sit and watch the massive, lake-like waters flow by. Sundays, however, were a whole different world on the plantation. Little or no work was done and the black slaves would congregate in one of the barns or one of the wide-open, shaded oak groves. It did not matter. All that mattered was that they got together and praised God as if Jesus Himself, in the flesh, was about to show up at that very moment. Ira had never seen anything like it, (except at one of the backstreet-wharf pubs in Ireland after a large successful haul). They lifted their hands up to the sky, clapping, singing, shouting and dancing in circles up and down the row with trance-like fervor. Ira would sometimes sit and watch, but from a safe distance, for if he got too close he was grabbed and pulled into the crazy mix to be thrashed about like a net full of fish.

Other times, he went into the city on a supply run. He was allowed to mill about the long stretch of docks, gaping at the endless row of ships from all over the world. He had been too exhausted, sick and frightened to get a good look at the port when he first arrived, but now the scene was simply grand. Every so often, he got to walk deep into the French Quarter to view the illicit sights of its backstreets, gaudy, debauched and carnival. He would stroll the Rue Conti to Bourbon, down to the Rue Dumaine, past the voodoo shops and back up to the French Market. Then he would go into the Saint Louis Cathedral to pray for the souls of his mother, father and sister. After crossing himself, he would light three candles and slowly walk the Stations of the Cross, recalling what little memories he had of his family. He never knew why he did this, and he never mentioned it to anyone.

Finally, one summer, something happened that would drastically change Ira's standing at the plantation. Back at the shipyards in Ireland young Bolivar had often been required to actually work in the water. He checked hulls and rudders for damage and retrieved items that had fallen overboard, turning him into a powerful, confident swimmer. Now he was a young man, nearly full grown at six-feet-tall, lean and muscled from the hard work, with strawberry-blond hair that fell in curls to his broad, chiseled shoulders. Still he would swim when the mood suited him, diving into the mighty Mississippi against the advice of others to play and frolic in the water like a fish. That summer a large, powerful storm blew in from the Gulf. Much of the plantation was flooded by storm surge and the constant driving rains. Three young girls, the plantation owner's two granddaughters and a niece, were stranded when part of the plantation home was literally washed away. After tying a rope around his waist and to a nearby tree, Ira ventured out into the strong, chest-deep currents. He made three trips, single-handedly rescuing each girl. The owner of the plantation actually witnessed the daring feat in a state of torpid panic. The man was so grateful afterwards, not only did he release Ira from his service, canceling the debt; he also gave him a lucrative position as a paid worker helping rebuild the plantation.

Then things began to go a little more Ira's way. The change in him was obvious to everyone, especially Tom and Peter. He did his best to accommodate his two friends without compromising his new position, or his new set of values. Tom responded favorably, working harder, seeking purpose in the more complex operations of the plantation. Peter, however, actually shirked his duties, thinking his friendship with Ira allowed him concessions regarding his responsibilities. Ira tried to talk to him, encouraging him to do better, but there was a deep-seated bitterness in the young man. He was repeatedly reprimanded but failed to show any improvements. His behavior even got worse, until finally the head overseer gave him a severe beating. Ira had tried to intervene in the corporal punishment, but it was too late. The master himself had been insulted, giving a cold nod to the overseer.

For a short while Peter showed reform and progress in his work. But his bitterness still remained. He seldom spoke to anyone, and he'd taken to heavy, daily drinking. One day, a couple of months after the beating, the head overseer was found bludgeoned to death. His living quarters had been ransacked, a large sum of money missing, and Peter nowhere to be found. Less than a week later he was found, passed out at a pirate's pub across the river at Algiers. For two days Peter was displayed in stocks at the corner of Charters and St. Ann with a sign around his neck that read; *Murderer Thief.* Before he was hanged his last words were, "Gimme a belt'a whiskey," which he was denied. Ira did not attend the public execution. When asked why, he simply said, "I d'nie think I know'm."

Within a few years the plantation was again showing a profit, Ira rising to even higher status among the paid workers. By that time, Louisiana had officially been admitted into the

American Union as its eighteenth state. But the nation was once again at war with England, a war that had become a disaster for the American experiment. Its economy had been wrecked by an embargo and a blockade. Invasions of Canada had failed. Enemy troops marched on the nation's capital, torching the White House. And the states of New England were threatening secession. By the summer of 1814, peace talks between the two warring nations began in Ghent, Belgium. But the British made constant objections, dragging out the process. Politics behind such a slow process was to have the strategic port of New Orleans in their possession by the time the treaty was signed.

Rumors of a British invasion had been heard in New Orleans since the war began. But no one knew for sure until the popular pirate, Jean Laffite, sent word to Governor Claiborne that he had been offered a very large bribe by the British to help aid in the city's capture. Now the question wasn't if the British were coming, but when? A call-to-arms was given and a local volunteer militia was organized under Major Jean Baptiste Plauché.

After signing up with the volunteer battalion, Ira went into town and bought himself a Kentucky rifle, a beautiful, powerful weapon that could knock a man down at a hundred yards.

"Ya know how to use this thing, boy?" asked the store keeper.

"Never fired a gun in me life," said Ira as he held the rifle, gazing at its craftsmanship. "But I'm a fast learner."

For several months Ira drilled in Plauché's outfit with the rifle he named Betty at his side. He practiced and practiced, learning as much as he could about marksmanship, becoming a crack rifleman. He did all this while still helping run the plantation.

Shortly before Christmas of 1814, General Andrew Jackson arrived with over 3000 men, weary and spent from the Creek Indian War in Central Alabama. He found the citizens of New Orleans in a panic, declaring a state of martial law. It was now known that a large British fleet was anchored in the Gulf, not far from the mouth of the Mississippi. Over 10,000 Redcoats were poised and ready to move on the city. Not only were the American troops exhausted and vastly outnumbered, but Jackson's men were low on flints, ammunition, gunpowder and other supplies. Again Lafitte came to the rescue, resupplying the American troops, also providing hundreds of well-seasoned fighters and gun crews. After an initial engagement on December 23rd that unnerved the British, stalling their advance up the river, the two armies spent 16 days preparing for battle just four miles south of the city.

Ira Hawkins had been made a squad leader in his ramshackle volunteer outfit. They dug trenches, helping build fortified earthworks along the northern bank of the Rodriguez Canal. It was still dark on the morning of January 8th when rockets and howitzers began to rip through the thick fog over Ira's head, crashing into the trees behind him. Major Plauché shouted words of support to steady his men. Ira was positioned with his squad at the top of a mound of earthwork, looking out at a dense wall of fog that covered the large field southwest of the canal.

Suddenly the fog began to lift, exposing several regiments of Redcoats moving along the tree line to their left. Ira made the sign of the cross and raised Betty to his eye, as all around him a thunderous crescendos of gun and cannon fire rang out. He took aim on a British soldier screaming at a phalanx of men marching to his side, a martial display of square shoulders and sharp, line-covered bayonets. After holding the man in his sights for several seconds, he squeezed Betty's trigger, emitting a violent cough of fire and smoke from the rifle's barrel. The Redcoat jerked, then buckled to the side, falling hard to the ground. As Ira reloaded he saw the British soldiers dropping by the dozen, the Americans blasting away from their well-protected earthen works. On came the enemy, bravely wading into an onslaught of rifle and artillery fire, moving ever closer to the canal, only to fall in teams. From the right, working their way diagonally across the field, came another British regiment of Highlanders and Dragoons, battle-seasoned men of the

Napoleonic Wars. General Jackson stood tall on a parapet fifty feet to Ira's right, a genteel principality directing waves of fire with his sword on the encroaching enemy. The young Irishmen continued to aim, fire and reload, over and over until he lost count. The Redcoats suddenly began to break and run, finally repulsed only yards from their objective, a chorus for songs to be sung.

The British suffered over 2000 casualties, including three generals killed, one of which was stuffed in a pickle barrel to preserve his aristocratic body. The Americans and their pirate allies lost less than 150 men. Andrew Jackson would soon become a household name, a legendary hero of the fabled city. It was later learned that the Treaty of Ghent had finally been signed, two weeks before the Battle of New Orleans.

Ira Hawkins became part of the local fraternity of men who participated in the battle, gaining him even more prestige in the community. He stayed on the plantation for another decade as the lead foremen, frugally saving his money, building himself a nice little nest egg. During these years Ira branched out, slowly reinventing himself, learning as many trades as he could. He even went into partnership in a few successful business ventures, grasping the lower rungs of nobility. Tom, who was now a free man, also chose to stay on the plantation as a supervisor, happily married with a child.

When he first arrived in New Orleans, Ira hated the place for obvious reasons. But now he loved the city's vibrant, diverse culture, its rapid ever-changing citizenry, and the many gainful exchange opportunities. He had become somewhat popular within the Irish bourgeois class. For the first time in his life he was experiencing true happiness. Ira eventually met a pretty Irish girl named Dorothea Miller, just arrived with her aging father, Gavin, a shoemaker from Dublin.

"Do you pray to the Virgin Mary?" asked Dorothea, after Ira had struck up a casual conversation with her at the market near the wharf.

"Aye, I do," he said, hoping to impress her with his faith. "Oo' else?"

129

"Why, the Lord Jesus Himself," said the feisty lass. "That's who else. You must be Catholic."

"A'course," said Ira, looking a bit confused. "An'oo idn't?"

"I idn't," said Dorothea, turning away, looking back over her shoulder. "I'm a Protestant."

"What's a Protestant?" he asked, getting no answer as she walked off down Decatur.

Six months later, after a rather stormy courtship, Ira converted to Protestantism and married Dorothea. He quit working on the plantation, and soon opened a dry goods business in the French Quarter, which also became their home. The business thrived, and they were very happy together during those hectic days.

Ira soon learned that a close friend, a slave named Rubin from the plantation, was in a bit of trouble. A few years older than Ira, Rubin had taken the fiery-tempered Bolivar under his wing when he first arrived at the plantation years ago, showing him the ropes and keeping him out of trouble with the overseers. Rubin was also a veteran of the Battle of New Orleans, having served in Plauché's volunteer battalion. But because he was black, he'd received few of the favors bestowed upon the white men of that honor.

Rubin explained to Ira that he had fallen in love with a slave girl named Nancy from the big plantation on Lake Pontchartrain. Nancy was pregnant with Rubin's child, and her master was known to be picky about who fathered children among his female slaves. The man already had a mate arranged for her within his own stock. If he learned Nancy was pregnant by a slave from another plantation, he was likely to become very angry. To make matters worse, Rubin had already been caught twice sneaking onto the plantation after dark to see Nancy. She was just beginning to show and was still able to keep her condition a secret, but not for much longer.

"She's my heart, Ira," said Rubin, almost in tears. "An' when dat man find out Nancy be wit child, he gonna know it's mine. Den he'll sell'er off somewheres faraway, just'a spite me. He be known to do dem kind'a things."

"Rubin, me lad," said Ira. "I d'nie think they'll sell off a healthy worker just 'cause ya got'r pregnant. But lemme give it some thought."

Ira had once met Nancy's master, drinking together at some holiday gathering. The next day after talking to Rubin he went to pay a call on the aristocrat at his vast plantation that stretched from the banks of Bayou St. John, to the shores of Lake Pontchartrain. He was very straightforward with the man, candidly explaining the situation and his long friendship with Rubin. Then he offered one thousand dollars for the girl, a price he could barely afford to pay.

"You were right," said Ira to Rubin the next day, his hand on his friend's shoulder as if to console him. "They did sell Nancy off."

Rubin's jaw dropped.

"She's help'n Dorothea mind the store."

"Alla'looya!" shouted Rubin, giving Ira a big hug, then dancing a quick little jig with his friend. "I gets ta be wit' my ya-ya girl!"

Rubin and Nancy were soon married, traditionally jumping the broom. Not long after that their baby was born, a beautiful girl they named Sarah. Ira let Nancy and baby Sarah, who were legally his, stay with Rubin at the plantation until he could find another way to keep them together. For the past few years, Rubin had been doing extra work, paying small amounts to buy his own freedom. So it wasn't long before Ira had enough to buy his old friend.

Trade was so good at the dry goods shop, Ira bought the small building next door, expanding the business. Rubin and Nancy had the large slave quarter in the back all to themselves, Little Sarah tucked snug in a papoose while her mother stocked the shelves.

Using his numerous connections throughout the city, and the many plantations that surrounded it, Ira found several other ways to make money in the hustle and bustle of the port of New Orleans. He paid young boys who ran the docks to gather and send out information. This allowed him to find out what was needed and wanted, when and where. Then, he'd deliver those goods and services, eventually becoming a reputable go-between, pocketing nice commissions and finder's fees.

Within a year Rubin and Nancy had more than paid for themselves. Ira gave them papers stating they were free blacks. Even Baby Sarah had her own little certificate of freedom. Ira now paid them a daily wage plus a percentage of any profits they produced, their contacts within the black community being quite invaluable.

Seven years after the official opening of Ira's Dry Goods, David was born, a big baby boy with bright, fluffy red hair. And little Sarah was the perfect babysitter for David; she adored him and played with him almost constantly.

But as good as things were, Ira could not ignore the fact that New Orleans was a dangerous town. There was always much of the element about. Disease and plague were not uncommon, and the city's sanitary works were almost nonexistent. Ira had often considered leaving to find more hospitable environs. He spoke about this many times with Dorothea, but Gavin could not travel and she would never leave him.

Gavin was a pleasant old man who'd been well past fifty when Dorothea was born. He would fix a shoe or two once in a while, but usually he'd just entertain everyone with stories of the old country. When the weather was nice, he would sit in front of the store mending shoes and striking up conversations with passersby.

One afternoon Dorothea stepped out to check on her father. It was a beautiful day, the sun shining through a cool breeze. Gavin was sitting slumped in his chair, appearing to be asleep. She had been preparing herself for this day. As she touched him on the sleeve, she knew he was gone, a pleasant look on his still face. After the funeral she turned to her husband, urging him to make a plan for leaving the city.

"It's time we go, my darling," she said, holding baby David, "and find those places you always talk about."

X

Ira Hawkins finally set his sights on Texas-Mexico, only ten years independent from Spain. They were offering generous land grants to Americans who would settle there. He also heard of something called the Texas Trail, a trace that ran across northern Louisiana to the Mississippi River at the port of Vicksburg. It was said to be a route of growing trade and travel. After studying maps of the region, Ira made a plan. He would take his family up the Mississippi to the Red River, then up to the Texas Trail, heading west to stake his claim.

Ira assumed that Rubin and Nancy would want to stay behind, where they could legally remain free. Outside New Orleans the laws changed from place to place regarding free blacks. In some areas people of color had no rights whatsoever. But Rubin and Nancy made it very clear to Ira, as long as they were welcome, they wanted to join them in search of a new home, even if it meant giving up the outward appearance of freedom.

After another year of careful planning and saving money, Ira sold his home and business and said goodbye to his many friends. Then his little crew of six boarded passage on a steam-powered riverboat, a new contraption of the 19th Century. The boat stopped briefly in Baton Rouge, picking up more settlers, soldiers and workers. Then it steamed up the Red River to Natchitoches, a little settlement that was even older than New Orleans. Workers were being sent to help break up the Great Raft, a massive logjam that covered the entire surface of the Red River from Natchitoches to Arkansas, over a hundred miles to the north.

"Jesus, Mary and Joseph," said Ira as he crossed himself, seeing the Great Raft for the first time. "What on earth could cause such a thing?"

"Some say it's from a big earthquake 'bout a hundred years ago off in the Rocky Mountains," replied an old soldier with master sergeant stripes and the grizzled look of a veteran. "But the Indians say a legion of giants once played a stick and ball contest long ago, far out West. The losing team was forced to relinquish their mallets to the river. What you see now is an ancient conglomeration of that sacrifice."

"Is dey really giants up dat way, mista'?" asked little Sarah.

"Don't worry, little girl," said the soldier as he lit his pipe. "The losing team died off, and the victorious ones hitched a ride on a shooting star that's now circling the sun."

Ira learned from the soldier that another small settlement called Shreve Town had been founded where the Texas Trail met the Red River, seventy miles north of Natchitoches. Farms and plantations were just being developed in the rich fertile region, but the Great Raft prevented a steady flow of goods downriver. Ira saw a business opportunity in this, and decided to blaze a freight line between the two points.

"I see even more prosperity in our future, my love," said Ira, wrapping his arms around his exhausted, smiling wife. "Hard work and heaps of prosperity."

"Well, let's get to it, then," Dorothea replied.

After a day of prayer and fasting, Ira decided to open another dry goods business in Natchitoches. He wrote letters of request along with a partial down payment to friends back in New Orleans, asking that they extend him a line of credit on the supplies he needed. Provisions were adequate in

Natchitoches, but Ira knew he could do better with his own supply line.

After a week getting settled in, Ira and Rubin set out to cut a path to the Texas Trail, over half-a-day's ride through tough, rugged country. They rode along the east bank of the river, amazed at the dense, century-old conglomeration of driftwood. Living islands of trees, grass and vines grew up out of the silt, a floating forest teaming with wildlife that stretched from riverbank to riverbank. Most of the work dispersing the Great Raft was done at its south end near Natchitoches. But for the past three years men had been using snag boats and explosives, clearing narrow canals up river that soon refilled with debris because of the lack of travel.

"A man could walk rat 'cross dat dair riv'va," said Rubin, "an' not get 'is feet wet."

"Maybe, but I d'nie think he'd make it to the other side," replied Ira. "Somethin' might eat'm."

By early evening, Ira and Rubin came to a well-worn wagon road running east and west. The Texas Trail. A few miles back they had accidently angled away from the river, The Great Raft so thick and loamy it was indiscernible from the land. They took the trail west a short distance until they came back to the river, surprised to find it completely cleared in both directions for about a quarter-mile. On the west bank they could see the small settlement of Shreve Town, no more than an outpost of sorts. A few snag boats and barges lined the little town's shore. To their right, off in the distance, a group of men cleared away trees on what looked to be the beginnings of a farm or plantation. Straight ahead of him, Ira noticed a large cypress tree ten feet from the river's edge. Wrapped several times around its trunk was an inch-thick piece of rope that ran passed a short pier. The rope then stretched all the way across the river, hanging slack but not touching the water. On the opposite side the rope ran to another pier with a barge-ferry parked next to it. After ringing a large bell attached to the tree, some men on the other side looked up noticing Ira and Rubin.

"Welcome to Shreve Town," said the ferryboat man as he docked back across the river. "Population eighty-seven, count'n you and your slave here." When Ira did not respond, the man glanced at him. "He is your slave, right?"

Ira looked at Rubin, who smiled and winked. "Aye," he said turning back to the man. "He's mine."

"Well 'at's good, cause we don't 'llow no free niggers round here."

"Well," said Ira, stepping off the ferry with his horse. "This one's for sale if you'd like'm."

Rubin gave Ira a puzzled look as the ferryboat man gave him a once over.

"Pretty strong look'n nigger," the man said, stroking his chin. "Wa'cha want for'm?"

"Ten-thousand dollars, cash," Ira said, looking away from the man, surveying the small town.

"Ten-thousand dollars!" balked the man. "Lord'a mighty! What's 'ee do, lay golden eggs!?"

"He might at that, my friend," said Ira, smiling and winking at Rubin who now looked slightly perturbed. "He might at that."

Ira spent the rest of the day learning what he could about the little township, named in honor of Henry Shreve, a riverboat captain from the Northeast. Now in charge of clearing the Great Raft, Captain Shreve was a bit of a legend on the rivers. Ira was familiar with at least one story about the man. He and a few others had hauled and poled a barge loaded with goods all the way from New Orleans up the Mississippi and Ohio Rivers to Browsville, Pennsylvainia, a grueling 2200-mile trek that took five months.

"Yes, that was no steamboat," said Shreve to Ira after they met at the Office of Western River Improvements, a small agency that fell under the U.S. War Department, tasked with the formidable undertaking of the Great Raft. "We made that trip on muscle, grit and little mule-power. That was the voyage that gave me my start. If I had not been late on my return trip for that fight with the British, I doubt that I'd been thrown in jail for breaking that stupid river monopoly."

"Nie only that, sir," replied Ira. "If you'd arrived just a day or so earlier with all the munitions you had, we'dov' captured the whole British expedition. Nie just run'm off. And you'd have a statue of yourself somewhere down there in New Orleans."

The two men talked for an hour. Shreve explained to Ira that a handful of plantations were already functioning in the area. Large loads of the raw cotton and other crops were piled high, everywhere to be seen. No set route was yet established in getting the crops down to Natchitoches, or the necessary goods up to Shreve Town. The task was done randomly in haphazard fashion with no routine schedule. Many loads had been lost to the river, or spilled somewhere in the thick, dense woods along its west bank.

The next morning Ira purchased two wagons full of raw cotton and two extra horses. After everything was ferried over to the east bank, he and Rubin carefully made the return trip to Natchitoches, arriving just before dark.

"Well, now," said Dorothea when she saw the two wagons bulging with cotton, "ya certainly made that look easy."

"Look'n easy an' be'n easy are two different things." Ira said, before kissing his wife. "Remind me to show ya later."

For the next two weeks, Ira and Rubin made seven more round trips to Shreve Town. Loads of flour, sugar, coffee and other necessities were taken up before returning the next day with two wagons of cotton. Ira's first shipment of goods had arrived from New Orleans by then, and his first barge of cotton was ready for transport down river. While the men were gone, Dorothea and Nancy fared well, finding the settlers and river men of rural Louisiana much more agreeable than the fussy folks of New Orleans. Little Sarah kept a close eye on baby David, who was himself venturing out getting into anything he could.

Ira had considered his stay in the area somewhat temporary, a year or two at the most. But as he inquired further about the land grants in Texas, he began to have second thoughts. As conditions to receiving the grant, the Mexican government would require him to convert back to Catholicism, and conduct all his official business in Spanish. And he had to settle no less than sixty miles from the American border. After learning all this Ira decided he liked the fertile, rolling hills of northwest Louisiana. Besides, Dorothea was pregnant again. And trouble was brewing in Texas.

Within a year passable trails had been blazed down both sides of the Red River from Shreve Town to Natchitoches. The Great Raft had been cleared to almost ten miles north of Natchitoches, and even further south of Shreve Town. A narrow canal that allowed one barge at a time had also been cleared through the Raft between the two settlements. Although it was occasionally clogged with large floating dead falls, it was still progress.

Not long after Paul was born, Ira moved his family and business up to Shreve Town, which had more than tripled in size and was still growing. Ira's Dry Goods and Freight Services was now at the corner of Commerce and Cotton, the town's third official intersection.

Ira made a deal with the indigenous Caddo Indians, buying two hundred acres of thick, wooded land just north of the town. A large swampy bayou ran from the west into the river, through the southernmost quarter of the land. The first thing Ira and Rubin did was build a sturdy wooden bridge across the bayou where he would make his home and grow his crops. The two men cleared the land while Dorothea and Nancy ran the shop, Sarah looking after David and Paul. The following summer the first cotton crop came in at a very nice profit.

"Here ya go, Rubin, me boy," Ira said to his friend, handing him a heavy fist-size bag of coins as they crossed over the bridge they had built, back to the farm from the market. "Three hundred dollars. Put it in a safe place where nie a soul can find it. For that hard rain surely to come."

"Tree hun'ard dollas!?" balked Rubin, his eyes bugging wide. "What'am I go'n do wit dis, Massa Ira?"

"That's your business," said Ira, shooting Rubin a playful glance. "An' stop call'n me, Massa. I've known ya since I'sa nip. An' in case ya forgot, I use'ta follow your lead. Remember?"

"Well," said Rubin, "maybe if ya started follow'n my lead again, I'd be get'n two'a deez here bags instead'a one."

Ira glared at Rubin, then threw his head back and laughed.

One day Ira was in town and saw two men beating on a slave that had dropped and broken a jug of whiskey. At first he considered it none of his affair. But when the white men started making the already battered black man lap the whiskey off the ground like a dog, he stepped forward.

"That's enough, don't ya think?" asked Ira, in his syrupy accent.

The two men looked at Ira as if he'd lost his mind. "Wad ju say?" asked one of the men.

"I tell ya what," Ira said, pulling out a few coins. "I'll pay for the whiskey. Now stop beat'n on'm. I'm sure it was an accident." He tossed them the coins and started to walk away.

"D'ya hear dat, boy?" the man said, reaching down grabbing the slave by his shirt. "Dat feller dair done paid fer da whiskey ya done slopped all over da ground." Then he kicked the black man in the stomach. "But I still gotta learn ya right."

Half expecting this, Ira turned on his heel and punched the man in the stomach so hard he fell to his knees and vomited. When the other man tried to hit Ira, the cagey Irishman ducked and grabbed his arm, twisted and bent it behind his back, slamming his face into a nearby post.

"Now, listen good, cause I'm only gonna say this once," he said after the second man crumpled to the ground. "I gave ya enough for the jug a whiskey and then some, so ya'd stop beat'n on'm. But ya kept beat'n on'm. Since I didn't get the services I paid for, consider this an official grievance." Then he reached down and helped the bleeding slave to his feet. "What's your name, lad?"

"Isaac, sir. My name's Isaac and I thank ya, but ya gonna gets me kilt later on when dey get's me alone."

Ira knew Isaac was right, and since he needed more help on the farm anyway, he pulled out a bag of coins and threw it at the first man's feet. "That should buy ya enough whiskey to get ya through the winter."

After the paperwork was done, Isaac told Ira that he had been sold and separated six months earlier from his wife and thirteen-year-old son who were at a plantation southwest of Shreve Town near the Texas line. The next day Ira went and bought the two slaves at well over their market value. But for Ira, it was well worth the look on their happy faces when they were reunited as a family. Mary, Isaac's wife, cried, laughed, then cried some more as she and their son, Jacob, huddled around the man who was taken from them on a mere economic whim.

The situation worked out better than expected on the Hawkins farm. Isaac proved to be a strong, competent worker and when paired with Rubin, under Ira's direction, the three men cleared more land, making way for even more crops. Mary turned out to be a remarkable cook, so good that Dorothea suggested they open a small cafe next to the dry goods shop using her recipes. The little restaurant was a hit, filled with hungry patrons most every day. Ira decided to open a produce stand across the street, forming a cozy little spot that would come to be known as Hawkins's Corner. A residual benefit Ira had only vaguely hoped for was his slaves' children. Jacob was a good-natured boy who followed instructions well and was capable of many tasks around the farm. He took an immediate liking to Sarah, adoring the little girl and the two made excellent babysitters for David, who was just beginning to blaze a series of trails along the river and bayou. And little Paul was now up and walking around, acting like the new boss.

Even before Ira and his family left New Orleans, it was known that Texas was challenging Mexican authority. On one of his early visits to Shreve Town, Ira met a man from the Carolinas traveling west on the Texas Trail, going to help the settlers there fight for their sovereignty. Ira wished him well and it became one of the many reasons he decided to stay put in Louisiana. He noticed that in the two decades since the war with the British, his thoughts seemed to dwell more and more on those that had been killed and maimed, and less on the victory itself. He could only imagine what kind of nightmares must haunt the survivors of the defeated. And he never stopped asking God to forgive him for the men he killed that day, especially that first one. Others had passed through Shreve Town to go and fight with the Texans, men from Tennessee, Kentucky and Virginia, men with a hard look of resolve and not an ounce of duplicity.

One day, seven-year-old David was playing near the bridge that crossed over the bayou when he saw a rare sight: two strangers riding toward town from the north. Everyone that traveled the road to the bridge was well known to David. The only strangers he ever saw were in town or on the Texas Trail. Both men were large and broad-shouldered, like his father. They had pistols tucked in their belts and rifles slung across their backs, an extra fully-loaded packhorse apiece with all sorts of gear, including more rifles. One man wore a coonskin cap, its tail hanging over his shoulder. The other had on a wide-brimmed leather hat and a huge knife about two feet long tucked into his belt.

"Howdy," said David, standing as tall as he could near the rail of the bridge. "Y'all lost or somethin'?"

"Well, son," said Coonskin Cap, leaning forward on his saddle with a handsome grin. "I don't think so, but maybe you could help us. How far to the Texas Trail?"

"Shoot, Mister," David laughed. "You could spit'n hit the Texas Trail from here. 'Cept we call it Texas Street in the town limits, but it's all the same. Just keep go'n straight after ya cross the bridge here, an' you'll run right into it."

"How's about a good place to eat?' asked the man with the large knife.

"Take a left on Cotton Street," said David "and you'll come to Mary's Manners, right on the corner next to my pa's shop, Ira's Dry Goods. They got chicken-sausage gumbo today or you can have a Delmonico steak with a potato and green beans. But mind your manners, my Aunt Mary don't put up with no nonsense."

"Oh, don't worry son," said Coonskin Cap. "We'll behave."

The two men smiled and waved at David, then crossed over the bridge into Shreve Town.

Sometime later, news reached Shreve Town of the bold yet futile stand made by the Texans at a mission-turned-fort in San Antonio, called the Alamo. Although the fighting was almost five hundred miles away, the Texas-Mexican border was less than a half-hour's ride from Shreve Town. A town meeting was called to discuss the matter. Three single men volunteered to set out and take up arms with the Texas-Americans. Ira and a few others donated weapons, supplies and even some cash.

"Give'm hell," said Ira to the men before they left. "But try to remember that you're men, not animals. Helps ya sleep better later."

In a little over a month, word came that Sam Houston's ragtag army had routed Santa Anna's troops at the Battle of San Jacinto, screaming "Remember the Alamo!" winning Texas their Independence. Later that summer, it was learned that all three men had survived the fighting and were now married, living on generous plots of land given to them by the new Republic of Texas.

By 1839, Shreve Town had become Shreveport, with a population of over a thousand by the decade's end. The Red River was now cleared of the Great Raft from a point ten miles north of the city, all the way south to the Mississippi. It had become a busy port, with daily steamboat traffic churning its dark rust-colored waters, bringing up the goods and folks that make a city and sending out its raw yields to be dispersed abroad. Besides cotton, there was sorghum, millet, oats, rye and many other crops that grew luxuriantly throughout the region. The native grasses also possessed rich nutritional properties, excellent for cattle grazing, and soon beef became second in the area only to cotton. Salt, lumber and oil were also abundant. More roads and bridges were laid as little towns began to crop up all over Northwestern Louisiana. Little towns like Blanchard and Vivian to the north, Minden and Ruston to the east, Greenwood to the west, and to the south were Mansfield and Pleasant Hill.

In Ira Hawkins's older years, when his health had faded and Dorothea and Paul were gone, when David was out West chasing his adventures, he would look back on those early days of settling Shreve Town as his fondest. Before the town became a city and the simple things became complicated. A time when Mary's Manners was the only sit-down restaurant in town, when Rubin and Isaac could set with their children to enjoy a meal and no one would complain. (Someone did complain once but they were tossed out on their ear by Ira and told to mind their manners.) Had Ira Hawkins been more ambitious, he too could have been a cotton king, owning the town and the city it became. But he didn't want all that. He was no robber baron. He only wanted his modest little portion. .

But for a while Ira earned himself a little bit more than modesty. The farm prospered and a gin was purchased, paying for itself in no time. The clever little contraption omitted the process of taking the raw cotton to one of the large plantations to be sifted of its seed, a costly time consuming affair. The fluffy, ginned cotton was then hauled into town where it was formed into large bales by a huge steam powered press. After making his sale to the speculators, Ira would always stand on the dock with David and Paul at his side, watching as his crop was loaded onto a steamboat, often stacked as high as the captain's helm. Sometimes Ira would look around, trying to find the exact spot where he had first arrived in Shreve Town, but things looked so different now. David and Paul would always wave goodbye to the cotton, pointing out the different bales that had come from their farm. It was only a fraction of the massive cargo piled three-stories-high on a two-hundred-foot-long steamboat sounding its horn, puffing smoke and spinning its gigantic red paddle wheel in a rainbow spray downriver.

XI

Ira's family lived in a fifty-by-thirty-foot log cabin, built an equal distance of about three hundred yards from both the river and the bayou. It was set at an angle facing the corner of land that looked out on where the bayou emptied into the river. Small trees and brush had been cleared away. But the large trees, broad oaks shrouded in moss, thick towering pines, magnolias and pecans had been left, giving the homestead a nice shaded canopy, a pleasant grove lined with cypress trees all the way to the water.

A hundred yards to the side of Ira's home was Rubin's cabin, also made of logs. After Isaac's family was reunited, they lived in Rubin's cabin, sharing the space until yet another cabin was built, giving each family their own little home. Behind the cabins, further to the west, was the first cotton field, thirty acres that when in full bloom looked like a patch of dirty snow in the 100-degree heat. A well-worn dirt road ran from the cabins, meandering south through the trees, turning sharply west along the bayou a short ways before coming to the bridge that crossed over into Shreveport.

Walking at a brisk pace, Ira could traverse the distance between his home and his dry goods shop in less than thirty minutes. On horseback, it took less than five. Within the first few years, the children had blazed a maze of trails along both sides of the bayou leading up to the river, winding up and down its western bank. The road that led to the bridge was called Market Street on the Shreveport side. As other farms sprouted up to the north the road continued on from the point where it forked off to Hawkins's farm, and was given the name North Market Road. Although the bridge itself, the land on both sides, and nearly the first mile of North Market Road belonged to Ira, he never made any fuss about folks traveling on it. And he always made a point to greet them whenever he could. As the Red River was cleared further north, even more farms and little towns sprung up. The local parish leaders eventually offered Ira a handsome price for the bridge and the road. Very soon the road stretched all the way to Texarkana, Arkansas, which sat partially inside the Republic of Texas.

In their early years of parenthood, Ira and Dorothea Hawkins found raising David and Paul quite simple. Most of the time they were under the watchful eye of Sarah and Jacob, who were thought of as older siblings, and their parents more like aunts and uncles of color. The two Hawkins boys were three years apart and Sarah, who was seven when David was born, was two years younger than Jacob. The children's difference in color was rarely mentioned and never seemed to matter. They never spoke harshly to one another, playing and joking like family well into their adult years.

Though both were healthy and energetic, David was naturally bigger, stronger and more aggressive, while Paul had more of a methodical, stick-to-itiveness to his character. When he was only four, Paul won the first of many fishing contests against his brother. At a special spot on the bayou, not far from the bridge, David had just showed him how to properly bait the hook, always spitting on the worm for good luck before casting.

"Let's see who can catch the most fish," said David to his little brother, who had just tossed his line in the water. "You gotta head start, but that's okay 'cause Pa's been teach'n me a lot 'bout fish'n."

Just as David casted his line, Paul got a bite. He did not jerk, but gently tugged up and back, then leaned slightly forward, letting the fish run a bit before tugging again, setting the hook. Seconds later, Paul had a nice little foot-long catfish flopping around on the bank, David looking on in disbelief. For the next hour, David moved up and down the little stretch of bayou east of the bridge, trying his luck here and there. Meanwhile, Paul stayed put at the same tiny little cove catching fish after fish, giggling and laughing at his older brother's frustration.

"It's a good thing Pa's been teach'n David a lot 'bout fish'n," Paul chirped over dinner that night, after winning the contest ten to two, "or else he might notta caught nut'n."

The following winter, the boys made a small raft of logs and cane poles and decided to float it down the bayou to the river. It was their first raft and a quick lesson learned. Winter wasn't the best time to test a raft. It lacked adequate buoyancy, tipping slightly after they pushed out. Paul fell in the freezing water first. For a moment David rode the raft like a seesaw, yelling as his legs worked it against the water. He then spun away from the bank as the raft shot out from under him. His arms flung out as he crashed backwards into the cold murky bayou. With their breaths taken away, David and Paul splashed and struggled together toward the bank, gulping and choking up water. Soon, Sarah and Jacob came running to help pull them up on land, dripping and shivering. Ira and Dorothea were furious at David and Paul over the silly stunt, and at Jacob and Sarah for not supervising them more closely. Realizing that everyone was all right, their anger briefly subsided, until they noticed the ruined mail-order coats they had bought the boys for Christmas that year.

When Ira first bought his land, a handful of Caddo Indians still lived there. They never caused any fuss or trouble, a quiet, peaceful, agrarian tribe that rarely showed themselves. Occasionally, they would be seen in small groups walking along the river, up the bayou to the bridge, dressed in humble, earthy raiment. Other times they would take the North Market Road, skirting west into town to sell their wares, always keeping a respectful distance from the Hawkins homestead. But within a few years, they had all moved north, off of Ira's land, further away from the ever-increasing white settlers. All except one, an old-timer called Brown Grass. He lived in a tiny hut near the river just inside the northern boundary of Ira's land, about a mile from the bayou. Brown Grass found fascination in the simplest of things, yet seemed to understand the complexities of the changing world around him. He possessed a serene thread of timeless wisdom woven into a charm of child-like wonder.

Ira had been out by himself early one evening, taking a casual ride along the river. He suddenly heard singing and turned toward the setting sun. He found Brown Grass standing in front of his hut, facing the sun with his arms raised, singing a song that sounded to Ira both very old and very new. When the Indian was done with his sun song, he turned and greeted the Irishman as if he knew he'd been standing there all along.

"I sing to every sunset," said Brown Grass, innocently speaking in an unusually-correct English. "They're all different, you know."

Brown Grass had been a shaman for his tribe in the decades before the white men came to break apart the living logs of the river. The two men had met several times before. Ira had told Brown Grass he was welcome to any crops he needed, knowing the man would take very little of the fruits and vegetables that grew in the various fields and groves. He sifted handfuls of cotton by hand, weaving it into the garments he wore, dyed a reddish-brown at the river's edge.

"You wish me to leave, Ira Hawkins?" asked the old Indian after Ira mentioned he was the last of his people to remain on the land.

"Mister Brown Grass, you are welcome to stay as long as ya like. I was just a bit curious as to why ya didn't leave with the rest of your people."

"My people's ways are not necessarily mine, and there is no right or wrong to this. It is simply the way things are." Brown Grass looked around, scanning the horizon in all directions. "Very soon, Ira Hawkins, I will also be going, but not with my people. I have a great journey to finish, and so much of that journey has been traveled here at this spot." Noticing something on the ground, Brown Grass then stooped over, admiring a trail of ants on campaign against a small brown scorpion, set upon by a collective mob of the tiny creatures. A late matinée for the Indian's entertainment.

Ira thought he knew what Brown Grass meant, for the Indian was very old, well into his nineties and quite possibly over a hundred. Although the two men came from very different worlds, they had two things in common deriving from their early childhoods. Both had been orphaned at a very young age, and both had spent several years in a Catholic monastery, receiving a somewhat formal education. Ira learned from Brown Grass, that long before the white American settlers came, even long before America was a nation, French traders had settled Natchitoches, bringing religion, as well as disease.

In his childhood, before his parents died, Brown Grass had heard the tales of his grandfather's grandfathers, tales of Desoto and the lost crying thunder dogs.

"What are crying thunder dogs?" asked nine-year-old David who would sometimes pay Brown Grass a visit with Paul always tagging along. "And why were they lost?"

"Horses," explained Brown Grass. "My people did not know what else to call them, for they had never seen horses. And just before they saw them the sound of thunder was heard. But it came up from out of the earth, not down from the sky that was clear of clouds, lightning and rain. Then they saw them, carrying men dressed in steel, crying and tossing their heads. It was said that they came from very far away seeking cities made of gold, but could not find them and were lost. Some thought the thunder dogs were laughing, but it was more like crying they said."

One autumn day when the air was new and cool, David and Paul went to see Brown Grass. They took the trail north along the river, then cut back west toward his little hut. When they got there, they saw him building what looked like a bed made from twigs, straw and grass. It was raised about five-feet-high on thick tree limbs. Underneath it was a large pile of logs. And next to it was something that at first frightened them. It was a huge, man-like creature over seven-feet-tall, harry, dark and looming like a guardian above Brown Grass's altar. Then they realized it was something he had made, probably out of mud and grass. Many times he had told them about the Halkom, the ancient giants who lived in the mountains to the north, fabled creatures of spell and mystery, towering guides to the afterlife.

"Hey, Brown Grass!" David called out with Paul standing warily behind him. "What'cha do'n!?"

The old Indian slowly turned and raised his hands to the boys. "Farewell, my young friends. I wish you peace and the strength to face all fear." Then, his eyes looked passed them toward the river, which could not actually be seen, only a large gap in the treetops. "The Halkom has come to take me where I must go. Please, tell your father to finish what must be done."

David turned, following the Indian's gaze and suddenly the earth seemed to tremble. The sun had just set but it was still light, the sky streaked with pink and blue. Over the years, whenever David Hawkins would look back on that moment, he could never be sure of what he saw that night, but he never doubted that it was real. A gigantic man completely covered in thick, dark fur was striding toward them with great purpose, churning his limbs in a lumbering gait. Paul screamed and ran. But for just a moment, David looked at the creature, seeing his terrible face, warped as if by eons. A once-beautiful angel, now fallen and feared, misunderstood yet necessary, seeking to make right its primordial sin. And when David could smell the huge creature, a foul stink that seemed to hit right at his stomach, he too turned and ran like he'd never run before.

"Do not fear!" Brown Grass's words echoed through the trees after the boys. "The Halkom will take me to even better worlds than this!"

Back at the house the boys were hysterical, Paul babbling incoherently, something about a monster. David was a little less excited, but confirmed his brother's ravings. After a short discussion, Ira, Rubin and Isaac got their rifles, lit torches and began making their way to the old Indian's abode. When they got there, all three men raised their weapons aiming at the huge figure standing in front of Brown Grass's hut.

"Wait," said Ira, lowering his gun. "I d'nie think it's real."

They approached slowly, the flickering light of their torches dancing on the bizarre scene. Brown Grass lay peacefully on his wooden altar, arms crossed over his chest before the towering figure of the Halkom.

"It's just made of grass and mud," said Ira, as he held up his torch, reaching out to touch the replica, gazing at its eerie, opaque features. He looked up, holding his torch higher. At the top, jutting from a band that was wrapped around its head was something that struck Ira with amazement. The distinguishable feather of a red-tailed hawk. "Wonder how'ee got that up there?"

Ira then looked at Brown Grass, as he lay on his sacred altar, chest-high to the Irishman. "An' I wonder how old Brown Grass got himself up on this thing?"

"Massa Ira," said Isaac. "I knows dat tang ain't real, but I'ds feela whole lot betta if'n we's ta get on outta here."

"Yeah," seconded Rubin, looking around nervously, "me too, Ira. No disrespect meant ta Mista Brown Grass here, but dair ain't much we kin do fer him."

"You two go on back," Ira said, not taking his eyes from Brown Grass and the strange figure. "Tell Dorothea, I'll be there shortly."

For a long while after Rubin and Isaac left, Ira stood looking at Brown Grass's body and the oracular shrine he had made. Then he reached out with his torch and caught fire to the logs, knowing it was what Brown Grass wanted. As the flames grew brighter, engulfing the body of the old Caddoan, Ira noticed an array of effects heaped on the little altar: rugs, tunics, headdresses, trinkets, and an assortment of artifacts to be taken with the old shaman to entertain him in his new and better world.

Growing up, the boys learned a good work ethic. The whole family pitched in, doing their part to keep the farm and businesses running. Before he was ten, David was making runs in the buckboard, back and forth between the farm and Hawkins's Corner, delivering goods and whatever was needed at a moment's notice. Both boys helped out at the café and the dry goods shop, but Paul's favorite job was working the produce stand, pacing around the barrels of fruit and vegetables wearing an apron his mother had made him. There was never a dull moment, even the tedium of working the field was made entertaining by the stories of Rubin and Isaac. Sometimes the two black men would fuss and argue with each other in ways so comical, it was the main topic of conversation at the Hawkins dinner table. David and Paul would often mimic their banter like a schoolhouse skit.

"Ya move'n like'a herd'a turtles dis mo'nin, Rubin," David would say in Isaac's deep voice. "Lil' too much molasses las' night, I reckon."

"Na'ugh," croaked Paul with his chest puffed out imitating Rubin. "Iss cause I had'a pick up afta' ya in da tool shed. We ain't got no lil'elves dat come out at night do'n dat. I hads'ta do it."

Ira would always bray laughter, while Dorothea giggled ladylike.

A few complications arose when a census was taken of the newly formed Caddo Parish. When Ira reported that he had six slaves, four adults and two children, the census taker asked to see their papers of ownership. Isaac, Mary and Jacob's he quickly produced for the man, but Rubin, Nancy and Sarah's had been disposed of years ago. In fact the only type of identification papers they had were the ones that stated they nnrrccssddw.m

were free blacks, documents they dare not show in the Shreveport area. As far as the paperwork was concerned, this was only a minor problem. After paying a small fee and answering a few questions, explaining how the papers were lost in the move from New Orleans, Ira had official titles of ownership to Rubin, Nancy and Sarah. But word had gotten out, and even though it was a matter of little importance to most folks, some of the more influential members of the community frowned on the insignificant discrepancy.

Dorothea Hawkins's mother, Patricia, had taught school at a small Episcopal Church in Bethlehem, Ireland, a little town on the outskirts of Dublin. She had been a strict yet caring woman who had demanded a lot from her daughter and only child, at the same time allowing for appropriate moments of playfulness. When Dorothea was seventeen, Patricia died from hemorrhagic fever. The sadness of the ordeal was too much for her and Gavin to bear. Two years later they decided to leave their grief behind and invest what little money they had in a new life in America

From her first moments of motherhood, Dorothea had been a teacher to her children. Even when David and Paul were still infants, she would hold up simple objects like spoons, wooden cups and balls of yarn. As they lay in their cribs she would tell them what the items were in a calm, clear voice. Then she would let them handle the object, but only for a second, before gently pulling it away. This would increase their curiosity. Then she would give it to them again, each time calling it by name and each time letting them handle and play with it a little longer. This was how she got them to say their first word. David's was *Ball*, Paul's was *Yarn*, both pointing at the same object three years apart, bringing a cheerful laugh from their mother. She would often read to them, even in those early years, and talk to them the way one might talk to an older child.

"Your Grandfather Gavin was given a gold watch by the town marshal for helping out the day the levee broke in

Cloverton, two years before we came to America. For two days straight he piled sandbags until…."

This had an uncanny effect on the boys' ability to learn, as they grew older, and even seemed to increase their desire for knowledge. Paul developed a strong interest in the practical goings on of the farm, the specifics of agriculture and animal husbandry.

"Hey Pa, how does the cotton get up from outta the ground?"

"How'd all the little pigs get inside'r anyhow?"

David, on the other hand, was more of the dreamer, wondering what kept the stars in the sky and where the rain actually came from. Sometimes, in the early evening he would run at the setting sun, hoping in vain to catch a glimpse of its other side. Other times, he would stare at the moon, thinking he saw the lights of great cities twinkling on its surface.

Dorothea had tried, with some success, to teach her slaves how to read and write. Growing up, Rubin and Nancy had learned the alphabet and could already read a little. Isaac and Mary, however, could not read at all. But Dorothea was patient with them and little by little, over the years, they picked up some of the rudiments of language and phonics. Because of their age, Sarah and Jacob took to learning at a much quicker pace. Dorothea had hoped this would change some of their crude speech patterns. But she noticed they simply read the words correctly, then later, spoke them in their usual slang dialect. The education of slaves was of course illegal. Many times the adults had warned the two black children about displaying the ability in public.

From the moment Jacob first set eyes on Sarah, he'd been in love with the cute little girl. He often wanted to tell her, but every time he had the chance, all he could do was look at her big, dark eyes and smile. At first she seemed indifferent to the boy, but gradually she started paying more attention to him, the way he worked so hard and the way he always seemed to be trying to impress her. Back in New Orleans young Sarah had had a handful of friends, but none that were close. She'd spent most of her time watching baby David. Now that she was a teenager, her feelings for Jacob were beginning to grow. He was now a strong, muscular young man, who spoke through his actions, reliable, constant and steady. The few conversations they had over the years were usually regarding the care of David and Paul. But lately Jacob had been practicing the priceless art of simply talking about the weather with Sarah.

One day at Hawkins's Corner Jacob found a pencil and a scrap of paper. He looked up and saw Sarah crossing over to the produce stand, noticing the lithe, supple characteristics of her body's movements. Then he looked back down at the pencil and paper in his hand and wrote down his thoughts to the girl in three simple words. *I love you.* After folding the paper twice, he nervously walked over to the produce stand where Sarah was helping consolidate some of the fruits and vegetables as the ever-precocious Paul tended to a few customers.

"What's dis?" she asked after Jacob handed her the note. Just as she read it, an animated smile breaking across her face, the scrap of paper was snatched from her hand.

"Gimme dat!" It was Chuck Manshack. He and his brother, Greg, had been haggling with Paul, trying to get a couple of apples on credit. But the boys still owed him for two peaches he'd given them the day before. The Manshack brothers were about Jacob's age, a couple of bullies whose father was the local blacksmith. There were a total of six Manshack brothers, Chuck and Greg being somewhere in the middle. Wilber Manshack kept a turbulent home where fighting and violence were a way of life.

"I seen it," said Chuck. "But I don't believe it. Dat nigger dair, done wrote dis nigger here some kina note. Wassat say, Greg?"

"I think it says, I love you," said Greg taking the note, holding it up high as Sarah grabbed at it. "Ain't dat sweet?"

"Dat's mine!" shouted Sarah, lunging for the note. "Now you gimme it back!"

"Who'da hell done taught ya how'da write, boy?" said Chuck, turning to glare at Jacob, who stood embarrassed, not knowing what to do, his arms down at his side. Ever since he was young, Isaac had taught Jacob how to protect himself with his fists, occasionally sparring with the boy. But Jacob had never been in a real fight.

For a short moment, Greg Manshack thought it was funny, playing keep-away with Sarah's note. But when she jumped more aggressively at the token, her fingernails scratched the white boy's forearm, leaving three long red marks.

"You little black bitty!" yelled Greg, jerking his arm away, then backhanding Sarah hard across the face, knocking her to the ground. Chuck brayed a long hard laugh of ridicule, holding his belly and pointing at the girl, sprawled out in the dirt.

Jacob, who had just turned nineteen, had never before lost his temper. He looked down at Sarah, grimacing in pain, and their eyes met. Seeing the pain was bad enough, but then he saw something else in her eyes, something that he too felt. Embarrassment. That embarrassment suddenly sparked a fury that lay dormant in his soul since the day his father was temporarily taken away six years earlier. He had not known what to do then as he'd listened to the wailing cries of his mother.

Suddenly his arms were no longer down at his side. He now knew exactly what to do with them. Jacob didn't really lose himself in his anger. A controlled rage came over him as he waded in to the Manshacks, throwing a whirlwind of hard, accurate punches. At first, he completely stunned them, knocking Chuck to the ground and Greg, who was a bit larger, back on his heels. But Greg recovered quickly, clinching Jacob in a hold that intertwined their arms. Just as Jacob was thrown slightly off balance, Chuck jumped back into the fray. Jacob was stronger than each of the Manshack boys, and for a moment was able to hold his own. But the Manshack's were seasoned, dirty fighters and the scrap soon turned into a nasty brawl with the telling weight of two-to-one odds. Chuck threw a handful of dirt in Jacob's eyes, then Greg kicked him hard in the knee. Just before he went down, Jacob threw a hard elbow, his first real attempt at treachery. The blow crashed flush into Greg's mouth, knocking out his two front teeth, one of which he swallowed. Chuck's boot caught Jacob square in the gut as he doubled over on the ground, Sarah screaming in protest. After spitting out the other tooth, Greg drove a clubbing right fist to the side of Jacob's head, slamming it against the dirt. Suddenly, a ripe red apple exploded on Greg Manshack's left cheekbone just below his eye.

"There's your apple!" screamed Paul who had stepped forward and launched the piece of fruit from point blank range. "Now you leave Jacob be!"

Greg, who could not see clearly out of his left eye, had just turned his attention back to Paul when Sarah punched him in his good eye. Chuck then lunged at Paul, grabbing him by the shirt and slinging him like a rag-doll into the produce stand, spilling bushels of fruit and vegetables to the ground. All of a sudden, ten-year-old David came to the rescue, sprinting across the street with a bison femur bone in his hands.

A year earlier Ira had traded a twenty-pound bag of cornmeal to an Indian in exchange for the bone. It was about three feet long, three inches thick and made an excellent club. David had been working at the dry goods shop when he looked out the window and saw his baby brother being tossed into the produce stand. He quickly grabbed the bone, which was kept behind the counter for incentive purposes, and bolted out the door. After leaping over Jacob, he cracked Chuck in the knee, then smashed Greg in the ribs like a battering ram. Young David Hawkins was about to administer even more punishment, when Dorothea, Mary and Nancy came rushing from the café to intervene, the two Manshack boys rolling in the dirt, howling in pain.

At first, the incident was a minor ruckus in town, simply a matter of kids fighting. But when Wilber Manshack found out his two boys had been whipped by a couple of slaves and their master's children, he took the matter to the sheriff. Late that night, Sheriff John Kotch and over two-dozen men, including

Manshack and his two eldest sons, rode out to the Hawkins farm. A cluster of torches lit their way.

"Ira," said Kotch. "I gotta take that boy in. Mister Manshack here's filed a complaint."

"David!" Ira turned and called back into the cabin.

"Yessir," said young David at the door, looking stern and unafraid of the group of man gathered out front.

"You'll have to go with the sheriff," said Ira, placing his hand on his son's shoulder. "Seems you're being arrested for protecting your younger brother."

"What in the good Lord's name, John!" Dorothea came from out of the cabin, standing in front of her husband and son. "He's only ten."

"D'nie ya worry, son," Ira said out loud, ignoring his wife, kneeling down to look David in the eye. "I'll be there to bail ya out soon, and we'll get a good lawyer. Ya have rights, son."

"Not him!" Wilber Manshack suddenly bellowed from the back of the crowd. "The nigger! The boy!"

"Ira," said Kotch, who now looked a bit confused and nervous. "It's the one called Jacob that we've come for, Isaac's son, not yours."

Ira stood and looked toward the other cabins where the two families of slaves began to come out and show themselves.

"Dat one, dair!" yelled Manshack, pointing at the furthest cabin where Jacob stood between his mother and father. "He attacked my boys wit' a club! Busted one 'ums teeth out, an' broke 'is ribs! Busted d'udders leg up, so my boy can't walk! My boys fought fair, wit' dair hands! Dat nigger dair done used a club! He needs ta hang!"

"Hang!?" shouted Ira, noticing the fear on his slaves' faces. "Why, Wilber Manshack, if ya are nie the biggest idiot in the parish! Everyone knows your boys are a herd'a goons that go about look'n for trouble! Nie only c'nie they win a fair fight, but they c'nie even win a dirty one!"

"No one's gonna hang!" yelled Kotch, looking back at Manshack and his boys. "Not for give'n a few licks with a club!"

"It was a buffalo bone!" shouted David. "And I'm the one that used it! I took it to Greg's ribs after wack'n Chuck in the knee, 'cause he threw my little brother into the fruit barrels! Jacob knocked Greg's teeth out with his elbow after they ganged up on'm! Jacob fought fair! Your boys were the ones fight'n dirty!"

"Yeah!" Paul yelled. "Jacob fought fair! Greg an' Chuck were fight'n dirty! An' they owe for two peaches I give'm yesterday!"

"Da only reason I jumped in," shouted Jacob from their cabin door, "was 'cause Chuck hit Sarah!"

"Yeah!" Sarah added from her cabin door. "Chuck hit me after I tried ta gets back da note dat Jacob gimme ...!" The girl's words were suddenly cut off as Nancy reached around, cupping her hand over her daughter's mouth.

For a moment everyone was quiet. What Sarah had said didn't seem to register in the minds of most of the men. A few had puzzled expressions, glancing back and forth between the Hawkins family and their slaves. But most of them just sat there on their horses, thinking the whole thing was being blown out of proportion, a few bullies who got their come-uppance.

"John!" Ira finally spoke up, breaking the awkward silence, "There's nie reason we c'nie settle this at your office tomorrow!"

"Dat nigger assaulted my boys!" screamed Manshack standing high in his saddle, spit flying from his mouth. "An' I want'm arrested now, or so help me ...!"

"Or so help you what, Wilber Manshack!?" Ira's voice roared through the darkness. He stared at the man for a second, then turned to the sheriff. "If ya take the boy, ya do it through me. I'll nie let ya have'm!"

"You'd give up yer own son!" shouted Manshack. "But not yer nigger!?"

"Me son's got nie'a thing to fear from ya!" Ira turned and reached inside his house and pulled out Betty, the rifle he had bought to fight the British. He then walked in a purposeful stride, past the men, past Rubin's home, stopping in front of

Isaac's cabin. After cocking the weapon, he stood with it across his chest. "Over my dead body you'll get the boy! It's late now, and this hubbub has gone too far over nie a thing! So, either do what you've come to do, or get off me land and see me on the marrow!"

A few more words were spoken that night, but Kotch was able to simmer things down by ordering Wilber Manshack to keep his mouth shut. After agreeing to be in the town with Jacob the next morning, Ira watched as the men turned and went back the way they had come. They all gazed in silence as the haunting trail of torches wound away from the farm through the trees, up along the bayou to the bridge. After the last torch was out of sight, they held hands in a circle and prayed. All of them.

At nine the next morning, a meeting took place at the sheriff's office on the corner of Texas and Market. The entire Hawkin's family was there, including their slaves. The Manshacks were also there, a foul, revolting bunch with large, inbred features. Chuck and Greg stood bandaged to the rear of the group, looking asinine and sullen as their kinfolk blustered and huffed. Sheriff Kotch had had enough foresight to temporarily hire a handful of extra deputies. Although Ira's family stayed relatively calm, the parlay was quite heated and the deputies' presence very likely kept it from turning into another brawl. In the end, Kotch made it clear to Wilber Manshack that he would only arrest Jacob after arresting Chuck and Greg. Because they were white they had more rights than Jacob. But Chuck had assaulted Paul, a white child under the age of ten, a much more serious crime than Jacob's assault on Greg and Chuck. That, Kotch explained, would very likely be deemed justifiable because of Greg's assault on Sarah, who was the lawful property of Ira Hawkins. Greg and Chuck would also be charged with the willful destruction of the produce stand. David's attack with the bison bone was deemed justifiable due to the testimony of various witnesses, as was Sarah's punch to Greg's eye, and Paul's assault with the apple.

However, if Manshack withdrew his charges against Jacob, the whole matter would be forgotten.

"Dey done taught dair niggers how ta read'n write," spat Manshack when the meeting came to an end. "What ya plan ta do 'bout dat, sheriff?"

"Don't get jealous, Wilber," said Kotch. "Just remember what we talked about here. An' you an' your boys best not cause any more trouble."

"I wouldn't give a hoot, Ira," said Sheriff Kotch when he paid another visit to the farm later that day, "if ya taught them slaves'a yours how to spin cotton into gold. But ya gotta keep things like that a little more hush-hush. Folks are start'n to talk, and some of'm don't like it."

"John, I'm sorry for the trouble," said Ira. "And I c'nie thank you enough. But most of all, I'm sorry about losing me temper last night. Sure glad no one called me bluff. Ol'Betty was nie even loaded."

About the same time Sheriff Kotch was patching things up with Ira, Jacob was standing off by the river, looking out across the water. The previous day's excitement had brought back nasty memories of his early childhood, visions of the cruel masters who had treated him and his mother and father like livestock, or worse, like dogs. He was stiff and sore from the fight, his head throbbed and his face was banged up, left eye half-closed, nose and lips busted and swollen. His whole body hurt. He looked at his swollen hands, the knuckles raw and starting to scab over. He made a fist with each, gazing at them like some new monumental discovery. The pain felt good to him, knowing he had given more than he got. For the first time in his life he felt like a man.

He heard a noise behind him and turned to see Sarah standing with something in her hand. As she stepped closer he realized it was the note he had given her, the note of much ado. Her eyes blinked and she smiled, inching her way even closer. Finally, when she was a foot away, she stopped and looked back at the note, then, back up at Jacob.

"Are ya's aw'right, Jacob?"

"Yeah, it ain't nut'n."

"Look kina like sump'n to me."

He didn't know what to say, just stood there mesmerized.

"Know what?" she asked.

Still he couldn't speak. She stepped forward and raised herself up on her toes, taking his face in her hands, pressing the note against his cheek as she kissed him softly on the lips.

"I loves you, too," she said pulling back with a smile, then turned and sprinted back to her cabin.

As he watched her run, ducking through the swaying moss, Jacob noticed the physical pain seemed to leave his body and nothing else mattered. Nothing at all.

XII

The Monday after his falling out with Johnny, David Hawkins sent a courier to the Ebarb farm with a message stating that he had the man's mule, and had sent forty dollars as a form of payment. Not that he doubted Johnny's honesty; because of the incident, he wanted to be sure. He also sent a letter to Amy Bolton, candidly expressing his feelings for her, but suggesting they try and take things a little slower. Seven attempts had been made in getting the letter to his liking, his awkwardness rising out of the woodwork of his study. Finally, after a moment of silent prayer, he was able to find the words that suited him. He also mentioned Johnny's visit with his friends, and the terrible quarrel they'd had. He apologized for this, saying that it was partially his fault. He hoped that Johnny would forgive him, especially for striking him.

That same afternoon, Hawkins was paid a visit by Lieutenant Colonel Grady Hackwith and a full colonel he had never met. When they arrived, he was still very bitter over what had happened Saturday and was in no mood for guests. But he knew it must be important, for they had come unannounced and in full-dress. The colonel was introduced as Robert Gastonel, a former lawyer from Baton Rouge who'd once made a close bid for the State Attorney's Office. He now owned a house in Shreveport, where he lived with his wife and three children. He was a short man in his early forties with thinning brown hair and a goatee that came to a sharp point under a pleasant face that seldom smiled. His dark, intense eyes told of a man who did not enjoy war, yet fought it with every ounce of his being, allowing its energies and powers to harness his very purpose. His fingers drummed nervously along the brim of a hat held at his side, occasionally rocking back and forth on his heels when he spoke.

Hawkins showed the two colonels to the porch, and soon Sarah brought them a large pitcher of sweet tea floating with lemon wheels. After filling their glasses, Sarah smiled and went back in the house to do some cleaning. As the three men sat drinking tea, enjoying the early waves of spring, Hackwith briefed Hawkins on the Union advance, occasionally turning to Gastonel for confirmation.

"This morning we received a dispatch from General Taylor," said Hackwith. "A large portion of his cavalry has been captured."

"Really?" Hawkins asked, more amused than concerned.

"And the rest of his cavalry was cut off when the enemy moved into the Red River," Hackwith continued. "They were patrolling the northern bank of the mouth of the river and had to retreat northward to keep from being captured themselves. It could take days, maybe a week for them to find their way back to Taylor."

"I'm forming an outfit, David," said Gastonel, "to ride down and support Taylor, and reconnoiter the Union advance. If you're feeling up to it, I could use a man of your caliber and experience to lead a patrol. Perhaps even two patrols working close together."

Hawkins glanced at Hackwith, then back at Gastonel. "When are we go'n?" he asked with a calmness that hid his internal trepidation.

"I told you not to worry, Robert," said Hackwith, laughing and grinning at Gastonel, then looking back at Hawkins. "David here loves to ride hard, straight'n early."

"There'll be seven patrols in all," said Gastonel, sitting up straight to look intently at Hawkins. "About a hundred men each, operating independently, setting up its own supply and communication lines, harassing and slowing the enemy advance. The first two patrols leave Wednesday. I want all patrols in the field no later than sunup Saturday. If you need more time than that, Major, I can allow it. But time is of the essence."

"I won't need more time, Colonel," said Hawkins. "I have a handful of affairs to attend to, but I'll be ready for duty by the end of the week."

"Excellent," said Gastonel before going over a more specific review of his plan for the mission.

Even before Hawkins' return, word had been sent out of a possible Union campaign to occupy upstate Louisiana. Since the expedition's official confirmation and onset last week, dozens of riders had been sent north, northwest and west, relaying the word through Arkansas, Texas and Indian Territory, even into Kansas and Missouri. A small regiment of Arkansas infantry with a detachment of cavalry was on its way south. Hundreds had already arrived from Texas, and dozens more were showing up by the day. Small bands of Cherokee and Choctaw Indians from were even casting in their lot, half-breeds and cut-hairs who dressed like white men but hated bluecoats.

Gastonel's plan was to send his seven patrols down the Red River, three down the east side and four down the west. Each patrol would split into three or four smaller troops of twenty or thirty men controlling the roads throughout the region. Relay points would be set up for re-supply and communication. Once the main body of Union forces was located, the different troops and patrols would seek out weak spots in the enemy's advance guard, attacking with surprise and stealth, then retreating before being fully engaged. These strike-

and-move attacks would be repeated over and over, keeping the enemy off guard, never knowing when and where the next attack might be. Dispatches would be sent back regularly through the relay points to General Taylor and the generals in Shreveport.

"General Taylor wants Banks's forces separated from Porter's gunboats at the river," said Gastonel, as they referred to a map they had brought with them. "If we can somehow lure him west at Alexandria or Natchitoches, into those woods and swamps near the Sabine River, then Taylor's men could be brought to bear using the element of surprise. Then we would have'm."

"Yes sir," said Hawkins. "I agree, but what about Porter? Once the rains begin, he won't have much trouble getting upriver."

"As we speak," said Hackwith, "several barges are being towed downriver about twenty miles, near Loggy Point. They'll be set lengthwise across the river, then scuttled.

"Tell David what they have at the shipyard," said Gastonel without looking up from the map.

Hackwith looked at the colonel, then back at Hawkins. "You know what a submarine is, don't you, David?"

"Yeah," said Hawkins, frowning. "A boat that goes underwater. Like the Hunley."

"That's right," Hackwith said, nodding. "And we have one."

"We have four," said Gastonel, still looking at the map.

"Four?" Hackwith said, looking at the colonel with some surprise.

"So," said Hawkins, raising his eyebrows as he turned to look toward the bayou. "That's what goes on over there."

"They're still in the developmental stages," said Gastonel, finally looking up from the map. "But they could be an important factor if Porter gets this far upriver. And," he added after glancing at the bayou, "they have a team of men crazy enough to operate them."

"Suicide missions," said Hawkins, slowly shaking his head.

"Yes," Gastonel agreed. "But I seriously doubt Porter will get this far. At least I hope not." The three men sat silently for over a minute, each of them thinking about the underwater boats, the strangeness of it.

"Well," said Hawkins, breaking the silence, looking at Gastonel. "Colonel, I honestly feel that it would be very wise to concentrate all of the patrols west of the river. It's very unlikely that Banks will send any large body of troops east of the river once he gets this far north. Even if he does, they won't be able to force a crossing. Not a large one, anyway." He paused and waved his hand over the center-left portion of the map, staring at it with animated certainty. "If we can control these roads the way we did at Chancellorsville, Banks would be blind, just like Hooker. Taylor could move into position, then we could lead Banks straight to'm."

"Where, Major?" said Gastonel stroking his goatee, his eyes on the map.

"Like you said, Colonel," Hawkins turned his palms upward, keeping his eyes on the map, thinking, "somewhere west of Alexandria and Natchitoches. And as you can see, that's a lot of ground to cover. We'll just have to be ready."

Gastonel slowly nodded still stroking his beard, looking at the map. "Chancellorsville was a masterpiece. If only we can duplicate that here."

"Chancellorsville was a very costly masterpiece, Colonel." As he spoke, Hawkins's eyes stayed fixed on the map, still thinking back on that bittersweet day. After a moment of silence, he turned to the colonel. "A victory like that would ultimately doom Shreveport."

A long silence ensued, interrupted briefly by a light breeze sounding the wind chimes that dangled overhead, the three officers taking turns looking at each other, looking at the map. Finally, Gastonel gave Hackwith a subtle nod, then turned to Hawkins. "You're absolutely right, Major. We must achieve something better," he paused, looking back down at the map. "And perhaps afterwards, we can."

"Afterwards, sir?" Hawkins queried with a slight frown.

"There is another matter, David," said Hackwith, clearing his throat and taking a drink from his glass. "It concerns the cotton and requires a bit of discretion."

Hawkins did not reply, only shifted his eyes back and forth between the two colonels.

"As you know," Hackwith went on, "by legal statute, all cotton that could possibly fall into Union hands is to be burned."

"Yes," said Hawkins. "I'm aware of that."

There was a long pause. Hackwith blinked, took another sip of tea then looked at Gastonel.

"There is a vested interest, David," said the colonel, tracing the rim of his glass with his finger, "in keeping the cotton from being burned."

"I'm sure there is," Hawkins replied coolly. "The value of the cotton in Shreveport alone must be in the tens of millions."

"That's right," said Gastonel. "And Grady tells me that some of that cotton is yours."

"About two-hundred-and-fifty bales," replied Hawkins, after glancing at his tea glass. "Worth a fraction of the half-million bales that are in the area."

"David," said Gastonel, "if the South loses ...."

"The war is lost, sir," Hawkins interrupted. "If you want to know if I'll help see that the cotton does not get burned, yes, I'll do that. As long as the money generated by the cotton stays here in this community."

Hackwith and Gastonel looked at each other, then Gastonel turned back to Hawkins.

"I can't promise that all of the money will stay here, David," said Gastonel. "But it will be more, much more that if it's burned."

"There are lots of places where we can hide the cotton," said Hackwith. "And I'm sure David knows a few good spots where those damn blue bellies won't find it."

Hawkins leaned back in his chair and nodded. "Yeah, I know a bunch'a places."

Gastonel looked down for a moment, letting out a long sigh, ran his fingers through his hair, then looked back up, smiling for the first time at Hawkins. "David, what do you think about giving the cotton to France? Somehow getting it down to Mexico?"

"To get them in the war?"

"Yes, as our allies."

"I think that would be a huge mistake."

"Why?" asked Gastonel.

"If France gets involved in this war, so will England. Maybe even the whole of Europe. The West Coast would become vulnerable to the Russia and Japan; they both have powerful navies. The entire North American continent would become a theater for some catastrophic world war. A war that we, the South, would ultimately lose."

"All over some cotton?" queried Gastonel with a chuckle.

"Cotton and those that work it," replied Hawkins "Giving France cotton for guns and ammunition is one thing. But actually getting them to fight with us is something I am very much against. The South cannot win this war; it's too late. But we can stop this campaign. I'll fight to protect my home."

The three men sat silent for moment, both Gastonel and Hackwith looking at Hawkins as he returned their stares without any emotion.

"Well, David," said Gastonel, finally. "I do appreciate your candor. Tomorrow morning at seven-thirty, there's a briefing at headquarters. I'd like you to be there."

The three men stood and shook hands, briefly discussing the pleasantries of Hawkins's homestead. As he watched the two colonels ride toward town, Hawkins stood on his porch noting an eerily familiar mix of fear and exhilaration. He then thought of the Man in White and looked up at the sky, the fathomless blue sky. The exhilaration suddenly increased. But so did the fear.

Gaby Heartshorn had just selected a collar blade hanging on a nail in the barn when the two Confederate colonels rode up to the Hawkins farm. He was about to use the sharp, hooked blade to clear a small patch of sugarcane he found down near the levee. Cook himself up a little rum in his spare time. But as he watched Hawkins and his two guests get cozy on the porch, he whacked the foot-and-a-half-long catch knife into the middle post of the barn. From a small cubbyhole by the door, he pulled out a bottle of sarsaparilla spiked with laudanum. He whistled for the two dogs sniffing around the hooves of the colonel's horses, tied to a post by the willow tree. When they came to him, Caesar trotting warily behind Jacko, he led them to the back of the barn where he filled a bowl with the sweet tasting tonic. He watched as they lapped it up in seconds. Within minutes, Jacko curled up by the door lying his head down to sleep. Caesar followed Gaby as he nonchalantly walked out to do a little eavesdropping. But the dog only got as far as the shade of the magnolia before curling up and falling fast asleep.

He had been a cutthroat all his life, killing his first man when he was only thirteen and making a living by treachery and violence. At nineteen he'd ridden with a band of marauders trailing behind the U.S. Army during the Mexican War, raping and pillaging along the disputed border. He killed his younger brother, and fathered a child by his older sister. Associated with pirates, prostitutes, bushwhackers and con men of all sorts. When the war began he first took up with the Confederacy, but soon turned coat when he saw the huge throngs of Union troops streaming into Southern Louisiana. The transition was slow, and occasionally he worked for both sides. He ran a string of prostitutes in New Orleans, pimping them to high-ranking officers, having the girls learn what intelligence was needed and wanted. Then he would get that intelligence or simply create it and sell it to the Yankees or the highest bidder. If the information proved reliable he got even more money. At Port Hudson he got an old friend, who was then a Confederate captain, drunk on whiskey and laudanum, finding out about troop strength and communication lines there before the Union siege. He exposed Confederate spy rings, getting several former colleagues hung. And did all this without revealing himself even once.

As the Red River Expedition got underway he was asked to go to Shreveport and find out what he could. As always, any reliable intelligence he gave to Union forces would pay handsomely. Because of his contacts in New Orleans, he was given Andrew McMillan's name, a high-ranking cotton spy already in Shreveport. But it was stressed to Gaby to keep that bit of information tightly under wraps, it was only for special circumstances. He got word of a former slave who had run off years ago, but had come back to find his family and was now trying his hand at espionage. Story was, the young black man had returned through a farm in Shreveport owned by a Confederate officer off fighting back East. The place was now said to be part of the Underground Railroad, and was run by the officer's wife. Eventually Gaby Heartshorn found Joshua Dubear tagging along with the 4th Corps d'Afrique, a colored infantry unit made up of former slaves from the New Orleans area. Gaby had watched the young black man from a distance for half a day. The black troops seemed uninterested in Dubear, probably because of the thick glasses he wore. Gaby, however, determined that he could be easily manipulated and simply approached him, making an offer sealed with an intriguing lie.

After leaving Caesar asleep under the magnolia, Gaby walked out toward the field. Once out of sight, he veered off into the woods, then doubled back to emerge at the opposite side of the house. Crouching low, he slowly crept to the corner just outside the porch, where he listened to nearly half-an-hour of valuable, candid information. Not only did he hear details of Gastonel's patrols, he also learned of the plan to hide the cotton, knowledge of several secret locations that could line his pockets even more.

As the three men said their goodbyes, Gaby traced his steps back the way he'd come. By the time he got back to the barn the colonels had left and Hawkins had gone inside the house. He hadn't given it much thought at the time, but he'd seen Sarah hurrying from the house to the other side of the field. He heard whispers as he entered the barn and turned to his left, noticing two figures in the dark shadows.

"Ain't nut'n changed since da las' time yooz here, Josh." It was Ruth and Dubear. Gaby knew the two had taken a liking to each other. And why not? She sure was a pretty little thing with dark skin, filled out nice like a woman, good teeth and the come-hither features of a happy life. How he wanted to put his hands on her, make her scream and whimper. If he could just get her down to New Orleans, she'd easily fetch three times what he'd get for the information he now had. "I still ain't never had me no real beau. Boosy come an' visit me sometime, but Pa found out an' run'm off. All we did was kiss over by the fallow cane poles ova' by da levee. But he don't kiss like you do. Na'ugh."

"Quit play'n footsy, boy," hissed Gaby, startling Ruth and Dubear, who pulled away from one another, "an' go'n saddle up my horse."

Dubear stepped forward into the light, Ruth standing a few feet behind him, embarrassed, unable to meet Gaby's leering eyes. "You want me to saddle your horse, now? Where you going, Gaby?"

"Never mind dat!" he snapped. "Jus' get to it. An' make it quick, boy. Got some biz'ness ta tend to."

Dubear nodded and looked back at Ruth, motioning for her to come with him.

"Na," said Gaby as Ruth started to follow Dubear. "You stay put. I'm in a hurry." He turned to glare at Dubear. "Go'n get my horse, boy."

Dubear glanced back at Ruth, hesitating before awkwardly walking from the barn.

Gaby's eyes shifted back to the pretty young black girl, again causing her to look away awkward and frightened, not knowing what to do with her hands. Greed and lust had ruled his life and now, as Gaby stared at the curves of Ruth's body, he began thinking of a way to ravish her off. Even though slavery no longer existed legally in New Orleans, he had the connections there to easily sell her as chattel. Or, he thought, investment in the girl might be wise. With the money he got for his spy work, he could refine the young girl, have her schooled in the social graces. He already knew she could read a little, and that was a good start. After she was taught how to properly talk, dress and carry herself, Ruth could be contracted to some of the finer brothels in the city, with the fashionably dressed Gaby Heartshorn as her sponsor.

After leaving Hawkins's farm, Johnny and his three friends had taken the same route by which they'd come. Silently they'd walked back along the levee, through the wharf area and past the train yard, to the trail that led back to the river, where they'd left the raft. Bobby, Randy and Robert had sat cross-legged in a little triangle on the raft as they floated back downstream. Johnny had sat off alone with his knees pulled up to his chest, arms wrapped around them, looking downriver under the brim of his father's cap. The trip had taken a little over two hours. A few times, one of the boys had to prod at the many logs that floated down the Red River like schools of great pre-historic fish. All night they walked west to Pleasant Hill. By the time they reached Ebarb's farm the sun was peeking over the trees behind them, and the boys were exhausted.

"I'm gonna go talk to Old Man Ebarb," said Johnny. It was the first time he'd spoken since they'd left Hawkins's farm. He pulled out the money and handed five dollars to Robert. "We can split this up later."

"We'll wait here for ya, Johnny," said Robert.

"Na, dat's okay. I'm just go'n tell'm ...." he hesitated. "I'll tell'm where Grey Stump is."

The other three boys walked back to their homes as Johnny approached Ebarb's farmhouse. Dogs were barking and before he could get close, a door opened and a man stepped out with a rifle in his hands.

"Who's there?"

"It's Johnny McRay, Mister Ebarb. Can I walk up an' talk to ya?"

"Yeah, come on."

Ebarb was well into his seventies. The top of his head was completely bald with little brown spots and he had wiry wisps of gray hair around his ears and neck. He wore coveralls and stunk of moonshine.

"You're Adam McRay's boy, aint ya?" he said, setting the rifle against the doorjamb.

"Yessir. But he got kilt in da war."

"I heard. Sorry 'bout dat."

"It's alright."

"Wha'cha want, son?"

"Me an' some friends took Grey Stump from ya dis morn'n."

"Well," said Ebarb, looking past Johnny at his field. "Ya bring'm back?"

"No, sir." said Johnny, reaching into his pocket pulling out the money and handing it to Ebarb in a large wad. "But I got dis fer ya. Iss forty dollars."

"Forty dollars!?" blurted Ebarb, taking the money and looking closely at the bills. "Good Lord, dis is Yankee money! Where'd ya get dis, son!?"

"From a man named Major David Hawkins up around Shreveport. He was my pa's commander in da war."

"Ya took Grey Stump all da way up ta Shreveport?" Ebarb's arms dropped to his side. "Gotta be outta ya mind, boy."

"He said, if'n ya didn't wanna sell'm, he'd bring Grey Stump back to ya an' ya can still keep da forty dollars."

"What?"

"An' if'n ya do wanna sell'm, he said da forty dollars is a down payment an' he'd give ya da rest later."

Ebarb looked at the money in his hand, then back at Johnny. "Dis Hawkins fella told ya all dat?"

"Yessir, he did."

"Mule ain't worth no forty dollars."

"I thought ya liked Grey Stump!"

"I do, but he ain't worth no forty dollars."

"Well, I gotta get go'n, Mister Ebarb. Sorry if I bothered ya."

Johnny walked the rest of the way home with his head down. When he stepped inside, Amy jumped up from the table.

"Johnny," she said. "I've been so worried."

He ran to her and fell into her arms. She held him close for a minute, taking off his father's cap stroking his hair.

"Where have you been, Johnny?"

He didn't say anything. He couldn't. She kept stroking his hair for a moment, then gently pushed his head back so she could see his face. A reddish-blue bruise ran from the left side of his upper lip to the tip of his nose.

"You've been fighting with Bobby Bernard again, haven't you?"

"No." Still, he wouldn't look at her. His eyes were lost somewhere off in the distance.

"What happened, Johnny?"

"I went an' saw Major Hawkins."

"What? Where, at his farm?"

"Yeah. Me an' Robert'n Randy'n Bobby went."

"How'd y'all get up there"?

For the next ten minutes he told her little bits at a time, while she coaxed each part of the tale from him by asking, "Then what?" Pulling teeth like she had done so many times since he was a little boy.

"An' den Bobby axt'm how many Yankees he done kilt."

"Oh no, Johnny."

"An' he said it was sump'n he didn't like talk'n 'bout. An' den he said killin' a man weren't like squirrel huntin', so I axt'm what killin' a man were like."

"Johnny, why did you ask him that?"

"Cause I wanna know."

"Ya want to know what it's like to kill a man?"

"Yep, I sure do." He looked at her. "Dair's sump'n else I wanna know."

"What's that?" she said, putting her hands on her hips, cocking her head to the side.

"I wanna know why he lives an' eats with a bunch'a niggers."

At first she didn't say anything, just stood there looking at him. She had the look she only got when she was very displeased, a look of anger with a hint of sympathy. "What has gotten into you, Johnny?" she finally said, before turning and going to her room.

He picked the cap up off the kitchen table and put it on his head, then went and looked at himself in the mirror, standing there a long time. He stood at attention, hands at his side, fingers turned inward along the hem of his pants. Chest out, shoulders back. Then he brought his right hand up, saluting his image, holding it for a moment before snapping his arm back down to his side, gazing at himself with admiration. Later in bed, still wearing the cap, he lay thinking of what it was like to kill men and win wars.

She lay in bed thinking of Hawkins and the day they first met. How he held her and kissed her and told her how beautiful and sweet she was as he ran his fingers through her hair, making her feel so alive. Since that day, he was constantly on her mind. When, she wondered, would she see him again? She pulled her spare pillow close to her, wrapping her arms around it wishing it were him. She remembered how he had traced slow little circles on her cheek, down her neck and shoulders. How she felt so comfortable and safe with him, so warm and attentive to each moment.

For a long time afterward, she had kept her face nuzzled into the nape of his neck. He seemed to have wanted her there, saying nothing, just positioning himself that way, pulling her gently to that spot as if calling on something good from his past. Something likely to slip away if held too tightly or left unacknowledged. A time to judge other times by, transcendental and spaced too far apart, like the dawning of a new day, still as short as the rest. And just before she closed her eyes and slept, she smiled, fearless and happy in a beloved presence of mighty angels.

Word was spreading through upstate Louisiana of a large Union force moving up the Red River. Fighting in the southern parts of the state had been frequent and fierce in the early years of the war. Bloodshed along the Mississippi River had been almost constant. First, outlaw marauders from Missouri and Kansas swept through eastern Louisiana, calling themselves Jayhawkers. Then, counter-marauders showed up, forcing those who were neutral to pick a side. During Grant's Vicksburg Campaign, the rape and pillage decreased somewhat. Afterwards, it returned with increased lawlessness. The northwestern part of the state had been spared the ravages of war, until now. Through the back roads and dirt trails, word was heard of "da Yankee man a'comin'." All along the little creeks, gullies and bayous, folks talked of it. The groves, hollows and coves where people live, now abound with fearful rumor, spreading to the points, bends and stretches where they work, hunt and mingle. In the churches, feed stores and shanty shops, they spoke of the coming invasion. Breaking out their long guns, muskets and pistols, they portioned out the black powder, shot and mini-balls. Sharpening their knives and swords. Adjusting their gun sights to offer a dose of Louisiana windage to the uninvited.

The Union expedition met its first bit of resistance at Marksville, several miles up from the mouth of the Red River. Fort DeRussy was easily overwhelmed and abandoned to the Yankees, both sides taking only a handful of casualties. From there, small pockets of Confederate resistance continued, slowing the campaign, stalling it out at several points along the river. Banks was cautious and Porter was impatient. The men were irritable and fights broke out regularly. Many times a boat would run aground atop an unseen sand bar in the middle of the river, stopping the whole flotilla. A whole day, sometimes two, would be wasted pulling the vessel free. From both sides of the river snipers would fire at the expedition, doing little physical damage, but causing tension and fear in the ranks. The further upriver they traveled, the more this increased. Constant uneasy glances at the trees, wishing it was over before it had even begun.

XIII

Sarah found Jacob and Isaac working at the edge of the field re-riveting a leather strap that had come loose from Gray Stump's harness. She had been doing her weekly dusting throughout the house when she looked out an upstairs window and noticed Gaby Heartshorn walking into the woods at the south side of the field. He'd glanced back over his shoulder a few times, as if to see that no one was watching. From the moment she first met Gaby she disliked the man, finding his very presence dubious and unsettling. She also wondered what Dubear was really doing back in the area, honestly hoping the young man's story were true. As she went room-to-room, window-to-window, tracking Gaby's obscure movements through the trees, she wondered what on earth he was up to. At first, she thought the Cajun might have a still hidden somewhere off in the brush. But after hurrying downstairs she entered the front parlor and saw him reemerging from the woods, creeping toward the south side of the house. She thought of David and his two uniformed guests.

Just before she had started her dusting, Sarah served the men some of her special sweet tea, an old recipe of Mary's made with honey and the juices of cane, sorghum, blackberry and lemon squeezed into the brew. She recalled how they abruptly stopped talking, David quietly smiling and nodding at her as she brought out the tray, as if the matter was of some secret military importance, confidential soldiers' business.

Fearing for her master and his guests' safety, she looked carefully at Gaby, his back only a few feet away through the glass. Could he be some kind of assassin? But she noticed, as he crouched low up against the house, his hands did not hold the large knife he always kept tucked into his green sash. He was perfectly still, listening intently to the little parley on the front porch. For nearly thirty minutes she stood watching Gaby, ready to scream if his hand touched the knife, but otherwise not knowing what to do.

Aside from the brief period between Emily's death and David's return, the war itself did not really interest Sarah. Most of what she heard she did not understand, except that thousands and thousands were being killed and maimed, and that the South was losing. She knew slavery had a lot to do with the conflict, and that slavery had once existed up North. But why were they suddenly doing so much to stop it? She truly feared their intentions were somehow based on greed, disguised as compassion for the plight of slaves. Even with all these questions, she knew what she was now witnessing had something to do with the war. Recently she had heard other slaves talking in town; "Dem Yankee gun mens a'comin' up da riv'va, free'n da slaves as dey go." Just the other day, Ruth had come to her with a strange question, "Mama, what do contraband mean?" And what about Dubear, Sarah thought, what did this mean about him? She could tell Ruth was falling for the handsome young man and the idea of them becoming involved actually appealed to Sarah. He was a bit aloof at times, almost uppity. But he was smart, kind and thoughtful in his own way, with an obvious shine to her blossoming daughter. But what secrets might he really hold?

When the little meeting on the front porch ended, she'd watched as Gaby made his way back through the trees, across the field and into the barn. Her hands trembled as she slipped out the back way, wanting to go to David and tell him what she had seen. Filled with uncertainty her mind raced as she approached her husband and father-in-law, telling them as they looked up from their work. Dumbfounded, the two black men looked at one another, then back at Sarah. Both were exhausted, working endless hours to get the crops in the ground. For a second, it seemed to Sarah that they thought she might be lying, or that the matter was none of their concern, that they simply did not care. Then, with earnest conviction she said, "David be our family. We's always 'posta look afta'm. Dat man might do sump'n to hurt David. An' if'n he hurt him, he hurt all'a us."

At that moment they looked up to see Dubear coming out of the stable with Gaby's horse, walking the animal into the barn. And lately, wherever Dubear was, Ruth was sure to be close by. The three slaves looked at each other, then began walking quickly toward the barn. Jacob and Isaac told Sarah to go and get Massa David, but she ignored them, instinctively moving to check on her daughter. She would not have made it to the house anyway, for just before they entered the barn, a scream pierced the mild spring air.

In the time it took Dubear to get his horse, Gaby Heartshorn decided what he would do. Murder for profit had never been hard for him, at least not in the emotional sense. Pretending to be an ally before turning the blade was something he actually enjoyed, having long since embraced his criminal self. Physically, however, the act could sometimes be quite demanding. For his diabolical plan to work, deception and timing were of the essence.

In his saddlebag was a pistol and another bottle of laudanum. He would take no chances with Hawkins. After luring the man together with his slaves, the gun was for him. The slaves he would dispatch with his knife. Many times he had single-handedly killed two, three, even four men with his blade. He was that good. Dubear and Jacob might prove difficult, so they would be after Hawkins. Quick slices across the throat and the rest would be easy. The woman, the old man, and then the little ones. And of course, if there was too much screaming, there was still the pistol.

The laudanum was for Ruth. Once drugged, he would carefully pack the girl like cargo, wrapped in a blanket on the buckboard. After hiding the bodies, he would take the back roads skirting south around the town. By the time the hideous foul play was discovered he would be well away from the area. Over the past few days, he'd considered contacting McMillan, but he wasn't even sure what the man looked like. And why bother now? It was known that Simmesport and Fort DeRussy had already fallen to the Yankees. If he pushed hard enough, he could be in Union-controlled territory in a little more than a day.

What Gaby Heartshorn did not know was that Joshua Dubear had his own plans regarding their relationship. He was fed up with being ramrodded by the man, disgusted at how Gaby acted agreeable and friendly when Hawkins was around, but turned vile and cruel when he was not. He was beginning to hate the man. But that hate, he knew, if left unchecked could cause him to act in ways most unreasonable. Dubear had grown up fast in a unique time of an ever-changing world, but suddenly he felt so young and ill-prepared for the path he had chosen. And for the first time in his life, he was in love. He decided he would stand up to Gaby. But as he walked the man's horse to the barn, his stomach in knots, he saw no easy way to do this.

When he'd entered the barn he heard a whimper and looked to his left. Gaby had Ruth pressed in the corner. In his left hand was a dark pint-size bottle that he had up to Ruth's mouth, the dregs of what he'd given the dogs. "Just a sip," hissed Gaby. In his right hand was the knife, its glistening blade at the girl's throat, her terror-filled eyes suddenly shifting to Dubear.

"Now listen, boy," said Gaby, looking at Dubear but keeping Ruth pinned against the wall with his body, creating the lies as he went. "We get'n outta here, me and you. Got me some good things to tell dem Yankees. An' dey'll be given us money fer it. Lots of it. Gonna take Ruth here wit' us. Ya like dat, don't ya, boy?"

"What are you doing?" gasped Dubear.

"Call out dat Hawkins fella," said Gaby. "Real natural like. Say it's im'potant."

"You bastard!" growled Dubear, releasing the horse as he moved toward them.

Gaby wasn't ready for Dubear's reaction. He dropped the bottle and turned away from the girl, meeting the young man's charge. But Dubear was able to knock Gaby's arm away, locking him in a clinch. For a second it worked. Dubear had both of Gaby's arms out to the side and was moving him back. But the wily Cajun brought his knee up hard into Dubear's crotch. He swung his knife arm down and around in a half circle, driving the blade deep into Dubear's thigh. Both Ruth and Dubear screamed. But Dubear's shriek of pain was cut short when Gaby struck him hard across the jaw. In one motion Gaby yanked out the knife as Dubear crashed to the ground, blood bubbling out of his leg.

"Guess we gotta do dis da hard way." With deceptive speed, Gaby snatched Ruth by the wrist.

At that moment Sarah entered the barn, almost at a run, with a panicked look on her face. Jacob and Isaac immediately followed. When he saw them Gaby spun Ruth around, holding his bloody knife to her throat.

"Please, Mista," pleaded Sarah, her eyes wide with panic and fear. Her trembling right hand reached out for her daughter. Her left hand pressed at her breast to steady her heart. "Don't hurt'r, please!"

Gaby moved toward his horse, which had lurched further into the barn, stirred by the excitement. When he got to the animal he drove Ruth to the ground, forcing her to kneel at his feet as he reached for the pistol in the saddlebag.

"Mama!" gasped Ruth.

"Quiet, Baby," said Sarah only ten feet away, just inside the barn. Jacob and Isaac were right behind her, also pleading mercy for Ruth as the girl shook uncontrollably on the dirt floor of the barn.

Gaby had just pulled out the gun when his eyes suddenly looked past them.

"MASSA DAVID!!" screamed Ruth.

The slaves all turned to see Hawkins standing unarmed in the sunlight just outside the barn.

He had been in the kitchen when he heard the screams. Not thinking to get his pistol, he ran, limping out of the house to the barn, expecting a terrible accident. But when he saw Ruth under Gaby's bloody knife as the man dug through his saddlebag, he wished he had taken the few extra steps to grab his Colt .45 hanging in its holster on the wall by the kitchen table. From where he stood he could have easily fired from the hip and nailed Gaby in the head before the man even saw him. But now Gaby had his pistol pointed at Hawkins, the two men glaring at each other. Hawkins wasn't sure what the matter was, but he suddenly knew that he would be the last to know. He stepped forward into the barn and raised his left hand in a steadying gesture, hoping to calm his terrified family of slaves.

Gaby's scheme wasn't quite working as planned, unraveling a bit at the seams. He had just decided to use the gun to finish off everyone, hoping the shots wouldn't draw any attention. Suddenly, a bluish-gray blur raced into the barn. It zipped past the slaves. With a low growl, Caesar's jaws clamped upward out of the shadows, onto the wrist of Gaby's gun hand. The weapon discharged harmlessly into the air. The dog thrashed its head, snarling, knocking loose the pistol that disappeared into the darkness. Gaby screamed, slashing wildly side-to-side with the knife. Caesar let out a loud yelp. The blue heeler fell off to the side, hurt, badly bleeding and limping. Gaby's horse reared and kicked and spun around lurching in a circle. A churning cloud of dust stirred through the barn. The horse almost trampled Ruth, then Dubear as it bolted outside. The slaves jumped together to the side, as Hawkins stepped calmly out of the panicked animal's path, his left hand touching its hide as it passed.

With his badly bleeding left hand, Gaby grabbed Ruth up off the ground and put the knife back to her throat. Jacko now showed himself, awakened by the commotion and the familiar cry of his companion. The sleepy dog barked, jumping in a half-frolic to shake loose the cobwebs, gaining his bearings at the feet of his master.

"Let'r go Heartshorn," said Hawkins as the dust settled. "She's just a girl."

"When I'm'a ready, Major. Now, somebody better go'n get my horse 'fore I slice this young'uns nose off."

"YOU TAKES DAT BLADE OFF'A MY BABY'S FACE!!!" shrieked Sarah.

"Go'n get my horse or she ain't gonna have no face!" yelled Gaby, spit flying from his mouth. "Ya hear!?"

"He were liss'nin to ya, David," said Sarah, looking at Hawkins, her eyes full of fear and tears. "Sorry I didn't come to ya, but …."

"Listening to me?" Hawkins looked intently at Sarah, then back at Gaby.

"You an' dem udder souljas on da porch," Sarah cried. "He's round da side liss'nin to ya, I seen'm."

"You're a spy?" Hawkins blurted out the question without even thinking.

"If someone don't get my horse, I'm gonna kill dis lil' nigga!" As Gaby screamed, he waved the knife at Hawkins. Seeing her chance, Sarah lunged, grabbed Gaby's arm and bit his hand. Gaby yelled, jerked back his arm, slicing both of Sarah's palms, allowing Ruth to squirm loose.

"You black bitch!" screamed Gaby, shaking his two bitten hands.

The four slaves fell together, looking at Sarah's wounds as they moved out of the barn. Hawkins moved past them toward Gaby as he staggered back and regained his balance, slouched over in a wide stance ready with the knife. Jacko and a maimed Caesar snarled and barked at the mayhem.

Gaby lunged at Hawkins's left. He was quick, real quick, thought Hawkins. Gaby lunged again. This time he caught Hawkins in the shoulder with the tip of the blade.

"Got'cha!" the Cajun taunted.

Hawkins grimaced in pain. Blood flowed down his left arm. He suddenly noticed a collar blade stuck in the post behind Gaby. He quickly dove to the ground and rolled to his right, grabbing a handful of dirt. As he came up, Gaby switched knife hands, making wide backhand slash at Hawkins's midsection. The Confederate sprang back, arms out, as the blade's tip cut a gash through his shirt, across the flesh of his belly. At that same moment, Hawkins flicked his wrist, throwing the dirt in Gaby's face.

"Ya bastard!" he screamed, spinning around, then making wide, violent sweeps with the knife keeping the dogs at bay.

Hawkins lunged, snatching the collar blade from the post with his right hand. He turned forty-five degrees and stepped with his bad left leg. Pain ripped through his body from his old wounds as he hurled the collar blade with all his strength. Just as Gaby's eyes cleared, the catch knife's sharp back hook ripped into the soft flesh just above his left collarbone. Gaby screamed and dropped his knife, spun around, both hands on the blade that protruded from the left side of his neck. A gush of blood spilled to the ground as he staggered out into the sunlight. He fell to his knees, still screaming, blood still squirting in arcs from between his fingers as he held both hands on the wound. Sarah then broke from her family, took three steps and kicked Gaby in the face as hard as she could with the bottom of her shoe. He sprawled backwards onto the dirt and quivered momentarily before going limp.

Seeing that Gaby was done, Hawkins turned to Dubear, lying in a pool of blood, soaked thick into the dirt. "Help me in here!" he shouted, taking off his belt. Jacob and Isaac ran to him, lifting Dubear at the waist as Hawkins tightened the belt around his upper thigh. "Get the buckboard ready. We got'a get'm to a doctor 'for he bleeds to death."

Hawkins turned to look at Sarah and their eyes met. She was crying, tears streaming down her face as Ruth wrapped her hands.

Hawkins then realized Caesar's left ear had been cut off. The dog stood proudly holding up his front left leg. It had been gouged badly by Gaby's blade. Jacko stood beside him, licking blood off the face of his one-eared partner.

Fortunately the medical facilities in Shreveport were quite good. Over half a dozen qualified doctors worked in the hospital that was adjacent to the headquarters building. At first, a couple of them took exception to caring for slaves, but Hawkins told them very bluntly that they had very little choice in the matter. "If you don't treat'm as good as your own young'uns, you're gonna need a doctor. Ya got that?"

Afterwards, Hawkins went to see Sheriff Wilhyte, explaining to his childhood friend how Gaby showed up at his farm ten days earlier with Dubear looking for work. He also told Wilhyte of the meeting on the porch with Hackwith and Gastonel and how Sarah had seen Gaby secretly listening in on the parley.

"If he'd gotten that information down to the Union commanders," Hawkins said as they looked at Gaby'a corpse laid out on the buckboard, "it could'a caused us a heap'a trouble up here. Banks would be a lot less cautious. He'd be send'n out a lot more cavalry ahead of'm. And we don't won't that."

"What about the other one?" asked Wilhyte. "The one that got stabbed in the leg?"

Hawkins shook his head and looked down at the ground. "That boy took a damn gator knife in the leg from this son of a bitch. Be lucky if he doesn't lose it. He didn't know noth'n. Just try'n to protect Ruth."

"But he did come up here with'm," said Wilhyte.

"He was just his slave, Austin," Hawkins said, wondering if it was true, still not looking at the sheriff, motioning at Gaby's body. "This fella here was a sly one. Had me fooled. That boy was just a tagalong unawares being used as cover."

After leaving Gaby's body and making an official statement, Hawkins went to headquarters to tell Hackwith and Gastonel of the violent events that had just taken place at his farm, but both men had already left. Next he made a statement to the department adjutant, writing a detailed report that took two hours to complete. Finally he went back to the hospital to gather up his slaves, and headed back across the bayou to the farm.

Dubear had gone through the painful process of having his wound cleaned and stitched with only a swig of whiskey and a spoonful of laudanum. The doctor said he was very lucky. Heartshorn's blade had missed the femoral artery, but done severe muscle damage. He would be weak from the loss of blood for a long while, and it could take a year or more for his leg to regain its strength. Sarah's right palm and the fingers of her left hand were cut almost to the bone, but no tendons were hit. Her wounds were cleaned, stitched and bandaged as she lay in Jacob's arms. Hawkins's cut to the belly was not deep and only required cleaning and a bandage, but his shoulder had a deep gash that mercifully only hit flesh. Almost a foot of catgut was needed to close the gaping wound. Even old Caesar was given top treatment. After a little whining the dog was stitched and bandaged, his head and leg wrapped in a clean white dressing.

It wasn't until they got to the fork in North Market Road, past the bridge where the levee began, that Sarah spoke up. It was the same spot where thirty years earlier little David had given directions to the two men looking for the Texas Trail. And where Sarah had told Emily of Tim's planned attempt to run. And the southern limit of young David and Paul's kingdom as young boys.

"Dair's sump'n we gots ta tell ya, Massa David," Sarah said, huddled in her Jacob's arms.

"I know, Sarah. I know," was all he said, until he stopped the wagon in front of the house. "Jacob, you Isaac and the kids, go'n get some of y'all's things and come on over to the house. I'll help Sarah and Josh inside."

"What'cha mean, Massa David?" asked Jacob as they all looked at Hawkins.

"Josh, here, can take Paul's old room. Isaac can take the guest room. You and Sarah can have my old room and the kids can sleep in the den.

"Massa David," said Sarah, leaning against Jacob. "Ya might wanna hear what we gots ta say first."

"I think I might already know a little about it, Sarah," he said, helping Dubear out of the buckboard. "Come on, let's go inside."

When he finally had them all gathered together in the living room, he put on his reading glasses and pulled a letter from an envelope, holding it up to the light. "Who are Clem and Noel?"

"Dey's a couple'a runaways from Texas," said Sarah. She then took a few minutes telling Hawkins how Ruth found Clem and Noel. And how Emily let them stay in the barn until their baby was born.

"A baby was born in the barn?" asked Hawkins, with a slight laugh.

"Yeah," said Ruth. "Dey named it Aaron."

"Yeah," said Hawkins, looking back at the letter. "I see that."

"Miss Emily wanted to bring'm in da house, but Noel were too fer along," said Sarah. "She's already start'n to holla out sump'n fierce."

"Den some slave huntas come 'round, Massa David," said Jacob. "An' Miss Emily reckoned it be better if'n deys left. So we took'm up to da mountains at a chicken farm up in Arkansas."

"Well," said Hawkins, after a moment of thought, "got a letter here, addressed to Emily from Mister and Mrs. Charles Etheridge up on Rich Mountain, Arkansas. Got here last Wednesday. Clem and Noel are do'n good, it says. Little Aaron's walk'n around get'n into everything he can. And Noel just had another baby. Last month. A straight and smiled back. "Pluck and Dee, whoever they are, moved on to St. Louis.

They hadn't heard from Jay and L. B. since they left last April." He sat in his chair and turned to look at Emily's picture on the wall. "Now, tell me all about this and don't leave out a thing."

They talked for over an hour, taking turns telling Hawkins of his wife's bold crusade. About Ruth's little slip to Pearl at the Christmas celebration, and Sarah and Clair's secret rendezvous in town. About the long trek in the buckboard, taking Clem and Noel to the Etheridge farm. How Emily drew a map for Tim and gave him a compass to find his way to Rich Mountain. They told him about the Emancipation Proclamation dinner she prepared for them and the others that were helped to freedom.

He sat listening intently to each word, occasionally looking up at her picture on the wall, falling in love with his wife all over again. In his mind's eye, he could see her finding purpose in such an endeavor, fussing over all the little details, troubling herself with delight.

Then Joshua Dubear finally came clean with his story. He had been born a slave on a sugarcane plantation in Houma, but when he was ten he ran away with his mother and father. For over two months they traveled north on foot, sometimes by boat upriver, all the way to Chicago. His father got work in a factory and his mother worked as a maid in a fancy hotel. By the time he was eleven, Joshua had his first pair of eyeglasses and was in school learning how to read. When he was fifteen his father was killed in an accident, so Joshua went to work in that same factory. By the time the war started three years later, Joshua's mother had remarried and seemed happy when he last saw her. He left Chicago and tried to join the Army but was rejected because he needed glasses to see. Determined to play some part in the conflict, Joshua made his way to St. Louis to become a spy.

"I really didn't realize what I was getting into," said Dubear as he sat next to Ruth holding her hand. "I wasn't expecting to meet people like your wife, Major Hawkins. And I sure wasn't ready for someone like Gaby Heartshorn. Our plan was to tell your wife the same story we told you. I told Gaby she wouldn't believe it, that she'd know we were lying, but he didn't care. Kept saying he knew how to smooth things over. He said that since she'd been helping runaway slaves, she wouldn't have much choice but to go along with whatever he said. But when we got to Shreveport, we heard that she'd passed away, and that you'd come back. I wanted turn around and leave, but Gaby said he'd kill me if I tried. I didn't know what to do, so I just went along with him. I'm so sorry for what happened."

Hawkins thought for a moment, considering what might have happened if Emily had been here. She would've shot Gaby in the foot with the scattergun, not caring a flip what the man had to say afterwards. She would've done what she could for Dubear, but Gaby would've been hanged.

"A man like Heartshorn plays the middle," said Hawkins thoughtfuly. "He never commits to anything until he's sure it'll go his way. And he'd do anything to get what he wanted. He was a violent criminal and he got what he deserved."

At sunset Hawkins paid a visit to Emily's grave, stopping to pick some wild-flowers along the way, placing them at the base of her headstone. After a long moment of silence, he smiled and said, "I'm so proud of you, girl."

The next morning at headquarters, Hawkins moved stiffly as Hackwith introduced him around the room of officers. He tried to play down his wounds, but Gastonel and Hackwith showed genuine concern, asking him repeatedly about his shoulder. Also troubling to them was the fact that a dangerous spy had been just feet away as they talked strategy on Hawkins's porch the day before. If Sarah had not seen him, Gaby Heartshorn could have easily slipped away, and at this very moment, been sharing what he knew with the Yankees. Banks and Porter would have a much better layout of what awaited them. Union counter-patrols could be sent to ambush the Confederate patrols, neutralizing their purpose, leaving the roads approaching Shreveport in enemy control.

"Are you sure you're up to this, David?" asked Gastonel.

"Yes, Colonel, I'm sure. I'll be ready by Friday," said Hawkins. "There's someone I'd like you to meet." He turned and motioned to Steven Jenkins, who was standing off to the side. After a brief introduction, Hawkins spoke very candidly to Colonel Gastonel. "I've ridden with this man from here to Pennsylvania and back, and I've known him since I was a little boy. I want him to command a troop in my patrol, but I need him promoted to lieutenant."

"What?" balked Jenkins. "Me, an officer?"

"Relax, Steve. You'll do fine," said Hawkins turning back to Gastonel. "He's more than capable, sir. He can ride and shoot as good as the best of'em, and he handles men like a charm."

"Consider it done," said Gastonel, extending his hand to Jenkins. "Welcome aboard, Lieutenant Jenkins. Grady will take care of all the formalities."

"Thank you, sir," Jenkins said, giving Hawkins a puzzled look. "I'm sure I'll get used to it."

Soon General Edmund Kirby Smith entered the room. Because of the events at Hawkins's farm, security had been increased and no strangers were allowed near the headquarters building. Smith stood before the men telling them what they already knew. A Union force of some 40,000 men was moving up the Red River with orders to capture Shreveport and confiscate the cotton on the plantations in the region. Huge loads of cotton had already been moved to secure areas around the town. A picket line now extended from Fort Turnbull, on the bluffs overlooking the river just south of Shreveport, to Greenwood at the Texas line. It was estimated that over 2,000 men had already arrived via Arkansas and Texas, and many more were showing up by the day. Taylor still had only 8,000 men in position west of Alexandria and so far Smith had only made a verbal commitment to send more troops, fearing an attack on Shreveport by Union forces occupying parts of Arkansas.

When the briefing was over, Hawkins met with the other officers in Gastonel's reconnaissance patrols. The first patrol, leaving the next day, would ride southeast along the river as quickly as possible, working with the already existing patrols to find the main body of the Union expedition. Brief but specific instructions would be left at the towns and communities along the way regarding supply and communication. Within twenty-four hours three more patrols would head out, each taking with them herds of fresh horses to be kept at various locations. One of these patrols would take the route of the first patrol, eventually splitting itself into four twenty-five-man troops, fanning out to the west of the river. The other two patrols would start by riding farther west, splitting and fanning out further still, covering as many of the roads as possible between the Red and Sabine Rivers. Relay points would be established in each of the towns in this area, enlisting civilian volunteers to deliver urgent messages up and down the line. By the time the last three patrols are in the field, the Union main body would have been located and the other patrols would be given a brief rest before harassment of the enemy's advanced units began. Coordination and support from Taylor's forces near Alexandria would help paint a clear picture of the state's south-central region for the commanders, keeping tabs on the enemy's movements toward Shreveport.

After eating brunch with the men, Hawkins left to attend to a personal matter. First, he went to see Sheriff Wilhyte. The two men walked over to the office of the Clerk of Court, Donald Mayfair, who also served as the Justice of the Peace. What Hawkins had to say, caught them both by surprise.

"If anything happens to me, I want my farm left to Sarah and Jacob."

"What?" Mayfair balked. "You can't give them your farm."

"David, that's illegal," said Wilhyte.

"I know. But when this war is over laws are going to change and you know that. By the laws of the United States of America they have a right to my property because I wish it so."

Mayfair and Wilhyte looked at one another. "David," said the Mayfair, "We are not in the United States of America."

Hawkins looked up at the ceiling and let out a long moan. He then held up his hands, palms out, and looked back at the two men. "In the event of my death, I want my estate placed in escrow until it is legal for them to own it. And," he moved close to Wilhyte, "they are to be allowed to stay there unmolested, just as they have been. I want your word, Austin, that you'll protect them just as you would me or Emily."

Wilhyte looked at Mayfair.

"I want your word!" Hawkins raised his voice.

"The community won't stand for it, David," said Mayfair. "After Emily died, I was constantly being pressured to put your farm up for auction."

"What!?' shouted Hawkins. "Who was trying to get my farm!?"

"You were believed to be dead," Mayfair said in frustration. "The war was going terribly and you hadn't been heard from since last June."

"Who wanted my farm auctioned off?" Hawkins said in a calm yet frightening tone.

"It was several of them, David," said the sheriff, looking a bit nervous. "They didn't like the idea of slaves being left unattended. I was riding out there every day just to keep'm from makin' a fuss."

"The only way I can do what you ask," said Mayfair, "is if you named a white trustee in your will. And there's still the matter of the outcome of the war."

"The war is lost," said Hawkins.

"And you're willing to die for a lost cause?" asked Mayfair.

"No. I'm not. What we're doing isn't about the Confederacy. It's about the well-being of the people and the land. My father helped found this town when it was no more than an outpost on an impassible river. I'll be damned if I'm gonna let a bunch'a half-ass Yankees take it over and burn it. We have to stop those bastards so there's something left for us after the war."

For a long while the room was silent. Hawkins walked over to the window and looked out on the street. There was little time to make a decision. His body and mind ached. Finally, he turned to Wilhyte and Mayfair. "I have an idea," he said.

Half an hour later the papers were drawn up and signed. Then Hawkins rode back to his farm to rest.

XIV

By the time Ira Hawkins had established himself in Shreveport he had been a Protestant for well over a decade. But out of habit he still occasionally made the sign of the cross. It was a gesture that had been ingrained since childhood, since the old country, to the movements of his right hand whenever tragedy or great calamity struck, or sometimes in moments of supreme awe.

"Jesus, Mary and Joseph," he would whisper as his fingers gently touched his bowed forehead before passing down to his chest, then to his left shoulder, then to the right. He refrained from performing the little ritual at the dinner table after grace because Dorothea disapproved. But still, young David and sometimes Paul would cross themselves, whenever their mother wasn't around, imitating their father as he had imitated his father back in Ireland.

Crossing oneself was something everyone did in Belfast. It seemed as common as waving or saying hello, and yet somehow its repetitiveness never cheapened the act. Little Bolivar Dunnydon's first memory of life was being taught to make the sign of the cross by his older sister, Macy, as their parents received word of a terrible accident that had claimed the life of a close family friend. A kind old seafaring man named McQuaylan, who always gave the children candy and trinkets, had fallen from the crow's-nest of a ship in the harbor. Death, it also seemed was very common, even in those days before he became an orphan. His family had attended mass every Sunday at a small Catholic church on the outskirts of Belfast, taking a little horse-drawn cart over a mile even in foul weather. When they became ill he did not understand and was soon quarantined in the rectory of the church. Strangely, his parents had died just hours apart and were buried that same day, along with many others that had been claimed by the epidemic. At the funeral he had boldly stepped forward, tossing a tiny handful of dirt in each of their graves. He had crossed himself each time, momentarily gazing down at the wooden caskets with sad, bewildered eyes.

In great detail, Ira told David and Paul of his lonely years at the orphanage, years that had been filled with both academic and ecclesiastical rigor. He described a walled community with drab, dingy passageways, untended gardens, stagnant pools of water and packed lecture halls patrolled by cloaked men of a divine, sometimes grim purpose. Still traumatized from losing his family, little Bolivar spoke very little that first year. And like a desperate prisoner, he began planning his escape the moment he set foot in the place. Solace was found in his own personal experience of God's love, mercy and grace. But even at his young age, Bolivar was well aware of the ever-present taint of man's iniquity on holy ground.

Gradually he came out of his shell doing his best to fit in while still maintaining his identity. He enjoyed learning and did quite well in his studies, but unlike the other boys, work became his favorite pastime. He often volunteered to do extra duty and even took on the chores of others. It seemed that any given task, no matter how mundane or dirty, brought him out of the grief of the past, at the same time keeping him from the fear of the future. While most boys his age seemed to naively fidget and twiddle, he developed a keen ability to live in the here and now. He savored every moment for all it was worth, a trait that would prove beneficial when he later came to America.

Every now and then he came across a shilling or two, a gratuity from one of the fathers or well-to-do parishioners for going out of his way to perform an especially difficult task. He saved each weighty coin, along with every pence he earned. But he wasn't the only one making tips on the side. Soon, he began charging fees from the boys whenever he did their chores, and sometimes their schoolwork.

As the years went by, he did his best to encourage the newcomers and the boys who had not adjusted to life at the orphanage. He once saw a new boy being picked on by two others and decided to intervene. After a quick scuffle, meting out a beating to the bullies, a young priest, who up until then had been very kind and fair to Bolivar, gave him a severe beating. A few days later he counted his money, carefully hidden under a plank in the floor of the sanctuary, over thirty pounds worth of coin. After leaving ten percent of his savings in the offering box, Bolivar poured a week-old chamber pot on the young priest as he slept. The man awoke with a start, howling in protest and dripping with filth, as Bolivar hurried down the hall crossing himself and saying a quick Hail Mary. He then slipped out a window to live life on his own.

He carefully made his way through the streets of Belfast, carrying himself as a boy much older. He was tall for his age, needed to fill out some, but had broad shoulders that conveyed strength not found in the average ten-year-old. All this and the stern look in his eye allowed him to easily pass for twelve, a questionable age that bordered on young manhood. The money gave him time to learn, watching the city's ways from the shadows of the background, keeping him from the traps of desperation.

More than once he had to fight to keep his purse, even though he was often outnumbered. Two boys that had been whipped fair and square by Bolivar stalked him the following day, enlisting the help of a cohort before cornering him in a back alleyway. Not only was he at a three-to-one disadvantage, but the third boy had a long chain, taunting Bolivar by twirling it in circles above his head. As he crouched against the wall, unsure of what to do, a thick wooden staff as clattered down at his feet from a second-story window. After snatching up the heavy rod, Bolivar gave quick glance at the figure in the window, then dished out a serving of hurt to the three boys. First, he let the boy with the chain take a swing, deftly catching the weapon as it wrapped tightly around the staff. Then, in one quick motion, he jerked the boy to him, kicking him in the crotch, before smashing him in the face where the chain was wrapped. The rest was easy. With the chain still attached to the staff, Bolivar beat all three to a bloody pulp, chasing them out of the alley as a round of applause echoed from the window above. Walking back, he looked up to see a very old man leaning out the window, clapping and grinning with delight.

"Marvelous, lad!" cried the old man. "Simply marvelous! Now, if you please, toss me back my swagger stick."

"Many thanks, sir," said Bolivar, throwing the staff back up to the window, the old man snatching it out of the air with ease.

"I see ya put a few extra notches in it."

"Sorry 'bout that."

"Adds character to it," said the old man with a smile. "Besides, I love watching these hooligans get what's coming to them. And you looked as though you could use a little help."

"That, I did, sir." For a while, Bolivar chatted with the old man, the first pleasant, carefree conversation he'd had in a long time. After telling his story, Bolivar was given directions on where he might go to find something of a livelihood.

"Find the Slago Wharf. It's down past the barracks at the west end. There's a ship that no longer puts out called the Barronda, an old caravel that looks as though she's sailed the ages. Ask for Captain Darrow, wears an eye patch and a gray skullcap over a black bandanna. Tell'm Icarus sent ya. He'll give ya work on the boats and a place to lay your head. But be careful me lad, it's only a wee step above where ya are now."

Bolivar found the Barronda, a vessel that conjured up images of passage through forbidden seas. Three masts were still furled with the tattered remnants of what used to be sails. Ropes, chains and strips of soiled canvas swayed lifeless from the yardarms. Knocks, clanks and pings echoed from somewhere in the rigging, off the deck and deep within its hull. A high, narrow stern faced the harbor, bearing its name scrolled in gothic red lettering, littered with an assortment of refuse, rubbish and discarded garments. A broad, ominous bow, similarly adorned, was encrusted with barnacles and scarred with the batterings of its endless nautical miles. A killer of sea monsters now put to its moorings.

"Is there a Captain Darrow on board?" cried Bolivar.

After a few moments, a shape emerged at the gunwale and right away, Bolivar could tell it was Darrow.

"An'oo might you be, young nip?" The man's voice bellowed effortlessly, sending a low, deep vibration through the air. Bolivar imagined the man capable of putting the ship in motion with just the force of his words.

"Icarus sent me," was all Bolivar could manage as he gazed up at the scary looking man.

A smile broke out on Darrow's face, completely altering his attitude. "Icarus? Ya don't say. And how is the old codger?"

Bolivar explained from the wharf's edge how Icarus tossed him his swagger stick to fight off the three young goons, and sent him to find the Barronda to get some work and a place to stay.

"Come aboard, me lad," said Captain Darrow. "Something in your eyes tell me ya already know the virtues of hard work."

Bolivar made the sign of the cross as he walked the short, narrow plank that ran from the wharf to the ship's starboard side, seeing a reflection of himself on the strip of black water below. Once onboard, Bolivar noticed the chaos was a little more organized.

"Barronda," Darrow said, "means organized chaos."

Piles of hooks, pulleys, and gaffs lined the deck, arranged in their various shapes and sizes. Coils of rope by the score, and stacks of folded canvas. One of these stacks had, at a glance, what looked to be a dead body laid on it. But suddenly, the man rolled over with a loud, growling moan, eyes closed, a large bottle of some brownish-red liquid cradled lovingly in his arms.

"'At's Greely," said Darrow without looking, "my quartermaster. 'Ee's on one. Lost 'is wife a few years back an'ee gets 'at way time an' again.

As Bolivar was shown below deck, past dozens of boxes and crates packed with more ship-junk, the boy began to realize that the Barronda was really just a floating warehouse. He was given a small cabin not much bigger than a closet, and after being told to rest, he fell fast asleep on a cot that would be his bed for the next three years.

At this point in his young life, Bolivar could swim, but not that well, something that would soon change. His first job for Darrow was helping replace a broken rudder on a ship that had just come in from a storm at sea. When he didn't immediately jump in the water after Darrow told him to, the captain threw him in.

"Might as well get used to it, lad. Sink or swim, as they say."

Darrow was in charge of maintenance on all the boats that came into the Slago Wharf, and there was plenty for Bolivar to do. Because of his early hardships and the fact that he was nimble and wiry, he caught on fast, learning to shimmy up a mast in seconds. In his first year, he learned to set rigging for sails of all shapes and sizes, becoming totally fearless of heights, crawling and dangling like a monkey from the ropes and yardarms. He learned to tie a wide variety of knots, and stitch ripped sails, even do rough carpentry work. Now all Darrow had to do was whistle and point and Bolivar would quickly cross himself and jump in the water like a seadog, often doing a flip in the air as he went.

He became attached to the other members of Darrow's crew, a band of misfits and retired sailors, who in turn grew very fond of the eager-to-please young boy. At night they would gather in a circle drinking rum, singing songs and telling old tales of adventure. Bolivar never grew tired of listening as they spoke of people and places he never knew existed. Some of them, like Greely, stayed on the Barronda, but a few, came and went, seeming to vanish and reappear like ghosts. Often Bolivar would be talking to one of them, coaxing a story of some exotic faraway island. The mysterious seaman would suddenly look up, his eyes off on the horizon. Bolivar would turn to see what it was, then look back to find the man gone, as if he'd never been there. A day or two later, he would be busy at his work and out of nowhere a calloused hand would ruffle his hair, that very same seaman walking by with a wink and a smile.

Eventually Bolivar began to make friends off the boat, spending his spare time running the streets. Stealing was a way of life on the docks and Darrow discreetly encouraged it, as long as it was not done on the Slago Wharf. There were plenty of other wharves lined with ships packed with a variety of goods. And little by little, small loads of merchandise began finding its way on board the Barronda. A whole cargo of fabrics was stolen, yards of cloth, rolls of silk and gigantic rugs from the Far East. Another time, they got enough spices, also from the Orient, to make the Slago Wharf smell of cumin, curry and basil for weeks, saffron staining the ship's deck a deep yellow-orange.

The big spice heist had drawn unwanted attention to the Slago Wharf, putting Bolivar in bad favor with Darrow and the others. But over time he was able to remedy the situation to some degree. Even though he was still just a boy, Bolivar and his little team of thieves brought Darrow a lot of loot. They could go places and do things adults could not. But still the damage had been done, and Bolivar knew it was only a matter of time before he was done in. He was learning a valuable lesson about stealing; no matter how good one was at it, no matter how perfect the crime, it always brought anxiety.

At the time, those three years seemed to pass slowly for Bolivar. But Ira now knew they came and went far too quickly, much more so than the next five years. He often wondered where his life would be if he had jumped another ship or if he had **not** been found out on Mercy's Wind. Surely he would have picked up where he left off, running the wharfs of New Orleans unchecked, or possibly some other American port. But he hadn't jumped another ship, and he had been found out, and he lost his freedom for it. Looking back on that time of being a servant, being bonded without choice to another man's land, another man's property, Ira realized, as bitter as it was, the experience had saved his life and changed it for the better.

Besides Dorothea and his sons, Ira's most pleasant dreams were of Chéri. How lonely and lost he had felt that day he found her, cold and wet on the ground, screeching and flapping her useless, downy wings. He had taken the bird, wrapped her in a cloth and lay with her in his bed talking to her, feeding her any bugs or worms he could find. One old slave, who was said to have been brought to the plantation from Africa decades ago as a small boy, noticed Ira cuddling the baby hawk, smiling and talking to her as if she were a child.

"Oh yeah, dass good," said the old slave, nodding at Ira, happy to finally see the boy with a smile on his face. "Ever'a one needs dem an *afa shay'ree* at diss heugh place. Yessa. Ain't nut'n wrong wit dat."

Ira had asked the old slave what *afa shay'ree* meant, but their accents conflicted and he could not understand what the man said. A housemaid who was hanging her linens out to dry overheard Ira and translated for him.

"Infant Chéri," said the housemaid. "It means 'loved child.'"

Decades later, Ira was walking with David and Paul one crisp autumn day along the western boundary of their land. Even though it wasn't really a hunting trip, Ira had brought Betty in case they happened upon any game. The boys were still quite young, but they had become skillful marksmen with the old Kentucky rifle. As they strolled along, David held the weapon, loaded, cocked and ready. Ira was in midsentence, telling the boys about his voyage across the Atlantic, when suddenly they heard a shrill caw off in the distance. Startled, as if hearing the voice of an old, forgotten friend, Ira stopped talking and turned to see a red-tailed hawk perched high in a tree across a clearing. Right away he could tell the bird was fully matured, wearing its winter feathers. Ira had told the boys all about Chéri and his unique companionship with the bird back in his hard days at the plantation. Often he would point out one of the reddish-brown hawks as it circled the sky, explaining to them how the noble bird of prey became their namesake.

The hawk cawed again, then took flight turning sharply back into the woods, disappearing through the trees.

"Afa shay'ree," Ira whispered, crossing himself. David and Paul followed suite, gazing, half-expecting to see the hawk reemerge from the brush.

For a long while, the three of them looked silently toward the trees, listening as the faint sounds of movement echoed from within the darkness of the woods. An image suddenly appeared. A great stag stepped from the shadows into the clearing, a huge buck crowned with an impressive rack of antlers. The majestic creature trotted for a second, flaunting its grandeur, then took off in a sprint along the tree line, the thick coat around its upper body churning with power and grace.

Without a word, without any instruction from his father, David raised Betty to his eye, leading the animal to his right as he fired. It was an excellent shot, striking the stag just behind the shoulder, causing it to lurch and stagger before continuing on, then veering back into the woods. They tracked the deer for nearly a mile, easily following the trail of blood sprayed on the trees and leaves from its punctured lung. The large buck was found in an upright position, slumped headfirst against an embankment, prostrate, as if praying to the earth.

"Jesus, Mary and Joseph," they quietly echoed one another, again crossing themselves as they viewed the eerie scene. In its last moments the animal attempted to burrow into the ground, its antlers driven in the miry topsoil.

Young David Hawkins made several friends growing up in the Shreveport area. Austin Wilhyte was the son of a planter who also settled on a nice section of land just to the west of the Hawkins farm on the north side of the bayou. He was a stout little boy, shorter than David but strong and always up for adventure. His mouth always seemed to be cocked open to one side in a partial grin, giving him the dumb bad-boy-look, even though he was actually quite smart and good-natured. Brett Edmonds's family owned the local general store on Lake Street, the only real competition for Ira's Dry Goods. Byron Edmonds, Brett's father, had passed away some years back leaving the profitable business as a nest egg. Brett's mother, Diane, drank heavily since Byron's death and was known to have had several affairs. An overly eccentric woman, she made it a top priority to always keep Byron's oil-on-canvas portrait well dusted and hung straight at the entrance of the store. She would often be seen with a feather duster in one hand, a glass in the other, sipping, dusting and preening away as she shamelessly spoke to her late husband. A bizarre yet touching sight.

And there was Philip North, David's best friend, whose father ran the Red River Shipping Company, the most powerful operation in the area next to the cotton kings themselves. David and Philip would team up with Austin and Brett, spending hours running the trails together. The boys built a series of forts along both sides of the bayou and west bank of the river, using tree limbs, driftwood and cane poles. Two of these forts were in oak trees that sat strategically at the mouth of the bayou facing the river. One was on the north side, closest to the Hawkins farm. The other was on the south side, closest to town. A rope and pulley system had been rigged between the two forts, stretching over the bayou so that urgent messages and special packages could be exchanged. Ira nodded and smiled at the boys when he saw the clever little contraption, happy that they were finding better things to do with their time than he did at their age.

Since David and Austin lived on the north side of the bayou, they would go to the north fort first, sending a battle plan for the day across to the south fort. Philip and Brett, who lived on the south side of the bayou, would then send back a reply. Eventually the four would meet up, setting out to vanquish the imaginary enemy of the day, whether it hostile Indians, roving bands of outlaws, ruthless river pirates, or the vanguard of an invading army.

As David pulled the rope one day, retrieving the message from the other side, he noticed the line had more weight than usual. At first he thought it might be some of Mary's house-baked cookies sent fresh from the café, or some pie or cake. But inside the bucket, curled in a disgusting heap, was a dead opossum, freshly killed and still warm. The boys were known to play practical jokes on each other from time to time, but not usually something as ghoulish as this. David looked across the mouth of the bayou at the south fort 150 feet away, its crude fabrications partially hidden within the oak's branches. He saw movement, but thought it odd that neither Philip nor Brett clearly showed themselves, something they usually did with heightened exaggeration, waving, hooting and making a show of their presence. His eyes began to carefully scan the trails of the opposite bank, many hidden by brush. But he knew exactly where their courses lay, for he'd blazed each and every one. He looked to his right at Austin, who was still examining the dead opossum, then noticed movement along the north side of the bayou. After adjusting his eyes, he saw that it was Brett racing up the trail that led to the north fort, running as if his life depended on it.

"They got Philip!" he shouted as he reached the base of the tree, then bounded up the rough-cut two-by-fours nailed to its trunk. He had a black eye, and blood was smeared across his face and forearm where he'd wiped the flow from his nose. He was angry and scared, trembling with excitement, his dark hair matted in sweaty tufts to his face and forehead. After being asked who *they* were, Brett started rattling off names, each time holding out a finger and striking it with the index finger of his other hand. "Robert Manshack, Kenny Youtts, Kyle Gill and that stink'n Merle Pemberton. That's who they is."

Robert Manshack was the baby brother of Greg and Chuck whom David had whacked two years earlier with the bison bone. Like all the Manshacks, he was a thug and a bully, the nasty type that enjoyed hurting the weak. But as bad as Robert Manshack was, he wasn't nearly as vile as Kenny Youtts whose father was shot and killed by Sherriff Kotch not long after Shreve Town became Shreveport.

Ben Youtts had just been deputized by the sheriff and was trying to arrest some off duty river workers who were drinking moonshine, camped near the south edge of town. They laughed at him, pointing out that they were in fact outside the town limits. Youtts became enraged, then violently smashed one of the men in the head with a club, killing him instantly, a senseless act of homicide witnessed by a half dozen other men. Youtts was so stupid and ill-mannered that when Kotch said he'd made a big mistake in hiring him, he became even more enraged over being fired less than four hours after starting the job. He was also totally oblivious to the fact that he had just committed manslaughter. When Kotch tried to arrest Youtts, he resisted, pulling his pistol. But Kotch had been voted sheriff for a good reason. Although his judgment was a bit questionable, he'd spent four years in the Army and was a seasoned Indian fighter. He quickly rolled to his left as Youtts fired, the ball striking another worker in the leg. Kotch then shot Youtts with his flintlock as the deranged man charged him with his knife. He hadn't killed anyone yet, but Kenny Youtts was definitely as dumb and uncouth as his father, with a temper to match.

Kyle Gill was another loathsome piece of work, a tag-a-long who would do whatever Manshack and Youtts told him. His family ran a pig farm west of town, south of the bayou and it was rumored that his mother was actually his older sister. He was so dense and witless, he made the other two seem bright by comparison.

There was never any question that Robert Manshack was the leader of their little group, Youtts playing a close second simply because he was less ambitious, and Gill was just glad to be there. But Merle Pemberton wasn't really part of their group, with them, but not one of them. The Pemberton's were dock workers and teamsters. Their family lived in a series of boats that sat moored along the river, south of town. They were a strange type that also had an inbred look, speaking little and always lurking about at odd hours. Merle would often be seen with Manshack and his bunch, but the boy was definitely his own man, if the word man could be used to describe him, for he somewhat resembled a wild animal. He wasn't very big, but at twelve he had the look of a boy in his mid-to-late teens. Dark fuzz already showed on his face, and his thick matted hair fell in coils to a pair of muscular shoulders, attached to a pair of equally muscular arms with thick bluish veins. His dark, beady, feral eyes looked almost intelligent, always making you wonder what he was thinking because his facial features lacked any kind of emotion.

A few months earlier Robert Manshack and his three sidekicks were fishing near the docks when Greg, Chuck and Troy Manshack happened along. The older boys began having a little fun picking on their brother and his three friends. Robert, Kenny and Kyle submitted quickly, without hesitation, and were whacked around a bit, given a headlock and an arm twisted behind their back. But when Troy grabbed Merle by his hair, the younger boy bit him, clamping down hard on the older boy's pinky finger. Troy screamed and tried to pull away, but Merle grabbed his wrist, pulling it to him as he bit down even harder, shaking his head and growling like a mad dog. The two of them started moving in a circle, spinning around and around each other, Troy screaming, and Merle growling, louder and louder. Then just as Troy was about to yank himself loose, Merle rammed his head into the bigger boy's stomach. All in one motion, he brought his knee up hard into Troy's crotch. As they sprawled to the ground, a disturbing guttural sound came from deep inside Troy Manshack. It was the sound of intense pain stifled by the inability to cry out. Not only was Troy's breath knocked out, he had been racked to the very tips of his hair. On the ground, Merle quickly squirmed loose and jumped to his feet. He stood there defiantly with blood dripping from his chin, then spit out Troy's chomped-off pinky finger.

"HE BIT MY FINGER OFF!" shrieked Troy, still gasping for breath as he gawked in disbelief at the blood squirting from where his pinky had been, his other hand reaching for the severed digit. "YOU SON OF A BITCH!!! YOU BIT MY FINGER OFF!!!"

Although David and his friends had not witnessed the wanton act of mutilation, it was common knowledge in the town. David thought for a moment after listening to Brett tell how he and Philip were bushwhacked by Manshack's little gang. Youtts had punched him in the face as he fought his way out of the attack, and the last thing he saw was Gill and Manshack tackling Philip to the ground.

"I tried to fight som'ore, but dat damn Youtts punched me again, right in da nose."

"I got'n idea," said David. "Come on."

As Austin and Brett followed David up the trail, they selected large pieces of driftwood to use as weapons. When they got to the other side, instead of taking the trail to the south fort, David turned left on Cotton Street and headed toward Mary's Manners.

"Ya go'n tell yer folks 'bout diss?" asked Austin.

"Heck no," said David, stopping to look back at the river. "Y'all meet me at the river trail."

Parked outside the dry goods store was a buckboard being loaded with supplies by a man and a short chubby boy David knew vaguely.

"Yer David Hawkins, aren't ya?" the boy asked as David walked by, mounting the steps to Mary's Manners.

"Yeah, I'm David." He stopped at the top of the steps.

"I'm Steven Jenkins," said the boy. "I'z in class with ya a couple'a years back. This is yer folks' place, huh?"

"Yeah, it's my pa's," said David.

"Come on, Steve," the man said as he threw on the last of their supplies. "Gotta get on back."

"Well, I'll be see'n ya," said Steven Jenkins, hopping on the buckboard with a wave.

David nodded, waved back, then hurried into Mary's Manners.

At a clump of bushes by the trail, Austin and Brett waited for David. They had a clear view Hawkins's Corner and could just make out the fort in the opposite direction. Soon, David came walking from the café carrying a picnic basket bulging with goodies, wrapped in gingham.

"What'n the world ya got there, David?" asked Brett.

"Blackberry cobbler and some cinnamon apple fritters," David said, walking past his two friends, taking the trail to the south fort.

As David approached, he saw Manshack and Youtts standing on a three-foot-by-six-foot platform that jutted out of the fort. It was a little balcony enclosed by a driftwood railing, open to the air.

"Well, look'ee here," said Manshack, oozing with nastiness. "Dey done brought us a snack."

"Whadja do, Hawkins," jeered Youtts with a crooked grin, "get dat nigger Mary to fry up dat possum we sent ya?"

David stood silent, keeping his anger in check. He wanted to say something smart, like reminding him that opossum was supposed to be baked, not fried. And that Youtts had surely eaten enough of it to know this. Anything to rile the boy, but that would go against his plan.

"Where's Philip?" David finally asked.

"He's up here," said Manshack. "Kyle's babysittn'm."

"Philip!" yelled David. "You aw'right?"

"Yeah," came Philip's voice from the fort. "They got me tied up."

Manshack and Youtts both grinned disgustingly.

David looked beyond the balcony, where a tree limb protruded out of the roof of the fort. Merle Pemberton was crawling out on the limb, finding himself a place to sit and watch whatever was going to happen.

"I brought y'all some fresh baked blackberry cobbler and some apple fritters," said David, "plus a jug of Mary's good 'ol sweet tea. But ya gotta let Philip go and don't hurt'm no more."

Manshack and Youtts looked at one another, their hideous smiles growing larger, spreading like the back end of a goat about to relieve himself. The cobbler alone would've been a fantastic treat. Everybody in town knew Mary made the best. But cinnamon apple fritters and a jug of Mary's sweet tea - that was almost like winning the lottery.

"Just let Philip go," said David pulling back the gingham cloth revealing some of the fritters, "an' I'll send up the basket."

Manshack turned, looking back into the fort. "Untie the mamma's boy."

A few seconds later, Philip slipped out of the bottom of the fort, climbing down the two-by-fours on the trunk. David had already tied the rope that hung down from the fort to the basket. As Youtts was pulling it up, David said, "When y'all are done eat'n, we want the fort back."

"What?" balked Youtts.

"We'll give ya the fort back when we're good'n ready," said Manshack.

David shrugged and looked at Austin and Brett, who were staring at their friend in utter confusion, while Philip dusted himself off, a little hurt but not injured.

"Since I know ya ain't gonna share none with Merle," David said, looking back up at Manshack, "there might be enough for the rest'a y'all."

"Whad'a ya mean?" asked Manshack, suddenly looking uneasy, his voice losing its usual tenor. He glanced back nervously at Merle Pemberton, who now wore the beginnings of a frown. Youtts had pulled up the basket, but was paying little attention to it after hearing David's remark about Merle.

"Well, there's only three slices'a cobbler and three fritters," said David. "Heck, remember that time Mary gave y'all them pork ribs she's gonna throw out? There was plenty'a them, an' ya didn't share none with Merle."

Now Manshack and Youtts both looked scared, pasty-faced as a couple of condemned criminals. Merle stood up on the limb, glaring at them, his expression cold and chilling.

"I think it was last May," David said, looking off in the distance, recalling the incident. "You an' Kyle an' Kenny here were walk'n past the café at close'n time. Aunt Mary called out an' asked if y'all wanted some ribs she's about to throw out. They's burnt a little an' kind'a old, but had meat on'm. Two whole racks I think it was. Some cornbread, too. 'Nough fer four or five'a y'all."

Merle, whose frown had changed to a menacing scowl, was slowly making his way back down the tree limb into the fort. Manshack and Youtts were petrified. Kyle Gill's scared face also showed itself as they listened to the testimony of young David Hawkins.

"Remember, y'all were 'round back eat'n the ribs? Then I came out with the trash an' told ya I'd seen Merle walk'n up the street look'n mighty hungry." David paused, noticing through the tree branches that Merle now stood directly behind Kyle Gill, breathing down his neck, staring at the back of the terrified boy's head. Just as a befuddled Manshack was about to speak up, David finished his story. "I'z about to holler at'm so he could have some, but you said you'd rather eat with a pig, and that Merle Pemberton could starve for all you cared. Then, y'all run off with the ribs, big ol' sack full."

A blur of activity suddenly erupted on the little balcony. Manshack, Youtts and Gill were all wrestled back into the fort, each screaming for mercy. David and his friends couldn't see what was happening, but they definitely heard it. Thumps, bangs, hollers and more screams. Somebody, and they couldn't be sure who, shrieked, "Nooooo!" at the top of his lungs, as a crescendo of thumps rattled the boards of the fort.

Merle Pemberton was about the same size as most boys his age. But pound for pound he was much stronger. He was deceptively quick and had the cagy fighting tactics of a weasel. And when angered, the word 'rattlesnake' came to mind.

Up in the tree fort there was another blur as someone suddenly flew out into the tree limbs, churning like a wild animal, and screaming to the high heavens. After a big thud Kyle Gill bounced up, bloody and bruised. He then sprinted past the other four boys like a cat, screaming like a banshee, a look of utter horror on his face.

Kenny Youtts came flying out next. He literally hit the ground running, without so much as a glance at David and his friends.

Again "Nooooo!" was heard from the fort, among other pleas for mercy. "Stop! It hurts! Pleeezzz!!" Finally, Robert Manshack's battered face poked out of the small hole in the fort's floor. "Help me!" he screamed, his eyes bulging with abject terror, before being jerked back up inside. "Nooooo!"

"Wonder what the heck he's do'n to'm," replied a snickering Philip North, causing David to mercifully intervene.

"Merle!" yelled David. The ruckus stopped after a few more thumps, moans and whimpers. Merle's face appeared over the edge of the balcony. Just below it was the face of Robert Manshack, a swollen mass of hurt held tight in a headlock. "Why don't ya let'm go? I think he's had enough."

And with that, Merle simply released the headlock, Manshack's face falling with a thud. A moment later, Manshack scurried like a frightened dog out of the hole in the bottom of the fort. After flopping to the ground, he quickly limped away, whimpering to himself as he went.

For a while it was quiet. The four boys on the ground glanced back and forth between the path of the retreating intruders and the boy up in their fort.

"Do ya mind if we come up, Merle?" David finally asked.

"It's yer tree fort, ain't it?" said Merle.

David crawled up first, and after the other three were inside, he noticed the basket of goodies still sitting undisturbed in the back corner of the little balcony.

"Well, Merle," said David, after an awkward moment of silence, pointing at the basket. "Break out the cobbler and fritters.

"But I thought you said there weren't enough," Merle bashfully replied.

David smiled. "There's plenty, Merle. I just kinda made that part up. We got us a whole cobbler there, an' a big ol' heap'a fritters. And, one big jug'a sweet tea, but no cups. So we'll all hav'ta drink after each other. Don't mind that, do ya Merle?"

At that moment, David and his friends saw their new friend, Merle Pemberton, do something they'd never seen him do before. He smiled.

XV

In the summer of 1844, cotton worms infested many of the farms north of Cross Bayou. All the way up to Caddo Lake, the small grayish worm's eggs could be found on the cottonseed pods, the tiny larvae feeding on the white fibrous bolls. Nearly two-thirds of Ira Hawkins's crop was free of any pestilence that year, as were a few other farms north of the bayou. But the parish leaders formed an ad hoc committee, voting eight to one to have all the cotton north of the bayou burned. Ira was the one committee member to vote against the burn.

"The cotton should be appraised batch by batch," refuted Ira at the meeting that was held at the Shreveport town hall in front of hundreds of local spectators, "nie by whether it's north or south of Cross Bayou. There is tons of good cotton north of the bayou, and I'm nie just referring to me own crop. Jessup Parker has a fine yield this year, with only a wee bit of infestation. Gerald Stucky has several fields that were nie touched by the damn worms. Arty Flowers was hurt pretty bad, but he still has at least ten good acres with nie a trace of the cursed things. And there's many others north of the bayou that have a good product to show at the market." He paused for a second, wiping the sweat from his forehead. "And, I say this with some hesitation, but I know for a fact that the worms have been found south of the bayou…"

At that moment Ira was cut off by chorus of loud objections from the clan of cotton kings. Actually, it was a team of hired cronies who made all the noise, troublemakers brought in from out of town. They had been paid by the local aristocracy to make sure that any word of the worms south of the bayou was shouted down. Since no large plantations existed north of the bayou, only small farms, they had no well-dressed thugs posing as cotton delegates to speak for them. But they did have Ira Hawkins, and shouting him down was no easy task. For nearly a half-hour the argument continued. But Ira was outnumbered, and not fully prepared to deal with these professional agents of deception, men he'd never even seen before, bringing up irrelevant and questionable rebuttals. He could tell by the way they glared at him from across the packed room, they knew exactly who he was.

When the meeting was finally called back to order, the chairman's gavel hammering incessantly, it was too late. The other committee members had been swayed, or possibly even bought out, paid off by a slippery unseen hand.

But deception can work both ways. Just before the burnings took place, Ira devised a plan to sneak some of the good cotton north of the bayou to the river, where it was secretly floated by night down to the market. The clandestine venture did not profit much and it took a lot of work, but it was a big moral lift for the small farmers. Ira only wished that he could have done better for his neighbors.

Not long after the cotton worm fiasco, Ira sold his small strip of land on the south side of Cross Bayou, nearly twenty acres that was little more than a playground for David, Paul and their friends. The tree fort where David rescued Philip North and won over the unwinnable Merle Pemberton was on that strip of land. It was bought by the town of Shreveport to be annexed into its limits. Times got hard for the Hawkins family and they learned to get by without some things they had grown accustomed to. But get by they did, stretching to make ends meet. Another thirty acres of land to the west was sold, and on it went, selling what used to be surplus as things got worse before they got better.

Business at the café and dry goods shop dropped off and both were eventually sold at a loss. Poor Mary cried for weeks. Next to Isaac and Jacob, that café was her life. Ira was able to keep the produce stand open, even though it didn't bring much of a profit. But it didn't cost much to operate, and Paul still gladly worked the barrels for free whenever he had the time.

One day both Rubin and Isaac came to Ira with an unusual request. The two black men approached him hesitantly, early in the morning, shortly before their work began. Even though Rubin and Ira had once been peers, servants together on the same plantation, with Ira actually being subordinate to Rubin for a time, the two seemed to have grown apart since settling in Shreveport. No jealousy, bitterness or harsh words, they just didn't talk like they used to. Isaac had never had any bad dealings with Ira. He enjoyed the hard work, and was forever grateful for having his life and family restored. The respect between them seemed to be mutual with regards to their status, but he couldn't claim to have a close friendship with the man, a situation both slaves agreed was fitting. Still, times were hard, and this made them wonder.

"We jus' wants ta ax ya," Rubin said with Isaac at his side, "if'n ya gots ta sell one or two'a us off, ya know, to pay fer things 'round heugh, we unda'stands."

"Please, Massa Ira," said Isaac looking intently at him as he spoke, his hands clasped together, "sell one'a us. Not da girls or Jacob. Keep dem ta'gedda, if ya please. We both heard tell dat da Collins Plantation, west'a here ain't too bad a place, an' it ain't too far need'r."

For a moment, Ira just stared at the two black men. Then he bursted out laughing so hard he had to lean against a tree, holding his belly. "First of all," he finally said when he caught his breath, "nie a soul would buy ya. Besides, I'd never get another lick of work out of Mary and Nancy. Dorothea would put me in the doghouse. And Sarah and Jacob, well, they'd just run off to find ya, and my boys would go with'm. Nie a thing would get done 'round here." He laughed some more as Rubin and Isaac looked at each other, a little embarrassed. Then he stood close between them, his hands on each of their shoulders. "Nie to worry, me lads. I'll sell the whole farm if I have to, and we can finally move to Texas. But you two and your families are indispensable to me now. Come on, let's get to work."

Neither Rubin nor Isaac knew what indispensable meant, but they both had a feeling it was a good thing. Early that evening, after the day's work was done, Ira broke out a batch of blackberry brandy he had made last winter. He took it to Rubin and Isaac and asked them to help finish off a bottle or two. The three men sat together in chairs under one of the oak trees, talking of their younger days. They made toast after nonsensical toast, laughing and singing songs well into the night as the ladies and the children watched from the porch, shaking their heads.

The following winter something happened that bonded the Hawkins family even closer to their family of slaves. Ira decided to make the best of the hard times and take a big hunting trip up into Arkansas. His plan was to take all the men and boys for a week up into the mountains to kill as much game as they could for the holidays. Ira figured they might even get lucky, taking enough game to last the whole winter, maybe even selling some of it at the market.

After asking Sheriff Kotch to check in on the ladies from time to time, Ira and his hunting party headed north with six horses and a wagon, loaded for bear and eager for a week of sport. They spent the first night in Eldorado, camping just outside the little town, the highlands looming off in the distance, a light flurry of snow setting the mood. As they set out, they were warned by the locals to be careful. Most of the mountain folk were friendly, but not all of them.

For three days they hunted, enjoying the chase and celebrating the kill. They took an assortment of deer, wild hogs and a black bear, and plenty of other small game; dove, turkey, squirrel and rabbit by the score. The weather kept the expedition a success, it was cold but bearable, preventing the meat from spoiling. The game was all skinned, cleaned and salted down, the men showing the boys the tricks and rituals of the outdoor trade. Steamy warm blood, smeared thick on the boys' faces, was left to dry in an opaque mask worn for the duration of the hunt.

A thin layer of snow had covered the ground since Eldorado. It had made a suitable canvas for their hunting grounds, offset by their tracks lined in rows, sprinkled and splattered with the blood of their kills. As they began the journey back, the snow increased, falling in large clumped flakes that veiled the trees in a slanted curtain of white. Rubin drove the wagon packed with salted meats and hides, barely visible now under the snow. Far off to the east, the sky suddenly cleared. The mid-morning sun gleamed brightly into the snowstorm, creating a fiery cascade of tiny mirrors floating down to the earth, reflecting the golden-silvery light.

"It looks like it's rain'n little bits'a fire, Pa," eleven-year-old Paul said, pointing up at the sky.

"The devil's beat'n his wife, son," said Ira. "But nie because she burned the supper."

"Huh?" said Paul, looking at the father.

"He caught'r play'n footsie with Abraham behind the fig tree." Everyone laughed at Ira's remark, even the boys.

They did not see the five men until they were right up on them, rounding a bend that led to a switchback. Ira said hello and the men nodded. Emotionless, they sported thick unkempt beards and were dressed in layers of homespun garb and animal hides. Rifles cradled like pets. A slow, unknown fear crept through the boys. Rubin subtly motioned for them to stay behind the wagon as Ira instinctively took the lead.

"Folks look a little lost," said one of the men.

For a second, Ira didn't respond, his hand finding the pistol tucked in his coat. "A family outing," he finally said. "Stock'n the smokehouse for the holidays, ya see."

"Well, there's a fee for hunt'n these here woods," the man said.

"Is that right?" Ira replied, cautiously watching the stranger's movements. "In that case, I'll give ya one quarter of our kill, plus the hides. That's more than fair and I'm not in the mood for haggling, mister, so let's get this done, and we'll be on our way."

"Ya talk kina funny, mister," said the man. "Where ya from?"

"Where I'm from has nie a thing to do with the matter." Ira glared at the man, cocking the pistol, carefully keeping the percussion cap in place with the tip of his finger. "Now take the offer, or clear a path. I've nie the patience for any nonsense."

"Keep ya game," the man said coldly. "We'll take that young nigger there, plus any coin ya got."

As the man said the last words he began to level his rifle. But Ira quickly pulled out the pistol and fired, hitting the man in the chest. What happened next was total confusion. More shots were fired from both groups. Rubin screamed for the boys to stay behind the wagon as he moved it into the trees to the right. Both Ira and Isaac's horses reared and fell to the ground. Jacob did his best to calm David and Paul as the three of them controlled the panicked horses. Soon the gunshots stopped and the reloading began. A barrage of curses came from the mountain men who had taken up a position behind some rocks a hundred feet down the path.

As Isaac helped Ira get behind the wagon, the boys could see that their father was shot in the shoulder. Rubin was slumped semi-conscious on the ground with a gunshot wound to the chest, stains of crimson on the fresh fallen snow around them. Isaac took charge, both tending to Ira and Rubin, and steadying the boys. His and Ira's horses were dead, so he quickly had David and Paul move the other four horses back into the woods to keep them from being shot. He then ordered Jacob to fire at the mountain men.

"Ya wants me to choot at'm, Pa?" asked Jacob, holding his

rifle with trembling hands, fear in his eyes.

"Dat's right, son," said Isaac, trying to remain calm. "Choot at'm. Try'n hit'm if'n ya can."

For a half hour, gunfire was exchanged across the path at the bend as the snow continued to fall. Ira was hurt bad and Rubin was hurt worse, both going in and out of consciousness. David and Paul were huddled around them, tears in their eyes as they reloaded for Isaac and Jacob.

"I got's an idea," Isaac said during a lull in the gunfire. They were running low on ammunition, so he told David and Paul to stay behind the wagon with their father and Rubin, firing one round every minute. He and Jacob would skirt back and to the left, cutting through the woods on the opposite side of the path. They would then veer to the right, hoping to come up behind the mountain men.

It took another half-hour for Isaac and Jacob to get in position. David and Paul were so low on ammunition, they'd reduced their fire to one shot every five minutes. The man Ira shot was obviously dead. A trail of blood was still visible beneath the new fallen snow from where the others had dragged him to the rocks. One man had been shot in the hip, the whole left side of his waist soaked in blood as he reloaded the rifles of his cohorts from a sitting position against a tree.

Isaac leaned in close to Jacob, his face only inches away, and said, "We ain't jus' choot'n at'm now, son. We go'n choot'm."

It was over with very fast. Isaac shouted and shot one of the men as he turned. Jacob then shot another man as he raised his rifle. Isaac pointed Ira's pistol at the other two and they immediately dropped their rifles and surrendered.

The man Jacob shot died where he lay, but the man Isaac shot lived. Over half the game was left behind to make room in the wagon for Ira and Rubin. The three mountain men were forced to ride their horses with their hands tied in front of them. The man that Isaac shot kept falling off his horse, and eventually he was put in the wagon. He kept complaining loudly, until finally David cracked him in the head with his rifle butt, knocking him unconscious. Later, when he came to, he started complaining again and this time Ira saw something in his son he'd never seen before, something that made him feel both proud and fearful.

"One more sound outta you," David snarled, grabbing the man by his hair, holding the blade of his knife to the man's face, "and I'll cut your damn tongue out!"

"David," said Ira, his voice very weak. When David looked at him, Ira slowly shook his head. "No, son."

Paul kept at a slow pace driving the wagon, tears streaming down his face as he talked to Rubin and his father. Isaac and Jacob rode ahead with their guns on the other two mountain men. David rode behind the wagon alert for more trouble. Paul was the first to know that Rubin was gone, calling out his name over and over. David tied his horse to the wagon, jumping on to take the reins as his brother crawled in back to lay and cry against his old friend Rubin, where he stayed until they reached Eldorado late that night.

Fortunately the doctor in Eldorado was a seasoned surgeon, an Army veteran of some obscure Indian war. He was able to easily extract the mini-ball from Ira's shoulder, patching it up nice and clean before working on the two mountain highwaymen. The next day they returned home with Rubin's body. It was an awful homecoming with Nancy and Sarah shrieking and wailing, Mary and Dorothea doing their best to comfort them.

A deep sadness fell over the Hawkins homestead, a visitation of grief and mourning. Rubin was buried at the far end of the first cotton field by a small clump of trees, a spot that would become hallowed ground for all the Hawkins family, both black and white. For the next month Nancy spent most of her time there talking to him. Ira's shoulder recovered slowly, but he was up and around in just a few days.

Two months later, the painful return trip was made to Eldorado for the trial of the three men. Ira, David and Paul's testimonies were necessary for the prosecution. Isaac's and Jacob's word could not of their own convict a white man, not even ones of such ill repute. The men were quickly found guilty and sentenced to life for the attempted murders of Ira and his two sons, not for the murder of Rubin, which was looked on as a mere property crime. The Hawkins family then did their best to put the men out of their thoughts as they made the quiet trip home to Shreveport.

Over the next few years young David and Paul went through the process of becoming young men. The events up in Arkansas had left indelible marks on their characters. Though they both still possessed their affable, good-natured traits, there was now a notable seriousness in their manner and they very rarely spoke of the ill-fated hunting trip.

For a long time, Ira blamed himself for the tragedy, often wishing out loud that they had hunted closer to home. At times he was quiet, going for long walks along the river in the early evening. Sometimes he would take Dorothea with him and they would stroll the trails their sons had made, holding hands among the cypress trees like teenagers. Gradually Ira came out of his melancholy, and he always did what he could to give Nancy and Sarah relief from their loss.

Jacob finally proposed to Sarah and they were married under the two oaks that stood beside the Hawkins home. They jumped the broom like their parents had, then danced around the trees. Everyone danced that evening, a happy occasion that lifted the spirits of the whole family.

By the time the United States was at war with Mexico, the Hawkins farm began to prosper again, and Ira decided to build himself a new home. The large two-story house was built at an offsetting angle to Ira's first home, which he then gave to Jacob and Sarah. Nancy lived with her daughter and son-in-law, and Isaac and Mary moved into Rubin's old house, while Isaac's house was converted into a set of stables. More livestock was purchased as the place took on the look of a more permanent homestead.

Twice David tried to run off and join the Army, wanting to go and fight in the war down in Mexico. American troops had passed through Shreveport on their way to the disputed border regions and David had been seduced by the pageantry of war. The first time, Ira simply grabbed him hard by his shirt, jerking him until his eyes bulged wide, telling him in a loud voice that he was not going. But David kept reading the papers, learning of places like Palo Alto, Monterrey and Vera Cruz. Ten months later he tried again. This time he got into a prolonged shouting match with his father until his mother intervened.

"David," she said softly, with her arms down at her side, "you don't need to go down there. It's just a bunch of nonsense."

What his parents did not know was that their son was fighting his own personal battle with the first girl of his dreams. Ever since he was eight, David Hawkins had had a terrible crush on a blue-eyed girl with curly blond hair named Kathy Mathis. Over and over, he tried getting her attention in all the silly ways that boys do. Showing off, doing silly tricks, wearing a spiffy shirt or combing his hair a new way. Nothing ever seemed to work. At best, she would give him a look like she thought he was a complete fool, but usually she didn't even seem to notice him. Until one day, not long after Rubin was killed, David told her how pretty she looked in a new dress she was wearing. And that seemed to do the trick. Before long, they were holding hands behind the row of red oleanders in town by the river, and it was there that she let him steal his first kiss.

Kathy's father had a small farm about a mile up the bayou on the south side. David would cross over on a small rowboat and they would meet at a special spot to kiss, pet and cuddle. The first time she rejected him sexually caused the frustration that led to his first attempt at running off to join the Army. And when he told her of his second attempt to leave, she finally saw the disappointment in his eyes. When he looked off to the west, something enchanting and shimmering in those eyes stirred her. Reaching out, she turned his face back to her, finally giving herself to him, ravishing one another and taking each other's virginity with fear and amazement.

As time went by, Kathy made it very clear to David that she was ready to settle down and start a family. But David hesitated. He'd been reading in the papers about the vast lands obtained by the war with Mexico. For a couple of weeks he grew distant from Kathy. Then another suitor stepped in and took his place. After a brief courtship, the son of a wealthy cotton broker proposed to Kathy and she accepted. When David found out, he struggled to hide his bitterness, turning his attention to the unexplored West.

When he was a young boy, his country's border was less than a half-hour's ride away. Now it stretched over two thousand miles, across unexplored mountains and plains, all the way to the Pacific Ocean. The day after he learned of Kathy's marriage, David Hawkins went to enlist in the Army.

This time when Ira found out, he did not even try to stop his son, and his mother simply looked off out a window, slowly nodding when he told her.

"If it's what ya want, son," she said, then turned to put her arms around him. "But you better come back and see me." She then held him at arm's length, studying her son for a moment. "And take care of that horse your father got you."

All of David's friends had moved on with their lives and settled down. Philip and Brett were both married and working their family businesses. Even Merle had himself a steady girl and a job working for Philip at Red River Shipping. Austin was married and working as a deputy for the aging Sheriff Kotch. Before he left, David went to each of his friends to say farewell, wishing them the best after reminiscing on their not-too-distant childhood. His family saw him off that day and he rode into town alone. He then traveled to Fort Worth with a group of men to begin training.

The weeks and months went by as the constant steady grind of farm work continued for the Hawkins family. Occasionally the different farms and plantations would bring their crops in all at the same time, flooding the market, driving down the prices. Ever the minimalist, Ira would wait it out, affording himself a better deal. Other times, he would have to sell his crop to one of the large plantations to get the best deal. But he never groveled, always standing tall before the kings of cotton.

David wrote long and often, telling his family of his new soldier's life. He tried to hide the disappointment of those first nine months, but they could tell he was not happy, all the constant marching and drilling, being yelled at for the pettiest infraction. And his beloved horse Kaffy had gone lame and had to be put down. But then one day a letter arrived stating that David had a new horse and had been transferred to a cavalry unit. Now his letters took on a more grand light. They moved with a quickness that told of a new pace set for his life.

During his brief furlough home, eighteen months after he'd left, David noticed his mother looked a little peaked. Things seemed heavier than usual for her, and she had to sit often to rest. But his father and brother were getting along fine without him, stirring a twinge of the bittersweet. Jacob and Sarah now had their own little baby, a girl they named Ruth. His short visit was pleasant, but they could all tell he was eager to get back with his unit. His new horse, a dark, overbearing stallion called Tempest, seemed out of place on the small farm. And when he left the second time, he was sent off with a little less sentiment. The never-ending obligations of farm life beckoning.

In those years it was really Paul who made the Hawkins farm. Even though he wasn't a big man like his father and brother, he was incredibly strong and sinewy with an endless reserve of energy, always getting by on very little rest. His organizational skills were so deft that Ira simply stood aside, letting his son take over without a bit of worry. He read books on how the large industrial businesses operated, applying and modifying some of the methods to his own knowledge and experience. He also pried bits of wisdom from his father, Isaac and even Jacob. He developed strategies that were specific to the different areas of the farm, and thought up formulas and plans of action for any problems that might arise. Soon the farm was running even more efficiently, turning an even higher profit.

One day Ira and Dorothea were in town shopping for

fabric at Edmonds General Store. Dorothea had been speaking with some of her lady friends when she turned back to her husband who was looking at a new stock of leather goods. Her hands were shaking and she had a strange, blank expression on her face.

"Oh dear, Ira," she said, reaching out to him. "Don't let me fall."

He caught her in time, just as she collapsed, and laid her gently on the floor as her whole body trembled. She was taken to the doctor's office down the street where she lay coming in and out of consciousness, unable to speak. At one point she seemed to smile, reaching out to touch Ira's face as he sat at her bedside kissing her other hand. Then her eyes fluttered, her hand dropping to the bed as Ira began to cry, knowing that she was gone.

Dorothea was buried about twenty feet off to the side of Rubin. Just behind them, flanked by an entourage of little pines, was a small clump of young trees, a black oak, a soft maple and a magnolia. It was where she and Ira had their first picnic together at the new homestead. Just the two of them, taking a break from building the first cabin, watching from a distance as Sarah looked after David and Paul.

It took David eight days of hard riding to make the long trek from Santa Fe to Shreveport, over a thousand miles of dangerous rugged terrain. He was now an officer, a single gold bar on each shoulder, a five-year veteran of more than a dozen expeditions throughout the southwest and lower plains. His youthful features still remained, but they had been hardened somewhat, sharpened, as if by the wind and sun. His long, curly red hair was highlighted in nuances of gold that matched his rank. His bearded face was tanned a dark reddish-brown like his muscled forearms. And his sad, fearless eyes openly revealed his innermost sorrows.

Second Lieutenant David Hawkins immediately put in for a transfer to be near home and was quickly approved. He was assigned to Fort Turnbull, south of town at the bluffs along the Red River. His off-duty time was spent helping out at the farm, amazed at how well Paul had the place running. He was now able to tell them in person what it was like out West instead of describing it in a letter. Many nights were spent with Ira, David and Paul sitting around the fireplace talking like old war buddies. There were also moments of silence after speaking of Dorothea. These moments would linger briefly, then they would smile and laugh together, recalling how she sang to herself in the kitchen every morning, the old jaunty Irish tunes from her childhood. Or how outwardly she acted as if she did not like the stray cats that Sarah sometimes kept around. But secretly everyone knew she adored the little creatures, feeding them when she thought no one was looking.

"Remember that one little gray cat with white socks and a funny tail? She'd always act like she didn't know it was there, but it followed her everywhere she went."

One afternoon David came in from the fort and asked to use the buggy. He said that he had a special picnic planned with a young lady he had met in town. That weekend he brought her to the farm to meet the family. Emily Rains was her name and she fit right in, as if she'd always been there, adding a special light to the place that would shine long after she was gone.

Paul had been seeing a girl named Alice Dalton and there was talk of marriage, with tentative plans for some time next year. David could not understand his brother's reluctance, he wasn't typically restless and Alice was a lovely young lady with a pleasant, outgoing personality. But he soon found out from his father there had been a little drama around the farm since he had been gone. Not long after David's last visit, three and a half years ago, Paul started seeing Gwen Pierce. Her best friend at the time was Alice, who was then promised to Michael Flowers, a good friend of Paul's. Ira didn't know all the details, he simply told David what Dorothea had told him. At some point Gwen secretly started seeing Michael and Alice secretly started seeing Paul. Eventually the two triangles of infidelity were found out and a long series of melodramas unfolded. There were rumors of a catfight between the two girls. One night Paul came home with a black eye, scraped knuckles, utterly flustered and unwilling to speak of the matter. More than once, Ira saw Michael in town with similar marks on his face, averting his eyes in embarrassment. Things had settled down since then, but Paul and Michael rarely spoke to one another. Alice and Gwen seemed totally estranged, as the two couples had switched out their affections.

"He still sees Gwen," Ira said to David, slowly shaking his head. "An' I'm sure Alice still sees Michael."

"Little too sophisticated for me," replied David.

David and Emily were married in the spring of '54 at the First Methodist Church, followed by a brief honeymoon. David booked them an overnight, first-class riverboat ride down to Alexandria and back. After a wonderful dinner at the captain's table, a band played and they danced on the veranda until the wee hours of the night.

Ira decided it was time for a larger barn to be built. The one they had was too small and had been damaged by a fire the previous fall. Within two weeks the structure began taking on its full shape, posts and beams set, rafters in place over forty feet high. David had taken the buckboard into town with Emily to get more lumber, nails and other materials. Paul was inspecting the joists and rafters, making his way along the top side beam, when he noticed one of the two-by-fours that supported the rafters at the apex had come loose.

It had been unseasonably hot that spring, even for Louisiana, feeling more like June. This caused the summer insects to stir sooner than usual. As Paul shimmied up the rafter to reach the unfastened board, straddled awkwardly across the rough-cut timber, he heard a distinct buzzing hum in his left ear. Adjusting his vision, he saw a nest of red wasps the size of his fist attached to the rafter, only inches from his face. It crawled with the demon-like creatures. The formidable hive suddenly swarmed upon him in a cluster of sharp, excruciating stings. He screamed as they attacked his face and hands. Forgetting where he was, he lost his balance, his bearings scattered, not realizing he was falling until it was too late.

"Oh, no!" Ira gasped, looking up from his work just as

Paul landed hard on a stack of lumber, his head violently snapping downward.

David and Emily returned with the supplies moments later finding a dreadful scene. Ira, Jacob and Isaac were carrying Paul's body toward them. He was taken into town to the doctor, but nothing could be done. Death had paid another visit to the Hawkins family, sitting down to dinner like an unwelcome guest.

Had it not been for Emily, the Hawkins home might have remained a sullen place. Her very presence was a tonic for Ira's recurring melancholy, and she comforted David while he dealt with his own anguish. She also grew very close to the slaves, becoming especially fond of the women and baby Ruth. She kept herself busy taking care of her husband and father-in-law, always smiling but never seeming fake or pretentious. And when David was called again out West, she handled it better than most, taking on the extra chores in her usual selfless manner.

When David returned a year later she leaped into his arms showering him with kisses, and the two decided it was time to have a child. Emily soon began showing signs of pregnancy, her monthly flow was two months late and she was having morning sickness. But sadly, a month later she miscarried. For three days Emily wept with David constantly at her side. Then she simply put her grief away, put back on her beautiful smiling face and got back to the tasks of living.

Not long after Noah was born, David was sent out West again, this time to Colorado. It was sunset and David was playing cards in the barracks with some of his men when a courier arrived with a message from the telegraph office fifteen miles away in Telluride. John Brown and his sons had led a group of over twenty anti-slavery men, attempting to take over the town of Harper's Ferry, Virginia. Brown had expected the local blacks to join him in his revolution to end slavery, but none of them did. Word came the next day that the insurrection had already been put down by U.S. Marines commanded by a Colonel Robert E. Lee. Already there was uneasiness in David's outfit, the inception of a rift that would grow deeper than any of them could imagine.

While David was gone Mary had taken ill and passed away. On her deathbed she had asked to have a moment alone with Nancy. They had known each other for over twenty years and become quite close, like sisters.

"You take good care'a my Isaac, Nancy girl." Mary had said holding as tightly as she could to her friend's hand.

"Is it aw'right if he take care'a me some too?" asked Nancy.

Mary smiled. "He like a lot'a butta'n honey in his grits."

Ira's heart had grown weak over the past few years, so David put in for another posting closer to home. He was soon assigned to an engineer battalion that was building a series of roads and bridges through the Broken Bow Cherokee Reservation in the southeast corner of Indian Territory. He would spend the week helping run a surveying crew, plotting layouts for excavation, then return to the farm on the weekends.

By late that summer the presidential election campaign was in full swing. Ira was sitting on the porch reading the newspaper, getting a dose of the southern angle on the pivotal campaign. He suddenly felt numbness in his left hand that quickly spread down his arm, followed by a sharp pain in his chest. He tried to breathe but the pain instantly multiplied as if his heart were caught in a brier of sharp thorns. The paper fell meaninglessly to the boards as he tried to call out for Emily. Soon she was there, kneeling beside him, holding his hand, and calling his name while she caressed his forehead. Momentarily his thoughts began to spin and it seemed his memories were suddenly chased backwards down the river, racing far across the ocean to his old home as a boy.

Two months later Lincoln was elected president, setting off a firestorm of rhetoric throughout the Deep South. By Christmas, South Carolina had officially seceded from the Union, taking the lead by calling the United States a failed experiment, and by February the South had its own president.

For a brief time David Hawkins was a civilian again, having resigned his commission in the U.S. Army and not yet joined the Confederacy. Two short, carefree months that were the happiest of his life.

"David," Emily's voice would sing as he stood on the porch deep in thought. He'd turn to see her running playfully toward the levee with a blanket under her arm, looking back over her shoulder, her hair dancing across her face. Suddenly everything else could wait. "Race ya to the tree!"

XVI

Ever since he was a little boy, David Hawkins had a strong affinity for horses. His earliest memories had been of riding on a horse named Piney in the French Quarter, straddled in front of his father, his little hands clasped tight into the animal's long, rough mane. There had also been a chestnut named Blocker and a sorrel named Paco. As a young child, Hawkins grew very calm and comfortable in the presence of the animals. He would talk to them in their stables, asking them how their days had been and how the food tasted as they nibbled it from the palm of his hand. Piney had been his father's casual riding horse and Blocker his mother's. Both were big, strong and gentle, being used for plowing and pulling loads. Paco was a bit smaller and sometimes skittish, but he was fast and always Ira's choice, when he was in a hurry.

Years later came Rooty, Mitten, Juno and young David's first personal horse, a dust brown mustang named Kaffy. He loved the animal and spent hours and hours with it each day. Kaffy had Paco's speed and Piney's good-natured personality. It was Kaffy that David had been riding on the ill-fated hunting trip to Arkansas, and Piney and Rooty that had been killed by the nasty mountain men. Old Piney was replaced by Ursa, and

Rooty by Hugger. Twice Kaffy was saddled up to take David off and fight in the war down in Mexico. And it was finally the old faithful mustang that took him to Texas when he first joined the Army. Ira had bought the yearling pony when a herd of horses had been brought into Shreveport from way out West. So it was only fitting that the aging steed met his end in the land where he had been born wild and free. After stepping into a prairie dog hole, Kaffy had to be put down by a shamelessly weeping Private David Hawkins.

Hawkins was still in the infantry at that time, and Kaffy had been kept mostly in a large corral until a courier was needed or Hawkins was given leave. Now without a horse and low on cash, life seemed odd constantly on foot. While watching some men break in a bunch of wild horses, he noticed a magnificent dark brown stallion that was throwing everyone to the dirt, almost at will. Hawkins stepped up and asked to try his hand. To the men's surprise, he stayed on for well over ten seconds before being thrown by the violently lurching, twisting and turning animal. Now it was personal. For over an hour he kept at it, helping lasso the unruly beast before getting it set to mount again and again. Finally the horse broke into a gallop and Hawkins knew he had tamed the animal. As he walked back to the barracks, exhausted and dirty, he was approached by a lieutenant colonel he had never seen before.

"How would ya like to have that horse as your very own, soldier?"

"Sir," said Hawkins after snapping to attention. "The private would do anything the colonel asked to possess such a fine animal, sir."

"Stand at ease, son. I'm Lieutenant Colonel Fletcher Riggins and that was an outstanding display of horsemanship. If you can shoot half as good as you ride, I'd like to have you transferred into my battalion, the 327th U.S. Cavalry. That horse you just broke comes with the deal."

"I shoot even better that I ride, sir," Hawkins said with a slight grin.

"Outstanding," said Riggins. "Outstanding."

He named the horse Tempest and a few days later was transferred to the cavalry and began nine months of advanced training. Many of the exercises he participated in were long rides through South Central Texas to the Gulf Coast, and observation patrols along the vast Mexican border. Hawkins had an endless thirst for adventure and with Tempest, he quickly earned a reputation as an intrepid trailblazer, always at the head of the pack, seeking out the challenges that most men shunned.

After his training was complete, he rode Tempest home to visit his family and see his mother for the last time. They marveled over his pretty blue uniform, his new horse and stories of travel. Old Blocker had passed on by then and Paco was out to pasture, his speed gone, but still just as skittish as ever. Mitten had given birth to Nitney. And Juno, Ursa and Hugger were still plugging along.

After his furlough, the 327th was ordered to New Mexico Territory where Tempest carried Hawkins to the source of the river that ran through his home. It flowed out of a rugged stretch of the Southern Rockies, burnt reddish-orange cliffs surrounded by plush poplars, sagebrush and eucalyptus trees. Along the base of those cliffs that gave color and name to the river, Hawkins had his first violent encounter with Native Americans. A patrol of 20 men riding separate from the battalion had stopped to rest and water their horses at stream running near the ridge of a plateau. Without warning, a rockslide crashed down, taking out half the men and horses. Suddenly a swarm of over forty Apaches rushed from the cover of the trees. Hawkins grabbed Tempest by his ear and bridle twisting his head until the animal lay down behind a large boulder to avoid the flying arrows and spears. He then blasted away with his new six-shooter. With no time to reload he snatched up the weapons of his crushed and fallen comrades, firing until they were empty, then finding another and another.

Hawkins would not recall it until a decade later, but there had been Someone beside him that day, a Man he did not recognize. He knew every man in his troop, but this Man had looked strange to him. The Man had been out of uniform, wearing a white blouse and white billowy pants. He had handed Hawkins a pistol, then another and another, as the crazed Apaches rushed their position behind the boulder. At one point Hawkins looked at the Man and saw that He was pulling the pistols out of the sand. He handed one to Hawkins, then He handed a pistol to another trooper and another.

Finally, seven wounded men made it out of the ambush on three wounded horses, racing as fast as they could back the way they had come. With arrows protruding from his rump, Tempest had carried Hawkins and two other men to safety. One of them was a young Sergeant Grady Hackwith, draped over the saddle horn hanging on for dear life with two good arms.

Looking back over his shoulder, Hawkins had seen the Man standing on a ridge near their boulder. His arms were out wide and the Apaches were swarming on Him. But the Man did not go down. White light shone around Him and the Indians could not touch Him.

After making their way back to the battalion, a large detachment was sent to the battle site, easily found because of the circling buzzards. Strewn over the blood-splattered dirt and rocks were thirteen dead, mutilated soldiers and over thirty dead Indians. Most of the dead horses had been butchered, their leg quarters cut off and carted away for food. Hawkins had been wounded in the back and shoulder, and was sent to a base camp with the others to recuperate. Meanwhile, Riggins sought out the renegade Indians. Two days later word got back to the base camp that a small settlement of Navajo had been found. Though they offered no resistance and had nothing to do with the attack on the U.S. patrol, they were wiped out, massacred to the last man, woman and child. That night Hawkins got very drunk, cursing the starlit sky.

After a while he fell silent. He thought he heard a voice whisper something. He looked around but there was no one, just the cactus, sagebrush, sand and the night. Then he heard the voice again; clearly it whispered, "I gave you guns from the sand. Why do you curse Me?"

For a long while afterwards, Hawkins just stood there looking up at the sky, wondering if he were going mad.

Tempest was a tough horse and his wounds healed quickly, the wicked-looking scars on his butt adding character to the animal's fast-growing notoriety. For the next three years he carried Hawkins through the southwest territories that would later become Colorado, Utah, Nevada and Arizona. They escorted pioneers across the mountains. Rescued settlers from floods, blizzards and avalanches. Protected shipments of gold and other valuables. Hunted down outlaws and checked Indian raids with swift retribution.

Once Hawkins and his troop were tracking a band of desperados across Southern California's high desert, flanked left and right by silhouetted Joshua trees. He was walking in front of Tempest, looking carefully at the ground. Suddenly he heard what sounded like a train, yet they were a hundred miles from any form of civilization. The earth shook violently, throwing the men and horses to the ground. Then, as suddenly as it started, it stopped. Hawkins looked at Tempest who was still lying on his side, his head up looking intently at his master like some bizarre sand-sea monster.

"What's a matter!?" screamed Hawkins, jumping to his feet and wildly waving his arms. "Ya never felt'a earthquake before!?"

After a moment's hesitation, the horse lurched up and shook himself off as if nothing had happened. The men they were tracking were eventually caught and hung at Bakersfield.

Not long after Hawkins was made an officer, he received word of his mother's death. He was given immediate leave, making an incredible cross-country trek, yet still missed the funeral by over a week. Not long after his transfer to Fort Turnbull, he met Emily and occasionally let her ride Tempest. With the exception of the men Tempest had quickly thrown the day Hawkins tamed him, and the two who'd been saved from the Apache attack, Emily was the only other person to ride the horse in its long well-traveled life. In many of the ups and downs of Hawkins' life, Tempest had been there like a steady and unyielding keeper. Hawkins often told his friends that he did not have the horse, but that the horse had him.

When Hawkins resigned his commission in the days before the war, he bought the animal with his own money, as the horse was officially U.S. property. And it was that bloody afternoon at Shiloh that Tempest was struck dead in a blinding drift of peach blossom petals, lying lifeless on Hawkins's broken leg. And as Adam McRay pulled his commander free, the bodies of men dropping by the thousands, Hawkins allowed himself one final backward glance at his beloved charger.

He had seen horses die before, but never slaughtered like they'd been at Shiloh. A team of fine animals running at a full gallop, then suddenly tripping over their entrails spilling from their bellies, laid open by pieces of hot flying iron. Horses with broken backs, up on their front legs trying to run, going around in circles, heads thrown back screaming like terrified children. Fountains of blood spewing from their mouths as they lurched and reared, slamming their bodies to the ground with horrifying thuds. Legless horses still alive, blown in half by cannon balls. Horses killing horses. And the screaming, the crying, the awful sounds that they made. A slaughter of the crying thunder dogs.

For a month and a half Hawkins had no horse. He had been transported in a packed ambulance wagon to Birmingham, Alabama, where he convalesced until the bone was healed. His leg had atrophied somewhat and walking was painful. But in early June his new outfit moved on to Virginia and he was soon assigned another mount, a creamy pale he called Dancer. Though not as fast as Kaffy or Tempest, Dancer was a larger, well-seasoned horse of almost draft size. He had already carried three men to their deaths and was Hawkins's first fully trained warhorse. Dancer was surprisingly graceful and utterly calm under fire. Though a beautiful animal, he bore the ugly scars of combat. His left ear was nicked in half down the center, the outer portion flopping like the tip of a dirty rag.

Saber slashes and gouges crisscrossed and marked his body. And just below the nose, his upper lip was split causing the animal to spill large bits of his feed. Dancer carried Hawkins through all the battles of the Seven Days and Second Manassas, savage engagements that brought the western style of fighting to the East, where it stayed till the war's end. While supporting A.P. Hill's late charge at Sharpsburg, Maryland, Dancer received several bullet wounds. One actually passed through the fleshy part of Hawkins's left calf before entering the horse's abdomen. As the Confederate's leg was being cauterized with a red-hot branding iron, Dancer slumped to the ground and died. Hawkins was back in the saddle in less than two weeks

Paige, a painted brown-on-white, was Hawkins's next horse. For eight months he rode Paige in skirmish after skirmish with the Union Cavalry. At Fredericksburg he had stood holding his horse's reins off to the side of the great southern generals. He'd watched in disbelief as the Yankees were slaughtered in countless waves of suicidal charges against the well-protected Confederates, hunkered down on a sunken road behind a stone wall. The following spring Hawkins' outfit was helping Jeb Stuart control the roads outside of Chancellorsville, nullifying Union intelligence there. This allowed Lee to split his smaller army in half, sending Stonewall Jackson's corps on a clever flanking maneuver around Hooker's army, arguably the Confederate high-water mark.

Hawkins was at an impromptu parlay, conferring with the regiment's top brass in a thick second-growth wooded area called Wilderness. Suddenly a badly-wounded courier was seen approaching from the Union encampment. After collapsing from his horse, the young lieutenant grinned at the score of officers that had gathered in a tight circle around him, blood flowing from his mouth.

"Where the devil did you come from, son?" asked a general, as two lieutenants tended to the courier, doing their best to make his last moments comfortable. The wound was obviously quite grave.

"Rode rat threw dat Yankee camp, sir," said the young man, who might have been twenty. "Should'a seen da looks ond'r faces. They's all shit'n an' gett'n, like a bunch'a cats at a dawg fight. Knocked me over a big'ol kettle'a stew, I did. Spilt it rat'n da dirt, yessir." He laughed, then began to choke and cough, reaching into his breast pocket, looking suddenly less flippant. "Bastards shot me in da back, but I still made it through. Dis here's a dispatch from Marse Robert. Wants it delivered, in hand to Stonewall."

The general quickly read the bloodstained paper, then turned and handed it to a colonel at his side. "Have your best man deliver this to General Jackson. Marse Robert urgently wants him to attack as soon as possible." The general then pulled out a flask and handed it to the dying courier. "Have yourself some good French cognac, son."

The colonel glanced around until his eyes found Hawkins. "David, Stonewall's men are due west'a here. Get this to'm, immediately."

It took Hawkins and Paige half-an-hour of hard, rough riding through the thick tangled maze of trees and brush to accomplish their mission. At one point he came upon an excellent view of the enemy's lines, taking note that they stretched just north of a turnpike. A mile further he finally reached the outer fringe of Stonewall's left flank, the many staggered formations plodding relentlessly through the gnarled forest. He was stopped twice and questioned, both times having to shout at the nervous pickets holding him up.

"I have an' urgent message from General Lee to General Jackson, you sons'a bitches, now let me through!"

Finally, within sight of the great general, he was confronted by an uppity lieutenant colonel that couldn't have been older than thirty.

"General Lee himself gave you this?" asked the staff lackey, looking over the dispatch with flaunted derision.

"No, sir," replied Hawkins, livid with exhaustion and impatience. "It was relayed to me from a courier about three miles east of here."

"And how do you know he wasn't a spy, Captain?" the young lieutenant colonel said with a contemptuous smile.

"Because!" screamed Hawkins, "He was shot in the back riding through the enemy's lines, you jackass!"

"Let'm through!" Jackson's voice roared through the trees.

Hawkins snatched the dispatch from the man's hand and approached the general on horseback. He saluted and handed Stonewall the letter, while giving a brief but candid explanation how he got it.

"Sir, there's something else you should know," said Hawkins. "If you continue on this course, you'll meet the enemy head-on, not on their flank. However, General, if you adjust your columns to the northeast for about a mile, then have it spread out and move south, you'll catch'm flush on their right flank."

"Double time the ranks!" bellowed Stonewall after reading the dispatch, tilting his head back to get the full effect of his cry. Without even looking at Hawkins, and not so much as a word of thanks, the general turned to the uppity lieutenant-colonel and said, "Have the men veer to the northeast until I give the order to cut back south."

As the order was repeated, echoing through the woods, the long line of Stonewall's corps perceptively lurched from a moderate trudge to a rapid steady gait, rising above and beyond, as only Stonewall's corps could. In unison, the columns angled quickly to the left through the almost impenetrable terrain. Endless rows of butternut-gray, conflicted with the spring landscape, waging something like war on the flora even before the battle began.

As Stonewall's men charged from the Wilderness, Paige was shot out from under Hawkins. Dazed and blurry, he found himself staggering through the thicket, his carbine in hand, saddlebags slung over his shoulder. Smoke rolled at him through the trees, the roar of battle off in the distance.

To his right he suddenly saw something that made him wonder if he'd been killed. A large wooden cross with a Man nailed to it loomed just twenty feet away. Blood rolled down the cross to the ground, dripping from its horizontal beam. Hawkins could smell the blood, the coppery scent reacting with his faculties. He could see the Man's face clearly, a prominent crown of thorns on His head. Was this the same Man who had handed him pistols from the sand? The Man gazed at Hawkins with sad yet powerful eyes, then turned His head toward the sounds of battle. The index finger of His tightly spiked left hand twitched, then, with herculean effort, pointed. Hawkins turned, and at that moment a large brilliant red stallion with a wild black mane emerged from the smoke that had enveloped the trees. Again he began to wonder if he were dead, this striking creature a guide to his afterlife. Shades of Brown Grass and the Halkom lingered in his thoughts. He watched the captivating animal as it trotted in a figure eight, like storybook movements of Greek and Roman mythology, tossing its head, the black mane dancing with a life its own.

Hawkins turned back to his right, but the cross and the Man nailed to it were gone. But the dominant coppery smell of blood remained. His attention was quickly turned back to the horse. He softly called out to it, whispering, talking to it with seductive inflections, even singing to it in soothing tones. He held out his hand, gently stroking the air, mimicking, as if to touch the lovely beast, slowly luring him in, enchanting the enchanter.

Eventually, the remarkable sorrel let Hawkins approach, its saddle askew, as if its former rider had been violently knocked off. He quickly fixed the saddle and hopped on the majestic creature, riding off to join back in the fight.

"Easy, boy!" shouted Hawkins as the horse bolted through the trees, weaving and churning its body with delirious fury. "My, but you're a wild one!"

Hawkins ripped through the enemy's lines like a child at play, feeling as if he'd found a new and secret weapon. When he found out Stonewall had been badly wounded, accidently shot by his own men, Hawkins decided to name the horse Jackson. From the moment he first saw him, there was something special about the horse that moved Hawkins. And the more time he spent with Jackson, the more impressed he was with his abilities. Not only was he the fastest, strongest horse Hawkins had ever ridden, but he had a striking beauty of another world. Jackson was as big as Dancer and had the speed of Paco or Kaffy. He had the tough, relentless fury of Tempest and the tireless endurance of Paige. Hawkins felt a connection with the animal, as if their souls had suddenly remembered being ripped apart ages ago, finally rejoined there in the Wilderness.

"Ya don't give a horse 'at looks 'at purdy an' fights 'at good a name like Jackson," said Jenkins the day after Chancellorsville. "Ya ought'a call'm Lucifer"

"Careful, Steve," replied Hawkins as he tended to Jackson. "He understands everything you say."

A few weeks later, Hawkins rode Jackson in a huge parade near the Rappahannock River. Over nine thousand mounted Confederates galloped past General Lee's reviewing stand, sabers glistening in the morning sun as cannons roared a martial salute. Hawkins had felt uneasy about the parade. It had seemed premature to him, an undeserving sense of glamour.

Massed on the opposite riverbank were over ten thousand Union troopers, hidden by a dense fog. After splitting their forces in half, the Yankee cavalry forced crossings east and west of Jeb Stuart's Fleetwood Heights headquarters. After checking one attack the Confederates were stunned to find another Union charge coming at them from the other direction.

The fighting lasted all that day. Jackson mesmerized the Yankees, moving through their ranks like a ghost, Hawkins slashing away with his saber, firing his pistol at all angles. By nightfall, the Southerners still held their ground, repelling the enemy attack. But for the first time in the war, Union cavalry showed cunning zeal and determination, matching their Rebel counterparts, a foreshadowing of the road to Gettysburg.

Back through Maryland they coursed, meeting the Yankees at every turn. They moved deep into Pennsylvania, where they first heard a new name for the history books: *Custer*. But even in the horrible defeat at Gettysburg, being thrashed again and again by a Union cavalry now come of age, Hawkins and Jackson stood out to the blue-coated riders, a gray-on-black-on-red blur of havoc slicing through their ranks. A spoiler, giving them the cold steel and hot lead, screaming the Rebel yell like none they'd ever heard before, then vanishing into the trees only to reemerge elsewhere, taking aim, always at the heart. Many times Hawkins would notice the Yankees bunching into tight groups, pointing his way, ganging together to end their frenzied spree. Jackson would lead them on a chase, and then suddenly turn and loop back on them slicing through their center, letting the blood fall where it may.

By Christmas of '63, it was brought to General Jeb Stuart's attention that four men in his division were all that was left of a battalion that had been purged at Shiloh. He asked to see the men. As Hawkins, Steven Jenkins and two others stood before the once flamboyant general, he showed the telling signs of frustration, fatigue and defeat.

"When was the last time ya heard from yer families?" Stuart asked.

"Been a while, sir," said Hawkins, looking to his men. "Not since early summer, when the Yankees took the river." The other three nodded in unison. "Nothing's get'n across, I guess."

"Well," said Stuart as he looked thoughtfully at the four men. "Do ya think y'all could get across that river if I gave ya a furlough home?"

Home. The word seemed to drip through the air like honey, a sweetness that flowed through him, affecting his balance and vision. He turned again to his men, seeing shameless expressions of longing, tears pooling in their eyes. He looked down for a moment, fighting his own emotions, then turned back to the general.

"Sir, we'll swim that river if we have to."

"At's right, General," said Jenkins, gesturing suddenly with vivid animation. "Our horses'll just ride right in 'at river, tote'n us 'cross da water like a ferry boat, while we's hang'n on tight to da saddle horn."

"I'll have your travel papers ready tomorrow," said the general, offering a faint smile.

After reminiscing on the better days, Stuart pulled out a bottle of whiskey and the five men toasted their fallen comrades in silence.

From Pennsylvania through Virginia all the way back to Louisiana, Hawkins could not wait to introduce Jackson to Emily. He knew she would love him, and not just his beauty and strength. The one thing that stood out more and more to Hawkins was the animal's intelligence. Jackson was the smartest horse he had ever known.

The day after he returned from taking Johnny the cap, Jacob told Hawkins something that had happened while he had been bedridden with fever. A small flock of crows had perched in the trees that surrounded the Hawkins family plot. One of them actually landed on Emily's headstone. At that moment Jackson let out a loud violent neigh, a prolonged angry cry that echoed across the farm, stopping the slaves in their work, causing them all to look up toward the corral. Even Sarah looked out from the window of Hawkins's room as she tended to him. Without so much as a running head start, the horse leaped up and out of its enclosure. Then it sprinted across the field stirring the ominous birds in a circling, cawing swarm that swooped back diving on the enraged charger as it reared, boxing the air with its front hooves. From their various locations around the farm, all six of the Hawkins slaves, including the children, stood captivated by the sight. A surreal conflict of equine-avian wrath over a small plot of sacred ground. Suddenly, like a prizefighter landing a lucky punch, a crow that had become snarled in Jackson's mane was struck hard by the horse's flailing front legs. The crow was knocked to the ground where it was then stomped repeatedly into a flopping quivering mass of glossy black feathers.

"Dat's some mean horse ya got dair, Massa David," Jacob had said. "Kilt dat ol 'crow 'bout near a dozen times."

And now, as Jackson paced swiftly around the corral, propelled by the simple nimble flicks of his lower legs, his master came out to greet him. The lovely beast snorted and tossed his head, nodding hello. The black luxurious mane spilled out, alive, dancing over the rippled muscles of his dark reddish-orange body, its hues changing with the obliquity of the sunlight. Eyes glistening like those of an artist, full of verve and wonder. Like something not a horse, but Achilles reborn. A killing deity, scary legend and myth.

"Hey there, my friend," said Hawkins, playfully putting his arms around Jackson's neck, cloaked in the stygian mane. "Wanna go'n chase some Yankees? Huh, let's go'n chase some Yankees."

XVII

Taylor's army marched north out of Hinestown, a quarter-mile-long column of Confederates moved with a steady swaying gait. That morning word had come that the Union expedition, nearly five times their size, was moving into Alexandria, just thirty miles to the east. They all wanted to stay and fight, hating the idea of leaving anything to the enemy. It wasn't the first time Alexandria had been taken by the Yankees. The town had been briefly occupied during the spring of '63. Once again the Confederates were vastly outnumbered, and now they must find a more suitable place to make a stand. There was already talk of small cavalry skirmishes along the different river roads, a trickle of wounded here and there.

But they had faith in their commander and did not complain, offering encouraging words to one another. They told stories of Shenandoah to those who had not been there, stories of Stonewall and the heady days of victory and spoils. A time of fire-eaters and firebrands, revolvers and rebels. A time when defeat and despair were as foreign to them as wings on a pig. When ink flowed from the press giving pageantry and glamour to the blood they invoked. Mere show, now replaced by loss, death and attrition.

If Smith had sent the reinforcements Taylor had asked for, a stand could have been made at the rapids south of the town, forcing Banks to maneuver west, exactly as Taylor wanted. Porter's navy could be held in place at the river by one well-placed regiment, while the Union Army was lured into the woods and back roads to be picked apart and surrounded. A separation of the enemy's forces, isolating and wearing them down bit by bit, then sieging them into submission, could very likely pull northern troops away from Vicksburg and Natchez. This would set up the possibility of retaking those crucial points on the Mississippi River, allowing the Eastern and Western Confederacies to reconnect, putting yet another snag in the Union works. But Edmund Kirby Smith sent no reinforcements, and for the second time Alexandria was abandoned to the Yankees.

By mid-March all of Northwest Louisiana knew of the coming invasion. Volunteers were still arriving daily as Shreveport took on the appearance of a city at war. Every road leading into the town and its surrounding regions was obstructed with a series of well-guarded check points, scrutinizing all traffic moving in and out of the area. Fort Turnbull had turned over its small battery of cannons to be taken south to engage the enemy. Telegraph poles had been cut into quarters and painted black with tar, then placed where the cannons had been. Later that day, the fort's commander inquired about the poles. When told of the hoped for subterfuge as seen from the river below, he simply replied, "Humbug."

As his two patrols gathered on Commerce Street, their backs to the river, Hawkins rode up and down their ranks, nodding and speaking briefly with the men. Jackson moved with ease, as if able to defy gravity. Some of the men Hawkins had known since childhood, old playmates not seen or heard from in a decade or more. Most were acquaintances from some time in his life, individuals he had come across here and there as a boy or a young man. A few were strangers, newcomers to the area having settled in during one of his many absences. Altogether, over two hundred men, lean and strong, with the stern, hardened look of a warrior class, mounted on a choice stock of gamey horses. A plucky team of Southwestern chivalry.

When Hawkins got to the end of the column he saw a face he hadn't seen since well before the war. Even on a horse he could tell his old childhood friend hadn't grown much in height over the years. And even with a thick bushy beard there was no mistaking the long, wild black hair, and the thick rock-hard forearms of Merle Pemberton.

Over the years Hawkins had run into Brett Edmonds many times and on each occasion he looked to have gained at least twenty pounds. He was now a fat, jolly father of seven, still running the most profitable retail business in town. Austin Wilhyte had been sheriff of Caddo Parish since five years before the war. He was commander of a volunteer unit that would defend the city limits if the Yankees got that far. Philip North's father passed away, leaving his son a small fortune. Shortly before the war began, he left the country to manage a sugarcane plantation he had purchased down in Honduras. Hawkins hadn't heard much about Merle lately, except that he still lived in a boat on the river south of town, and that he'd had an on-again-off-again relationship with the same girl for over fifteen years.

"Howdy, David," said Merle in his usual awkward manner, sporting a mischievous coon-like grin.

"Merle." Hawkins offered his hand and pleasant smile. "What in the world have you been up to?"

"Been haul'n loads now an' again, back'n forth from Dallas." He leaned forward on his saddle horn, looking down at the ground. "Molly done kicked me out again, so I'm try'n to set things right by help'n wup these Yankees."

Hawkins smiled and slowly shook his head. "You remember Steven Jenkins, don't ya, Merle?"

"Sure, I know Steve. Talked to'm just a minute ago."

"I want you to stay real close to'm. Do whatever he says, aw'right?"

"Sure thing, David."

Hawkins nodded and was about to ride off when he turned back to his friend. "They pay'n ya anything for this, Merle?"

"Nope," said Merle, adjusting his hat. "But if dem Yankees get within fifty miles'a Shreveport an' we stop'm, I get ten acres somewheres here in da parish. I got my sights on'a little piece'a land up around Mooringsport. I think Molly'd like dat."

"She's gonna love it, Merle," said Hawkins. "You just do your thing."

Hawkins's first patrol was made up of just over a hundred men. It would be led by Captain Keith Novak, an able young officer who came highly recommended by Colonel Gastonel. Novak, who was just twenty-five, had been born and raised in Texas and had come to fight in Louisiana during Grant's Vicksburg Campaign. Tall and slim with a baby face and blond hair, he did not have the appearance of a cavalry officer. But once he opened his mouth all that changed. He had the deep clear voice of a leader, could holler out the rebel yell, shout orders and call cadence as good as any Hawkins had ever met. And when the two shook hands, he offered an iron grip and a serious unflinching look in his eyes.

"What part'a Texas ya from, Captain?" asked Hawkins.

"San Antonio," replied Novak. "Had a few kinfolk got killed at the Alamo, an' my pa fought for Sam Houston. Still got us two-thousand acers'a land down 'air. Nice an' pretty, an' we aim to keep it 'at way."

"Yeah," said Hawkins. "Let's get to it."

Jenkins, who now wore a gold second lieutenant's bar on each shoulder, would lead the second patrol. Though he was new as a commissioned officer, Jenkins was by no means a stranger to delegated authority. Over the past two-and-a-half years he had seen to the needs and responsibilities of hundreds of men, on countless occasions in some of the direst situations imaginable. All this, while still maintaining his fun-loving, good-ol' boy personality.

They moved south out of town at a slow trot, past Fort Turnbull, paralleling the river. Hawkins ordered Novak's patrol west to Forbing, then to split his men into four equal troops, familiarizing themselves with every path, trail and road they could find. He told them to make their way to Natchitoches, looping back southeast, all the while splitting up and regrouping, paying quick calls to every community and homestead along the way. Hawkins then ordered Jenkins to do the same with his patrol, scouring the area inside Novak's loop to the west bank of the Red River. The two patrols split, leaving coppery dust trails corkscrewing into the air at offsetting angles. Not only would this etch the topography into their memories, it was excellent practice for the days to come, allowing time for the men to become better acquainted with each other's bents and habits.

Hawkins accompanied Jenkins's patrol. By noon they reached Natchitoches and found a small group of wounded Confederates from one of the earlier patrols resting at the river's edge. A dozen battered and bandaged men sat in the shade of two large cypress trees as they were tended to by the local town's people.

"We was surprised early yesterday evening by what we thought was a bunch'a Union infantry, but turned out to be a battalion of enemy cavalry," a young sergeant told Hawkins, his head and arms wrapped in bloody rags. "Chew'd us up pretty bad, sir."

"Where?" asked Hawkins.

"Just south'a Crump's Corner, futher west'a here."

"How big'a cavalry?"

"Close to a thousand of'm. We saw a bunch'a Yankees on foot stand'n near a thick line'a trees. We knew they saw us, but we's just gonna watch'm for a bit. Their horses was hid in dem trees, an' we didn't even 'spect it. Next thing we knew, a whole heap'a blue bellies was come'n at us on horseback. Mean, nasty bastards they was."

"Yeah, I'll bet," said Hawkins looking off to the southwest. "Where's Colonel Gastonel?"

"Haven't seen'm since an hour or so before sundown yesterday, not long after we got chopped up. He ordered us to fall back here'n wait," the young sergeant let out a long sigh, kicking his boot at the dirt. "We wasn't 'spect'n that many of'm this far north yet, sir."

About that time Novak's patrol arrived, riding in from the west with more bad news. "All of Gastonel's patrols have been engaged in heavy skirmishing since yesterday, Major," said the young captain, his boyish features now taking on a more sinister animation. "And the colonel himself has been badly wounded, but refuses to relinquish command until he's spoken to you personally."

"You've seen him? Where is he?" asked Hawkins.

"No, sir," replied Novak. "We've been com'n across bits an' pieces of the first patrols that left Shreveport on Wednesday. All of'm pretty banged up, like these guys here. Gastonel and what's left of his men have teamed up with some mounted detachments of Taylor's division. They're about twenty miles to the southwest 'a here."

"Aw'right, listen good!" Hawkins said to Jenkins and Novak, speaking in a loud deliberate tone so that all could hear. "Let's keep it kind'a tight from here on. Keep the different troops separate but in eyeshot. Captain Novak, if we encounter the enemy, I want your patrol to immediately loop out and attack from our right, just like the ride to Natchitoches. Me an' Steve here'll take the rest'a the boys an' hit'm head on."

As they moved southwest out of Natchitoches, more remnants of the first patrols were found, dazed and down-cast by the side of the road. Within an hour Hawkins's lead scout brought news of a group of riders, over a hundred strong, claiming to be volunteers from Texas and Indian Territory. The volunteers had by-passed Shreveport riding south by southeast from Waskom at the Texas line. Hawkins wanted to meet the men, sending back his scout to arrange a quick parlay up the road.

"There's 'bout four, maybe five hun'erd of'm, sir," said the leader of the rag-tag bunch, who was obviously a full-blooded

Indian, but spoke with a white Southern accent. His eyes were wide with excitement as he pointed back down the road. He was surrounded by a band of men who looked to be an assortment of outlaws and trouble-makers dressed in all types of get-ups and trappings, armed to the teeth with pistols, rifles, swords and knives. "Yankee cavalry. Come'n up the road 'bout four miles due west'a here."

"What's your name?" asked Hawkins, pointing at the man.

"I'm Toby Whitefox from Broken Bow in da territory and these are my men, the Kodabacks. We don't like Yankees much and we can damn sure prove it."

"Yeah, I'll bet you can," said Hawkins, continuing to point. "You used to peddle whiskey on the reservation up there, and steal horses and wagons from the Army."

Whitefox's face went blank, then flashed a crooked grin. "That's right, I sure did. The U. S. Army," he added, sitting up straight in his saddle. "An' how would you know that?"

"Long story," replied Hawkins.

"Well, if it matters any," said Whitefox holding up his right hand as if he were taking an oath. "I'm a Christian man now. I work for God."

"Amen to that, Toby Whitefox," Hawkins said, looking around, examining the terrain. "You say them Yankees are headed this way, up this road right here?"

"Seen me a few turn-offs and bends back 'air," Whitefox said, looking over his shoulder. "But they very well could be come'n up dis here road any minute, Major."

"Toby Whitefox," Hawkins said turning to Jenkins. "This here's Steven Jenkins, my lieutenant. I think you'll like'm. I want you to take a handful of your men and ride up an' show'm where these Yankees are. Steve, take Merle and a few others. Y'all ride up the road a ways with Mister Whitefox here, then cut off into the woods. See if you can find them Yankees without them see'n ya. If it looks like they're come'n this way, get on back here. We'll be wait'n for'm. If they go another way, turn off or something, ya'll split up. Steve, you follow'm. Whitefox, you come back here an' let us know."

"Don't like Yankees much myself, Mister Whitefox," Jenkins said to the Indian as they headed out. "They'll spoil a damn good barbecue if ya let'm."

"Keith," said Hawkins to Novak, "get your men over in them trees. I'll take the rest and these volunteers over to that small clearing by the tree line. Anyone come'n up this road won't see us till they're right up on us. Wait for my lead, and then come hard and loud. Got it?"

"Got it, Major," said Novak, spurring his horse to move his men in position.

"Got some Yankee cavalry head'n this way, boys!" shouted Hawkins to the band of volunteers, standing high in his stirrups. "So fall in with us, but don't bunch up too tight! When ya hear me holler, scream like the devil, an' give'm hell!"

It took Jenkins and Whitefox just ten minutes to find the Union cavalry patrol. They spotted them from a thicket a quarter mile across a sparsely wooded meadow that led up to the road. The blue line of riders was four abreast and over a hundred yards long, rumbling to the north with the Stars and Stripes flowing at their point.

"Yeah," said Jenkins, "'at's 'em. Whad'a ya think Merle?"

"I think we ought'a put a dose'a wup-ass on'm," Merle casually replied, peering at the Yankees from the cover of the trees.

"I like the way he thinks," said Whitefox with a nod.

"Yeah, me too," said Jenkins, turning his horse. "Come on. Let's get on back an' get ready."

Hawkins guessed that he now had about 300 men, about two-thirds the size of the Union force he was about to attack, according to Jenkins's report. "They look fresh an' spunky, but I don't think they're ready for us."

In this war Hawkins had learned that Southern troops often had a slight advantage when it came to surprise attack. Not only did their uniforms, or lack thereof, tend to blend more with the landscape, but they were usually on the defensive, turning the tables by deciding to fight on familiar grounds of their choosing. A narrow sloped clearing, that extended about two-hundred yards along the road, would soon become a field of battle. Hidden in the trees at the back of the clearing, was Novak's company. Waiting in the trees past the sloped clearing, was Hawkins's other company and the volunteers.

The Union patrol was halfway past the clearing when Hawkins gave the signal, a loud banshee squall that ripped through the air like a weapon itself. They spewed from the trees, each imitating their commander's war cry, creating an atmospheric salvo that preceded their charge. Wild looks of surprise were seen on the Yankees' faces as Hawkins's men crashed into the front of their column at a sharp ten-o-clock angle. Suddenly halting their movement, the Union troopers buckled onto themselves. Then Novak's men slammed straight into the column's side, jarring their numbers off the road into the trees, forcing them to fight on unsuitable ground not of their choosing.

It was moments like this that caused Hawkins to truly ponder his eternal fate, moments when he seemed utterly removed from his better half. There was little time to think during battle. All one really did was feel and react. Fear, anger, rage and horror were the companions of the moment. But later, when the chaos had ebbed back into the still life of routine, the two-faced messenger of thought would come, the Janus of his conscience. He would look back in meditation, able to see the chaos more clearly, knowing he'd been touched by special angels of a sacred canon. Marked by powers that wrenched space and time, permitting concessions to that other half, allowing the moments when he slashed carnival-like, channeled by pure malevolent grandeur. Besides God, there was only one other soul he spoke of this with - Jackson, his accomplice, stomping with bloody hooves the men that fell, ramming his head into them, even biting to jerk them free of their mounts. Better to kill them.

For nearly ten minutes the Union soldiers held, fighting tenaciously, using their superior numbers to crowd and maul their attackers. Many had dismounted or were knocked from their horses to regroup on foot and fire with carbines and pistols. But now their numbers were no longer superior, and the skirmish had changed from a close-quarter brawl to a precision shooting match. Soon the Yankees began to fall back the way they had come. Dozens of them were running on foot, their horses dead or run off. They fired back in desperation, stumbling over their comrades. The Rebels eased off and started tending to their own wounded, men from both sides crawling, bleeding on the ground.

The Union troops stopped down the road after the firing had ceased, waving a white flag of truce, wanting to gather their dead and wounded. Hawkins shouted for his men to hold their fire, allowing a moment of humane solidarity, a spectral stage where not a word was spoken. Federals and Confederates came within feet of each other to help and take up their own, looking briefly into one another's eyes. Looking for some note of contrast save their uniforms, they found only naked similarity.

"Wonder what they'll call this one?" Jenkins said to Hawkins as the Union troopers rode away.

Hawkins looked around again at the terrain, at the sparse dead and wounded still in his charge. "This place gotta name?" he asked without looking at his lieutenant.

"Not that I know of," replied Jenkins. "Don't even know what road this is."

"Well, then," said Hawkins turning back to his horse, "they probably won't call it anything."

For over a week Hawkins's two patrols worked with other patrols and volunteers to keep the roads around Natchitoches clear of Union cavalry. They focused most of their efforts south of town. But as the days passed the Yankee patrols grew larger and closer, blazing their own trails through the woods, occasionally surprising the Rebels. Finally, two weeks after leaving Shreveport, Gastonel's dirty, ragged bunch of Confederates was found moving into Natchitoches from the south along the river. The colonel was lying in an ambulance wagon being escorted by his men when Hawkins rode up alongside. His right leg, hip and shoulder were dressed in clean bandages, and he looked obviously weak and pale, the pain showing in his pensive eyes.

"Taylor's men are just south of here," said Gastonel as he lay on his back, his voice barely audible. "Banks is taking his time. Probably waiting on the rains and making sure he has the roads. The man outnumbers us nearly four to one and still he seeks an advantage. A lot of Union cavalry has been spotted southwest of here, David. Have you been able to deal with them?"

"Yes, Colonel," said Hawkins. "So far, we're keeping them about ten miles to the southwest by using a connection of different roads and trails the men have grown familiar with. But just yesterday we spotted a large body of infantry less than fifteen miles southwest of here."

"Infantry?" said Gastonel, somewhat surprised, a weak smile showing on his face. "Away from the river?"

"Yes, sir. We've been getting a good deal of help from these volunteers. Every day they ride down from Shreveport in groups of ten, twenty or more. They don't have much in the way of training, but they're tough and always ready to fight."

"Has General Smith sent any men from Shreveport?"

"None, sir. Not yet."

"Bastard," said Gastonel. "What's he waiting for? With just one more division, Taylor could crush Banks and this campaign of his would be over with."

"I sometimes wonder about Smith," said Hawkins.

"The patrols are all yours now, David." Gastonel extended his hand to Hawkins. "Play your cards right and when this is over, I'll see that you make lieutenant colonel. Get you a nice, cushy job at headquarters."

"Thanks, Colonel," said Hawkins, tightly grasping the wounded man's hand. "But I'll just stick to playing my cards right. Don't think I'd fit in much at headquarters." Hawkins looked back down the road, noticing the lead elements of Taylor's army. "Will Taylor make a stand here at Natchitoches?"

"No," said Gastonel. "He'll turn west, away from the river. And Banks will follow."

Hawkins looked off to the west. Less than twenty miles away was Pleasant Hill.

Admiral David Porter stood with his arms crossed on the bow of the Cricket, one his lead gunboats. The Eastport, his largest vessel was still stuck on the rocks near Alexandria. His thick beard did little to hide the bitter frown on his face, his eyes scanning the sky as a slight drizzling rain began. It wasn't enough; he wanted a downpour. The temperature was also dropping, a late spring chill blowing down from the northwest. He had opposed the expedition ever since Henry Halleck, who at that time was Union-General-in-Chief, told him of it six months earlier. Grant was now the top general and had recently sent word to Banks to proceed with the capture of Shreveport as soon as possible. Banks's men were now moving west away from the river, planning to turn north and attack Shreveport directly from the south.

Porter had thought that Mobile should be taken first, or the invasion of the Texas Gulf Coast. But this Red River Expedition was absurd, the river itself being nearly as much a threat as the Confederates. His only consolation thus far was the huge quantity of cotton being taken by his men as they combed the river valley. Cotton speculators had been brought along from New Orleans, corporate yes-men sent to put a price tag on the expedition, and so far the numbers were growing.

Two days earlier Porter had met with Sidney Brooks, giving the New York reporter from a short interview. Brooks was preparing to go ashore and follow along with Banks's men, when he saw the admiral on deck and approached the commander.

"Did you enjoy the ride, Mister Brooks?" asked Porter.

"It was very interesting, thank you," said Brooks. "Tell me, Admiral. When and where do you think the Confederates will ultimately make a stand against this campaign?"

"Hard to say," Porter replied with a shrug. "To be honest, I'm surprised we haven't encountered more resistance."

"I've noticed most of the ranking officers are of the opinion that Taylor will finally stand and fight just south of Shreveport at Fort Turnbull, I believe it's called. However, I have met a few that think an engagement will occur elsewhere. Any thoughts on this, Admiral?"

"Richard Taylor's a crafty devil," said Porter. "He'll do what he can to keep Banks away from Shreveport. I've no doubt that he's got something tricky planned. But if the rains come early, I'll get there first."

Brooks nodded, then asked, "What about Natchitoches? Will Taylor make his stand there?"

"I don't think so, but we'll see."

The two men chatted a little while longer, Porter sharing some of his knowledge of New York City, Brooks giving some of the grim details of the riots there last summer. Brooks then boarded a rowboat and was taken to a pier on the west bank, leaving the admiral to his dreary river work.

With many boats still catching on unseen sandbars, Porter's fleet crawled at a snail's pace, precariously negotiating the shallow river. Meanwhile, the Union flotilla was still being harassed by Confederate snipers, back-water sharpshooters and ornery Louisiana locals just itching to take a shot at a boat full of Yankees.

For nearly three weeks heavy cavalry skirmishing had become a daily ritual on the roads of Central Louisiana, two or three bloody engagements a day. By the time Gastonel was transported to hospital in Shreveport, Hawkins and his men had ridden into Pleasant Hill from the south, wet, filthy and utterly exhausted. The small town now had a number of men nearly twenty times its size camped within its limits, and thousands more spread through the woods to the south and southeast. Platoons, companies, battalions and regiments of Confederates bivouacked across the landscape, scattered in teams of gray, camped within the trees.

As he approached the schoolhouse, Amy Bolton stepped out on the porch, the same spot he'd last seen her a month earlier. Although she looked tired and weary, her beauty still showed through the subtle hints of her character. When she saw him her shoulders dropped as she heaved a sigh of relief. He dismounted and slowly walked Jackson over to the railing and stood there looking up at her, offering a weak, but genuine smile.

"I meant to write, but...." His words trailed off.

"You did write," she said. "Remember?"

"Oh, yeah. I forgot." He slumped against Jackson as the horse folded his head around Hawkins in a partial embrace.

"I think your horse is jealous of me," she said, running her hand along the rail.

"No, actually," said Hawkins, "he thinks you're jealous of him."

She laughed, gently tossing her head back, causing her hair to bounce in waves against her shoulders, a sound of wind chimes playing in his ears.

"What does a guy have to do to get a hot bath around here?"

"If all you want is a hot bath, the livery will accommodate you."

"And if I want more than a hot bath."

"I'll heat the water."

They walked together through the crowd of soldiers to her small house on the opposite edge of town. After Jackson was rubbed down, washed and rubbed down again, Hawkins let the horse graze free in Amy Bolton's fenced-in front yard. There was little room elsewhere for the animal and when he asked, she simply shrugged and pointed to her little yard. For the last few weeks Johnny had been spending most of his time at Randy's or Robert's house and Amy rarely saw him except at school, and even there they seldom spoke. She finally got the whole story about what happened at Hawkins's farm the weekend Johnny went to visit with his friends, the bitterness that had been left out of his letter. Though painfully disappointed in her cousin, she was not completely shocked by his actions. Losing both parents at such a young age had taken a toll on the boy, and his misunderstanding of Hawkins's personal views aggravated the situation even further.

After tending to Jackson, Hawkins went inside. When he entered the house he saw Amy had a large, high-back tub of hot water prepared. As she undressed him she saw the stitched up wound on his shoulder, its threads now coming loose from the stale, scabbed over scar. When she asked, he simply shook his head not wanting to speak of the matter. She sat in a chair washing him from behind, letting her arms drape over his shoulders, mindful of the wound. Gently rubbing his chest and arms, she brushed the hair from his eyes, caressing her cheek to his. Like before, they talked very little, falling into an instinctive, rhythmic flow with one another. After she was done she dried him and put him in bed, then undressed herself and got in to hold him. At first they just lay there holding and cuddling each other. Then she began to softly whisper to him, and their movements became slow and fluid, filling the empty spaces caused by the world outside.

Afterwards they lay facing each other, running their fingers through one another's hair, kissing and smiling, sparing them something better when other worlds came.

"My horse is going to eat those flowers you have growing by the side of your porch."

"I know. It can be his reward for bringing you back to me."

"In that case, he deserves a garland of bouquets."

She laughed and kissed him.

He smiled and looked at her for a long time, not saying anything. Studying the contours of her face, seeing the subtle likeness to Emily, he now felt a strong bond to Amy. He knew that their time could be short, and he did not want her memories of him to be transient.

"Marry me," he finally said. "Right now. Today."

Now it was her turn to just look at him, her lovely eyes searching his face, not for anything in particular, just looking for the enjoyment of it, just to have the moment. Her fingers ran across his beard. She put her face close to his, gently caressing her cheek against his beard. It felt soft to her, and she loved it. She kissed him again, a long, lingering kiss, loving the softness of it.

"Yeah," she said, sweetly, after pulling back, nodding. "Let's get married."

They quickly got dressed and went to Amy's pastor, a tall slender man who smiled easily and wore a pair of round spectacles. Although he thought it quite irregular, he agreed to marry them and a few witnesses were rounded up. A couple of Amy's friends stopped what they were doing and came. Steven Jenkins and Merle Pemberton made a showing. Amy sent for Johnny, but he could not be found. They both knew he would not come, unless it was to start trouble. But still they felt they should at least try and let him know that he'd been invited.

A short impromptu wedding was held in the small chapel. Vows were exchanged as they both looked awkward but very happy. Hawkins wore his uniform, which was still dirty. Amy wore a white dress, barrowed from a friend. Two rings were found, a couple of keepsakes from someone's old jewelry box. Neither seemed to care about the formalities; they just wanted to be married and have the sweet permission to kiss in front of spectators.

A little rice was thrown and a few congratulations given. Then they went back to Amy's little house and got back in bed.

School and most other businesses in the town had been suspended due to the conflict. For the next three days he stayed with her, a time not unlike his best days with Emily. She fed and waited on him, almost constantly at his side, therapeutically rebuilding his strength. They never spoke of the terrible possibility to come, and that last night together was the sweetest for the both of them. But that next morning activity stirred and he awoke, reluctantly leaving her for the wretched call to arms.

XVIII

The four boys wanted to enlist, having discussed it amongst themselves for some time now. Ever since Taylor's army had arrived, streaming into the town from the south, they had talked of it, talked of signing up and receiving their issued gear, joining up with the Rebels and fighting for their home. If only they were a little older, just a year or two. Maybe then they could pass for men instead of boys. How they wanted to dress in the gray uniforms, marching about with rifles and stern looks on their faces, jocular and carefree with those in their common units, but aloof and harsh to those who were not.

"Maybe we could jus' walk up an' ax one'a'm," said Randy as they watched a group of soldiers camped at the far end of the schoolhouse clearing. It was a spot where they had played countless times over the years, a staging ground for their many excursions deep into the woods to fish and hunt or just walk and explore. It was the ground Hawkins and Johnny had walked on the day they first met, watching as the hawk took the hare up into the pecan tree.

"Na, dat's not how ya does it," said Bobby. "Ya got's to ack kind'a like ya don't' wanna be in wit'm. Din, dey'll wan'cha in wit'm. If'n ya acks too much like ya wanna be in wit'm, dey won't wan'cha in wit'm."

"Why, dat don't make no sense, Bobby," said Robert. "We's too young anyways. Dey sure ain't gonna want us none if'n we ack like we don't wanna be wit'm."

One of the soldiers had been watching the boys as he sat with his platoon, watching the boys talk about the soldiers. For some time they had been standing off by the trees, gazing in his direction, talking back and forth among themselves. Except for one of them who stood off to the side; he wore a Rebel cap and didn't seem to be involved in the other three boys' conversation. Finally, the soldier motioned for the boy in the Rebel cap to come to him.

"What's yer name, boy?"

"Johnny."

"Where'd ya get dat cap, Johnny?" asked the soldier. "An' don't lie to me none."

"It was my pa's."

"Yer pa? Well, where's he at?"

"He's dead." When Johnny said this, several of the other soldiers turned and took notice. "Got kilt in da war."

"Yer pa got kilt, where?"

"Up at Shiloh. Few years back."

The soldiers looked at one another, swapping glances of doubt and suspicion.

"If your pa was at Shiloh," asked another soldier, "how'd ya get 'is cap?"

"Man dat was wit'm brung it to me," said Johnny, taking off the cap. "See. Dat dair's 'is blood."

"Well, Johnny," said the soldier after glancing at the other men. "My name's Emery, an' we're awful sorry 'bout yer pa."

"Das aw'right, Emery," Johnny said, putting the cap back on his head. "I kind'a gotten used to it now."

"Say, Johnny," said Emery, licking his lips and wiping them with his hand. "Me an' my friends here, well, we's kind'a hope'n ta get us some good'ol fire water. If ya get my mean'n."

"Ya mean moonshine?"

"Yeah," said the other soldier, leaning forward. "A little moonshine'd do da trick."

"Ya know where it is, don't ya Johnny?"

Johnny looked across the clearing at the trail that led to Ebarb's farm. "Yeah," he said, looking back at Emery. "I know where's it is."

Throughout most of the South, Confederate money wasn't worth the paper it was printed on. However, in regions that so far had been spared the ravages of war, it still had some value. Some, but not much. The soldiers gave Johnny what they had and told him to get as much moonshine as he could.

"How da ya know Ol'Man Ebarb's got'm self a still, Johnny?" asked Robert as the four boys headed up the trail.

"I thought everyone knew dat," shrugged Johnny, leading the way. "Shoot, whenever Pa use to take me hunt'n 'n fish'n, da first thing'eed do was pay a quick visit ta Ol'Man Ebarb."

"Heck," said Bobby. "My pa's been buy'n shine from Ol'Man Ebarb since 'fore I's born."

"Y'all wait here," Johnny said when they got to the edge of Ebarb's property. "I'm go'n ax'm."

"Aw, Johnny, can't we come wit'ya?" whined Bobby.

"Heck, no. If all'a us go up 'air, Ol'Man Ebarb'll think we's gonna drink it. I ain't even sure'ees gonna sell it ta me."

This time, as Johnny approached the house and the dogs began to bark, Ebarb stuck his head out the window by the door.

"Zat you, Johnny?" Ebarb said, squinting in the sun.

"Yesser, Mister Ebarb, it's me. How are ya?"

"Mighty fine, Johnny. Say, heard from dat Hawkins fella ya told me 'bout. Sent word to'm ta jus' keep ol' Gray Stump. He probably likes it better there anyway, an' forty U.S. dollars is one heck'ova deal. Get me a young mule an' a couple'a milk cows with a little change ta spare. Heck'ova deal indeed."

"Oh good," said Johnny. "But dats not why I come ta see ya, Mister Ebarb."

"Well, what'cha need, Johnny?"

"Wanna buy some moonshine from ya. Got forty dollars, but dis time it's Confedertate."

"Ya wanna buy some moonshine!?" shouted Ebarb. "Good Lord, son! Ya wanna get me put'n stocks!? Can't give ya no shine! Shine's fer grown ups!"

"Ain't fer me, Mister Ebarb. It's fer some'a dem soldiers dat's camped over by town. Dey's da ones dat gimme da forty dollars Confederate." Johnny stepped to the window and handed Ebarb the money. "Dey's jus' some good ol' Rebels wanna drink fer dey gotta fight dem Yankees."

"Well," said Ebarb, looking at the money. "Dis here's not worth a dime a dollar, but ya gotta gimme yer word ya ain't gonna drink none, not even a nip."

"Lord no, Mister Ebarb," Johnny said, crossing his heart and holding up his hand. "Pa gimme a sip once after I begged'm fer it. Made me sick as a dawg."

Ebarb glared at Johnny a moment then disappeared from the window. After a few minutes the door opened and the old man stood there with two half-gallon jugs in his hands.

"Don't normally take Secesh money. Purdy soon, won't be good fer nut'n but wipe'n. Ya tell dem soldier boys dis here's da best shine west'a da Miss'ippi an' south'a da mountains."

On the way back Bobby kept asking Johnny for a sip, but he refused, holding the two jugs close to his chest. Finally, about halfway back down the trail Johnny gave in, handing one of the jugs to Bobby.

"Jus' one sip, an' ya best not get sick."

Bobby asked Randy and Robert if they wanted to join him. They said nothing, just shook their heads side to side staring at the jug. Bobby then took a mouthful and swallowed it. At first his eyes closed tight and he made an ugly face, squishing his cheeks against his nose. His lips then spread, grotesquely furrowing his features like a sufferer clown at the circus. Then, he made a deep keening moan as his eyes and mouth opened wide. With a strangled gasp, he looked at each of his friends as if he were about to plead for help, but was unable to speak.

"Ya aw'right, Bobby?" asked Robert.

"Yeah," he said as the word was cut off by another gasp followed by a whimper. "Think so." He stood there looking at his friends through red watery eyes. Then he slowly turned to his right holding the jug out with his left hand. Just as Johnny took back the moonshine a long stream of vomit spewed from Bobby's mouth. Doubled over, gasping, he stammered, "G-gosh, I…uhm…." His words were cut off as he threw up again, hands on his knees, puking all over his boots.

"What's dat ya said dair, Bobby?" asked Randy. "Didn't catch dat las' part."

"Shut up," was all he could say between dry heaves.

The boys were trying hard not to laugh at their friend. As soon as he straightened himself up and turned back to them with a sour look on his face, they saw he was all right. First Johnny, then Randy and Robert began to laugh so hard they fell to the ground in stitches, tears flowing as they rolled in the leaves and pine straw. Bobby sat on the ground propped against the base of a tree, his legs bent, hands on his knees, looking back down the trail with his mouth hanging open. At that moment he saw Emery and three other soldiers walking toward them packed with all their gear.

"See, I knew dey came down dis here trail," said Emery. "Johnny, ya got us our moonshine?"

"Oh, yeah," Johnny jumped to his feet, handing Emery the two jugs of liquor. "Sorry, but I let my friend Bobby here take a swig an'ee throw'd up." Johnny giggled. "We's laugh'n at'm."

"Good stuff, huh, Bobby?" said Emery, handing one jug to his friends while taking out the cork from his own. "Here ya go, Seth. Let's play pin da tail on da elephant." The two soldiers clinked their jugs together before taking an ample swallow apiece, then made their own whiskey faces. "Ooooweee doggy! If he ain't a frisky fella!"

"Ya rat 'bout dat!!" roared Seth, passing the jug to the next man. "Dis here'll curl ya hair, put a twinkle in ya eye and give ya happy feet!"

"Ya didn't think I's gonna run off wit ya money, did ya?" asked Johnny.

"Heck, no," said Emery. "We's move'n out. General Taylor's ordered us to fall back to Mansfield."

"What fer?"

"Yankees is headed dis way, 'bout ten miles down da road."

"Can we come wit ya?" Johnny said as the other three boys gathered around him, Bobby suddenly looking like himself again. "We could tote yer stuff fer ya. We won't get'n da way none."

"Wha'da ya think?" Emery said, looking at Seth.

"Sounds like a good idea to me," answered Seth taking off his pack. "Free up my drink'n hand."

"Aw'right," said Emery, taking off his pack and handing it to Johnny. "Ya can carry dis, but I don't wanna hear no belly ache'n later. Ya hear?"

"Yessir," said Johnny, slinging the large, heavy pack on his back. Soon, the four boys were happily carrying a pack apiece as the soldiers stepped more lively, drinking from their jugs of moonshine.

David Hawkins stood holding Amy in her little front yard while Jackson ate the last of the flowers. An hour earlier Jenkins had come with word that Banks was finally moving his 20,000 men west from Natchitoches away from the river. And that Porter had at last traversed the rapids north of Alexandria. Confederate intelligence had confirmed that Banks's men were currently heading toward the Shreveport Road that ran north straight through Pleasant Hill.

"I've arranged transportation for you up to Mansfield," Hawkins said, gently running the back of his hand across Amy's cheek. "From there, once things get more organized, I'll get you and Johnny up to Shreveport."

"I'm not going to Shreveport unless you're going there," she said looking into his eyes. "I'm going to stay close to where the fighting is and help however I can."

Although he had known her only a month and spent just a few days in her company, he was certain he would not be able to change her mind. She had already decided what she was going to do. It was just the way she did things. He suddenly realized he was very much in love with the woman he had just married.

"Will you at least promise to stay in Mansfield until this is over?"

"No," she said calmly, wrapping her arms around his neck. "The only promise I'll make is to stay as close to you as I can, and since I know you're going to be where the trouble is, that is where I will make myself useful."

"Stubborn woman." Hawkins gazed into her eyes, slowly shaking his head.

"The past few days you seem to have found me quite agreeable, and now suddenly, I'm stubborn."

"Yes, you are indeed stubborn and I love you."

Her calmness broke, tears welling in her eyes, spilling down her cheeks. But she did not look away, rays of the morning light shimmering there. He mounted Jackson, still holding her hand as she stood there pressed up against his leg, looking up at him with an enchanting expression of bold fear, similar to the one Emily wore the last time he saw her.

"Try and find Johnny," she said. "I know he's with those other boys and I'm sure they're out following around with these soldiers. I haven't seen'm since the day before y'all showed up and I'm worried."

"I saw'm yesterday," Hawkins said looking away from her.

"You did? What did he say? Why didn't you tell me?"

"It was in the afternoon. You were taking a nap and I came out to tend to the horse. He walked up with his friends as if he were coming inside. When he saw me he said, 'What the hell are you doing here?'" Hawkins paused and looked at her. "I tried to talk to him, but he just stood there staring at me." He looked away and let out a long sigh. "God, I wish I hadn't hit'm."

"Adam never did," she said, causing Hawkins to look at her. The words held no trace of contempt or conviction, just an acknowledgement of how things were for the boy. "Try'n find'm. Please, David. You and him are all I got. And I promised Adam and Carla I'd take care of'm."

"I'll find'm," he said after a moment of silence, still looking into her eyes.

He released her and cupped his hand under her chin, bending to kiss her lips, delicious and fine. Medicine for the infliction to come.

Like the first time they parted, no words were spoken. But again they looked and watched after one another for as long as they could, grateful for another new day much longer than all the ones past.

It didn't take long for Hawkins to find Johnny. The Confederate was riding with his men along the columns of troops that marched a half-mile or so north out of Pleasant Hill. He suddenly looked to his right and there was the boy, walking with his three friends and some soldiers. Hawkins took note of the bloodstains in Adam McRay's cap sitting crooked on Johnny's head, cocked slightly to the left. A delicate stigma nuanced in warning to the hostile dimensions that pursued them. Four young boys trying to be men, bent against the heavy ruck sacks, burdens of initiation to a fraternity of measure. Rites of passage Hawkins was all too familiar with, the politics of a cadre.

"Johnny!" Hawkins called out.

The boy looked up and saw the Confederate. He shrugged up his shoulders in defiance, hefting the pack higher, straining to stand more upright, swaying against the weight.

"Wha'da you want?" said Johnny.

"I want you to stop whatever it is you think you're doing and go back to Amy. All'a ya." Hawkins looked at the other boys, motioning with his arm. "Get on back with your families."

"You can't tell us what to do!" Johnny shouted. "I ain't one'a yer men!"

"I **can** tell you what to do!" shouted Hawkins. "Whose gear do you have there!? Put it down, now!"

"It's our gear, sir," said Emery stepping forward after hiding the jugs of moonshine. "Da boys jus' wanted ta tote it fer us a ways, Major. Dat's all."

Hawkins glared at the soldier, then at Johnny and his friends who still held the men's packs. "I told you to put that gear down and get on back to your families. They gotta be worried sick about ya, an' they need your help move'n valuables. Now, drop them packs an'get go'n."

"Aw, Major," said Emery as the four boys handed over the packs, Johnny scowling up hatefully at the Confederate. "Dem boys is help'n us. 'Sides, da Yankees is back dat way an'…"

"Shut up! Or I'll have ya up on charges!" Hawkins barked at Emery. Then he turned again to the boys, Bobby and Randy moving away as Johnny stood fixed and unyielding, Robert looking fearful but holding. "Get move'n!"

"Come on, Johnny," said Robert, grabbing his friend by the shoulder. "He means it."

"Major Hawkins!" a voice cried from back down the road. Hawkins turned to see a young captain riding toward him, weaving through the columns of men. The man looked familiar. When he got close, Hawkins recalled being introduced to the captain three weeks earlier at the briefing back in Shreveport. After saluting, the man said, "Major Hawkins, I have orders from General Green. Your men are to fall back and take up a position as rear guard. The general is waiting just south of town. He wishes to confer with you immediately."

"Tell the general I'm on my way," Hawkins said to the young captain, who quickly turned and rode back the way he had come.

Hawkins looked to the side of the road noticing Johnny and his three friends as they made their way back toward town through the crowd of soldiers and civilians. For one brief moment Johnny looked back over his shoulder, the scowl still on his face, the hate still radiating from his eyes.

"Steve!" Hawkins bellowed, turning to find Jenkins, who was fifty feet back on the opposite side of the road. "Find

Novak and get the men turned around! We've been ordered to guard the retreat!"

Jenkins turned the men about, forming yet another column moving south down the west side of the road. Hawkins confronted Emery and his team before following his men. "I'll tell ya something for nothing 'bout dat whiskey ya got, soldier. Little bit goes a long way. And a lot'll take ya nowhere but da grave. Or if ya lucky, a set'a shackles."

"Robert," called Johnny as he ducked off into the trees on the east side of the road. "Holler at Bobby an' Randy 'for dey get too far ahead."

The four boys huddled together in the woods watching from the trees as Taylor's army moved north on the Shreveport Road in long segmented columns. Hawkins's patrol raced south in contrast, elevated beyond the ranks, a single line of horses and men.

"Come on," said Johnny to the other three. "I'm go'n back to find Emery."

The four boys filed out of the trees, heading back up the road, quickly catching up to Emery, Seth and the others. When the Confederates saw the boys they busted out laughing, complimenting them on their slippery, backtracking tactic, slapping them on the backs, almost like peers. Again they took on their jobs as menial beasts of burden, happily taking back the ruck sacks, as the cadre of Confederates hoisted their jugs, making sport of the moment.

"Gave da mean ol'major dair da slip, didn't ya Johnny?"

"'Notha one like dat, an' we'll make ya a gen'yew'wine ree'crewt."

"Teach ya how ta dig a latrine."

"Heck, I bet'ee can fry bacon an' mix up a good ol' corn pone, too."

All that morning the boys walked with the soldiers, carrying their packs as the men sipped the moonshine. Moving at a steady loaf, they covered a little over two miles every hour.

By mid-day they arrived at the Sabine Crossroads, just south of Mansfield.

Johnny proved that he could in fact make a corn pone, delighting the tipsy Confederates by frying the large strips of bacon, then, pouring the cornmeal into the grease, forming a thick, yellow, doughy mix. After the mix cooled, it was packed around the ramrods of the men's rifles, a two-inch-thick, foot-and-half-long corn pone that was roasted to a golden-brown over an open fire. As the men reclined in a grove of oaks, Johnny worked like an expert, showing his friends how it was done, making eight of the crispy, bacony treats.

"Where'd ya learn all dat, Johnny Boy?" asked Emery after finishing off his corn pone wrapped in big slab of bacon, a glimmering look of satisfaction in his eyes.

"My pa taught me."

Pleasant Hill was a quaint, refined little community, founded two decades earlier by a small family of settlers from central Alabama. Its inhabitants were predominately well-educated, well-bred and for the most part well-off. Even its lower class flourished in a general sense. There was a post office, a bank, places of higher learning and a theater where plays were put on regularly, drawing moderate crowds from the surrounding areas. There was a chamber of commerce, an art gallery and museum, a small public park with a walking path lined with flowers and a handful of gazebos. And of course, there was a little public schoolhouse that sat at the bottom of a hill north of town. To its side was a thick towering pecan tree that looked out over a clearing with a plush layer of grass that would soon be soaked in the blood of men.

There were no documented cases of extreme physical violence or molestation by Banks's men against the citizens of Pleasant Hill. The men of the town had taken a good portion of its valuables north to Mansfield. Many of the women stayed behind almost in defiance to the Northerners mere presence in their community. They refused to even acknowledge the Union soldiers as they smashed open their unlocked doors and windows. They turned up their noses as the Yankees took whatever they pleased. However, a few of the women of Pleasant Hill stared sadly at the Union soldiers as if they felt sorry for them. How on earth would they live with themselves when they went back home to their women? When they went back home to their mothers and sisters, and wives and daughters, and the sweet girls that they knew. When they stood once again like perfect gentlemen in the dens, parlors and sitting rooms they had so often taken for granted. Surrounded by the delicate, fragile womanly things that make a house a home, now broken under their boots. The women wanted so badly to tell them how welcome they would have been if only they had come under different circumstances. After all, they were Americans.

Almost everything was taken or broken. Some of the small houses and sheds were taken completely apart, stripped of their lumber. All food and livestock were confiscated. But even more tragic was that this was just the beginning of the end of the small town's innocence.

About the same time Johnny and his friends were cooking up corn pones for the team of Confederates, Hawkins stood not far from where he last confronted the boy, watching as the huge Union column rolled into Pleasant Hill. He was now third in command of a hastily formed cavalry battalion ordered to patrol the narrow gap between Taylor and Banks. The battalion had been provisionally attached to General Thomas Green's cavalry, a well-seasoned division that had just arrived from Texas. Tom Green, a veteran of San Jacinto, was a fearless commander who always led from the point, much beloved by his men.

"Howdy, Major," said Green in typical Texas style when he first met Hawkins. "Ready to kick some Yankee ass?"

"Yessir." replied Hawkins. "'At's what we do."

"Good ta hear it," said the general, then began explaining his battle plan to Hawkins, a grandiose strategy that involved killing or capturing the entire Yankee expedition.

Hawkins had come to hate the bravado of warfare almost as much as war itself. But sometimes he caught himself falling in with it, agreeing with it, knowing he would latter drag that part of his conscience out into the holy light of God to plead forgiveness.

Shortly after sunset Hawkins was standing off alone watching his men get settled when he was approached by a young general he had met earlier that day. Carmille Armond Polignac was a French nobleman-scholar turned soldier who came to America in the 1850's and joined the Confederacy at the outbreak of war. His father had been chief minister during the reign of King Charles X and his family had distant lineage to the Crown of Monaco. Prince de Polignac had initially served in the Eastern Theater as a lieutenant colonel on the staff of General Beauregard, then later under Braxton Bragg in Tennessee. After receiving his first star he was transferred to the Trans-Mississippi Department and given command of a Texas brigade. In his early thirties, Polignac was a few inches shorter than Hawkins and had a lean, wiry frame that moved with deliberate fluid grace. He smelled of perfume and wore a blue cravat around his neck. His long mustache was waxed so that the ends curled up, adding to his already animated features. Narrow deep-set eyes fixed aside an angular prominent nose. Because of the contrast between his suave, debonair nature and his strong, tenacious field presence, his men affectionately dubbed him "Prince Polecat."

"They tell me you were at Shiloh, David," said Polignac in perfect French-accented English.

"Yes, General. I was with the 13th."

"C'est la guerre," uttered the Frenchman after a long sigh.

"Indeed," said Hawkins. "That was war."

"You speak French?"

"No, sir. I'm sorry. Picked up a little here and there. Verai petite." Hawkins then looked intently at Polignac. "You were there, General, at Shiloh?"

"I was a staff liaison officer for Braxton Bragg," Polignac paused, looking off as if thinking back on that horrid day, "helping organize the regimental chaos."

"I see." Hawkins nodded. "You must have served in the French Army before coming to America, General?"

"Yes, I was in the Crimean War."

"Really?" asked Hawkins, raising his eyebrows. "Tell me, General. Are those Cossacks as tough as they say?"

"They are very tough, David. Like wild animals. But, they had one distinct disadvantage."

Hawkins raised his eyebrows again. "Pray tell."

"They stunk," said Polignac, leaning in close to the Southerner. "Even in the freezing cold we could smell them for miles."

Hawkins laughed. "Seems I read that somewhere."

"One of Bonaparte's memoirs, perhaps," said the General, coaxing another chuckle out of the major.

Little contact was made with the enemy that night. Hawkins and his men slept on the ground, their horses' reins wrapped tight in their hands while the animals stood by gazing into the darkness like mute sentinels of the cause. But just as the eastern sky began to turn purple, shots rang out in the distance, the shouts of men and the pounding of horse's hooves resonating through the trees.

"Mount up!" yelled Hawkins as he bolted up out of a half-sleep, hopping on Jackson to begin riding up and down the line of men. Many were still sitting or lying on the ground, arms out, as they held tight to the reins of their stirring animals. "Mount up!"

"Yankee cavalry!" shouted a voice from out of the darkness. "Just to the south at the Wilson Farm. General Green has ordered a full advance on their positions."

"Hear that boys?" Hawkins bellowed. "We got work to do."

Through the trees they rode, fifteen hundred strong, streaming out onto a large field that ran along a narrow bayou. In the twilight well over a thousand Union troopers could be seen clashing with Confederate cavalry, mauling the much smaller force. At that moment a huge chunk of the Yankees broke off and swarmed on the newly arriving Rebels. Together they converged in a crescendo of screams, yells, saber clanks and pistol shots, spinning into a vortex of equestrian brilliance, highlighted by the tempo of human madness and its clamor. The ebb and flow of violence was personified by the blood, sweat and guts left to the fertile ground, a glistening stain sprinkled on the morning dew.

As the sun broke over the horizon more legions of horsemen came. A brigade of Texans beckoned by the sounds and swirls, echoing and dancing anathema across the landscape like some rough beast born anew. Bit by bit, each part adding as another fell away, groping at the earth dead and lost. To every thrust a counter, moved like a chess piece at Godspeed, cutting frightful paths, only to be filled again and cut away over and over. Everything left exposed to the glaring white light of the seer. Off in the distance a farmhouse looms as the wind cries witness.

At some point the Rebels fell away, back to the trees along the slow bayou, spent and wasted and the Yankees glad of it. A time to breathe and reload, glance off at the resting enemy and lick the hard earned wounds that none dared complain of. This they did out of respect for the freshly killed dead and the dying.

General Green called a parlay, dismounting, stamping his feet, drawing crude, urgent maps in the dirt. Cursing the enemy, he pointed at them, seen just off in the distance as they forged their own sinister plans. Architects of a killing work, festering out designs in a bloody woad for the archives. A martial study to be shelved until time slows again and even plowshares are beat to dust and ashes.

"I wanna lure'm along the bayou," snarled Green, "into the woods an' fight'm again at the clearing we just came from."

And that they did, as even more Union cavalry showed. Feigning retreat, they ducked back into the trees by the bayou's edge, as if to draw strength from the black water's presence. A curse cast into the murk, waiting to spring back on the enemy as it passed without rites. A violation from its shallow depths to its opaquely mirrored sheen.

Back at the clearing, the Confederates fanned out left, right and center, taking up positions of attack as even more Texans arrived. Blades at the ready, guns aloft. Horses rearing, lurching, giddy with anticipation. Their steel giving back collective glints of the mid-morning sun. When finally the enemy came, emerging from the woods along that Ten-Mile Bayou, the Confederates swooped on them in a three-pronged charge, working the curse to its confines. The Yankees stumbled, falling over themselves, trampled by their own, trampled and hacked by the Rebels. Spun in a web of howling, slashing country boys seeking retribution for their coming down here, for their crisis of the Union.

Eventually Federal reinforcements arrived and for a while the large skirmish continued. But the Yankees never regained their step, and they soon fell away, back into the trees, overwhelmed by the Confederates. Throughout the day there were many more cavalry skirmishes along the Shreveport Road and the woods north of Pleasant Hill, but the engagements at Wilson's Farm and Ten-Mile Bayou were the largest. For Hawkins it was the most severe fighting he had encountered since last summer in Pennsylvania, and he knew the worst was still to come.

By nightfall Taylor had made up his mind; he was ready to make a stand. Tomorrow Banks would move north out of Pleasant Hill, thinking Taylor would continue to fall back to Shreveport, thirty miles away. But Banks was a politician not a soldier, and wars are seldom won by the popular vote.

XIX

For over three weeks General Albert Lindley Lee, commander of the Red River Expedition's cavalry division, had been encountering stiff Confederate resistance. He was Banks's advanced guard and every day since Alexandria, his patrols were returning mauled and battered, giving detailed reports of brazen, vicious attacks by much smaller Rebel units. Some of these enemy units, he was told, were not actually Confederate regulars, but ragtag bands of locals and volunteers from out of state. This gave an inaccurate account of the enemy's overall strength. These were stellar, hardened men the he was sending out, many who had ridden in the epic campaigns back East. But even in victory they came back looking whipped and defeated. As the days passed the attacks grew more and more ferocious and better organized. The general himself had observed some of the skirmishes from a distance. On more than one occasion he sent word to his superiors that he felt a major engagement was near, but his warnings were ignored. What did he know? Albert Lee was only a one-star general recently promoted to the grade, only a general of brigade, a mere imp of Satan. After Wilson's Farm and Ten-Mile Bayou Lee wrote yet another dispatch to his immediate commander, Major General William

Franklin, who was chief-of-operations and also a personal confidant of General Banks. Maybe he would help?

"Sir, it is just mid-day and two of my battalions have been all but routed by these so-called unprepared Rebels. It is therefore my assessment that the enemy is in fact not falling back, but concentrating the bulk of its forces somewhere in the vicinity of Mansfield. Request immediate support."

By noon the following day General Lee still had not received a response from his superiors. But he was getting word from his lead elements that a large contingent of Confederate cavalry was camped at a plantation just north of his current position.

Lee had achieved his rank by being a daring, competent man. But politics and petty, internal bias had somewhat impeded his career aspirations. If the expedition were his, he would have pursued Taylor's army much more aggressively, forcing him to fight weeks ago. Now, the general thought to himself as he read an incoming report, was his chance to commit to those aspirations. His curiosity having got the better of him, he had to know if he was right about the Rebels. After sending another dispatch to his commander stating his intentions, General Lee ordered an attack on the plantation.

In the shade of two huge cypress trees, their statuesque trunks covered with vines and high tendril climbers, Hawkins stitched a four-inch-long gash in Jackson's left jaw muscle. The horse seemed totally impervious to the pain. After threading each stitch he dabbed the wound with the sticky, pungent resin from one of the bolls that hung in clusters on the cypress trees, a little trick that impressed even Toby Whitefox.

"Where'd ya learn dat, Major?" asked the Indian.

"Out West," Hawkins replied. "An old Kiowa friend showed me."

"I didn't know dair was any cypress trees out in Kiowa country."

"Well, actually," said Hawkins, keeping his eyes on his work, "it's believed that cypress trees grow everywhere except the Polar Regions."

"Polar Regions?" Whitefox asked with a puzzled look. "What's dat?"

"North and South Pole," said Hawkins. "Top and bottom of the earth. Nothing much grows there, they say."

"Oh yeah," said Whitefox. "How do ya know somp'n like 'at, Major?"

"Read it in a book about trees," Hawkins shrugged. "They even got cypress trees in a big ol' park up in New York City."

"Well how 'bout dat," Whitefox replied, looking up at the trees. "An' it grows horse medicine. Who'da thunk it?"

"Saw'm stitch up a horse he had once back in Virgin'ee, called Prancer," said Jenkins, who was off to the side patching up Merle Pemberton's gun hand.

"The horse's name was Dancer, Steve, not Prancer. An' it was probably Paige that ya saw me stitch'n up."

"Dancer an' Prancer. Dey both rode wit' Sant'ee Clause from da North Pole, right?" Jenkins grinned at Hawkins, then turned to Whitefox, who was tending to his own minor leg wound. "Say Toby, what kind'a Indian are ya anyway?"

"Well, I'm whach'a call a full-blooded half-breed."

"Full-blooded half-breed," Jenkins pointed at Whitefox. "Dat means yer ma an' pa was both Indians, but from different tribes, right?"

"Dat's right. My ma was full-blood Cherokee an' my pa was full-blooded Chippewa. Dey met at some kinda rain dance at a reservation in da territory. Both of'm got sick'n died when I'sa baby. I's raised by some white folks up 'round Fort Smith, Ar'kansas. My step-mama tried, bless'r soul. But I's kinda hardheaded, as ya can probably tell."

"Dat's aw'right, Toby. We's all kinda hardheaded," said Jenkins turning his attention back to Merle, reaching to pull his friend's pistol from the holster. "See haw dat feels, Merle."

"No," said Hawkins. "Let him do it."

Since joining Hawkins's outfit, Merle Pemberton had more than proven himself, not only in the fighting, but also in the daily routines of soldering. Unlike the other volunteers, he kept mainly to the regulars, as if he were one of them. He never complained and anytime something needed to be done, no matter how menial or tedious, he was always the first to jump at it.

At Ten-Mile Bayou he sustained a nasty cut, opening the fleshy portion between his thumb and index finger, a gaping wound that squirted small arcs of blood. Merle had cauterized the wide gash himself, quickly packing it with gunpowder and lighting it with a match, then joining back in the fight. After the bloody skirmish, Whitefox cleaned and stitched the wound, giving Merle a few gulps of whiskey beforehand. This whole time he had sat quietly on a tree stump, a stoic expression on his face, watching as Jenkins changed the dressing on his hand. He would often look up toward the tree across the field, ever alert for the enemy.

Merle slowly stretched open his hand and gently grabbed his gun, gritting his teeth as he pulled it out. For a moment he held it up, just staring at it, then slowly squeezed the handle as the grit changed to his trademark weasel grin. Hawkins, Jenkins and Whitefox laughed as Merle shifted his eyes to them, twirling the pistol once around his finger.

"Merle," said Hawkins, pulling the last stitch through Jackson's wound. "I think ya missed yer call'n, buddy. But don't worry, it ain't too late."

"Dem Yankees better steer clear'a dis'n here," said Jenkins, slapping Merle on the back.

"Keep practicing, Merle," Hawkins said, "till ya get used to the pain."

"I'll bet you're part Indian, aren't ya, Merle?" asked Whitefox with a grin.

"Yeah, I guess I'm a half-blooded half-breed. My ma was half-French an' half Creek an' my pa was half-Spanish an' half Caddo. But I never really learned me no Indian ways, 'cept hunt'n an' fish'n, I guess." Merle stood twirling the pistol again.

"Thanks, Steve, feels purdy good." His eyes then shifted off in the distance, a sudden look of concern on his face. "But it don't look like I'm go'n get no time to practice. Look'ee here."

To the south was a quarter-mile wide clearing sparsely populated with half-a-dozen oak trees, the ancient, unkempt type, bearing great rangy limbs that bent back to the ground, regrown into the earth. At that moment Hawkins thought the oaks resembled a team of gigantic spiders creeping toward their lair, strangely wishing they'd do his bidding. Just emerging from the long shadows of the trees on the other side of the clearing, preceded by a rumbling under their boots they'd only now become aware of, were more blue coats than Hawkins could count.

"Jesus, Mary and Joseph," Hawkins whispered as he crossed himself, then let out the loudest Rebel yell his lungs could muster.

The swarm of Yankees enveloped each of the oaks, wrapping around them in a blue, liquid-like flow as they crossed the clearing to meet the outnumbered Confederates. Fortunately Hawkins and his men, and the other outfits they were teamed with, knew immediately what tactics to use. They surged forward, splitting their numbers just like the ride to Natchitoches, until just making contact with the enemy. Then they turned in staggered waves of retreat, only to turn back and fight again in an undulated method of attack. Grappling on horseback, the cagey Rebels let themselves be pushed back passed their campsite, taxing the Yankees before falling into a full retreat, pushing their animals at an all-out, dangerous tilt.

On the day Union forces moved into Pleasant Hill, Hawkins' patrol was attached to a small battalion of General Green's cavalry. After Wilson's Farm and Ten-Mile Bayou, they were added to another brigade of Texas cavalry under General Polignac, making up the center of the Confederate rearguard. They had been spread out along a line of trees on the southernmost edge of an old plantation, resting when the Yankees attacked. Not only were they caught off-guard, they were outnumbered more than two-to-one. Less than a mile behind them, through a series of small fields, trees and another wide clearing, was the whole of Taylor's army, bivouacked in the oaks, pecans and maples, under a canopied sanctuary of moss.

For three weeks an infantry division under General Alfred Mouton had comprised the last of the columns of that army as it trudged north from Alexandria. It would soon become the front line of the bloodiest battle of the war west of the Mississippi, an insignificant record that would stand only till the next day.

"By tomorrow all this retreating will come to an end," said Mouton to Polignac, his second-in-command. The two generals were looking over a detailed map of the Sabine Crossroads area, conferring with an entourage of staff officers under a tarpaulin that hung within a cluster of yellow pines. Mouton was the son of a former Louisiana governor and had been raised in Opelousas, French being his primary language. When he was sent to West Point in the early 1850's, he actually had trouble with the constant, daily use of English. He and Polignac often spoke French to one another while making their battle plans, causing them both to be more expressive in their passions. "And with it, Banks's Red River Expedition."

"The day is not young, Alfred," said Polignac, who just moments before meeting with Mouton, sent a dispatch to his cavalry units requesting an update on enemy movements in the area. The two had met at Shiloh, becoming close friends on that frightful day. Even before Polignac came to Louisiana, Mouton had requested to have him as his number-one officer. "But it is far from over. Perhaps additional patrols should be sent out."

"How many patrols are out now?"

"Four, I believe. I'm expecting a report from General Green any minute."

"Perhaps you're right, Armond," said Mouton, looking up from the map. "Send out the extra patrols. But I want the bulk of our cavalry to stay close. As you've just said, the day is still very ripe."

"Yes, sir," said Polignac, turning to a courier.

Mouton's last battalion was now his lead battalion, and in its forward ranks was a company of men from the Lake Charles area. In that company's second platoon was a rifle team led by Corporal Emery Blaine, who had in his employ as bearers four boys led by the brash young Johnny McRay.

"So I kept on pullin'r skirt up, ya see," bragged Emery after taking a swig of moonshine and passing it to his friend Seth Eubanks. "An' den she said, 'But Emery, do ya still love me?' So I says to'r, 'A'course I still love ya, baby. 'Member, told ya dat da last time. Ain't nut'n changed since den.' "

Laughter filled the air around the small group of Rebels, as they reclined in the shade of the trees, lying on the ground in a circle passing round the jugs of hard corn liquor. Levity and glee filled the moment, a moment fleeting and soon forgotten. They were all tough country boys who had seen very little combat, a few small skirmishes here and there, glimpses of the enemy from afar, but not yet knowing the truly grim depths of fear. And as they sauced their minds, adding relish to the moment, they made it that much harder to part with when the time came to simply kill and die.

Just outside the circle of regulars sat the four boys. They had all been in the company of men drinking and carousing, but not like this. Armed and ready to kill, or seemingly so, they felt a sense of careless mirth utterly foreign to them until now, contagious and spreading, laughing at things less dangerous than themselves, and some unknowingly that were not. The boys joined in the laughter, letting it clamor uncontrollably from their months in a high-pitched chorus that contrasted with the men's hysterical roar. But sometimes Johnny would look off to the side at one of the other squads of men, thinking for a second that he had seen his father. He would stop laughing and stare at the phantom image, losing it in the crowd of Confederates, wanting to run and chase whoever it was, but knowing it was no use.

"Den whad'ya do, Emery?" asked Seth, whiskey dripping from his chin.

"Well, wha'chew think I did, Seth ol' boy?" Emery looked wide-eyed at his friend. "I gave'r da business rat dair in dat barn."

Suddenly the sharp peal of laughter was broken by gunshots off in the distance. They all stood and looked to the south where a small regiment of auxiliary cavalry waited at the trees's end. Across the wide clearing riders approached looking urgent and distressed, hundreds of them shouting warnings and orders, the last of their file turning to fire back the way they had come. Then, for the first time, they saw the enemy bounding from out of the trees across the clearing. A blue wave meshed with the woods and etched in the dust of the earth, its dark leather tack and bridle compelled in a numbing roar of hooves. A quick and deadly horde highlighted by the shimmering steel of their swords and guns, crashing the day in a phalanx as wide as they were deep, and their end could not be seen for the trees.

"Yankees!" Johnny gasped loudly to himself.

He was so excited he did not realize that he and his three friends were slowly huddling close together. They gazed in wonder through the shade of the trees, looking past the stirring Confederates, out into the sunlight that shone brightly on the approaching throng of Union troopers.

The view they had was spectacular, a grand exhibition of Rebel cavalry rushing out from all angles to meet the enemy and cover their retreating comrades. At that moment Johnny saw Hawkins among the incoming units stopping at the tree line, battered, bruised and beaten.

"It's him!" he said out loud, but no one heard him over the commotion, a chorus of orders, screams and shouts echoing through the trees. The quick, noisy rustling of an army of men jumping to their work. "He ran! He done ran scare't!"

General Green's brigade, along with Hawkins's men, was ordered to take up a reserve position at the right flank. As they filed off along the tree line, the Confederate infantry began to form up within the trees while large reserves of auxiliary cavalry clashed out in the open with the enemy. First they grouped by team, then by platoon, then company and battalion and brigade, forming a series of long columns stretching through the grove of pecans, oaks and pines. Stepping forward, the boys stayed close to Emery's rifle team until the whole of Mouton's division, close to 4000 men, were bunched up in a line over 200 yards long just inside the trees.

"Y'all know how ta load'n shoot?" asked Emery to the boys who nodded nervously, eyes darting here and there, still glancing out at the large cavalry skirmish. "Dat's good, cause in a minute ya's each gonna find a rifle out dair in dat field. When ya do, start'a load'n an' passin'm up. Den we'll give ya ours ta reload. YER IN MOUTON'S DIVISION NOW!!"

"FORR'WORRD!!" came the call to the infantry, rippling down the chain of command. They stepped from the trees out into the sunlight behind the last of the cavalry, revealing themselves to the enemy across that half-mile stretch of land, a thick wall of gray emerging from the woods.

The Union cavalry could have pushed back the Confederate cavalry, but they saw the large body of infantry stirring in the trees and withdrew to a rise called Honeycutt Hill on the opposite side of the clearing. They set up a defensive position along a wooden rail fence that ran across the top of the hill, waiting for General Albert Lee to arrive. Soon he was there, looking through his field glasses at the full strength of the Rebels at hand, his men busying themselves with the preparations of battle. Lee spent only one minute assessing the enemy's size and formation, then sent one last dispatch to his commander.

"Here at last, Sir, is Taylor's army. Drawn up and determined to give no more ground without a fight. In order to hold my current position, I must receive immediate infantry support."

Not long after sending the message, one of the general's staff officers called to him and pointed to the west. Far off in the distance was the Shreveport Road that ran the length of the plantation. Partially screened by the trees on the other side of that road was another one of Taylor's divisions moving into position along the Union left flank.

"Damn!" Lee shouted, pounding his fist on the top rail of the fence. "We could have taken the day! Now, we'll be lucky to survive it!"

Amy Hawkins was angry and scared, a continuous ringing of gunfire echoing in the distance. Not only was her new husband off fighting nearby, but Johnny was still missing. After David had left nearly two days earlier, she had gone to look for Johnny, but he was nowhere to be found. To make matters worse, his friends, Randy, Robert and Bobby were also missing, not seen since the Confederates had pulled out of their small town.

She had traveled in a caravan the day before, escorted by soldiers from Pleasant Hill to Mansfield. She had actually witnessed some of the cavalry skirmishes from the road, far-off glimpses of men on horseback, slashing with swords and firing at one another with pistols, charging through the trees like madmen.

Now she was helping roll bandages, anything to assist in caring for the wounded that were already arriving in small numbers, numbers that were sure to grow. As the other ladies busied themselves with the many tasks at hand she could not help but look off toward the trees wondering where Johnny was, and if David was all right.

By early afternoon the sound of gunshots increased off to the south, and soon more wounded were brought in, each man bleeding from severe lacerations or a bullet or worse. One poor young man's horse had been shot out from under him and he was thrown violently to the ground. As he was laid out on a table, completely limp from paralysis, it was determined that his neck was broken. He soon died from suffocation, unable to breathe on his own. Another was brought in ranting and raving and flailing about, bleeding profusely from a gaping hole in the side of his head. Eventually, after the bleeding was stopped, he had to be strapped down as he shrieked and screamed in utter madness, finally going into a seizure and dying. All that afternoon the badly wounded came as the preliminaries to warfare unfolded, a bitter foreshadowing of things to come.

Hawkins and his men had moved into a position to the right of the Union high ground, dismounting and having their horses sent back to the trees. At a dry creek bed that wound from the west end of the plantation, they took cover lying prone on the slight incline. Over five hundred men side-by-side, ready with their carbines.

"Steve," Hawkins said to Jenkins. "Organize a squad of runners for ammunition and tell General Polignac that General Walker is moving his division to our right."

"What?" said Jenkins, turning to look back over his right shoulder, seeing over 3000 Confederates step from the woods southwest of the plantation. "Well, I'll be damned. Looks like we got ourselves an engagement."

"Get go'n, Steve!" shouted Hawkins. "And find Keith. Tell'm to make sure some men stay with the horses. I gotta feel'n when the kill'ns done, we'll be do'n some chase'n."

For over an hour Hawkins watched as two Confederate divisions moved into an "L" formation north and west of Honeycutt Hill. Off to the east he noticed another large Confederate cavalry brigade taking up a position on Mouton's left flank. The time to attack was now, he thought. But soon a thick, slow-moving wave of blue could be seen coming from the south and Hawkins realized the chance for a decisive victory was now questionable. The bulk of Bank's army was now at hand.

"Hey David," said Merle, after crawling up along the creek bed, moving low on his belly and elbows. "'Bout how far away are we from Shreveport?"

"'Bout thirty miles, Merle," said Hawkins looking at his friend. "Think'n 'bout dat land, aren't ya?"

"I hate to count da chickens 'fer dair hatched, David. But if'n we wup deez here Yankees an' I don't make it, will ya see to it dat Molly gets 'at land?"

"Don't ya worry none, Merle," said Hawkins. "You an' Molly both are gonna get dat land."

Hawkins had noticed a 100-foot-wide gap between the enemy's left flank and the dismounted Yankee cavalry that had been brought forward to match Walker's division to the west. He sent word down the line to charge that spot when the time came.

Just to Hawkins's left, about fifty yards from where the creek bed turned sharply to the north, was a battalion of Mouton's infantry. As the outfit's color bearer stepped past the creek, Hawkins took notice of the commander, a lieutenant colonel he had only met in passing whose name he could not recall. The man had been a schoolteacher before the war and was said to drink a lot, a bitter man who'd also been at Shiloh. He had little control over his undisciplined battalion, an arrogant outfit always complaining of never seeing any action. Fortified with brandy, he turned to face his men. With his pistol drawn, he drew his saber and held it high, then shouted vehemently, offering chilling words to those who'd been flippant till now.

"TODAY, MEN!!" he screamed, spit flying from his mouth. "YOU WILL SEE BLOOD TILL YOU ARE SATISFIED!!"

Hawkins stifled a laugh when he saw the pallid expressions of fear on the men's faces, then turned to Jenkins, who wore a rare serious look. "I think Mouton's going to advance any minute now, with or without orders from Taylor."

"I do hate a showoff," said Jenkins with Novak at his side.

"Listen, Steve," said Hawkins, "when the advance begins, have your men concentrate their fire on the enemy's infantry, at their left flank. And Keith, have your men fire at the dismounted cavalry facing Walker's men. When I give the signal, we charge 'at gap."

By comparison to all he had seen during this war, Mouton's charge was as gallant and bloody as any Hawkins had witnessed. Just after the silent clouds of black smoke erupted from Honeycutt Hill, a sickening crescendo of thuds was heard half-a-second before the roar of Union gunfire, a wave of bullets slamming into the first line of Confederates. Whole sections of the division folded to the ground under the ravaging Union fire, screams and shrieks accented by a heavy mist of red. Gouts of spurting blood changed color as it passed through the sunlight. Men grabbed their companions, grabbing the dead as the order to move forward was howled again and again. A few yards were gained in the interim as the Rebels prepared to fire back, answering the Yankees with their own question of ruin. Remnants of a battered brigade paused against the hail of bullets, discharging their weapons simultaneously, aimed at the legions in blue on the hill, protected by only a wooden rail fence.

At one point the charge seemed totally futile until finally the Confederates established their own organized line of fire. Little by little the Louisiana and Texas troops clawed and crawled their way closer and closer to the rail fence held mainly by men from Illinois and Ohio. The Union troops would unleash a barrage, then the Confederates would form a line launching their own salvo, only to advance further into the next stream of Union bullets. A death-for-death tradeoff, with the Southerners slowly grinding out a grisly advantage, eventually rolling up to fire point blank at the fleeing Northerners.

Johnny lay on the ground quivering with fear next to his three friends. In front of him dozens of men were scattered dead, sprawled in every attitude, while hundreds more fired, reloaded and fired again and again. The fused, mingled roar of musket fire and screaming filled his ears, reverberating through his body like waves in a shallow trough. He looked to his left to see Emery and Seth, each loading their rifles, ramming the barrels, cocking back the hammers and setting the percussion caps. They would lift the weapon, almost like a desperate lover to their faces, momentarily taking aim and firing with a quick burst from the breech, then, a sudden violent explosion from the barrel. Then, they would spin the piece forty-five degrees counterclockwise, setting its stock to the ground and tear at the cartridge box to reload, all the while screaming and screaming.

Johnny noticed a large portion of the Confederates had surged up ahead and were grouping together in large numbers to return fire. Although this readily exposed them to the enemy, it also allowed them to pour a more concentrated, well-aimed wall of lead on the Yankees. He watched with almost maniacal glee as a long stretch of blue uniforms at the rail fence disintegrated in a discernible fine red mist, fringed with hats, bags and bits of clothing flung high into the air.

"If'n ya ain't gonna help us none, get on back!" yelled Emery. "Otherwise, start grab'n up dem rifles ya see an' start load'n'um fer us!"

Just in front of him, Johnny saw a dead man still clutching his unfired weapon, two bloody marble-size holes in his chest. He snatched the rifle, having to pry it loose from the man's death grip and was just about to hand it to Emery. Suddenly its warmth enchanted him, its supple wood tones encasing the dark cold steel. Gently he curved his finger around the trigger, justifying his thoughts as he raised it to his eye. Taking aim on a clump of blue across the field, he squeezed the trigger and the hammer fell bursting the percussion cap. He had fired many guns in his life but never one as powerful as this. It slammed against his shoulder with a numbing jar, knocking him back and to the left.

"At'a boy!!" screamed Seth, as he and Emery advanced forward. "Now keep at it!!"

Johnny turned to the other boys and shouted, "Y'all jus' gonna lay there!? Come on; grab a gun!"

Robert moved first, then Randy, then Bobby. They each grabbed two or three rifles off the dead men around them, cartridge boxes, ammunition, and a cap apiece. Now they looked like Rebels, falling in, taking up a position behind the advancing Confederates. For over a half hour they reloaded weapons that were passed back to them as the battle raged. At first only Johnny would occasionally fire a rifle at the Yankees. Then, as the Union line began to falter, the other three boys joined in the assault, each taking a turn to fire at the thinning blue line.

"We got'm run'n now!" screamed Emery, as the enemy's flanks collapsed and the Yankees fled Honeycutt Hill.

"Come on, boys!" Seth yelled back, waving his rifle in the air. "We got ourselves a blue belly hunt."

The four boys ran with the pack of Confederates, surging up the hill and over the shattered rail fence now hung draped with the bloody enemy corpses. They were together in a row, shouting as they ran, screaming the cry of victory, pushing forward after the Union pell-mell retreat.

Hawkins was not surprised when the Union line on Honeycutt Hill began to falter. He took his men along the left edge of the field. Then they charged the ever-widening gap in the enemy's right flank. By that point most of the dismounted Union cavalry had retreated. What did surprise Hawkins was the large number of Union soldiers already surrendering. Well over a thousand men in blue were throwing their weapons down and their arms up. The Confederates were forming a circle around the prisoners when General Mouton rode up on his horse assuring their good treatment.

"Have the horses brought to the base of the hill," Hawkins told Novak as his men assisted in securing the enemy soldiers. "We still got a lot'a work to do."

Suddenly, a handful of Yankees that had just thrown down their weapons snatched them back up and shot General Mouton. The beloved commander was killed instantly, his body riddled with bullets. In a fit of rage dozens of Confederates fell upon the killers. They were beaten senseless, their skulls bashed in with rifle butts. The Rebels jeered and swore at them, spitting and kicking dirt on their dead bodies. Hawkins's men were forced to intervene before an all-out massacre took place. Generals Polignac and Green were soon there, openly displaying grief and disgust, while still maintaining control of the troops.

"David," said Polignac, tears of anger and frustration showing in his eyes as he looked south in the direction of the retreating enemy. "Take your men and ride with General Green and pursue the enemy along the Shreveport Road. General Taylor wants to keep up the attack, pushing them back as far as we can by nightfall."

The Yankees continued to fight in a retreating formation, a chaotic mass of close to 15,000 men strung out over a half-mile, many of them not even participating in the first phase of the battle. At some points the line was moving in both directions as whole battalions and regiments still rushed north up the Shreveport Road only to encounter the fleeing forward units, an army bent back on itself. Banks was in a tizzy trying to rally his division commanders, at the same time expressing doubt in his own strategy. For a brief moment he considered falling back to the river and regrouping with Porter. But a member of his staff quickly reminded him that the Navy had already moved further north.

Finally, about a half-mile south of Honeycutt Hill, a second line of defense was set up by the Yankees, a brigade of muskets laying waste to an onrushing wave of Rebels. But it soon gave way under the momentum of the Confederate surge, sweeping over the Union reinforcements, breaking their line and capturing more prisoners.

Just past this second stand Hawkins and his men came to an abandoned U. S. wagon train blocking the road. The Union teamsters had obviously panicked and while attempting to flee trampled scores of their own comrades. Crushed Yankee soldiers were strewn across the road, pinned under the wheels. Whole companies of Confederates were now looting the wagons, holding up the flow of attack, giving the enemy much needed time to fall back and regroup. Goods and supplies littered the roadside as Hawkins fired his pistol into the air.

"WHAT THE HELL ARE YA DO'N!?" he screamed at the startled men, pointing his weapon south. "THE FIGHT'S THAT WAY, YOU BASTARDS!! NOW MOVE!!"

"Well, I aim to get me a lil' sump'n extra," said one man, ignoring Hawkins, still pulling at the wooden cartons of dry goods.

Without hesitation, Hawkins fired into the box the man had in his hands, shattering it in a spray of splinters, spilling its contents to the ground.

"NOW, GET MOVE'N, OR I'LL SHOOT YA WHERE YA STAND!!"

Eventually command and control of the Southern troops was reestablished and the pursuit continued until a third line of Union forces was encountered. This time the Union lines held on a ridge overlooking a small tributary called Chatman's Bayou, repulsing the Confederate charges on their position.

Hawkins's men tried moving on the enemy's left flank, but they were checked by a crack regiment of Union cavalry. Violent skirmishes filled the thick woods of the dusk twilight, a blur of sabers and horsemen charging from all angles. Both sides finally broke off the way they had come as darkness took the day.

The Battle of Mansfield was over. Nearly half of the casualties were captured or missing, but in less than four hours of fighting well over two thousand men lay dead or badly wounded, strewn across a battlefield that stretched nearly three miles. Union forces could not draw from the precious water supply of the bayou. So, unbeknownst to the Confederates, Banks fell back to Pleasant Hill, where a fresh reserve division awaited.

As Hawkins's outfit returned along the northern edge of Chatman's Bayou, the night's first stars glistening off the glassy black water, a rider he recognized as one of Polignac's staff officers approached him.

"Major Hawkins," said the man. "General Polignac would like to see you."

At a small farmhouse off the Shreveport Road, Hawkins found Polignac in conference with General Taylor and his staff, studying a collection of maps and dispatches. After being offered a cup of hot black coffee, he stood wearily to the side as the generals discussed plans for the following day. Before long, the parlay ended with the different colonels and generals dispersing, some looking like inmates from a madhouse gaining one final chance at freedom.

"David," called Polignac, who was standing with Taylor at a table. He motioned for Hawkins, introducing him to the general when he approached. "How are your men?"

"Surprisingly well, Sir, thank you."

"Have we met before, David?" asked Taylor.

"Briefly, in Richmond, Sir," said Hawkins. "A few days after Sharpsburg. I dropped my cane as I shook your hand."

Taylor nodded, looking off. "Yes, I remember."

"General," Hawkins said, shifting his posture. "I'm very sorry about General Mouton. It is a terrible loss for us, but we will prevail."

Taylor nodded again, meeting Hawkins' eyes. "We will indeed, Colonel. We will indeed."

"Excuse me, Sir?"

"You've been promoted, David," said Polignac, placing his hand on Hawkins's shoulder. "I'm giving you the third battalion. Colonel Hudsmith and Major Pernell are dead, and Lieutenant Colonel Voltz has been shot in the stomach."

"Yes, I heard, Sir," said Hawkins, hesitating. "Thank you, Sir."

"Tomorrow," said Taylor to Hawkins. "I want you to move on their left flank again. Charge hard and I think something will break."

"I'll be there first, Sir."

She had never cried so much in her life. Well over a hundred wounded men had been brought to the small church turned hospital. They filled the sanctuary and its outer foyer, its back halls and anterooms, forever staining its hardwood floors with puddles of blood, its walls forever hallowed by their screams and pleas to God. She had tried to wipe up the blood, senselessly mopping it with a towel, but was told by one of the older women not to bother.

She had carried herself well in front of the men, doing her best to comfort them and show strength. But the hideous work of the surgeons played hell on her spirit. Twice she had to run off to find a place to weep, a solitary place, expelling the lurid images from her mind and soul, exercising the other self in powerful sobs that carried a distance, as if to a final plea of the damned.

She had not seen him among the maimed, but that was no comfort to her. She knew he could be out there suffering alone or dead, but she tried not to think of it. Impossible, with the many contorted faces or the ones so lost, fallen in despair. A montage of pain and misery, inescapable and bound by all things save hope, mercy and love. And the boy, she thought. Where on earth was the boy? Her heart seemed to barely hold itself in place, teetering at the edge of a dark emptiness.

Finally she became somewhat accustomed to the screaming, in spite of it, as she reached even more to the broken. She prayed with them, touching their frightened faces as they sought rest in the arms of grace and mercy. And it was that that finally saved her. The Helper, that shield of the better half.

That night Johnny and the boys camped with the men just northeast of Chatman's Bayou, a few minutes' walk from where Hawkins's men rested. Emery and Seth were already asleep, exhausted from the fight and the moonshine. The other two men in their team had been killed, along with many more in their company, their whole battalion suffering grave losses. The boys talked very little, eating hard tack biscuits, beef jerky and a few apples. The four of them sat in a small circle, off to the side, but close to the men, having earned their right to be there.

All the way from Honeycutt Hill for nearly two miles to Chatman's Bayou, they had kept up with the men as they chased the Yankees, helping reload and firing at the enemy. It was a wondrous, terrifying trek through grounds most familiar to them, now made complicated in a context strange and new. The boys had collected an assortment of weapons along the way, and now each had a pistol or two tucked into their belts and a rifle apiece. Bobby had a sword. Randy had a pair of field glasses and all four of them wore gray coats they had found. They dispensed most of the ammo and cartridge boxes they had to the men, who accepted it with a nod, some even saying thanks.

A slight chill was in the air and they huddled together wrapped in blankets, trying to sleep. Listening to the sounds of the night, they each quietly pondered their choices, knowing what was to come. Everything was the same, yet somehow different as seen from within, a simple fascination of their becoming. And why not? They were Confederates now.

XX

Lieutenant Colonel David Hawkins was lying prone in a thicket, observing through a pair of field glasses a spot that was quite familiar to him, a spot of some sentimental value. Through the trees on the other side of the clearing, he could just make out the little schoolhouse where he had first met Johnny and Amy. Union soldiers were formed up all across the clearing to the road. Thick columns of blue stretched from the woods before the town, extending to the base of the rise that was Pleasant Hill. He lowered the field glasses and looked to his left, studying the ground and trees around him, the road only yards away. It was the spot where he'd lost sight of her that day, rescued by her sweet gentle touch from the clutches of despair.

Just before sunrise that morning a small Confederate foot patrol had slipped across Chatman's Bayou with orders to quietly assess the posture of the Union forces. Taylor planned on sending his cavalry around the enemy attacking its rear positions, then throwing the bulk of his infantry at their front and left flank, repeating the success of Mansfield and cutting off any possible retreat. What the patrol had to report surprised Taylor. Despite the fact that Banks held the high ground overlooking the bayou, giving him a strategic leg-up to go along with the numerical advantage, he had abandoned the position. Polignac was then ordered by Taylor to send a mounted patrol to find the Yankees. Without hesitation the job was given to Hawkins.

After selecting ten of his best men, Hawkins had forded the bayou upstream to seek out the enemy. They rode cautiously through the woods far off to the side of the road, gently pushing their horses at a slow walk before dismounting to continue on foot. And here is where Hawkins found them, ready and waiting at Pleasant Hill.

He began writing on a piece of paper, occasionally looking up at the enemy, jotting down detailed specifics of their new positions. He then turned and handed the paper to Novak, who was also lying prone in the thicket.

"Take this directly to General Polignac. Then bring the rest of the battalion to the woods west of town. I'll meet you there."

"But what if the general orders otherwise?" asked Novak. "An' what about General Taylor? He's gonna wanna know this right away."

"Don't worry, Keith," said Hawkins looking back through his field glasses. "Polignac's gonna tell Taylor immediately, an' neither of'm's gonna order otherwise."

Hawkins studied the line of Union troops a little while longer, then turned to the rest of his patrol: Steven Jenkins, Merle Pemberton, Toby Whitefox and six others who had been with him since leaving Shreveport three weeks ago. They were all lying in the dirt and leaves, propped up on their elbows, tired and haggard yet still full of fight. The lines on their faces enhanced the determination in their eyes, a steady glimmer of resolve still fixed on a single purpose. Talking very little they cautiously moved through the trees, slowly walking their horses west, then gradually turning south until they found Banks's extreme left flank. Again Hawkins wrote down details of their location and the course they had taken in relation to the enemy's lines.

"Merle, ya think ya can get this to General Polignac? It's real important."

"Sure, David. I can do dat."

"Now listen. If someone stops ya, don't get in a fight with'm. Understand? Just tell'm it's an urgent message from me to General Polignac an' they'll let ya through. Then find Keith, aw'right? Help'm get the rest'a the men here."

"Yessir, David." Merle gave a quick, funny-looking salute before heading out.

The rest of the morning Hawkins's patrol covered the enemy's entire left flank as more dispatches were sent back, laying out a clear picture of Banks's emplacements for the generals at command. Shortly before noon Hawkins's battalion arrived at the spot he had chosen to rest before the battle, plodding slowly in a single file through the trees. They were a small battalion, less than 800 men, nearly half of them being the balance of Gastonel's original patrols. The rest were a mix of volunteers and Texas, Arkansas and Louisiana regulars. They took repose in a half-acre grove of yellow pines, surrounded on all sides by gnarled thickets of young oaks, magnolias and cottonwoods, a well-shaded sanctum with an ample view of the sky.

As he stood stroking Jackson's wounded face the horse nuzzled against Hawkins, nibbling lightly at his coat sleeve. All around him, as many of the men lay resting on the ground, something seemed to beckon from the woods, a presence he had felt many times. The earth and sky seemed to call out a silent warning. Would he be here today? Hawkins wondered. That Man? The Man in White? He was sure of it.

Like a legion of ghosts convoked to haunt his thoughts, he suddenly recalled some of the hours leading up to Shiloh. The night before the battle he had been off walking alone by the edge of his company's bivouac when he heard someone singing an old song from his childhood. He looked up to see Adam McRay strumming a guitar, singing in a surprisingly pleasant tenor voice. When McRay had finished the song, Hawkins approached him and for the first time found a simple common bond with the man. Both still wore bruises from their fight a week earlier in Mississippi.

"Hadn't heard 'at song in about twenty years," said Hawkins. "When I's a boy there was a fella named Banjo Jo, use ta sings it down by the river on Commerce Street in Shreveport."

"Banjo Jo!?" McRay looked up at Hawkins in surprise. "The Banjo Jo? Half-nigger an' half-injun? Always smile'n? Kept 'is hair kind'a long, braided in funny lil' knots, wit all kinds'a color'd up ribbons hang'n from'm? Like'a clown?"

Hawkins laughed and nodded. "'At's him."

"Banjo Jo'sa one taught me da strum dis here gee'tar, Lieutenant," said McRay with a grin, "down in New Or'leans when I's a boy."

"You're from New Orleans?" asked Hawkins.

"Born an' raised, rat dair on da Mississippi River at a dime-a-dance whore house on da corner'a Conti an' Decatur."

"The French Quarter," said Hawkins. "I's born in the French Quarter. Corner'a Barracks and Burgundy."

"You was born in New Or'leans?" McRay asked with even more surprise.

"Yeah, but my folks left when I's 'bout six. Don't 'member much about it."

"Ya don't say," McRay said, looking off to continue strumming his guitar as if he suddenly remembered their differences.

The next morning the 13th Louisiana Cavalry was in formation along the western edge of the peach orchard, still a strong proud battalion, only moments from their demise, looking straight into the coming dawn. A clearly distinguishable horizon crossed the East in hues of purple, pink and blue. The pink blossom petals were still on the trees. A luscious, cloud-like blanket of pastel hovered above the ground, its gentle beauty an absurd irony of what was to come.

Shortly before the order to advance, Hawkins and McRay looked at one another, their eyes meeting through the ranks, holding for a moment. McRay shifted in his saddle, turning to look out across the peach orchard at the massive files of the enemy, the strange yet noble look of fear on a brave man's face. Gunfire and the shouts of men echoed through the hills as the epic battle began in its many other places.

Hawkins now considered that brief exchange with McRay the night before Shiloh. Was that what compelled the man to come to his rescue? Or was it that short moment they had had just minutes before the bloody charge? He also realized how that act had ultimately brought him to Pleasant Hill. He blinked, thinking he saw his mother's image glistening in the pool of Jackson's eye. When he turned there was nothing but a deep aching loneliness that he knew would pass with the approach of battle. An instinctive kinship to the Man in White, a kinship of blood. Shades of Gethsemane lingering off.

Many of the inhabitants of Pleasant Hill who had left their homes and gone to Mansfield when Banks's army arrived were now following the Confederate Army as it pursued the Yankees back down the Shreveport Road. All of them had seen bits and pieces of the Battle of Mansfield, and feared what was to happen next. Another terrible battle would soon take place, spilling into their homes and quaint dooryards, tearing apart the sweet happy world they once knew.

Amy repeatedly asked about David Hawkins to anyone who would respond. Many were traumatized and either could not or would not speak, while many others either did not know him or knew nothing of his whereabouts. She also constantly looked for Johnny, knowing the boy would be somewhere near the Confederate soldiers. Several times she thought she saw him, calling out his name, once even jumping from the wagon, running to a boy she noticed following behind a group of soldiers. A boy Johnny's age with golden locks of hair, but not him.

While the caravan of soldiers and refugees stalled out along the road just north of Pleasant Hill, she walked through the multitude looking for the two, wearing a blue dress stained dark with blood. She walked back and forth, up and down the crowded Shreveport Road, calling out for Johnny and asking over and over for any news of David, any news of her husband.

"Yeah, I know'm," said a man on crutches.

"Is he well?" she asked, taking the man by the hand. "Is he alright?"

"He looked aw'right, ma'am," said the man.

"Do you know where he is?"

"No ma'am, but he was ride'n dat way." The man pointed south. "Dat was 'bout sunup, ma'am."

She thanked the man and started walking south, increasing her pace until a line of soldiers stopped her. A chorus of heavy shouting and yells could be heard coming from just ahead of where she stood, and no refugees were allowed to pass. Suddenly, as the large column of gray began to march forward, drums and bugles off, she looked to her left and saw Randy Randall. Gasping, she ran to him. Next to him was Johnny. They looked at each other and at that moment she did not know him. He was as strange to her as some alien creature born of another world. Standing out to her even more than the knives, guns and cartridge boxes, was Adam's cap, suddenly looking so well-placed on Johnny's head.

"Johnny," she cried painfully. "What are you doing?"

"We go'n fight dem Yankees," he said almost with a growl. "Dat's what we're do'n."

"But Johnny …," she said with a hopeless gasp, moving to take him in her arms. "Please, baby …."

"Stop call'n me dat!" he snarled, pulling away from her. "I ain't no baby! We done fought dem Yankees an' wupped'm! An' now, we fix'n ta wup'm again!"

"But what about David, Johnny?" she cried.

Johnny stood looking at her, growing stranger by the second. Then he hissed, "What'a 'bout'm?"

"Have you seen him?"

"Yeah, I seen'm."

"Is he alright?"

"Don't ya worry none, Aunt Amy, Major Hawkins done ran scare't. I seen he did. He's probably half way to Arkansas by now." He took one step toward her. "Don't ya worry none 'bout me nee'der. If'n ya wanna worry 'bout someone, worry 'bout dem Yankees." He walked backwards a few steps, then turned and walked away. The other boys fell in behind him, boys she'd known since they were very little, now with stern looks on their faces, grave and resolute.

"Johnny!" she said out loud. "Johnny," then again, quietly, as she began to cry, wrapping her arms around herself and crying.

As the line of Confederates moved forward, pushing toward the enemy to do battle, she stayed as close as she could. Walking, shuffling her exhausted feet, arms wrapped around herself and still crying, praying, dusting away the demons inside until she could do more, until she could do better.

The Battle of Pleasant Hill began late in the afternoon. Approximately twenty-four hours after the onset of Mouton's charge, Taylor sent Walker's division crashing into the Union center with devastating effect. A New York brigade just north of the clearing by the schoolhouse had held that center. The fighting quickly became close and intense as the Union line buckled back on itself forming a horseshoe with the Confederates mauling the Federals from within, a steady, ugly grinding of the other's enemy. Then out of the trees came the Yankee counterattack. As bodies piled up in a dry gully, a brigade of Iowa troops slammed into the Texans, shearing off the backend of the Rebel surge. An obdurate scraping of the ranks left in its wake the grasping arms of the late and the slow. Polignac's infantry was sent in and the fighting flowed past the schoolhouse, leaving bloody gouges on its boards as the two armies poured into the little town of Pleasant Hill.

The battle became a layered blue and gray field of men doing their killing work with frenzied thrusts and desperate lunges. Men fired their weapons, reloading and firing again, shooting at each other in tight quarters of insanity. A constant mingled cry filled the air as the two flags crept closer and closer, jerking side to side, back and forth. The killing was intimate, close and impermeable, wet with the mixed blood of the states. Blood to feed the grass, to scream out at the sky and gulp at the westering sun. Hands pulling, pushing, utterly absent of thought, seeking to end a conflict born of compromise lost. And still the constant mingled cry.

The Union troops were pushed back, overlapping onto the embankment south of town. Slowly they gave way like a sturdy old structure razed by a weary team of workers, falling back bit-by-bit, expiring piece by corporal piece, taking what it could of the town with them.

Then came another Yankee counterattack, two divisions unleashed in a stampede as if to show how and why. The spent Rebels were waylaid from behind like a band of freebooters, a reciprocity of ruin abridging the old-fashioned town even further, knocking loose its hard-earned human shoring. They ripped at the underpinnings tooth and nail to pry and gouge at every little part that was once whole, then pitched back again into the mix, only to be torn apart smaller and thrown back again. A spell of perdition cast in heaps on the agreeably curious artifacts of a community strewn to the dirt.

A few pieces of Union artillery stolen by the Confederates at Mansfield were brought to bear, firing into the surging blue horde. The rear file of the Yankee counterattack was pelted with a gory shower of madness, a spray of blood and body parts that rained down like a scene in the inferno. But in a grim reversal of fortune their owners recaptured the cannons. Misadventure reared its head like a haughty drunken whore, cackling at the downcast and trodden, taming the ever-slipped dogs of war.

Suddenly clouds gathered out of nowhere, quickly forming into the shape of a Man. The Image stirred, slowly animating in fluid movements that gradually quickened, as if awakened from a long sleep. His garments were white and made of the clouds, accented by the wind and sky.

All the killing suddenly stopped. Both Rebel and Yankee paused to look at the vision above. Dumbfounded, they pointed, causing others to look. A sudden deafening silence rang like a city of belfries. One could even hear the flies buzzing, drawn by the coppery scent of blood. Then the Man stretched forth His arms. In each palm was a gaping hole, a wound from the ages. Water began to pour from the wounds, raining down on the battlefield. Then the water turned to blood, baptizing the combatants of Pleasant Hill.

As suddenly as He appeared, the Man in the sky began to dissipate. In a powdery mist, He was slowly swallowed by the clouds, fading with the blood-rain, cueing the slaughter to resume.

Seth Eubanks was dead, shot point blank in the face. He had just killed four Yankees in rapid succession, shooting one in the chest, spearing another with his bayonet, then clubbing two with his rifle, cracking their skulls. Then out of the mass of humanity death came looking, choosing and pointing. Always it waited, sudden and quick.

They had been part of the early Confederate surge smashing through the western wall of the horseshoe of Yankees, striking them from behind, crushing the blue line against the bulging gray middle. At first they peeled away at the Federals, filling the gaps left behind, falling into places that at first seemed strange and new. Then a balance was found, locked in to the reckonings of a homicide fair. The economics of attrition luring them on to judgment. Rattlings of a birthright swapped for a glance at the abyss.

Bobby was missing and Robert had been shot in the leg, pulled away screaming by the men. Randy was dead, falling backwards into Johnny's arms, blood gushing from his mouth, eyes still open, sightless and gone. And now Seth, one moment triumphant, crushing the enemy, the next crushed, broken in ruins. Now he saw Emery struggling in the mass. Their eyes met; he motioned with his hands. Something in the dirt was calling, an *intruder in the dust*. Something flowing, wicked and immeasurably finite had stopped him. Something sharp, hard and tricky in its simplicity. Emery pitched forward and was gone, swallowed into the foreground. Johnny was screaming now, all hate and love forgotten, wanting out as the next counterattack came. All around him, war, men and killing. All around him, his dreams.

There had been a protector for Johnny that day, just like always. Someone he couldn't quite place, a Man that moved around him, shielding him from the raging elements. A fulfillment of plans made in another world, brilliant arrangements of the Almighty, appearing as utter folly to man. A sharp and painful footstool for the boy.

Hawkins's tattered battalion had been part of the charge that raced along the base of the rise, checking the first Union counterattack. They had waited in the trees to the west until late afternoon, when finally enemy troops came and the skirmishes began. At first they handled the Yankees, dashing their efforts to steal the day. But the enemy collected themselves and the trees became a maze of blue and gray. Finally, the Confederates fell back somewhat to the south, regrouping just as another charge was called.

Again they gushed from the trees, racing past the pecan tree and the schoolhouse, past his place of sexual healing, to where he witnessed the good kill of the old hare, omen-like for his procession to the good kill of men. Their collision with the enemy was horrific. Men, horses and steel splashed with men, horses and steel, spilling their very souls to the dirt and wind. A gathering of all the moments of his life, spectral and kaleidoscopic. All things suspended now save this sinister game of man. War, this bastard child of invention.

Hawkins pushed deep, well into the fray, pistol drawn, saber loosed. His legs clasped tight around Jackson, making him one with the animal. A mythic black-on-red stallion bounding through the ranks of men. Together they became a killing fury, blasting, slashing and kicking their way through the thick blue line. A horrifying premonition of death forever etched in the memory of every soldier who saw them then. A fallen angel atop a demonic charger unchained for a season from the surly bonds of hell.

Suddenly Hawkins saw the boy caught in the middle of the warped line where both sides had meshed together. He was screaming from under his father's cap. One moment he fought, struggling against the mass of crushing humanity, receiving his wishes. Then he pled for mercy, begging release, protesting his grisly inheritance, needing the Helper.

Hawkins turned Jackson toward the helpless child. The warhorse seemed to recognize the boy, leaping to the left, his front hooves clearing a path. Just as Hawkins got to the boy, bending low to the side to gather him up, a saber sliced diagonally across Johnny's face. The flesh was ripped open over his left eye, across the bridge of his nose and deep into the right cheekbone. The boy shrieked in pain and panic as the Confederate pulled him up and over his saddle, blood spilling into his lap. The blade that struck Johnny then plunged deep into Hawkins's side. As the Confederate turned, a bullet struck him in the back. On instinct he spurred Jackson and the animal bucked, lurching free of the madness. As he kicked his way out, a mini-ball tore into the beautiful creature's chest. With his last bit of strength, the magnificent horse tossed his head and raced toward the little schoolhouse. Blood spewed from the charger's mouth and nostrils as he carried the two wounded Confederates.

The whole town of Pleasant Hill was broken, its houses wrecked and destroyed, its two schools of higher learning demolished. Its post office, bank and public buildings had been ransacked, then razed to the ground. Its museum and gallery destroyed, its tiny theater riddled with bullets, its marquee fallen, snarled around a bloody corpse lying on the stage. A once-fanciful little park strewn with the dead and dying. Only the small schoolhouse north of town stood fast, a makeshift Confederate hospital filled with the wounded.

She found a place where she could do better, again giving care and comfort to the wounded, helping mend the broken and the disheartened. As the slaughter raged in the nearby field, her childhood place of play and solitude, she would sometimes look up from the men she was tending to and try not to grimace. But it was no use; she could not keep herself from being affected by the awful sights and sounds. She no longer cared that the men saw her crying as she worked, tearfully watching as more men were brought from the field.

Amy Hawkins was coming down the steps of the porch carrying a bucket of water and a bundle of bandages when she saw her husband ride up with Johnny draped across Jackson, each splattered with blood. The horse reared to the right, collapsing on the ground. Hawkins embraced Jackson's neck, whispering to him.

"At ease, boy. At ease."

Amy dropped the bucket and ran to them, laying herself between the man and the boy, taking them both in her arms, as they enveloped the dying horse.

"If you live," said Hawkins, turning to the boy, his face only inches away, "tell people what you saw."

Then the Confederate turned to his wife, touching her face and smiling as best he could. He tried to sit up, but could not, the life ebbing from his body. His bloody hand ran through her matted hair as she kissed his face, trying to find words that would not come.

"I really did mean to write," he finally managed in a weak voice.

She laughed as she cried, kissing his face, stroking the hair from his eyes. "You did write. Remember? I told you."

"I's kind'a hope'n we'd have ourselves a nice honeymoon after all this is over." His hand was holding and caressing the line of her jaw, his thumb touching the soft part of her ear. "But they got me on extended duty." He sighed painfully. "Damn Yankee expedition."

"Oh, David," she finally said, almost keening. "What can be done for you?"

"Everything I own is yours," he said. "My house. My land. My slaves. Take care of them. They are all that's left of my family." He paused, enduring a deep spasm of pain. "Go live there. You'll like it."

David Hawkins then looked up at the sky. As he whispered a last prayer before dying, he saw the Man in White in the clouds. Behind the Man he could see a levee covered with spring flowers.

The schoolteacher now realized she had suddenly come to the point where all she could do was hold her dead husband and weep. That was now her duty until she could do more, until she could do better.

Johnny ran his hands over his slashed face, grabbing hold of his father's cap, adding his blood to its threads. Then he looked out at his ruined home, and the killing field it had become.

All around them people ran to and fro. More wounded were brought from the still-raging battle. Both blue and gray lay where there was room. Moans and weeping filled the air, blending with the sound of gunshots, screams and war cries. A community forever changed by the unnatural deviance of war.

He could see her now. She was running toward the levee, looking back over her shoulder, smiling playfully. Wind chimes of laughter played in his ears as he chased her through flowers, her raven hair playing in the breeze. Her graceful legs danced over the grass, skipping to the spin of the good earth, the new earth. At the tall pine where the trail led off to the other grove, he almost caught her, but slipped and stumbled off to the side, pausing to catch his breath, his fresh new breath. He watched her with amazement as she giggled, quickly picking a handful of ripe blackberries, bordered with honeysuckles and guarded by a swarm of harmless bees. She put one to her lips and gently bit the juicy fruit, then laughed again. He laughed, too. She took off running, and as he sprinted after her, she let out another chorus of sweet giggling laughter. They raced the last stretch to their special place under the old oak where she finally let him catch her. A dreamy tumble on the soft plush clover.

"My darling," she said, touching his face. "My dear sweet darling."

Bobby Bernard was moving along the edge of the main line, to the right of where the horseshoe had formed. He had fallen back a bit when the others had charged, thinking of all he had seen the day before. No longer feeling the moment at hand, but still he wanted to kill a Yankee. He was at a spot where the wounded were being pulled away, carried back toward the schoolhouse. Suddenly, as he skirted the fray where it had spilled over the Shreveport Road, a young Union soldier came screaming out of the dust and smoke, bayonet fixed at the ready. Bobby had a large pistol in his hand, but before he could act he was run completely through, skewered with the long sharp steel. At that same moment, Bobby fired the pistol into the Yankee's belly, knocking him back as they both fell to the ground. Within arm's reach, the two teenage boys stared at one another. Their faces were masks of fear and pain, each knowing they would soon be dead. They both realized that in another place and time they might have been friends. Good friends. Dear friends.

"I'm sorry," said Bobby, starting to choke and weep, blood coming from his mouth. "I killed you."

At first the young Union soldier could not speak. He was also weeping and choking up blood. Then he calmly asked, "What's your name?"

"Bobby. My name's Bobby Bernard."

"My name's Josh," said the Yankee, his voice breaking some. "Joshua Peak."

"Where ya from?" asked Bobby, grimacing in pain, his voice also faltering.

"Me, I'm from Rhode Island."

Slowly the two boys crawled together and embraced, knowing just before they died they had finally become men.

Sidney Brooks had been standing behind a thick oak tree at the top of the rise overlooking the battle. He looked to his left just in time to witness the two soldiers kill one another. He had missed Mouton's charge, because he was too far in the rear of the Union column. And he was not able to find a safe place to watch the defense at Chatman's Bayou. But Pleasant Hill was a different. The hill that overlooked the town and large clearing north of it offered a perfect spot to observe 25,000 men slamming away at each other. Although the previous battle had approximately the same number of combatants, it had been strung out for well over two miles. This was a much more confined theater of killing with a view.

When Brooks first saw the two soldiers kill each other, he was only amused at their amateurish method, how they seemed to come across one another off to the side, almost by accident. It had been just another intrigue of war, just another spectacle of man's inhumanity to man. But then he saw them embrace and suddenly his bourgeois curiosity was challenged. They appeared to be speaking to one another in pensive tones. After a while, when it was safe, he slowly walked down the slope to the two bodies. He was surprised at their youth. One was certainly no more that eighteen or nineteen, the other younger still. Studying their faces he saw neither hate nor anger. Aside from their uniforms they looked quite similar, like they could have been brothers or best friends. For a long while he stood and stared. Then he began to write. He wrote of what he saw that day, the bravery and the carnage, the loss and the gain. But mainly he wrote of the two young men who lay dead at his feet, under his pen and told to the world.

XXI

At dusk the fighting stopped as if both sides suddenly decided there was nothing left to fight for. Tactically Union forces had the upper hand and the Battle of Pleasant Hill would go down in history as a Northern victory. But strategically it was a stalemate. Confederate troops simply left the field first. The Yankees stood exhausted holding the unwanted grounds with moderate authority. They watched the Rebels slouch wearily back to the schoolhouse, all that was left of Pleasant Hill. Through the last seconds of twilight the two American factions studied each other like a classroom of pupils gazing at failed exams.

In less than two days, less than ten hours of actual combat, the two armies had inflicted over 6,000 casualties. Banks had more than that waiting in reserve just a few miles down the road. If he'd regrouped and attacked the next day he would have very likely overwhelmed Taylor's smaller badly-mauled army. Shreveport could have easily been taken. But the politician lost his nerve and retreated, abandoning the Red River Expedition.

About 20 miles downriver from Shreveport, Admiral Porter was amused to find the New Falls City, an old steamboat that had been strategically scuttled by the Rebels blocking the river's course. Clearly painted in bold lettering on its starboard bow was a personal invitation to both Admiral Porter and General Banks, requesting their presence at the Accolades Ball in downtown Shreveport. "Proper attire required."

Porter was standing on the bow of his flagship, watching as his men cleared the river of the steamboat and its overture when a young ensign pointed toward the west bank of the river.

"Banks has been defeated," said Porter when he saw a large column of Confederate Cavalry riding up the river road, winding their way onto the levee. "And now the enemy is looking for us."

Only moments later the admiral received official word of what happened at Mansfield the day before. The Union flotilla was then turned about moving back down river. Their own captured cannons were used against them as Confederates lined the river's edge constantly peppering the Yankees as they fled south.

It took Banks two weeks to regroup with Porter, harassed by the Rebels all the way to the river. Several days after Pleasant Hill, General Green was killed in a skirmish along the river, decapitated by a Union cannonball. The spring rains were late and the river was at a twenty-year low. The whole fleet was soon trapped before the rapids north of Alexandria. The ingenuity of the Confederates had dropped the water level even more by digging channels to divert water out of it. Stopping the Yankee expedition wasn't good enough for the Rebels, they wanted to kill or capture the whole lot. But Smith had relieved Taylor of his command and no other major offensive was attempted against the aborted Union campaign, only urgent spats of continual harassment. Even though they were geographically quite vulnerable, the Yankees still had a large advantage in manpower and weapons, especially artillery.

At one point the Union commanders discussed burning the boats and fighting their way out on foot, a near impossible feat. But the Yankees were desperate. Porter's chief engineer, Lieutenant Colonel Joseph Bailey, proposed building a wing dam to raise the level of the water. Soon Midwestern and New England lumberjacks were braving Confederate sharpshooters. For two brutal, grueling weeks they fetched logs used to build the dam. After Bailey's clever innovation was loosed, Porter's fleet, loaded with Banks's army, successfully negotiated the rapids arriving in Baton Rouge as the spring rains began.

With Keith Novak as its new commander, Polignac's 3rd Cavalry helped chase the Yankees out of upstate Louisiana. Steven Jenkins was promoted to captain and given his own company with Merle Pemberton as his first sergeant. Toby Whitefox and what was left of his Kodabacks also continued to assist the Confederates, before returning to Broken Bow that summer.

Sidney Brooks' article *The Battles of Sabine Crossroads* appeared in Harper's Weekly and several newspapers throughout the United States and Europe that summer. It opened by describing the scene of two young soldiers, a Confederate and a Union, found dead, locked in an embrace at the edge of the battlefield.

When Andrew McMillan learned what happened to Banks at Mansfield and Pleasant Hill, he had quickly left Shreveport early the morning after the battles, riding south on horseback along the river road in the pre-dawn darkness. He knew Banks wasn't a brilliant commander. But the man possessed such an advantage in men and material, McMillan thought surely the politician-general would at least reach his objective. This would have made things much easier for the Union spy posing as a Confederate colonel. He would now have to find the Union navy in order to rendezvous with Casey and Butler, and get his share of the cotton.

Besides his rank, McMillan had travel papers signed by General Edmund Kirby Smith allowing him easy passage through Confederate checkpoints. In one of his saddlebags was his Union uniform, folded neatly in a Confederate battle flag. At a secluded spot outside Natchitoches he decided it was safe to change, the morning sunlight breaking through the trees. He'd seen no Rebel troops for the last few miles and knew that Natchitoches was still held by Porter's men. Besides, things were very quiet, no sounds of battle.

As he removed the gray uniform he smiled to himself. Along with the Rebel flag, it would make a great conversation piece back home in New York City. He thought back on his time in Shreveport, nearly three years of lies and deceit, and how he planned to return after the war. Maybe then he would finally get the Hawkins Farm. He'd had designs on the quaint little place since first seeing it shortly before David Hawkins left in the fall of '61. McMillan and a few other officers had been riding along the river one day and paid a short call. Upon meeting the strapping cavalry officer, he had hidden his envy well, offering a friendly yet duplicitous greeting. That had also been the first time he had laid eyes on Emily, and he had wanted her too.

After David's deployment, Andrew McMillan had aggressively made Emily Hawkins's acquaintance whenever he saw her in town. She'd always been courteous and polite, but showed little interest in him otherwise. As the months passed this embittered him. He had always been a lady's man. The thought of any woman, even a married one, refusing his affections angered him. During the Christmas holiday of '63, McMillan heard that Emily had been feeling ill, and that David Hawkins was feared dead. This had given him a very diabolical idea, one of personal gain unrelated to the war effort.

It was known that Emily Hawkins loved pralines. McMillan made a little batch of the pecan sweets, laced with a tasteless poison that had a delayed effect. Such things were tools of his trade. He started carrying them in a small tin he kept in his coat pocket, knowing he would eventually cross her path in town. A few days into the New Year he noticed her leaving McBride's one afternoon, looking peaked and unwell as she shuffled down Lake Street. First, he pulled out a good praline he kept wrapped in wax paper in his shirt pocket. Then he pulled out the tin and casually approached her, opening it to offer her one as he nibbled on the harmless praline. She smiled and refused, saying her fever had taken her taste away. But he had insisted, using his charm, saying his feelings would be hurt if she didn't at least try one. Reluctantly, she had relented and ate one of the poison pralines. In her already weakened state, Emily collapsed that night in the kitchen and died nine days later.

Using an anonymous broker, McMillan then made plans to buy the Hawkins Farm. It would make a great winter home after the war. But then David returned and his crafty scheme was lost. 'Oh well', he had thought to himself after ample shots of brandy. He still had claim to twenty percent of Casey's and Butler's cotton, enough to make him very rich.

McMillan was buttoning his blue coat, admiring himself in a small mirror when he heard the distinct double-click of a gun being cocked. He looked to his left and saw a man in plain clothes pointing a large pistol at him as he emerged from behind a tree.

"Well, look'ee here," said a voice from the other direction. McMillan turned and saw two more armed men walking up behind him. Both looked to have been recently wounded, bloody bandages on their arms and legs.

The three men were volunteers returning from the battles at Mansfield and Pleasant Hill. Although they had never served in a proper military outfit, they were seasoned fighters, hardened marauders who had killed and pillaged for the Southern cause. Their horses had been killed and they'd received no pay, just a piece of paper signed by General Richard Taylor attesting to their participation in fighting the Union Army. They were heading back on foot to what was left of their homes near Monroe. After stopping to rest under a tree, they saw the colonel ride up and dismount about a hundred yards away. As they helped each other up to go ask if he had any food to spare, the colonel began to undress. At first they weren't sure what to make of this. But when the colonel unfolded the Confederate flag, wearing only long johns, and pulled out the blue Yankee uniform, they knew exactly what he was.

McMillan kept his cool at first, claiming to be a Confederate spy sent to learn more about the Union campaign. But the men knew he was lying.

"The Yankees is retreat'n!" shouted one of them. "Ya don't' need a spy to know dat! Hell, da whole state knows dey done turned tail'n run!"

When the man tossed a rope over a thick tree limb, McMillan began to plead with them, changing his story. He explained that he would make for a very profitable ransom, friends in high places, Washington, New York and Boston. Why, he even knew Lincoln personally. This time the men believed him, and became even more set on hanging him.

Early in the war they had each chosen to remain neutral. But then the Jayhawkers came, and they were forced to take up the gun. They had not wanted war; it had been thrust upon them, a torch literally thrown into their bedroom windows, burning their loved ones. They explained this to McMillan as they put the rope around his neck.

It was thought to be bad luck to ride or use anything from a hanging-horse. But the men needed all they could get, including the ten-thousand Yankee dollars in the other saddlebag. So they didn't use the horse to hang McMillan. After using their knives to cut the Confederate uniform to shreds, they pulled the rope with their bare hands, hoisting him up till his boots kicked three feet off the ground. Before leaving they pinned a sign to his chest: **Yankee Spy**.

Samuel Casey and Frank Butler weren't too concerned about Andrew McMillan. They both knew he was a resourceful man of wit and cunning, quite capable of finding his way back to Union-controlled territory, to claim his share of the cotton. And oh what a claim it was! Admiral Porter's cargo barges had made it ten miles north of Natchitoches before turning back.

Even without reaching Shreveport the cotton haul was very large. It was so plentiful, Casey and Butler had more than double what they had expected. Their only worry now was getting safely out of Confederate territory. Both sides of the river were lined with angry Rebels taking potshots at the Union flotilla. The Yankee gunners did a fair job of keeping the enemy at bay and little damage was done. But it would be very bad luck to get hit by a stray bullet, so Casey and Butler retired below deck. Casey produced a bottle of cognac and the two men toasted their success, vowing to give McMillan an extra five percent, an added bonus for his troubles.

But when Porter's boats were trapped at the rapids near Alexandria, Casey and Butler began to worry again. And when sailors and marines started throwing their cotton overboard to lighten the load, they protested vehemently, but still lost a third of their haul. For the time being their fortune was still in hand, albeit greatly reduced. McMillan, they both agreed, would have to do without the bonus.

For over a week Casey and Butler waited pacing their quarters below deck, daunted by the sporadic gunfire outside. It was rumored that a special engineering feat would save them, a clever Yankee trick to get them past the shallow rapids. Another bottle was opened, this time whiskey, to drink to their final achievement.

However, it was Casey's and Butler's cotton bales that were used as buttress supports for the logs of the wing dam. By the time the flotilla returned to Baton Rouge, the value of the cotton they still had left in the cargo holes did not cover the cost of their fruitless endeavor.

A year after the Battle of Pleasant Hill, Amy Hawkins stood in front of the graves of the Hawkins family holding her three-month old child, a girl she named Cheri. David had been laid to rest next to Emily, a lady Amy never met but envied greatly. A light breeze blew through the infant's fine red locks as she spoke to her lover and husband, the precious child's dark brown eyes glimmering in the new day sun. With no shame

Amy would even speak to Emily, imagining herself a close friend and second to the brave constant woman.

The moment Amy met Sarah and Jacob, she fell in love with their little family and told them they were free. If they wanted she would sell the farm and take them north to begin a new life. But they would hear nothing of it. They would never go, and they wanted her there with them. She was a Hawkins now.

Amy was surprised to learn that David had willed the farm to her more than three weeks before the battles. Exactly twenty-one days before he proposed to her. As instructed in the will, she would give Sarah and Jacob fifty of the seventy-five acres that made up the Hawkins farm. Amy would keep the house and the twenty-five acre corner of land between the river and the bayou. She also gave them a majority of the farm equipment and livestock. It was all theirs anyway she thought.

There was also a personal letter to Amy from David sealed with a large glob of red wax. It was stamped with the image of a hawk in flight, a sprig of cotton bolls in its talons.

My Dearest Amy,

When I first met you my heart was broken in pieces. Bringing Adam's cap to Johnny was simply a duty of honor, a promise to keep to the man who died saving my life. From the moment I first saw you my heart began to heal. Yet I still grieved for Emily. And as I write these words I grieve for her still. As strange as it sounds, I wish you could've met her. The short time I spent with you can only be matched by my time with Emily. If I never see you again, know that I fully intended to ask you to marry me. If and when I do see you I will ask, and I know you will say yes. You have her eyes, by the way.

Do not worry about giving the land to Sarah and Jacob. Just wait a while, and it won't be long before they can legally own it. You can trust the sheriff, Austin Wilhyte. I've known him since I was a boy. He will protect you. All of you.

I hope that Johnny can someday get past his bitterness and anger. Deep inside I believe he's a very good boy. But he's far too young to be carrying around so much hate. Work with him Amy, as I know you will. Invite him back to the farm.

Find yourself a good man and marry him. Raise a family and be happy. You deserve it, my love. Think of me often, especially in the springtime. And don't be sad. Surely we will meet again and smile at one another in the presence of angels.

All of my love and blessings,
David Hawkins

But Johnny refused to live on Hawkins's farm. His face had been mended as well as possible, but the scar was terrible to look at. Randy and Bobby were dead and Robert had lost his leg.

"Can't run no mores, Johnny," he had tearfully cried when the two boys saw each other the day after the battle. "Can't run no mores."

Robert had always been the fastest of them, the fastest boy in Pleasant Hill. But not anymore. Things were very different now.

The town was relocated to the top of the hill that overlooked the battlefield. It was still a beautiful place, but few seemed to think of it that way anymore. Talk of ghosts and hauntings were not uncommon. And many would say they could still hear the sounds of battle at night when the wind blew through the trees. Folks would sometimes swear they had seen a loved one that had been killed in the fighting, walking through the woods or down the road, often in broad daylight.

One rumor began even before the battle was over. David Hawkins's body was being prepared for transfer up to Shreveport. Steven Jenkins and Merle Pemberton were there; both had been wounded. They asked about Hawkins's horse. The animal had fallen only a few feet from where they stood. But now its carcass was gone, vanished in the death throes of battle. That very night sightings of a great red horse with a black mane occurred from Pleasant Hill to Shreveport. Even the retreating Union Army was haunted by the ghost of Hawkins's horse.

For three months after the battles, Johnny lived with Robert's family, helping his friend adjust to his handicap. But Johnny seldom spoke. The two would often just sit silently looking off toward the trees. Or sometimes they would take a walk, Johnny helping Robert with his crutches. Robert would not go near the battlefield. But Johnny would sometimes be seen walking in his father's cap, tracing the steps he had taken with Hawkins. He would stop now and then, looking up at the tall pecan tree or the spot in the road where he'd last seen his father. Once he broke into the little schoolhouse, now boarded up and soon to become some sort of historical site. He sat at his old desk and stared where the chalkboard used to be, imagining his Aunt Amy talking to the class. He began to cry, thinking of how his life used to be before the war came to Pleasant Hill.

Every weekend after the battles, Amy had come down to see Johnny. She had tried to get the boy to come back with her to Shreveport. But he always shook his head, and would not go. After a while even Robert told Johnny he should go stay with his Amy, but still he wouldn't go. Finally, one day in the summer after the battle, he left without a word. Just vanished. And the only thing folks knew for sure that he took with him was his father's cap.

A few days later Ruth had been at her favorite spot picking blackberries. She looked up and saw a boy on the other side of the bayou wearing a Rebel cap. She lifted her hand to wave thinking he looked familiar. But the boy ran off. Ruth ran and told Amy, and ever since then Amy had repeatedly asked Steven Jenkins and Merle Pemberton to look for Johnny, but to no avail.

Shreveport, Louisiana rarely gets snow. When it does it's usually just a few flurries resulting in a thin layer of the white stuff. Two or three years might pass with no snow flying at all. About every fourth year, the old timers say a nice snow will pass through leaving a good blanket two or three inches thick. Unaccustomed to the element, the town slows down a bit. But it's usually a delightful treat for the locals, especially the children. They learn how to make snowmen, snow angels and snowballs, and have fantastic snowball fights. They leave a multitude of tracks crisscrossing the lovely white snow, where they played, danced and sang. But it doesn't last long, a day or two at the most. It soon melts to a dingy, mushy slush, floating in puddles of brown and gray. A few stout, well-made snowmen might remain, adorned and lonely, as they too fade back to mere water.

On the night Cheri was born a terrible snowstorm hit the area, one of the worst on record. The temperature had been in the thirties for weeks, since the New Year began. The ground was already hard and cold, the trees and brush brittle. Freezing rain and sleet came first, laying an inch of ice on everything just before dark. To the west the gray sky was lit pale purple by the setting sun, as the sleet gradually turned to snow. Clumps the size of marbles floated down in an endless shower of white crystals. By the time it was dark it looked like huge flocks of white birds attacking the earth from out of the black sky.

Not long after it began to snow, Amy went into labor. Her screams were so urgent and piercing, Jacob wanted to go get the doctor, but Sarah insisted that he stay. She was a very experienced mid-wife, unable to count the number of babies she had helped into the world. She'd even been there holding extra blankets and towels when baby David was born in New Orleans.

As childbirth typically goes, things seemed alright. But suddenly Sarah saw the baby's feet, and felt the presence of something evil. Her eyes opened wide with fear.

"Wassa matta, Sarah?" asked Jacob, noticing his wife's expression.

"Dat Ol' Scratch try'n to get Miss Amy's baby," Sarah replied.

"What can I do, honey?" Jacob moved close to her.

"Pray!" she cried, turning to look at her children standing at the door. "All'a ya! Pray!"

For the next hour Sarah tried but could not get the baby turned around. To make matters worse, Amy was bleeding badly, and beginning to grow pale and weak. Her screams became feeble cries and moans of desperation.

Next to the bed, Jacob, Ruth, Noah and little Rachel held hands and prayed. Occasionally Jacob would reach out and touch his wife on the shoulder.

Amy suddenly seemed to faint. Her eyes were still open, but she'd gone totally limp lying there lifeless on the bed.

"Nooo!" screamed Sarah. "No, please, Lawd! Please! Don't take'm both! Dats Massa David's baby, Lawd! Please!"

Just then Sarah saw that someone else was in the room. Standing by the door was a Man in White. For a second she actually thought it was David. The rest were still praying with heads bowed. They didn't see the Man. He moved up next to Sarah and placed one hand on her shoulder. His other hand He placed on Amy's swollen belly.

At that moment Sarah was looking into the Man's eyes. But then she heard a baby crying, and looked down. Not only had the child come out head first, Amy's eyes were open and full of life. As Sarah's family looked up, gathering around to see at the new-born, they all smiled, laughing and rejoicing in tears.

"Where dat man went?" asked Sarah, looking around the room.

"What man?" asked Jacob.

Amy spent over an hour out at the plot talking to David and Emily, a bit longer than her usual devotion. A blanket was laid out and she sat and played with Cheri on it while visiting. She would speak to all of them, Ira, Dorothea and Paul, as if they were there, even to Rubin, Nancy and Mary, responding to things they might have said.

It was known in the town that she did this, but only the most brazen gossip spoke of it openly. Amy had been changed by her war experience, hardened to some degree. Her kind, thoughtful side still remained, but she now had a look in her eye that went beyond scholastics. The things a person has seen often reflect in their eyes. And there were places in her heart and mind that she could only go with Cheri.

When she'd first arrived early the morning after the battles, Austin Wilhyte remarked that she favored Emily. Although the likeness was subtle, it would be the first of many times she was told this. Emily had been a bit taller, her hair black and features a little sharper, whereas Amy's features were softer and her hair was chestnut brown with auburn highlights brought out by the sun. There was, however, a striking similarity in the way her hair fell down past her shoulders, the way it flowed and bounced when she busied herself, the way it danced when she laughed. Her laughter and many of her movements were like Emily's, but especially her laughter. Amy also had the same figure and shape as Emily, healthy and eye-catching. They had the same work ethic, and were skillfully outspoken in the appropriate moments. And just like Emily, Amy knew well the constant power of silence.

Most folks in the community had welcomed her, greeted her with condolences and best wishes. They warmed to her, realizing the circumstances of her hasty marriage to David. But a small few had not welcomed her; these were the same ones who'd frowned on Emily's unorthodox ways. They couldn't find it in their hearts to receive her.

After saying her good-byes to each member of the Hawkins family, Amy headed back across the field to the house. Cheri giggled as she bounced the baby on her hip. In an hour it would be dark, the sun low behind her to the west.

As she ascended the steps to the porch she saw a rider approaching. Her eyes played tricks on her, and for a moment she thought it was that Man she had glimpsed the night Cheri was born. The horse looked like Jackson. Amy suddenly recalled rumors she had heard of the ghost of David's horse haunting the roads in the area. She blinked her eyes and for a second thought she was going to faint. It looked like David. Placing her hand against the post to steady herself she looked down and took a deep breath. When she looked back up she saw it was Steven Jenkins riding up in his captain's uniform.

He stopped at the willow tree and dismounted, walking toward her with a limp. He had a strange look on his face, a mixture of sadness and relief. At first she thought that he might have found Johnny and the boy had met with a bad end. Or maybe that the Yankees would return. Taking off his hat, he told her. Lee had surrendered to Grant. The war was over.

EPILOGUE

New York City 1917

Amy Bolton-Hawkins smiled as she took in the sights of the big city, a smile that gave her the appearance of a much younger woman, a woman in her early seventies or late sixties. She had lived a full life, a great-grandmother at the age of 81, now on her first visit up North. Her gray hair was pulled back hanging in waves past her shoulders as she walked with a cane in her right hand, surrounded on all sides by a loving family. To her left, their arms folded together, was her only child Cheri, herself a mother of four and a grandmother of nine. With the husbands and wives of Amy's progeny, their group of twenty was making a day of it exploring the trails of Central Park.

They zigzagged through a rocky section of the park, massive gray-black boulders and granite-like slabs jutting from the green foliage that surrounded them. A large brown historical marker explained that the trails they were walking had been cleared fifty-four years earlier with a stockpile of gunpowder later used at Gettysburg.

Amy stopped and looked at three familiar trees on the left side of the trail. Three very old, tall trees that had a certain wizard-like quality to their presence.

"What is it, mother?" asked Cheri. "Do you need to rest?"

"No, I'm fine," she said pointing with her cane. "Look! Cypress trees."

"I didn't know they grew this far north," said Cheri as their family group admired the trees.

"Your father once told me they grew in a park up here." Her eyes almost fluttered as she gazed at the trees. "It was just one of those things he said as he looked out the window of my old house the day before ...," she paused and looked at her daughter and smiled. "He said they grew everywhere but the North and South Pole."

"Hey, Gran-Gran," said Amy's seven-year-old great-grandson, Paul. "Those trees look like the ones by the river at your house. 'Cept they ain't got no moss on'm."

"Why yes, they do, Paul. Except they don't have any moss on them," Amy said with a smile, correcting the boy's English.

"Oh, yeah," he said, smiling and bashfully rolling his eyes. "They don't have any moss on them."

"Gran-Gran," said eleven-year-old Bethany. "Cypress trees make gopher wood and that's what God told Noah to build the ark with, right?"

"That's right, sweetheart," Amy said patting the child on the head. "That's what the Bible says."

After a short while the family moved on, at times feeling as though they were far off in some wilderness hiking trails through jutting rocks and thickly wooded terrain. But then a break in the trees would reveal rows of seven-and eight-story buildings not too far off.

Amy never re-married. She added Bolton back onto her name shortly after the war. When asked why she had done this, she said so that people would ask. It was her name after all, and she enjoyed telling people about it. Besides the letter to her in David's will, he had left another one with her name on it sitting on top of his desk. Next to it were five large diaries. Ira, Dorothea, Paul, Emily and David himself had all kept detailed journals of their lives. David invited her to read them and become acquainted with the family she had married into. She read the diaries, studied them over the years and decided to write a book about the unique family. During her pregnancy she had hoped for a boy and planned on naming him David of course. But when she saw the baby was a girl, she knew exactly what to name the child, the *loved child*.

The Trans-Mississippi Confederacy did not officially surrender until June '65. By then Keith Novak was a full colonel. With his right hand raised he swore allegiance to the United States, promising never again to take up arms against her. But still he was bitter, having lost a brother and many close friends to the war. He stayed in Shreveport for a while, and all that summer he and Amy spent time together. They took long walks by the river, and picnicked in the many arbors nearby. Although Amy greatly respected the man, enjoying his company and conversation, she said no to his proposal of marriage, and soon he returned to his family's large ranch near San Antonio.

Both Steven Jenkins and Merle Pemberton also swore their allegiance to the United States. Merle continued to work as a teamster, while Jenkins built houses in the developing southern part of Shreveport. Both men worked as volunteer firemen and because of their war experience they were often deputized when extra law enforcement was needed in the area.

When Jacob's first cotton crop came in a group of masked men had ridden out to the farm one night making threats of violence if the cotton showed up at the market in town.

"You ought to be ashamed of yourself, Danny Crowder!" Amy had hollered from the porch with a shotgun in her hands as the leader of the night riders flinched, "acting like a bunch of mindless pigs and wearing grain sacks on your heads like children with no sense! And you, Michael Webb! And you, Keller Chaney!" she began to point at the different men. "And you, Derek Lester! Your boy is in my class! I know all of you! So get on out of here and don't you dare come back or I'll shoot you AND report you to the sheriff!"

The next day Sheriff Wilhyte was told about the masked riders. He could not arrest the men; he had no proof. But he did let them know in no uncertain terms that they were the ones who would be harmed if it happened again. Jacob also hired his first employee that day, Merle Pemberton, hauling loads of cotton to the market in town. For the rest of his life, Jacob had to deal with prejudice and bigotry, but he simply took it as a measure of course, and through it all he emerged as a successful, prominent businessman.

Ruth and Joshua Dubear were married and their first son, Desmond, went on to become one of the first black architects in the area. Noah and Rachel also earned college degrees, and with Amy's help developed advanced educational programs for people of color throughout the region.

Sarah showed Amy some of the writings she had kept over the years, a stack of papers nearly three inches thick. "My Lil' Stories'n Poems," she called them. Amy asked if she could borrow them for a while, promising to return them later. After correcting some of the spelling, punctuation and capitalization, she arranged the lines of the text in a proper format. Then she returned the original writings to Sarah and asked her what her last name was.

"Well, Miss Amy," she had said, "we talked 'bout dat, me, Jacob'n Issac. Dey las' name always been Burk, from da firs' man dat owned'm. An' I never know'd my papa, Rubin's lass name." Sarah paused for a moment, then looked at Amy, smiled and said, "I wanna be Sarah Hawkins. If'n dat's aw'right."

Amy smiled and said that it was.

Six months later a large package arrived in the mail from New Orleans, addressed to Sarah. In it were fifty books, dark-blue with gold lettering that read: **My Lil' Stories 'n Poems by Sarah Hawkins**.

At first Sarah could not believe her eyes, Amy giggling as everyone gathered round. Then Sarah put her hands to her mouth and began to laugh and cry as everyone hugged and kissed her on the cheek.

The little book was a moderate seller, a few copies here and there, some to travelers who passed through the area. Becoming a published writer gave Sarah a sense of accomplishment she never even knew existed and she was forever grateful to Amy for the special surprise.

"Ya know what, Miss Amy?" Sarah had once said. "You kind'a reminds me'a Miss Emily."

And to Amy that was a marvelous compliment indeed.

A few years later Sarah received a letter of thanks from a Dutch nobleman in Amsterdam, a baron of some high standing. The man's wife had passed away from a sudden illness and to quell his intense sorrow he set out traveling the world. After arriving in Shreveport on a steamboat, he purchased Sarah's book at the shop on Lake Street before catching a train out West. He had gotten very drunk that night and put the book in his bags, forgetting about it till much later. For two years the man traveled exploring remote areas, climbing mountains, visiting exotic faraway cities, anything to pry loose the grief that held him so. At a posh hotel in Singapore, a pistol and a half-empty bottle of cognac by his hand, the baron decided to take his own life. While rummaging through his bags for bullets, he came across the little blue book he had bought half-a-world away and finally began to read. Sarah's simple poems and stories lifted his spirit. Especially the one that told how her kind master had returned from a terrible ongoing war only to find the grave of his precious wife. And how he then found the bloodstained cap of a man who had died saving his life, remembering a promise to take the cap to the man's son. The southern nobleman would eventually die saving the boy's life when the war later came to his very homeland, but not before leaving a large portion of his estate to Sarah and her family. The story, the baron expressed in the letter to Sarah, touched his heart causing him to put away the pistol and carry on with his life.

A few years after the war Amy had a small schoolhouse built near the bridge where the road forked leading to the Hawkins farm. It was open to anyone who wanted to learn regardless of color. Most of her students were black, but there were also a few Indians and some of the poor whites that lived along the river and bayou. Essay, short story and poetry contests were organized on a quarterly basis. A play was put on every month and spelling bees, science fairs and field trips were frequent. A little library with a broad compendium of books and resource materials was also built, most of it paid for or donated by Amy herself. Some of her students went on to study at institutions of higher learning, but many were content and grateful to have simply learned how to read and write and do math and gain a deeper, more fundamental knowledge of the world around them. And Amy Bolton-Hawkins was more than happy to provide that opportunity.

Merle Pemberton came to Amy one day and asked if she would teach him how to read and "do some figger'n." And soon, whenever he had some time off, Merle could be found sitting in the front row of Amy's class.

Every day right after lunch was a special time for Amy's students; for a half-hour she would read to them from a book. Her students loved all the stories she'd chosen, but one day she was reading a marvelous tale that especially enthralled them: **The Adventures of Tom Sawyer**, recently published by a former Confederate named Mark Twain. The little novel told how three wayward boys, Tom, Huck and Joe, had run away from home to live as pirates on an island where the Missouri River meets the Mississippi, if only to learn that even life's bases simplicities all come with a cost.

"...........*Another fierce glare lit up the forest,*" Amy read with dynamic emphasis, captivating her students. "*And an instant crash followed that seemed to rend the treetops right over the boys' heads. They clung together in terror, in the thick gloom that followed. A few big raindrops fell pattering upon the leaves.*

'*Quick boys! Go for the tent!' exclaimed Tom.*

They sprang away, stumbling over roots and among the vines in the dark, no two plunging in the same direction. A furious blast roared through the trees, making everything sing as it went. One blinding flash after another came, and peal on peal of deafening thunder. And now a drenching rain poured down and the rising hurricane drove it in sheets along the ground. The boys cried out to each other, but the roaring wind and the booming thunder blasts drowned out their voices utterly......"

Suddenly, Amy stopped reading, staring at the pages of the book as tears formed in her eyes.

"What'a matter, Miss Amy?" asked nine-year-old Jessica Scruggs.

"Oh, nothing." she said, putting her hand to her face. "A speck of dust got in my eye." But still she stood there for a moment, not saying a word, thinking of Johnny.

One of the field trip's Amy would take her students on, was an annual overnight excursion every spring to Sodus, formerly known as Pleasant Hill. (Wanting to forget those "days of terror," and feeling that it was inappropriate to keep such a name, the local citizens had chosen a moniker.) Accompanied by Merle and a few chaperones, Amy and her students would pile onto a couple of buckboards and ride down to Mansfield. Amy would tell how Taylor's smaller army turned back the Red River Campaign, now the official post-war name for the failed Union expedition. Then they would travel further south down what was now called the Mansfield Road to Sodus, stopping at the different spots where the Union army made their stand. After asking her students to be quiet and reverent, she would show them the little schoolhouse where she once taught, telling them of the horrible battle that was fought on the very ground where they now stood.

At first some inhabitants of the area frowned on the little field trip. But when they found out who Amy was, and that Merle was a veteran of both battles, they somberly nodded, allowing the interruption. Amy still had property in Sodus, a small house built after the battle on a half-acre lot. That evening a big cook-out was had at her place, a pig and a deer roasting on a spit. Everyone was invited but few of the locals chose to attend.

Amy spent as much time as she could in Sodus helping preserve the little schoolhouse, tending to the grounds and the small memorial set up for those who had died there, both North and South. She would often stand on her porch thinking of David and their few intimate moments together, sweet memories that kept her strong and graceful. She would go for walks near the spot where his horse had turned bringing him back to her the day they first met. Jackson, that beautiful, dangerous horse that had nibbled lightly at her sleeve, softly nuzzling her hands, now a feared ghost of the roads. And every time she looked up at the tall pecan tree she would think of Johnny, sometimes crying even decades later, but always praying for his safety, praying the boy would someday come home.

By the turn of the century Amy published her own book entitled, **"The Legacy of Bolivar Dunnydon and the Tails of the Hawkins Family."** It met with notable success allowing her to give back even more to the community, accommodating those she cared for and furthering her interests.

In 1904, after 40 years, the town of Sodus was once again officially named Pleasant Hill. Reunions and re-enactments were organized, drawing northern veterans who had been there, now old and gray wanting to recapture a sense of their past. Over the years, the local adolescents of Pleasant Hill often played a simple practical joke on these visitors.

"Excuse me," said a young man one day with a hearty New England accent. He had just driven an automobile up the road stopping the noisy contraption in front of the schoolhouse while Amy gave a tour to some visitors from Florida. In the passenger seat was a man well into his seventies wearing an old Union uniform with sergeant stripes, looking around, peering at the landscape through a pair of round spectacles. It was April and the re-enactments that weekend brought small crowds and much-needed dollars to the area. "Can you please tell me where I can find the town of Pleasant Hill?"

The new town was not actually visible from the old battlegrounds. Before Amy could respond, a young boy about thirteen, the leader of a small group of local pranksters, stepped forward and pointed up the hill. "It's 'at way, Mister. Top'a da hill. Ya can't miss it."

"Timmy Andrews," Amy called out in a chastising tone, hands on her hips.

"Well," said Timmy with a laugh and a slight pout. "He asked where Pleasant Hill is, not where it was."

"You'll have to forgive him, kind sir," Amy said after excusing herself from the small crowd of tourists and approaching the auto. "The boys get a kick out of watching newcomers ride up the hill, only to find out that what they are looking for is right here."

"Oh?" said the man with a puzzled look.

"Are you looking for the Pleasant Hill Battle Grounds, sir?"

"This is it," said the elderly gentleman in the passenger seat leaning forward to look at the schoolhouse. "This is where it happened."

"I'm sorry," said the driver. "My name is Eric Preston Fuller and this is my grandfather, Eric Preston Fuller, Senior."

"I was with a group of Vermonters," said the man in uniform, pointing toward the clearing past the schoolhouse. "We were bunched up in those trees over there, between a New York brigade and a regiment from Delaware. Forty-six years ago it was."

"Forty-seven, sir," corrected Amy reaching in to take the man's hand. "Forty-seven years this Sunday. Welcome back. I'm so glad you made it."

The Fullers enjoyed the re-enactment that year. Eric, Sr. was a charming old chap who had lost his right foot during the battle, but got around well enough with a cane and a wooden prosthesis. He asked Amy if she would accompany him in a quick search for the missing foot.

"Oh, some rabbit probably got off with it," he replied, coaxing a giggle from Amy after a stroll around the grounds.

They were invited up to the Hawkins farm, where they stayed as guests for two days before heading out for New

Orleans. Cheri's husband, William, told them the roads south of Alexandria were quite dangerous during the April rains and nearly impassable for an automobile. They were advised to make their way to Simmesport where they could easily park the car on one of the large riverboats, taking safe passage down the Mississippi to the city.

"Yes, I remember Simmesport," said Eric, Sr. as they set out. "If we had turned back then, I might still have my foot."

A few weeks later, Amy received the first of many letters from Eric, another one of sundry correspondences she had acquired over the years with friends from all over the world.

"I wonder how that dear Milo is doing," said Cheri as the family made its way through the fields and meadows of the southwestern portion of Central Park, observing an airplane flying overhead.

"He's probably somewhere in the skies over France," replied William. "Searching for that bloody Baron von Richthofen, whatever his name is."

"Well, I hope he's alright," said Amy as the others began to regale themselves with recollections of the only other Vermonter to visit the Hawkins farm. "I sure liked him."

Three years after meeting the Fullers, a large family brunch was being prepared under the two oak trees beside the Hawkins home. As the table was being set, a droning buzz was heard off in the distance. Suddenly an airplane was seen flying low over the farm from the north. Its engine sputtered as it banked to the left, for a moment looking as though it might crash into downtown Shreveport. But then it turned back sharply as the engine stalled out with a metallic cough, gliding in eerie silence to touch down on the narrow clearing between the cypress trees at the river and the oaks that led up to the house.

"My name's Milo," said the pilot, a handsome, wiry young man with light blond hair. "I'm sorry, but not only am I out of petrol, I'm a bit lost."

"Well," said Amy, as she and her family greeted the pilot, admiring the aircraft, "we can get you some gasoline in town later. You must be hungry. Please join us for brunch. Blackberry pancakes with strawberry and peach preserves."

As it turned out, Milo had flown a parcel from Burlington, Vermont, to Dayton, Ohio. There, he was asked to fly an urgent package to St. Louis. After delivering that, he took a short nap, then, was given some important legal documents going to Little Rock, Arkansas. Somewhere in the mountains he was blown completely off course, and by the time he came out of the storm he was flying over lowlands and small foothills. Having no idea where he was, he began looking for a place to land.

"The weather was so nice and beautiful," said Milo as he sat at the table, "I lost track of time. Next thing I knew, I was flying on fumes. I was going to land on the other side of the river, but then I smelled pancakes and saw your little picnic."

After some coffee the men took Milo into town, fetching a big drum of fuel for the plane.

"There's enough here to get me to Little Rock and back again," said Milo slapping the side of the drum and grinning at Amy and Cheri. "How about a bird's eye view of your farm?"

First Amy, and then Cheri went up with Milo, both of them shrieking and screaming with delight as the plane soared through the air, circling the sky over Shreveport.

"This would make a great spot for an airfield," shouted Milo as he gunned the engine, waving good-bye for his trip up to Little Rock. Since then he had written several times and not long after the war began, a letter arrived from Montreal. Milo had joined the Royal Canadian Air Corps and was soon being shipped to England. His last letter was from France, stating that he had twice seen Berlin from the air.

"I thought I was going to have an accident," said Cheri, thinking back on her plane ride as they made their way down Central Park West.

"I know," Amy laughed, looking at the children. "So did I." And the children all giggled.

As they approached 58th Street, a crowd was gathering there, drawn by a ruckus of some sort. A man was yelling, screaming at the top of his lungs, something about the war, something about a terrible reckoning sure to come.

Amy and her family tried to skirt around the crowd, but suddenly a Man was there standing in Amy's way. He was dressed in white and the others didn't seem to notice Him. The Man in White looked at Amy with sad powerful eyes, eyes that seemed hauntingly familiar. He pointed into the crowd. Amy turned and could clearly see the man who was yelling, screaming at the audience gathered before him. She was then pushed into the crowd as more people came pressing forward to hear what appeared to be a raving lunatic. Amy wanted to look away, but could not. With the Man in White at her side she slowly moved through the crowd toward the screaming man. Was there something familiar in his ranting movements, in the piercing glow of his eyes, the desperate twang of his voice? Or was it the filthy old cap on his head?

He had grown mad over the years, reversing himself over and over. Double minded. Unstable in all his ways. A nomadic wanderer, restless and discontented. He spoke of things most people did not understand. Maniacal warnings of the end, warnings against the necessary evil. Black moons and bloodstones. Rude utterances of past lives, offending the living as well as the dead. Shaking his fist at the moon and stars, while waving intimate to shadows off. Mystic faux pas slipped in a mire of knowledge, inherited by an orphan of wisdom. The waiting seed of a wanted cure to a self-inflicted dream. Even slitting throats and unfurling the black flag. Hope for the happy idiot. Despair for the brilliant fool. Something shiny wrapped I gray.

When he first set out on his own as a boy, the war had still raged like a dangerous predator in its death throes. Keeping to himself he had traveled northeast, mainly on foot, avoiding any large groups of men he saw. He hunted some, becoming a decent shot with the pistol he had, a .44 caliber six-shooter from the battle that day. But he stole most of what little food he could find. Occasionally he came across a newspaper and read about the series of great battles between Lee and Grant, then, the siege at Petersburg.

In the mountains, close to where Georgia and Tennessee become the Carolinas, he came upon a small, secluded homestead being pillaged by a handful of marauders. The dead bodies of a man and two teenage boys were sprawled out front, faint screams of a woman and girl coming from the house. Two of the marauders stood satisfied on the porch, cinching up their pants as another joined them from the house, filthy and bearded. He crept low to the side of the house with the pistol drawn. Holding it with both hands, he rounded the corner and took careful aim. Fast and deliberate, he shot each man in the chest before they could do anything but bellow with shock and surprise. He then bounded quickly inside the house. Then shot the other two as they fumbled in confusion with their pants.

Both the woman and the girl had been beaten severely and most certainly had witnessed the murders of their husband, father, brothers and sons, only to endure such a vile desecration. The woman had died first, never regaining consciousness. But the girl, about his age, had opened her eyes and smiled at him, holding tight to his hand before she slipped away. He worked all day digging graves for the family, leaving their murderers where he had killed them, and a note explaining what he had seen and done.

Not long after that, the war ended and he drifted out West, vowing never to return home. For over ten years he tried an assortment of occupations, a ranch hand, a teamster, digging for gold, farming, even a short stint as a sheriff's deputy. Although he was able to save his money, he could not find any sort of peace within himself. In a Wyoming boomtown he met and fell in love with a young showgirl, a fickle child who toyed with his affections like a ball. He asked her to marry him and she said yes. But in less than a year she spent all his money and ran off with another man.

"C'est la vie," he said and moved to Chicago where he began to associate with intellectuals, giving himself to study and reflection. He embraced romanticism, flight from reality into a world of impressive dreams, rich and sublime, a vague fog of self-deception that yearned for deliverance from the here and now, a willingness to face anything but the truth. With a sufficient education he read what he could of the early philosophies, neat schemes concerning the unity of life and thought. He made his way to New York, then Europe, learning bits and pieces of its many languages, exploring the realms of an artist and a scholar, finding only a sphere of subjectivity.

Then one day at a coffeehouse in Vienna, nearly two-and-a-half decades after his baptism of fire back home, he met a very complicated man whose name he could not pronounce, reading a book by a writer whose name he could not pronounce. The man claimed to have been a professor of classical philology at some obscure university, now on sabbatical designing his own curriculum.

"Just by looking at you," the stoic professor had said, "I can tell that you live dangerously."

"I used to," said the American with a pensive smile. "But now I try to live more peaceably."

"Peaceably?" the professor scoffed. "How old are you?"

"Thirty-seven."

"You're much too young to be living peaceably. And much too old not to know what I am about to tell you."

The professor paused and the knowledge-thirsty American sat up straight and said, "Please, enlighten me, sir."

"That's your problem. You seek enlightenment, but you don't even know what real enlightenment is. You are about to be forty, and mark my word, the time will pass very quickly, my friend." The professor held up the book, *L'espirit Souterrain*, open in one hand, striking a scholarly pose as he read.

"To live longer than forty is bad manners, is vulgar, immoral. Who does live beyond forty? Answer that, sincerely and honestly. I will tell you who: fools and worthless fellows."

Every day for a week the American met the professor at the coffeehouse reading and studying the book, pondering its complicated meaning, albeit shrill and glaring. He learned that nothing can justify self-deception or even a slight deviation from the ugly truth. All of his soul, his mind, emotion and will, must be laid bare in almost child-like honesty, then thrust like a charade into the world of men. Only then, would he find the enlightenment he sought.

"And be sure to die at the right time," said the daring professor, bidding the American farewell with a paradox to linger at his newfound turning point. "Not too early, as it appears you have come very close. But definitely not too late."

Now it seemed his ability to think and reason grew within him, all previous knowledge swelling with a refusal to belong to any school of thought, repudiating the legitimacy of any body of beliefs. It was strange, this enlightenment, an excellent desolation of his already crippled ego. A gestation of loneliness, counterpart to spending many years in a single room filled with a library of books, then suddenly finding a secret door out of the room, only to learn that he is on a deserted ship with a workable sail and rudder in the middle of a vast ocean.

For over a decade he traveled, literally circling the globe. From Naples he took a fishing boat to the Isle of Cyprus, a deck hand working the nets and riggings. Then a cargo vessel to Cairo, where he joined up with a group of explorers seeking the source of the Nile. A year in dark, seething jungles fighting wild beasts, crazed savages and malaria. The expedition was inevitably aborted, and from a remote mountain village he found passage on a wagon to Nairobi, resting for a month, sick with fever and delirium. After making his way to Madagascar he jumped a ship, sailing through a cyclone before reaching Perth. Another year, a blur of days, weeks and months working fishing boats, staggering seasick in rat-infested cargo holds, onward to the next port-of-call. Sydney. Manila. Hong Kong. By the light of a full Honolulu moon, he scaled a taut rope from a pier to a ship's bow. Twenty days later he awoke in San Francisco.

While walking the hilly streets he came upon a gathering, a group of striking harbor workers listening to a speech by a young lady with an Eastern European accent. Her words enthralled him, seduced by her passionate oration. It was an election year and her last statement before leaving the podium struck him as simple yet most profound.

"If voting ever changed anything, they'd make it illegal!"

Her name was Emma, and for the next year he traveled across the country with her group of anarchists, telling the masses of the evils of capitalism, and any shape or form of government. He fell in love with her, trying to win her heart, wanting to share her bed. She engaged him in deep conversation, challenging his beliefs and confronting his theories. But she would not sleep with him, politely refusing him entry into her little fold of lovers. Again and again he had heard her cries of pleasure in the night, as he held his one and only companion, the always-faithful whiskey bottle. His long suffering never paid off, and finally, after seeing a newcomer slip into her cabin, he left without a word, having only the satisfaction of becoming a ghost to her.

Alcohol became his lover. Soon he was living bottle to bottle in a haze of back alleys, street corners and jails, the curse of delirium tremens lurking in the shadows, the image in the mirror chilling his heart. He seemed to lose his passions as large bits of his memory began to fade. Often he would wake up in strange places having no idea where he was or how he got there. Once he woke up near a railroad track in Denver, swearing on all that was holy he had been in Albuquerque the night before. Another time he came to in Memphis with his last recollection being in St. Louis.

Late one night he jumped from a train desperate to find a drink. Wandering a small city in the wee hours, he passed a store window with a shelf full of liquor just inside. Without even thinking, acting completely on impulse, he smashed the window. As he made off with two bottles someone tried to stop him. A short scuffle ensued and he broke one over a man's head and got away. Later, when daylight came, he was found passed out in some bushes not far down the road. He was sentenced to four years hard labor on a Georgia chain gang, but was given another four after striking a guard and attempting to escape. Eight years of beatings, abuse and solitary misery grinding away at his identity.

By the time he was released back into society, he was a late-middle-aged man, a bitter man trying to recall some of the ideals of his past. He learned more about the Great War raging in Europe, finding it hard to believe that many of the places he had toured as a young man were now obliterated, laid completely to waste. And what about the people? Were they not above that? That kind of madness? Could it be true that literally millions had perished within a few short years? It seemed impossible and yet he knew firsthand the realities of such things.

He made his way again to New York, not sure why, but somehow feeling drawn to the city. And it was here that his passions returned, thinking back on a soldier he once knew, a Confederate of chivalry and valor. Taking off his coat and rolling up his sleeves he clinched his teeth as if to settle a score, and began to speak. It was an April day not unlike a certain April day of his past, clear and beautiful and stirring with fuss and racket. He started calm but deliberate, slowly rising to a fevered pitch. And as people stopped to hear him, a blue light seemed to emanate from his eyes. Eyes once innocent, now brazen in *flagrante' delicto*. Emma would have been proud he thought. The words he spoke were illegal, illicit locutions, words of protest and anti-war, but certainly not of peace. Vernacular paroxysms gushing seditious anarchy.

"Why?!" he screamed with his arms reaching out to his transfixed audience. "Why do we send boys to die for the Crown of England, France and the Czar of Russia?! To die in a subterfuge of valor pitting Germany as our surrogate foe! Blinded from the more nefarious crime, a mass pogrom of the individual, a generation of artists, scholars and craftsmen snuffed out at the whim of a royal family squabble! Besides filling its belly and coffers, what has the monarchy done but give sanctuary to the capitalist and safe harbor to the socialist?! Watch as they blend together rhetorical words and the passive acts of the aggressive mongrel coward to poison freedom, issuing in the next Dark Age!"

As he spoke the blue light from his eyes seemed to grow brighter, washing over the crowd in a baptism of fear, sympathy and wonder. And for a moment he had them all, a passionate cry in the urban wilderness, saying things that might have sometimes been on their minds, but never on their tongues. But just as it seemed he would ascend to the heavens, the police came. They took hold of the feral-eyed man and began to drag him away. He kicked and continued to scream to deaf ears of contentment. Shaking their heads the crowd began to disperse with raised eyebrows, yielding back into the routines and habits of the day, a slight ado now forgotten.

"Wait!" shouted an old woman stepping forward with her hand out, motioning for the police to stop. Although she was elderly, the woman had youthful piercing eyes, the kind of eyes a person who works for God might have. "Please!"

"Lady," said the officer in charge, his authority suddenly seeming to be in question. "You know this man?"

At first she didn't say anything, just looked with sad grateful eyes at the man held by the two officers. With her hand out, she moved slowly toward him, studying his face, studying his eyes. The man was now silent, gazing at her. He became lost in that gaze as she came closer, vaguely noticing the concerned family behind her. When he saw the Man next to her, a Man he instantly knew was risen from the dead, he suddenly knew everything else had been lies.

The lady touched his face, gently caressing it as he began to cry. And for the first time in years, he heard someone say his name. His first name.

"It's time to come home now, Johnny," she said, wiping the tears from the hideous scar on his face, gently taking the old blood-stained Rebel cap from his head. "It's time to come home."

ABOUT THE AUTHOR

Dris Horton was born in California, raised in Louisiana and lived in the New Orleans French Quarter for many years. He now lives in Atlanta, and is currently working on his second novel, *Sam's War*, based on his late grandfather's experience as a B-17 pilot shot down into Nazi-occupied Yugoslavia. Dris has also written a flash novella entitled *The Angst and the Blur-A Tale of Katrina*, and numerous short stories, and screenplays for both novels.

Made in the USA
Monee, IL
29 August 2021